Marilin

Very Good

JUST BEFORE DAYBREAK

JUST
BEFORE
DAYBREAK

AUDREY COULOUMBIS

ST. MARTIN'S PRESS
NEW YORK

Design by Claire Counihan

Library of Congress Cataloging-in-Publication Data

Couloumbis, Audrey.
  Just before daybreak.

  I. Title.
PS3553.082J8 1987   813'.54   87-79
ISBN 0-312-00586-5

First Edition
10 9 8 7 6 5 4 3 2 1

For Polly,
who gave me words,

For Arline,
who let me go on alone,

For Akila,
who makes all things possible,

For Harvey,
who gave me Hope, who made this book better.

JUST BEFORE DAYBREAK

1

As the Korean war ended and our uncles began to come home, my cousin Tucker noted that the last of the war marked our last summer as children, being we were twelve years old at the start of it and we'd be teenagers at the end. As I look back on it, that statement turned out to be a greater truth for me than Tucker meant it to be.

I wanted to write it all down, that being the best way to pass it on to those who'd need to know. But I myself don't understand how it got so bad, with none of us making a move to stop it. I found myself staring at this sheet of blank paper for the longest time, not knowing where to start. Everything caught together in a clump like Grandma Taylor's morning glories. Finally, I remembered what Tucker'd said. I knew the exact moment when childhood ended for me. It had to do with being

1

in the right place at the right time, as I've heard said so often, the thing that put me there being the sixteenth of July—my grandmother's birthday and the traditional date of the family reunion.

Tucker yanked on my braid. "Let's get out of here."

"Not now." Tucker and I sat against the wall, knees drawn up to rest our chins on. Children who sat were safe from Grandma Taylor's sharp eye.

"If we go now, we'll fall between the cracks."

"Or we'll get up and remind her we're here." Uncle Ted, Tucker's dad, had taken my mother home with him earlier. If we were careful, it was likely we'd be overlooked. Grandma Taylor rocked gently in her chair, checking who was sleeping at whose house, and putting people in wherever there was an extra bed. She was happiest when she had all her children around her. That happened at the family reunion and whenever there was a house to raise. This year both those things came at the same time.

"You'll be going home," Grandma said as she counted off Uncle Collin and his bride of nearly a year.

They leaned against the big black woodstove with their arms around each other. I'd had my eye on them for most of the day, and although they were attentive enough when spoken to, it seemed each found the other to be something of a distraction.

"No, Ma, we're not planning to," Uncle Collin said, reluctant to take his eyes off Aunt Suzie, "so if somebody needs the bed, they're welcome to it."

"The sheets are fresh put on," Aunt Suzie said shyly into the hush that fell over the room.

Uncle Collin pulled her closer, his lips brushing her face. "I may as well say this out so there's no mystery and no unwelcome callers, either. Suzie and I are sleeping in the orchard tonight."

This broke up the poker group, eleven people hunched around a table meant to seat four. Late last summer, Uncle Collin and Suzie were discovered in the orchard when Grandpa took Grandma for a late stroll. Despite their protests that nothing had happened, they were married two weeks later. Grandpa Taylor said it was Uncle Collin's duty to do right by the girl, and Grandma said she wouldn't have Suzie's mother calling on her for anything but an afternoon's conversation. "We like to never got over it," Uncle Collin told us indignantly. "I'm standing here to tell you we was three weeks married and both of us still virgins." That made everyone laugh harder.

I couldn't think why that struck them funny. From what I've seen and I've seen plenty, there's nothing funny about it. Not that I could ask. I don't know how old you have to get before someone will answer your questions. I do know that every question I ask gets the same answer: Don't bother me with that now. So it was with some interest that I watched Uncle Collin's manner with Aunt Suzie.

I thought back to Christmas, which I spent in Paris with Daddy and his wife when the variety show stopped there. They stayed in a tiny room on the darkened top floor of a hotel that kept the hallways better lit down below. It was a feature that went unnoticed by everyone else since I was the only one there during the day. In our room, there was a single window high on the wall, remarkable only for its view of the Seine. The management put a cot beneath the window for me, affording me the advantage of the view if I stood on it, though I don't think that's what they had in mind. That's where I spent most of my time, Daddy and Lisa being in rehearsal all day as well as the better part of the evening.

One night they worked quite late. I was asleep when they came in, waking me somewhere in the middle of their dinner—sandwiches wrapped in crisp waxed paper and a bottle of wine. I dozed in and out as they gossiped, hearing nothing that drew my attention until they were getting ready to go to sleep.

"Robert!" Lisa whispered sharply as Daddy came up close behind her. He laughed as he reached around her to turn down the lamp. I don't think he saw the way her eyebrows pulled

3

together in a frown as she got into bed. "Turn off the light, Robert. I'm tired."

"Leave it on for a while," Daddy said, speaking in the same near whisper that Lisa was using. He slid in next to her.

"Robert!" Lisa complained.

"She's asleep."

"What if she wakes up?"

"She won't." The bedsheets rustled.

"Not tonight, Robert."

"Come on," Daddy teased.

"No."

"It's been a while, Lisa," Daddy said, his wheedling tone fading fast.

"Well . . ."

"Let's see what we have under this blanket," Daddy said, the tease returning to his voice. He sounded like he was playing a game with a child.

"Let's see what we have under this nightie," he went on. "Come on, Lisa."

"All right."

"Let's see what we have under this nightie," he repeated.

"Ooh," Lisa said in a high voice that seemed to be part of the game.

"Let's see what I have in here for you."

"Ooh," Lisa said again.

I peered through my eyelashes once more as Daddy lifted himself over Lisa and began to rub up against her. She stared off toward the door. I knew what they were doing. I'd seen dogs do it, the male bent energetically to his task as the female stood indifferent to his efforts.

Clearly, it was not the same for Aunt Suzie, whose color rose and fell with her breathing when Uncle Collin came near her. I couldn't help wondering what made it so.

"Allie, if we don't go when the poker table clears, we'll be sleeping in Dorrie and Florrie's bed!"

Tucker was right.

I didn't move when the first three people got up to go. Too

4

young. Tucker wriggled with impatience. When Uncle Matt and Uncle Brian got up, we slipped out alongside them. You can go almost anywhere if you're walking beside one of the old uncles. Just as certainly, you'll be questioned if you're looking too chummy with one of the younger uncles. Outside, Uncle Matt put a hand on Tucker's shoulder. "You two aren't spoiling for trouble, are you?"

"No." Tucker's answer was too quick. Uncle Matt, at twenty-eight, was the most serious of all our uncles, more so since his marriage to a woman of yet sterner stuff.

Uncle Brian stepped in. "I got my eye on 'em tonight, Matt. Carrie's been waiting on you for better than an hour now." Uncle Brian, although three years older than Uncle Matt, was as yet unfettered by marriage. Uncle Matt gave in with a small sound in his throat, fitting a cautious frown in place as he headed in Aunt Carrie's direction.

"You two have plans?" Uncle Brian asked.

"No," Tucker said again, this time with an air of great prospects.

Uncle Brian smiled. "Well, I'm as good as my word. Climb into the pickup." And as we hurtled across the yard, "Keep your voices down."

We weren't the first into the truck and we weren't the last. During the wait, Tucker took to picking at sores. "I notice your stepdaddy didn't make it to the reunion this year."

"I saw that." I hoped he'd drop it.

"My ma says he's drinking again."

"He just didn't feel inclined," I said firmly.

"She says he's out of work again."

"I'll let my mom know. She never hears anything till the last."

"Not much use moving from one place if he does the same thing at the next place." That's when Uncle Brian got into the driver's seat and we set off. A good thing, too.

It never occurred to Tucker or me to ask where we were going. This time last summer, we'd have been safely tucked in along with our younger cousins; it was with considerable awe

5

that we found ourselves included this evening. Uncle Brian pulled up in front of the building site and inside half an hour the light of a bonfire shone on the golden frame of the new house. The floor, laid this afternoon, would see hard use tonight. Trucks pulled up as regular as a heartbeat, unloading what looked like the entire teenage population of Polk County, Iowa. Some brought beer, some brought banjos, and some brought news of more on the way. My hair, twisted into a thick red braid, slapped against my shoulder blades, marking me a child. I tucked the tail of it under, securing the folded braid with hairpins, the way Aunt Florrie'd shown me. It made me look much more grown up.

The music started, and we moved as one body toward the house. Tucker is an energetic dancer and unlike some boys, enthusiastic about it. We stayed on the dance floor through three changes of musicians, finally stopping to lean wearily against a raw two-by-six. Someone pressed a cold soda into my hand, his breath washing over me as he leaned in to pass another to Tucker. He was drunk. It didn't sit well with me at all. "Here, lemme sweeten that up some," he said and added something from a small square bottle to my soda. I snatched it away so quickly he ended up pouring some on the floor-boards. "Hey," he yelled.

"Here, Allie, trade with me," Tucker said. "Thanks, but Allie likes her soda plain." Tucker didn't notice his friend's condition. Or maybe he didn't especially mind.

"Let's get back up there, Allie," Tucker urged, pulling me to my feet. "It's okay. He's a good guy," Tucker told me when we were out of earshot. "He's just out having a good time, you know?"

By the time we left the floor the dancers were thinning out, although there was no sign that the celebration was coming to an end. We worked our way toward the edges of the party. The fresh air felt good. "I'll go get us a soda," Tucker said.

I pulled my braid down and poked my fingers into it. Not very far away my mother slept in Tucker's bed with my little sister, Crystal. Uncle Collin and Aunt Suzie were making love

6

in the orchard. All these people doing whatever they always did, and none of it changed by whether I was here or not. I thought about that a lot when I was younger. I'd stand in one place, wondering if I were to disappear right that minute, what would be different? After a few times, and not being able to find an answer, I stopped that.

Tucker came back with a crowd. They were new faces, they were rowdy and they were passing around a bottle. "Here, try this." Tucker offered me his soda. His had been sweetened regularly, thanks to his friend.

"No, I'd better not."

"Just one, so you'll know what it tastes like." He held the bottle out. I took it finally and swallowed some of it. Tucker was right. It was good. Sweet. Like spinning through a Virginia reel when you were supposed to be asleep in bed.

"I thought whiskey tasted awful."

"This is sloe gin. I got the tail end of the bottle. Have some?"

Sloe gin does improve a bottle of pop.

I don't remember much about the ride home. I do remember stumbling along beside Tucker, more supported by him than not, as we made our way toward the boys' shacks. It was just before daybreak, when the murky gray air sticks to you the way a spiderweb will. A time when all things are possible.

Tucker clapped a hand over my mouth, whispering, "What is it?"

"We're the only ones in the whole world who are up."

"Let's keep it that way."

That was the funniest thing I'd ever heard.

He shook me. "You be quiet now, Allie, you hear? Just be quiet."

We stopped outside one of the shacks, Tucker's hand on the doorknob. "Quiet now, hear? You don't want to wake anybody up."

I nodded. I was nothing if not cooperative.

Tucker shoved me into an empty upper bunk, taking the one across the way. "Stop that giggling, Allie!" I covered my mouth with my hands so the laughter could only seep out around the edges. After a while I slept.

It seemed only a short time before Grandma Taylor was shaking me out of the bunk. "Roll out of there. These children been tearing around the yard in their pajamas for the better part of an hour." She reached up to give me a less gentle shake. "Allie, are you awake yet? Come on, child, we've got work to do. We're raising a—"

The whole shack seemed to lurch to one side as Grandma stepped up on the bottom bunk to reach me. "Allie, how can you sleep so—are you all right?"

"Sure." I swung off that bunk the way I'd done so many times before. But this time I landed on one hip with a leg in the air. "Ow-w!"

"Allie!" Grandma helped me up. "Lord! You've been drinking," she said as I located the main source of my discomfort. It was all I could do to get outside.

Grandma Taylor followed shortly, pushing Tucker in front of her. "I know she didn't take to drinking alone"— Grandma yanked him into place beside me,—"and it ain't hard to figure out who her cohort would be."

Uncle Joe, who'd last night been to the drive-in movies with Uncle Little Mike, stumbled to the door. "Ma."

"Don't 'Ma' me! Letting these two get drunk at their age." "But—"

"You say one more word, and I'll take another hide to hang on the wall," Grandma warned. Uncle Joe disappeared from the doorway.

"Acting," Grandma muttered as she steered us around the house, "like you was raised by stray dogs! Allie, what do you suppose your mother'd say if she was to find out?"

That wasn't hard to guess. She raised a terrible noise at Daddy Jim when he was drinking. Or she used to. Now that I thought, she didn't say that much about it anymore. What did she used to yell about? He couldn't keep a job. That's what. He drank at work and couldn't hold a job. But he got a new job. A better one, Mom said. Until just before school let out.

8

Grandma Taylor dropped us on the porch with a thump. "Set here," she ordered, "till I can see to you."

We sat. She rounded up the little kids and put Dolly, who's only ten herself, in charge. We held our heads in our hands and listened to the goings-on in the kitchen. We'd set the tone for this morning's breakfast, that's for sure. Uncle Harry and Uncle Darryl came through the back door on the end of a broom. "Hot damn! That woman's in some mood."

"Whoa! What have we here?" Uncle Darryl knelt to look into our faces. "You two look to've had a high old time!"

"Allie got drunk," Tucker said.

"Drinking!" Uncle Harry chortled.

"You got drunk, too," I groaned. "You drank as much as I did."

"I didn't get sick."

"Who'd give you booze?" Uncle Darryl asked.

"Tucker's friend."

"He gonna help you out with Ma?" Uncle Harry wanted to know.

"You two certainly are enjoying an adventurous frame of mind this summer." Uncle Darryl's voice held a definite note of admiration.

"I guess we know what that means." Uncle Harry was absolutely gleeful.

"We got fried chicken to look forward to for dinner," they said together.

Grandma bustled out the door in time to catch them once more with the broom. "You got nothing to do but torture these children?"

Uncle Harry and Uncle Darryl flew around the corner of the house, hooting and yelling like wild things even as they piled into the pickup truck.

"The two've you follow me," Grandma said as she grabbed onto our shirts and charged full speed toward the henhouse. I had a glimpse of Tucker's feet scrambling in the wrong direction, but Grandma didn't let him fall behind. "I just don't have time to fry chicken for twenty people today," she told us, "so

9

it looks like you're gonna get off easy. But that's for today," she threatened, "and it ain't likely I'm gonna forget this real soon." She marched us into the henhouse. "So you'd better see to your best behavior." Half a dozen chickens squawked and fluttered wildly about until they could escape behind us, nervous souls or old enough to know this was no egg trip.

The floor was crusted with chicken shit and in some spots, sticky under our bare feet. Grandma quieted down now that we were inside but she didn't waste any time. She chose two worn-out birds with stringy necks, tucking them under her arm. "Outside," she ordered. And there she found two more victims.

"Tucker, grab that Red. The one with the torn foot." The other one, strolling past with a queenly air, was snatched up and thrust at me. We trotted along behind Grandma as she started back to the house.

My grandmother can wring a chicken's neck before it can blink an eye. She doesn't much like it, she says, but it's humane. It'd like to tear her heart out when Grandpa whacks a chicken with an ax and the body picks itself up to run a few steps before it drops. The head lays there on the block, the beak opening and closing as it gasps for air, the eyes blinking in desperation as Grandpa's big hand reaches for it. I can see what she means. The thing is, I can't believe it was humane the first time she put her hands around that thin neck and twisted. And maybe not the next few times either.

It was so fast that the last chicken was handed over as easily as the first. No fuss, no fretting, no boggling eyes for me to try not to notice. Then she chopped their heads off with hard sharp whacks, giving the chickens to Tucker and me to hold by the feet, one for each hand.

The blood dripped in a thin bright stream, first soaking the dusty earth, then splashing onto our ankles as we held them at arm's length. Ants swarmed to the dark rich color and carried tiny drops away. Our shoulders ached with the strain and we lowered the chickens slowly, so slowly that the red splotches formed a trail that moved closer to our feet, yet never letting the dead birds rest in the dirt. That was, in some unspoken way, against the rules. Sweat stood out on my forehead and my upper lip, clinging until I shook my head and then only creeping lower like a lazy fat fly. By then the flow had lessened to a steady drip and the thick sickening smell of warm blood clouded the air.

"You look hot," Tucker said through gritted teeth. With a visible effort, he raised his arms back to shoulder height. "And white. You look awful white."

"Shut up." I tried to wipe my face against my upper arm.

"I don't mean to make you mad," he muttered.

Last summer I'd gotten sick standing in the sun. While Tucker wasn't exactly happy that I was sick, he didn't overlook the opportunity to suggest that girls can't take the sun. I'd gone to lay in the shade while Tucker held the chickens for both of us and never said word one to anybody about it. It was humiliating. I'd paid him back good and proper later that day. I didn't think he'd try that again.

I dropped my chickens, running to vomit behind a bush. When I finished I found Tucker'd pumped water over the chickens and taken them in to Grandma. This time he didn't come around to collect some further punishment from me. This time he headed straight out to the barn to help Uncle Matt with the chores.

"What'll we do now?" Dolly likes to be the one to ask that question because she likes for someone else to come up with the answer. We were lying in the shade of the yard's single oak tree. Dolly was full of boiled chicken and dumplings and the satisfaction of being Grandma's favorite. I'd spent most of the morning in the cool darkness of Dora and Flora's bedroom with a wet cloth on my forehead. I couldn't eat lunch. The smell of blood was still strong in my nostrils.

I was on the verge of telling Dolly I had no intention of moving from that spot, when the screen door opened. Four of our uncles spilled out, headed for the afternoon's work. "Let's wave them off," I said as I got up. Something exploded beneath my foot. Not with a big noise but like a balloon that's down to a last puffy bit that bursts as you step on it. A soft little pop as something gave way under my foot.

A small toad, as big around as a quarter, lay in the grass staring calmly up at me. One of his legs had separated from his body, connected now by only a little mass of entrails. He didn't try to move, didn't do anything terrible like gasping or writhing in the grass. My stomach tightened into a guilty knot. I wondered how long he would lie there.

Long enough for his skin to dry out. Slow suffocation.

"Ugh! It's squished!" Dolly squealed.

"I stepped on it."

"Oh, no!" she wheezed, half-horrified and halfway to laughter. "It's too disgusting. Let's get away from it." She started toward the gate.

Sweat ran from under my arms, soaking into my halter. "What am I going to do?"

"It'll die in a little while," Dolly tossed over her shoulder. "You don't have to worry about it."

I circled the toad, wondering if I could leave it like that. His eyeballs swiveled so he could keep watching me. I realized he couldn't accuse me or even worry about what would happen to him. It didn't help to know that. I raised my foot, not at all sure I could do what had to be done. My skin felt scrunched up all over, the way your mouth feels when you suck on a lemon.

"Allie!"

I stomped down hard and turned my heel. A nasty sound bubbled up out of my throat as I scraped my foot over another patch of grass.

"Allie! Are you coming?"

I turned and ran without looking again at the toad.

"What were you doing over there?" Dolly scolded.

"Nothing. Stop acting like you're so grown up," I snapped. I skittered toe and heel across the softened tar to the dry grass on the other side of the road. We climbed onto the fence rail, taking care not to pick up splinters where our halters didn't meet our shorts.

"Hey, you gals comin' along?" Uncle Brian teased. Heads turned in our direction and we hung there awkwardly, tongue-tied. Grandpa leaned out the truck window, smiling with a soft sparkle in his eye. I looked at Dolly and right away I knew she didn't want to go. Another wave of uncles was coming and we dropped back to the ground. When they started jumping that fence, you might as well be clinging to the back of an angry bull.

That would have been the end of it but Uncle Darryl came up behind us. He put a hand on each of our shoulders, hugging us against his sweat dampened flannel shirt that was all ribs underneath. "I'm coming," I called out, but Dolly shook her head and pulled away. Uncle Darryl lifted me over the fence to Uncle Collin, who handed me into the back of the truck. I sat behind the window between Uncle Little Mike and Uncle Harry.

I knew why she had refused to come along. Being with our uncles was something of a mixed blessing. You were there to go along, like that bear that went over the mountain, to see what you could see. That didn't mean anyone had anything to say to you in particular. Or that anyone wanted to hear what you thought. I don't know when it happens that what you say begins to count for something.

But you were bound to hear talk, if you know what I mean. Uncle Little Mike began whispering to Uncle Joe about his date the night before, now and then erupting into high-pitched masculine giggles. Uncle Joe was sixteen, a year younger than Uncle Little Mike, and inexperienced. A perfect audience.

Uncle Brian sat listening to them, joggling from side to side with the motion of the truck, his eyes so nearly shut that he was looking through his pale eyelashes. I closed my eyes like his and stared at him. It wasn't long before a little smile turned up the corners of his mouth.

On my other side, Uncle Harry talked about the navy and

how it offered opportunities for young men to learn a trade. A subject of great interest to him ever since three of his brothers had returned from Korea full of stories. His sleeves were rolled up to the middle of upper arms that were as thick as some tree trunks, burned an Indian red by the sun. He was nineteen, same as Uncle Darryl, but his slow manner made him seem like a child.

No matter how hard I listened to Uncle Harry I kept hearing choice bits from Uncle Little Mike's recitation. The drive-in movie was scary, which is a *guarantee.* Playing like he was going to bite her neck. Bouncing titties. Touching it. Next time will be *it.*

The sun seemed to be beating on my head and in fact, my hair was hot to the touch when I ran my hand over it. We pulled to a stop where the morning's work had halted. The sweet dry smell of alfalfa filled my nostrils. It stretched across the fields for as far as I could see. The thresher sat silent, waiting, the sunlight glinting off the blades. Uncles Harry and Joe and Darryl jumped off the truck. "C'mon, sweetheart. I'm putting you up front."

Uncle Darryl calls girls sweetheart. Even Grandma.

"Let Allie ride up here, Pop. The talk in back is pretty joyous. Her ears are as red as her hair." He dropped me onto Uncle Ted's lap, who shunted me over to the middle with an assortment of tools.

"Hold on there, boys. We're pulling a lot of lumber downt the sawmill. How is it three of you are getting out here?" Grandpa hooked a thumb in his overall strap, a sign that he was going to sit there until he knew what there was to know.

"I want to hear what that recruiter had to say to Harry. We can't hear ourselves think in the mill, let alone do some private talking." When Grandpa looked doubtful, Uncle Darryl added, "We can spell Joe and then we'll come up to the mill."

"Suppose I don't ride this way again. You gonna waste an afternoon sitting on a fence rail?"

"You'll bring by water in a couple of hours?" Uncle Darryl

turned his big-toothed smile on Grandpa like a shaft of sunlight in winter. Grandpa thawed right down.

"You be ready."

"Thanks, Pop."

The saw mill was Grandpa's answer to three problems. A couple hundred acres of woodland that could be turned into producing farmland was one. And how to keep fifteen boys at work all year round was another. Last, it made money year-round, whether or not the crops were good and prices were up. It ensured each boy a farm of his own when he married, which, as I heard him say himself, was the deal he made them.

Some of Grandpa's sons are what Reverend Allen calls the children of his loins. Don't frown on me. It's written in the Bible that way. I think it must be what men say once they're married and talk of bouncing titties falls by the wayside. The rest of Grandpa's sons are what Grandma calls her latecomers. They are boys who, for one reason or another, were to be found destitute and homeless during the Depression. I gather that also means they were found by the side of the road.

There isn't any point in asking which ones are which. Grandma sometimes sits in her kitchen rocker, where she rocked all her babies, and tells you a story about how this one was so cute and smart. This one will promptly interrupt and say it couldn't have been him because he didn't get there till he was eight. Grandma just shrugs and laughs. Her boys nudge each other and joke about how it couldn't be that one either because he isn't cute. Or that one because he surely isn't smart.

It doesn't do much good to try to tell from looking either. Nearly all of them have blond or light-brown hair and blue eyes. Uncle Zeke, named after Grandpa, is an exception to this. He has black hair, as straight as I've ever seen, and is tall and thin like no one else in the family. But he was born right after my mother, who's the eldest, so there's no question there. Uncle Darryl and Uncle Tommy are also exceptions with their curly dark hair. They're latecomers who are true brothers and who've retained their last name. Burns. Uncle Tommy brought

Uncle Darryl to Grandpa when their parents died and it worked out they both stayed.

If you were really determined, you could begin to collect stories. Like Uncle Little Mike coming to them the year before Uncle Big Mike got married. That tells you only about Uncle Little Mike, though. Or you could compare their ages. Uncle Jake and Uncle Brian are the same age and so are Uncle Matt and Uncle Ted. That answers you for sure about a few of them but if you let Grandma hear you, you'll be outside hanging chickens before you know what got hold of you.

Uncle Ted chewed on Grandpa's ear about college, which is The Way Education Is Going. Uncle Ted took it hard that he couldn't go to Korea, and he's since become an authority on almost everything else. He says by the time Tucker grows up, a man won't even be able to get a job without having college. "Why, the way the world is going, there may even come a time when this little gal will need college." Uncle Ted smiled his fat, rubber-lipped smile. I looked at him then in a certain way that's meant to be polite. But I'd like to be in front of a mirror some time when it comes over me. It feels closely akin to the look Mom calls Being Smart.

Grandpa listened because he says you should always listen, take the best and leave the rest behind. Mom once said Grandpa will pass the time of day with anyone. Grandpa didn't seem too disturbed to hear it. By the time we reached the sawmill, Uncle Ted had talked himself out. Grandpa's face settled into the lines it has when he sits in his chair out in front of the house. He smiled at me the way he smiles at grandchildren. That's mostly all he ever does with grandchildren. All that I've known him to say, I've heard him saying to other people. He's never said two words to me.

We stopped at the little house on the way back. My Uncle Collin lived there with Aunt Suzie. I'd met her the summer before, although at the time she was just a friend of my aunts, Dora and Flora. She was fourteen then, like my aunts. But there was something different about her. She was more womanly in her appearance. And shy, even more so than my Aunt

Dora. She smiled a lot, blushing easily. By the end of the summer she was married to my Uncle Collin which, as my mother said, was young.

No one answered my knock, so I stuck my head inside the door. Because the little house had only one room, I had no trouble seeing that Aunt Suzie wasn't home. There was a red-and-white-checked cloth on the table, a surprise because table-cloths were something I had seen only in restaurants. A glass jar stood on the bed table, filled with daisies and a handful of grass. That's what caught my eye. It was regular lawn grass, grown tall enough to stick out of the jar some, making the daisies look like they'd been wrapped with a wide green ribbon.

Grandpa finished filling the bucket at the hand pump and I ran to get in the truck. Grandma was as young as Aunt Suzie when Grandpa built this house for her. They lived here till they had Mom and Uncle Zeke. By then Grandpa'd built the big house. It had a big kitchen, a sitting room that eventually became the dining room, and two bedrooms. After a while the two bedrooms were chock full of beds, and Grandpa built a shack out back of the house. He moved the first four boys out there, the youngest being eight. It wasn't long before he had three shacks out there and each of the little boys counting the days till he would be six years and old enough to move into his own place. Dora and Flora shared the second bedroom after all the boys were out.

Grandpa added porches on to each side of the house, screen-ing in one of them so he could sit outside with Grandma of an evening without being eaten up by bugs. He put in a bathroom last year. I heard him tell Uncle Zeke it was because Grandma would make a late trip to the outhouse, come in with cold feet, and he was getting too old to warm her feet every night. It didn't sound like much of a story to me but it sure tickled Uncle Zeke.

"What're they doin', horsin' around over there?" Grandpa said to himself as we came over the ridge. I sat straighter on the seat, trying to see over the nose of the truck.

Uncle Darryl and Uncle Harry ran alongside the thresher, yelling and laughing. Uncle Joe, sitting deep in the noise of the thresher, took no notice of them. I was with Uncle Harry once when he shot a rabbit. It saw us and began to run, not scared but smart. It zigzagged across the field, leaped over a bush— and dropped out of the air like it ran into a glass wall. Dropped straight down.

That's how Uncle Darryl fell.

Uncle Harry stopped still, picture of a farmer in the sunlight, and the thresher moved on, slow and steady as time. Grandpa jammed his foot down on the gas pedal. I clung to the seat, one arm thrown over the back and one hand glued to the door handle. I kept my eyes on the spot where Uncle Darryl fell, willing him to get up and start running again. Uncle Harry didn't move, even as we pulled to a stop behind him.

Grandpa jumped out of the truck. "Your belt," he yelled at Uncle Harry. "Your belt, Harry. Give it to me," he yelled again, dropping to his knees next to Uncle Darryl.

"I don't know how it happened, Pa." Uncle Harry began to cry as he fumbled with the buckle. "We was just playing around. I didn't think he was so close to the blades." Uncle Darryl's right pants leg ended in a bright red band that grew wider as he lay there watching all of us. Not saying anything. Not even crying.

The leather slid through the belt loops with agonizing slowness. It wasn't that Uncle Harry wasn't moving fast. He was. But my eyes weren't taking anything for granted. I was seeing everything so completely it seemed to be in slow motion. Grandpa must have felt it too, because he snatched at Uncle Harry's belt, nearly yanking him off his feet as it snapped free. Grandpa's hands were fast and sure, not shaking the way Uncle Harry's had. He pulled the belt tight. At the end of the row, Uncle Joe turned and started back, speeding up when he saw there was trouble. The thresher blades turned faster, making a sound like a faraway freight train bearing down on us.

"Pull up that pants leg."

Uncle Harry bent to do what he was told, stiff with fear. He went chalky and I thought he was going to pass out. I wasn't prepared, either, for how it would look. Neat. The leg had been sliced through, neat as cold butter. Grandpa yelled at Uncle Harry again but neither of us could hear what he said over the racketing of the thresher. Grandpa strained to pull the belt tighter, sweat dripping off his face like rainwater. Uncle Harry moved to help him.

The thresher stopped. Something beat in my ears where the sound of the thresher had been. Uncle Joe dropped to the ground and ran to us. "The bleeding's slowed," Grandpa told him. "Let's get him into the truck."

They were all moving now, not wasting words. I clambered into the back as Uncle Joe slammed up the tailgate. Uncle Harry planted his feet against Uncle Darryl's hip and pulled tighter on the belt than Grandpa had been able to do. Grandpa pulled off his shirt, bunching it up under Uncle Darryl's head. I braced myself against the side of the truck and clung to Uncle Darryl's hand as if I could keep him there by needing him so much. He squeezed my hand. "It's all right, Allie," he said in a thin voice. "It doesn't even hurt."

"That's it," Grandpa told Uncle Harry. "It's all but stopped."

"I can hold it." Just as Uncle Harry said that we hit a rut, loosening his grip on the belt. A fresh flow of blood spread over the floor of the truck. He bit down on his lip and pulled tight again. It was then that I saw tears in Grandpa's eyes.

It's funny the way one thing connects with another in your mind. And the way it can stay there, going round and round, like a record with a skip in it. What kept going through my head was something that happened last summer. We were in the hayloft, Dolly and Tucker and I. A beam runs across the barn, all the way to the back. Near the end, it connects with a riser before it goes on to the other end of the loft. "Betcha I can walk across there," Tucker bragged.

"So what? Uncle Matt does it all the time," I said.

"Betcha you can't."

"Tucker, don't start something that will get us into trouble," Dolly warned.

1 9

"I ain't startin' nothin'. You're just chicken to try it."

"I don't want to do it. It has nothing to do with being chicken."

"You say! You can't talk for Allie." That was the moment I could have helped Dolly and helped myself as well. But the thing about Tucker is he never lets go. Some things are better to have over with.

"Let's see you do it, Big Mouth," I dared him.

Tucker's eyes narrowed as he measured me. "You're chicken. I'll get across and you won't even try it."

"You never want to climb trees and you never go up very far," Dolly said to me. She was nothing if not helpful.

I could sit like Dolly and tell him that it proved nothing whether or not we could cross the beam. But until one of us crossed it, he wouldn't be listening.

"You're chicken," he repeated.

"That's as may be, but I've never been chicken at any of your games," I told him. All the tease went out of it for Tucker. Now he had to walk it faster, better. My stomach twisted into a knot. He'd push it. He'd do something that would frighten even him.

He stepped out on the beam and brought one foot down hard in front of the other for a few steps. He let out a long whistle, and I realized none of us were breathing.

Two more steps and he broke into an Indian dance, complete with war whoops, his hair flying up with each step. Dolly's hand gripped mine as we sat in petrified silence. Midway he stopped and looked back, grinning. Then he began to lurch across in a drunken shuffle. "How dry Iyam," he sang. He ran the last few steps and lounged against the column. "Your turn."

"You ain't finished yet," Dolly screeched.

"Okay, okay." He stepped over to the other beam and crossed quickly to the edge of the loft. "I'll wait here."

I started out, taking small steps, telling myself it was more than wide enough for my feet. As wide as two bricks laid together. Fear prickled over my scalp.

Tucker had done it.

So could I.

The floor of the barn fell away, dropping faster than I could cross the beam. Sweat trickled down my neck, followed by a wave of dizziness. I swallowed and tried to go faster, ignoring the weakness that crept through my shoulders.

"Allie, you can do it," Tucker whispered.

My stomach churned furiously as I forced myself to go faster. The beam didn't stand out so clearly in the fading light. It was soft beneath my feet and the skin on my abdomen crawled as that weakness rushed lower. The beam sank with my next step but I caught myself, arms out for balance, before it could spill me off.

"Allie," Tucker called, far off now, "you can do it, easy. Just think of it as the strip of tile on Grandma's kitchen floor."

I nodded.

His voice went on, nearly drowned out by the buzzing in my head. I wiped the sweat away from my eyes and peered into the deepening twilight. It was strange, this darkness, and as I wondered about it, everything went black.

"Allie!"

Tucker's scream brought me up to help myself. The beam caught me under one arm as I fell and I clamped onto it. The jolt nearly pulled my shoulder apart. Somewhere behind me Dolly wailed, "Hang on, Allie! Get your other arm over!" Tucker started out for me, driving Dolly to hysterics.

"What's going on out here? Oh, Christ!" Uncle Darryl was miles below me. "Get back from there, Tucker!"

"I'm gonna help her!"

"Get back!"

My arm began to cramp. "Allie." Uncle Darryl's face floated beneath me. "Allie. Sweetheart. Are you listening to me?"

His face came into sharper focus. He smiled, not the terrified grimace that Tucker's face held as he tried to will me across the last few feet, but a real smile. "That's it, sweetheart. I know it looks bad."

I tried to answer.

2 1

"Don't worry about that, sweetheart. We'll talk when we get you down."

My eyes filled with tears.

"I'm right under you, Allie. I can catch you." And then, "Allie. Let go of the beam." I screamed and swung wildly. "Allie! Allie, don't be afraid. I can catch you. I promise, Allie."

Trust is a funny thing. Uncle Darryl was nowhere near as tall as most of the boys, and skinny as well. Wiry, Grandpa said he was. And I wouldn't have let go of that beam for Paul Bunyan. I let go of it for Uncle Darryl. The beam roughed the inside of my arm as I slid over. The strangest thing was, I had time to wonder if I was doing it wrong. I was facing the roof of the barn as I fell, instead of Uncle Darryl. Then he caught me.

I know it sounds selfish that I sat there holding Uncle Darryl's hand, thinking about what happened to me last summer, as we raced up the road. Only once, as they lifted him into the truck, did he ask, Pop, am I gonna die? Grandpa's eyebrows lifted in surprise. "Why, no, son, I don't think so." Now I began to wonder if he'd been right.

Uncle Harry cried, not loudly, just tears running down his scrunched up face. Grandpa reached across to clap him on the arm.

"Pa. You know what he said when he fell? 'It's cut clean off, isn't it, Harry?' Just like that, Pa, without so much as a twitch of his eyebrow." A sob escaped him, just one, before he sucked himself back inside and tears rolled down his face.

"I'm thirsty, Pop," Uncle Darryl's voice sounded cracked.

Grandpa slid the water bucket across, sloshing water over the truck bed. It picked up enough blood to run red by the time it got to the other end of the truck. Grandpa looked stricken but he didn't say anything. He filled the ladle, then lifted Uncle Darryl's head to help him drink. Uncle Harry wiped one hand on his jeans and went for a better grip, pulling till Uncle Darryl's face showed pain.

"Hurting some?" Grandpa asked.

"Just an achy feeling."

"We'll be there soon, now."

Uncle Darryl's skin looked dry and thickened somehow. His coloring was the worst. Bluish.

"Are you doing okay, Uncle Darryl?"

"I'm feeling a little poorly, sweetheart," he breathed. He gave my hand another squeeze, finishing with a tremor.

Grandpa moved over by Uncle Harry and helped him to tighten the belt. It took the two of them to manage as well as Uncle Harry had until now.

"Pop?" Uncle Darryl tried to focus his eyes on Grandpa.

"What is it, son?"

"Just in case, Pop . . . I want to tell you . . . I love you and Ma. . . ."

"We know, son. Darryl, you're going to be all right. We're nearly there."

"Just needed . . . to tell you. . . ."

"Pa?" Uncle Harry's voice shook.

Grandpa raised a hand, warning off the question.

Fresh tears rolled down Uncle Harry's face as he reset his grip on the belt. It couldn't be pulled any tighter, but Uncle Darryl didn't flinch. I squeezed his hand and it gave me some relief to feel a weak response.

Uncle Joe pulled into Doc Petersen's driveway, continuing across the lawn, where the doctor was climbing out of his flower garden. He followed Uncle Joe over the side of the truck and I let go of Uncle Darryl's hand to get out of the way.

"Lost his foot in the thresher," Grandpa explained as the boys got ready to take Uncle Darryl inside. The doctor sat quiet, a finger pressed to Uncle Darryl's throat. He shifted his hand to another spot and pressed again. Uncle Darryl's hand lay where I'd dropped it, still curved to hold mine. "The boy's gone, Zeke."

It looked like a family reunion all over again, aunts and uncles and children scattered across the lawn with paper plates and iced tea. Except that the men wore suits, looking taller somehow with the jackets flapping in the breeze and their hair slicked down. The women were in their Sunday best with white collars and neat cuffs on the puffed up sleeves of summer dresses.

Uncle Harry cried uncontrollably over breakfast, and Tucker went off by himself after returning from the funeral. I was surprised myself that I had no desire to go along, even if he would've had me. The thing that got to me was, everyone else seemed to be taking it so well. Not that they weren't sad or that they didn't miss Uncle Darryl. But they weren't particularly interested in talking about it.

I almost understood it when I was sitting in Mrs. Petersen's kitchen. She fed me milk and cookies and kept up a pleasant conversation that we both agreed would take my mind off things. It wasn't as bad as it sounds. She had some interesting things to say and even though the afternoon seemed to go on forever, what with wanting to know where my grandfather had gone (they're going to be too busy to have a little girl tagging along), and what would happen to Uncle Darryl (don't you bother yourself about that now), she never made me feel like she wanted to pat me on the backside and send me outside.

I let myself drift away from Mrs. Petersen's voice and stared at the garden just outside the window. If someone were to look in that window right then, I thought, they'd see Mrs. Petersen at some business in her kitchen while she enjoyed the company of, who do you think that could be, a granddaughter? Sitting there for that moment, I could smile at Mrs. Petersen the way my aunts and uncles were smiling now.

And just when I thought I had it—it was gone.

Looking at my aunts and uncles was much like looking through that window. You looked at all those dressed-up smiling faces, not talking about Uncle Darryl (child, there's no point in upsetting yourself), denying they were even thinking about Uncle Darryl (Allie, if you don't go outside and find yourself something to do, Florrie and I are going to lock you in the pantry!), and you barely saw that all around them, Uncle Darryl wasn't there.

He was gone—just gone—and it hardly even made a sound.

Even now I can't get my mind around it in quite the same way, which is good because I don't think I could live with it all the time.

I found Grandma in one of the shacks, sitting on the edge of a wooden bunk. She smoothed the cotton slip over the pillow, a gentle motion that made my heart feel easier. It didn't come to mind to say anything, to think what to do. I went to stand beside her, to breathe in her cinnamon scent as she swept the wrinkles from that pillow. My chest was so tight it pained me, but I took the first really deep breath I'd managed all day.

"He slept here, Allie. He and Harry shared this bunk the first winter they slept out here, both of them babies six years old," she said wistfully. "I'd come out to see they was warm and the two heads, one light, one dark, would be here in the moonlight, their faces so little and sweet.

"That's how you always saw them, together. Darryl was like a gift to Harry, Darryl being so quick to pick things up and so patient to show Harry what to do. Darryl spoke for both of them, saw to it Harry's shy ways didn't hold him back. And Harry tromped anybody that even looked sideways at Darryl, half-sized little snip that he was." Grandma spread her hand over a corner of the pillow, crushing it till her knuckles showed white. "He looked half-starved, like a baby bird too early out of the nest, right up till. . . ." She swallowed noisily. I bent to stretch my arms around her shoulders, reaching to cross them in front the way I'd seen Uncle Darryl do so often, and squeezed her up in a hug. A little whimper escaped her and I felt her tears on my wrist. In spite of being a different thing than I'd ever done, it felt so right, the way Grandma and I fit together.

"Allie. Dear." Her voice was hardly a sigh. "Darryl's own arms were about this size when he took to holding on to me. I don't know that I ever told him how it warmed me to have one of my boys so affectionate in his ways." She began to cry. "I don't know how I'll face the mornings."

2

THAT afternoon Mom took me back to Carlisle with her, saying Grandma Taylor could do with some time to herself. Grandma followed us outside, stopping Mom when she was half inside the car. "You could stay a few days, Nora. I could do with your company."

"I want to get home, Ma, to Jim and Crystal."

Grandma let her held-in breath go in a little sigh. "You always were one to hold yourself to yourself."

Mom didn't answer, but her face seemed to close over itself, refusing Grandma's words, and bringing out the truth of them. Grandma leaned forward, resting her hand on the open window edge. "I never meant, Nora, to wear out your patience with me. Helping me with the others, I mean."

"I was your only girl until the twins," Mom said, more in agreement than by way of excusing it.

"It was more to me, Nora. You were my only friend. To talk to, like."

Mom struggled to come up with a smile. "It's different now, Ma. The boys have brought you so many daughters."

"Yes." Grandma's voice went faint. "Well, you're right, of course."

Relenting, Mom reached out to pat Grandma's hand. "I love you, Ma. I just need to be with my family now." Mom pulled her foot in and shut the car door. I saw as I climbed into the backseat that the toe of her shoe left a deep print in the hot tar.

Tucker sat in back with me, having been dragged along as company for me. We felt little inclination to talk. I don't think we'd exchanged ten words all day, and most of those had been that morning, when Uncle Darryl's funeral had been something less of a solid fact. Even Uncle Ted was at a loss, talking in spurts about one thing and another as he drove, then letting the ends of sentences die out unfinished. Mom nodded now and then, whether he was talking or not.

Daddy Jim waited for us on the front porch, with Crystal on his knee, both of them looking far too fresh and crisped up for such a hot day. Daddy Jim was putting a good face on for Uncle Ted's benefit. He'd never felt a call to do that before so it was clear to me he had fallen out of grace with my mother. In spite of that, or maybe because of it, things were quiet that evening.

On each of the few mornings since Uncle Darryl's death, I'd awakened with a sense of a bad day ahead, remembering in the next moment why I had that feeling. Waking in my own bed changed that in only one respect. It added the certain knowledge that Uncle Darryl was gone forever, that there was no chance that I would wake one morning in one of the wooden bunks my grandfather built and find it had been a terrible dream.

I peered across the room and into the crib where Crystal slept, wondering if she was awake yet. There was nothing to see but a small mound of yellow curls at the edge of her blanket. Crystal always threw off her blanket before she woke up.

It was the start of summer two years ago that Mom sat on the hard front steps of the apartment house in Des Moines and told me what Crystal's name would be. She leaned on the black metal railing, cradling her huge belly while she watched me crouched over a solitary game of jacks. The memory had the feeling of long ago and far away, like some fairy tales say.

"What will you name the baby, Mom?"

In a way that didn't hold herself to herself at all, my mother smiled and answered. "If it's a boy, we'll name him James, after Daddy Jim."

"And if it's a girl?"

"Well, then I think I'll name her Crystal."

"That's a funny name."

"It's a pretty name," she answered back in a dreamy way. "It makes me think of a pretty life. Full of flowers and blue skies and fluffy white clouds."

"Like Grandma's?"

"It can't be a pretty life if you have to work so hard you never notice." There was a sharper edge to these words and I thought carefully before I went on.

"What kind of name is Allie, Mom?"

"Alexandra," she said.

"Alexandra," I agreed.

"It's a growing-up-and-being-something name," she said.

"Is that why you gave me that name?"

"Your father named you, Allie."

I was quiet again, going back to my jacks.

"There was a time when I thought that was the same as a pretty life," she said, almost to herself.

"Isn't it?"

"Maybe sometimes."

Crystal had turned two just before I'd gone off to Grandma's. In my absence she'd added a word or two to the few she'd had before, and she'd come up with a trick. She threw her leg over the side of the crib like she might climb over, and dangled there with both feet in the air, clinging tightly to the rail. Mom said not to encourage her because she would likely fall out. However, encouragement or none, she was eager to show her new trick at every opportunity and she'd found several opportunities in the course of a single evening.

I thought about waking her up. I thought about Mom rushing in to pick her out of bed and Daddy Jim calling us all into the kitchen. Daddy Jim usually got up first on Saturday mornings. He made breakfast, saying Mom worked hard enough during the week, she ought to have a morning to call her own. I wanted to feel like this could be any Saturday, not just the Saturday after Uncle Darryl died. So at first I tried to ignore Daddy Jim's voice. He was angry and yelling, and my mother was yelling, too. They'd been fighting like this for months. Mom thought it would stop when we moved, and for a while it did.

Daddy Jim said it was like having our own house, except for the couple living upstairs. We had the big apartment which took in the use of the basement and the backyard. It was mostly dirt with a fringe of grass around the edges like a bald man's hair grows. Daddy Jim put in a layer of pink shale so we wouldn't have to play in the dirt, and Mom planted flowers along the fence, where she could stand dreamy eyed on a summer's evening.

Daddy Jim went on yelling, the words coming fast and not very clear.

I thought about being back in Des Moines on a Saturday. After breakfast, Daddy Jim would give me a quarter and walk me to Woolworth's where I could spend it. We passed a candy store, but if I stopped to buy penny candy I didn't have enough to buy what I wanted at Woolworth's. We figured out that the thing to do was, go to the dime store first and try to save over some money for candy. What I liked, Daddy Jim let me feel like I figured it all out for myself.

We'd stop in the library on the way home. It used to be that I could get books only from the school library. That meant taking out the books my teacher liked, books directed to a girl's interests. I had to sneak out the books about dinosaurs under my sweater set. When Daddy Jim found the books under my pillow, I was sure he'd be mad. I guess he was, because he made me take them back to school the next day. But on Saturday we stopped at a pretty red-brick building that we always passed right by before. He sat down with Crystal to look at picture books while I took as long as I wanted to find a book to read.

I got up, heading for their bedroom. Stiffly starched, ruffled curtains were neatly closed over the lower half of the kitchen windows. Morning sunlight drew broad stripes on the rounded surface of the new refrigerator. The pale green woodstove had been polished until it was glossy. She hated it but she would never neglect it long enough for it to collect fingerprints. My mother didn't have a woodstove in Des Moines.

I think I was going to knock on the door. Sometimes it ends an argument if I just show my face, partly because they don't want me hanging around asking questions. Mostly because they think I'll talk out of turn, especially now that fairtime is close and my father will be here. That's what I had in mind as I went through the living room to their room. But when I got there, they were yelling so hard I couldn't butt in. I stood outside the closed door, listening.

"I've seen the way he looks at you. Like he sees something the rest of us don't know."

"Jim, you're wrong. . . ."

"Wrong! How can I be wrong? Didn't I used to look at you that way when you walked down the street with your arm through Robert's?"

"Please, Jim. . . ."

"It's that kind of look, Nora! Who would know better than me? Don't walk away—"

"Stop it! Not now. . . ."

"Is that what you used to tell Robert? Stop it, not now," he mimicked her. "Have you been with that man? Is that it?"

"I've been here with you! Don't!" Something crashed to the floor.

"Run from me? You think you can run?" Glass smashed against the door. I jumped and even screamed a little but they didn't notice.

"Please stop! You'll wake the children," my mother cried over the creak of the bedsprings.

"Last week it was the neighbors you were worried about," Daddy Jim yelled hoarsely. "You're always worryin' someone will hear. You know what I figured out? You ain't worried what they'll think of me. You're worried what they'll know about you." I heard the bedsprings again, someone's feet slapped down on the floor. "You don't want them to know what kind of woman—C'mere, dammit!" Someone, my mother I guess, grabbed the doorknob but the door never opened.

"Not like this, pl——ow! Jim, I stepped on . . . no, please, Jim, no. . . ."

They slid to the floor with a scrabbling sound of feet and elbows. Then nothing. Just this terrible silence. Sweat stood out on my forehead. I only wanted to hear something. Yelling. Glass breaking.

Then I heard my mother crying. A soft crying that got louder for a second, then soft again and louder for a second. It went on that way and I only wanted it to stop. My knees shook right up to my elbows. I went back to bed.

It seemed like a long time before they finally came out. They headed straight for the kitchen, Mom going to the medicine cabinet that hung over the sink, still crying softly. I pretended I was asleep. I learned long ago that if you lay on your stomach with half your face turned into the pillow, it isn't so hard to keep your eyes closed. People will always believe you're asleep.

Daddy Jim made Mom sit on the chair while he got her a band-aid. "You have to be more careful, Nora. What would we do if you got laid up with an infection?"

Mom began to cry harder.

"Nora, Nora," Daddy Jim said gently. "You're such a baby about these things. Your foot is going to be fine in no time at all." He pulled her onto his lap. Mom went on crying, holding in the way she really wanted to cry. I could tell.

One morning soon after we moved here I went in to wake them up. Daddy Jim cuddled Mom in his arms while they talked in low voices. I climbed up on the end of the bed to listen. Building, Daddy Jim said, building was what he was doing. Same as her brothers did for themselves. Building us a home, Mom and me and Crystal. Mom looked so soft and sweet then, listening to Daddy Jim, letting her hand drift up and down his arm. I didn't believe he would treat her like this if he could remember that morning like I could. I wiped my nose and flipped my pillow over. It wouldn't do for them to see wet spots when they came to wake us up.

"I don't see why we have to go to church. We never have before."

"Don't make out like you've never seen the inside of a church, Allie!" Mom said, tying pink bows onto Crystal's tiny tailbobs. Mom was always careful to keep Crystal neat and clean, but when Mom took her out she made a special effort. Everyone always commented on what a pretty little girl Crystal was. "Your Daddy's family sends you to Bible school whenever you're visiting them."

"I only visit a few weeks out of the year. I can put up with it for that long."

"Allie. I don't want to hear any more of that kind of talk. It's—"

"It's talk of the devil," Daddy Jim leered, turning away from the mirror. He'd brushed his moustache until it separated in the middle, sweeping gently off toward his cheeks.

My mother looked worried. "Please, Jim. Don't encourage her."

"There's no good reason to turn ourselves into churchgoers. It can't do Darryl any good."

"It means so much to me, Jim," she said, her voice catching in her throat. "Please do it for me."

Daddy Jim shrugged. "I'll be waiting outside with Crystal. Don't be long."

Mom began to brush my hair. "The church was so beautiful,

33

Allie, the morning we were there for Darryl. The sunlight so bright, the wooden pews smelling of lemon oil and when we sang—afterward, the minister was so nice to Ma, and to me too. He's the kind of person who's always so sure about things, and strong. Do you know what I mean, Allie?"

I nodded. It was what she expected.

"I just knew that if someone took a problem to him, he would have the answer. That's when I realized it had been such a long time since we'd been to church." I guess she could see I wasn't convinced, because her face went a little pink. She twitched my dress into place and fluffed up the skirt. "I think going to church will help us. I want you to be on your best behavior."

I don't want to sound nasty here. I mean, I saw Mom's face, all lit up like a little kid putting an empty stocking under the Christmas tree. But she'd never had a good word for church-going.

"Did Grandma ever take you to church, Mom?"

"Why do you ask?"

"I was just wondering when you ever did go to church much. Except for weddings, I mean."

"Allie, are you being smart?" She pulled sharply on my ponytail to move it up higher.

"No, no. I'm just wondering. When did you?"

"Before we were married, your father used to drive to get me early Sunday mornings and take me back to Grandma Drew's for breakfast. Then we'd all go to church together."

I stood quiet while she began to dress, hoping she'd forget to tell me to wait outside. She hardly ever talked about Daddy and when she did it was never like this, remembering. It was usually because his plane was late or because She always waited in the taxi. Stuff like that.

Mom made a real production of putting on stockings. First checking her fingernails for rough spots, then scrunching the stocking up real tight before she put it over her foot. She looked very nice when she got dressed up, in a city kind of way. Wearing this gray skirt, black and white flecked, with a white blouse, quite old and very soft. She added a thin blue scarf around her neck, called a smoke ring. She took out her pocketbook, filling it with tissues before she put in her comb and lipstick.

Usually she got dressed up for PTA meetings and trips to the doctor. And weddings, of course. It seemed to me, and of course it's probably because she was my mother, that she always stood out a little bit. Maybe it's because she used rouge, though it was only a little bit so no one would know. Or maybe it's what I heard someone say once, that she was a great beauty in her day. I'm not quite sure when that was or when it ceased to be, but it may be that there was some of it left over.

It was a good day for her. It was boring for everyone else but you could see it was a good day for Mom. She listened to the preacher for all she was worth and when we stood up to sing, she sang for all she was worth. Especially when we sang "Leanin' on the Everlastin' Arm". Tears came to her eyes. It made me a little nervous, if you want to know the truth.

The preacher stood at the door saying good-bye to everyone, knowing who usually comes and didn't today, and also seeing the new faces. While he walked around the lawn a time or two, everyone stood looking like they had something important to talk about and couldn't leave just yet. It wasn't hard to figure out they were hoping he'd have something nice to say to them and that everyone else would notice. Everyone would. Whatever a preacher has to say is said in a carrying voice, just in case anyone might have been genuinely distracted and likely to miss it.

Every preacher I've seen is very careful to spread his attentions around so that after a few Sundays he gets to everybody. He came up to us after services the way Mom hoped he would. Of course, this was a different preacher than the one who'd been so nice to Grandma. I don't know quite how it happened, but the next thing I knew he was coming to the house for Tuesday night supper. This may not sound like anything but I can't remember that we ever had anyone over to supper.

* * *

3 5

When Brother Wayne first arrived, I was up to say hello. He perched on the edge of Daddy Jim's favorite chair, hunched over so he could rest his elbows on his spread knees, huge hands folded and hanging down. I don't mean to be disrespectful but he looked just like a spider sitting in a web. Mom popped me into bed at six thirty, along with Crystal. I lay there, too hot and sticky to sleep. It was broad daylight. A lawnmower clacked up and down the Kellys' lawn.

"Would you like to take your coffee into the living room?"

"Sister Nora, there's nothing I appreciate like a place to rest my elbows. Let's just sit here if you don't mind."

They closed the door between the kitchen and my bedroom and I figured that was it for me. But Brother Wayne's voice carried well enough to keep sinners in the back pews awake and it carried well enough to be heard clearly through that door. It wasn't long before things began to liven up.

"Forgive me for asking, Brother Jim," the preacher said, sounding concerned, "but with looking at the two of you, by all appearances in radiant good health, and strong in your love for each other, just what is bedeviling you?"

"I . . . I'm an alcoholic. I'm drinking again." Daddy Jim was about as pitiful as I've ever heard him.

"You say 'again,' Brother Jim. Am I to understand you had it licked for a time?"

"I didn't touch it for four years. I kept my word to Nora. I kept it." Daddy Jim's voice went lower with shame. "Till that day at work."

"What made that day different from so many days before it?"

"I don't know as I can say it right out."

"There's nothing you can't tell me, Brother Jim."

"Jim worries that I don't love him anymore," my mother spoke up. I crept from my bed and put my ear to the door.

"I don't like the way men look at her."

"You feel she comports herself in a way that attracts men's eyes?" Brother Wayne asked sternly.

"No, I guess not," Daddy Jim answered with some reluc-

3 6

tance. "But one man in particular is plainly attracted to her."

"Who is this man?" Brother Wayne purred.

"He lives upstairs," Daddy Jim answered.

"Is he alone?"

"He's married," my mother said. "We hardly ever see them. There's no good reason for Jim to suspect me."

"Why, then, do you think Brother Jim is so disturbed?"

"Well . . . I don't know."

After a moment, she added, "I don't try to make any man look at me. I like to look nice but I don't—"

"I see you wear lipstick, Sister Nora."

"Yes," my mother said in a breathy voice that I could hardly hear.

"And powder." His voice grew stronger. "Does your mother wear these accoutrements, Sister Nora?"

"No."

"When did you begin to use them?"

"During the war. All the women—" My mother's voice went higher, a sign that she was getting upset.

"You said something earlier about a factory?" My mother must have nodded. "And Brother Jim here was off to war?"

"I was married. . . . My first husband and I were divorced just after the war," she answered shakily.

"Nora's a good woman. I don't believe she laid with anyone but her husband before me."

"Amen. I'm glad to hear you speak up so surely, Brother Jim." And then his voice went lower so that I strained to hear. "Could it be your fears are not with your wife, Brother Jim, but with yourself?"

There was a space when I began to wonder if they were talking at all. I sat on the edge of my bed. It wasn't until Daddy Jim opened the door a crack to reach in for tissues that I realized my mother was crying. He left it ajar and I was able to hear everything clearly, even though they were almost whispering now.

"Do you sometimes look at other women, Brother Jim?"

Daddy Jim didn't answer.

3 7

"Do you think," Brother Wayne went on, "that I'm immune to those kind of thoughts because I speak the word of God?"

"You think of women other than your wife?" my mother asked, sniffling.

"I do." And then, not at all regretfully, "and I'm ashamed of it."

I wanted to peek through the crack of the door to see what kind of faces they were wearing. I really did.

"The thing you have to realize, Brother Jim"—he was speaking in a steadily rising voice—"the thing you have to realize is that while I'm a man of God, I'm also a man. We can't hold these thoughts against ourselves. Most importantly"—I was beginning to worry about how loud he was getting; somebody was going to get up and close that door—"you have to realize that we can have them and still not yield to temptation."

Mom and Daddy Jim were silent, digesting this information.

"Sister Nora," he said, "what would you like Brother Jim to know of your innermost feelings?"

"I . . . I want him to know I love him. I love our children."

"Good. Good, Sister Nora." And after a pause. "Do you feel you miss the attentions of a new man? Do you need to feel desired once more after so many years of marriage?"

"No," my mother gasped.

"Sister Nora," Brother Wayne coaxed her. "We're here before an understanding God. You have nothing to hide."

"I don't have anything to tell." My mother sounded bewildered. "I need . . . I need. . . ." She broke off, beginning to cry again, "for Jim to . . . believe in me. That's all I need."

"Those are fine sentiments, Sister Nora. Fine sentiments. . . ."

There were several moments of sniffling and whispering between my mother and Daddy Jim. I let out a long breath I'd been holding.

"I'm ashamed," Brother Wayne droned. "Pure ashamed."

Daddy Jim stepped nervously into the web. "We don't understand."

"Nora, you're a good and virtuous woman." I could see him

in my mind's eye, hunched over his folded hands and shaking his head, tut, tut. He might be a man chosen to speak the Lord's words, but I was none too fond of him personally.

"Ever since I met you and your lovely wife . . . oh, I don't know that you can forgive this, Brother Jim."

"We're all friends here."

"I'm touched to know you feel that way, Brother Jim. I feel I must confess to you some of my own wayward thoughts, and I'm grateful to know they'll be taken with understanding."

"Oh, yes." My mother sniffled.

"You, Sister Nora, have the innocent face of an angel, wreathed in the softest hair. Standing in the pulpit Sunday morning, I was speaking straight to you, I was that infatuated. Since then I've so many times seen your image before my starving eyes, that it's no exaggeration to say that you have become an obsession. I see you before me, a vision of such loveliness it steals my breath away."

I wasn't at all happy with the turn this conversation had taken.

"Such is the power of your beauty, Sister Nora, that in full awareness that I commit a sin"—his voice dropped to a throbbing whisper while "sin" still rang in the air—"I reach out and take your submissive body into my arms, hold you so closely I can feel the breath enter you and depart with a shudder. I step away, embarrassed by the proof of my manhood"—his voice quivered with pain—"telling myself this is enough! I must be strong enough to stop it here.

"But I can't," he cried out raggedly. "My fingers slip to the buttons of your blouse, unfastening them one by one, my eyes devouring the pink slit disclosed to me. Sucking in a thirsty breath, I slowly draw the fabric apart and let it slide back over your shoulders, caressed by its silky rustle as it falls to the ground. I cradle the soft pink globes of your breasts in my grateful hands. . . ." Brother Wayne's hands hung descriptively in the air, his every word a string that held my mother and Daddy Jim suspended.

3 9

"I need a drink of water," I mumbled sleepily as I slid around the door.

His hands dropped into his lap. The anticipation on Daddy Jim's face collapsed, and I thought I saw my mother's shoulders sag. Her face was unusually pink when she turned to me. "Allie, what are you doing up?"

"It's hot. I woke up thirsty," I whined.

"Of course you are," Brother Wayne agreed, defense coming from an unexpected corner. "Sister Nora?" Brother Wayne's right hand lifted slightly and my mother got up to get me a drink.

"Was there more?" Daddy Jim asked in that tone grown-ups use when they're about to go on talking about something they think children won't understand.

"No, Brother Jim. The Lord intervenes and I get down on my knees to beg his forgiveness. We are but men as his son was."

My mother gave me a little shove into the bedroom, shutting the door smartly behind me. I could hear their voices, lowered now that they knew I was awake, but I couldn't make out the words.

At last there was a scraping of chairs on the floor as they were leaving the kitchen. When their voices faded entirely, I got up and carefully twisted the doorknob, cracking the door so I could peek through. They stood clustered at the front door.

"You've set my mind at ease," Daddy Jim said.

"I'm real glad to hear that," Brother Wayne said, taking one of my mother's hands in his. "Sister Nora, I want you to know that if you need to talk further, I'm available to you."

My mother shook her head.

"You don't need to thank me. You're feeling that hum of excitement that comes from communion with the Lord," he said, letting his hand slide up to her elbow. My mother nodded, blushing. "You folks make me feel good. I want to see more of you. Promise me that, Sister Nora."

I shut my door and got back into bed, sure they would look in now. It seemed like forever went by before I got up to peek again. Dirty pots stood on the stove, dishes in the sink, and coffee mugs stood pale sentry on the table in the dimming light. As my mother says, there's a first time for everything.

The next couple of days were remarkable only for the silence. Even though Daddy Jim stayed home, he was in the basement most of the time, puttering in his workshop. Mom seemed to be waiting for something, stopping her housework every so often to go to a window and stare out. The sun got hotter, the air was almost too thick to breathe, sweat popped out on your skin and stuck there in itchy little droplets.

It was late afternoon and I was on my way back home from town when I turned onto our road to see a small group of people standing in our yard. They were all clumped together in a way that brought back the last time I visited my father. We were walking along the street in what passes for darkness in a big city: the sky is dark but the night around you is bright with wide, white window displays and blinking traffic lights and huge signs in glowing colors over each store. Tires screeched, the smash of glass, then silence. A long horrible silence before a woman's voice rose in a long wail. My father stopped at the first squeal of brakes, his hand gripping mine tightly. He made no move to help or to walk on. Horns honked, a few people left their cars, others leaned out their windows to stare as one man was pulled from his car and laid out on the street, unmoving.

We were pushed closer to the accident as a crowd formed, layers of people coming together elbow to elbow. The woman continued to cry in noisy, gasping sobs as someone tried to comfort her. I wanted to leave. I didn't want to get any closer to the still form of the man in the street and the frightening dark patch on the side of his head. A siren whined in the distance.

Still my father made no effort to leave. His eyes glittered black and green and electric blue as he watched the woman being placed on a stretcher. The police car managed to create a path for itself, an ambulance following close behind. "I want to go," I said loudly, yanking on my father's jacket sleeve.

"In a minute," he said in a way that meant he'd paid no attention.

"I have to go to the bathroom," I said as loudly as before.

He pulled me through the crowd behind him with no regard for the elbows and pocketbooks at my eye level. "Can you wait till we get to the hotel?"

"I don't know. I guess."

"It's a restroom, Allie. Ladies say restroom, not bathroom, unless they're in their homes."

"Okay." I stretched my legs long, trying to keep up with him.

"And ladies don't talk about it in loud voices, no matter what they're calling it. . . ."

This crowd was standing in my front yard. My footsteps slowed as I got closer; I thought of turning around and walking away. "Allie!" Mrs. Kelly ran to meet me. "Your Daddy is real mad. Do you know why?"

I shook my head. It was all I could do to breathe around the heavy thudding in my chest.

"Do you want someone to call for help?"

I nodded, wondering who could help. I didn't see whether Mrs. Kelly rejoined the onlookers. I saw her little boys standing in the crowd. They looked at me with the same pale eyes their mother had, and with the same mix of interest and fellow feeling. Mrs. Kelly and her boys looked at everyone that way but this time it held little appeal. I could hear men's voices as I walked around the house, yelling and carrying on. Crystal's voice rose and fell like a siren.

I heard Mom as I let the screen door close behind me; a cry, desperate at first, then working its way down to a false calm to reason with Daddy Jim. I listened as I crept through the kitchen. "You were here all week, Jim. How could I have seen anyone you didn't know about?"

The couple from upstairs stood in the open doorway. The man looked half-frightened, half-indignant, with clenched fists raised. His wife stood with her arms crossed over her chest.

4 2

"I heard you whisperin'." Daddy Jim's hand tightened on Mom's upper arm so that her skin was white around his fingertips. "I was downstairs and I heard you whisperin'."

"I work at night." The man made angry motions with his fists as he talked. "I'm asleep all day. My wife is there all day with me. How could I visit your wife and not have mine knowing about it?"

"I don't have to know how you go about it," Daddy Jim yelled him down. "I know it happens," he said, releasing Mom. Crystal's cries grew louder and Mom tried to comfort her.

"You been drinking," the man said. "You got no reason to think—"

"Reason? You think I don't have a good enough reason?" Daddy Jim raged. "Don't you know there's a witness to all that you do?"

"A witness?" The man looked at Mom as if he thought she'd been telling the stories. "What are you talking about?" His wife began to pull at his sleeve but he paid no attention.

"Ha! You don't look so sure of yourself now!"

"Bullshit! You tell me who's been saying they seen things."

"You, missus!" Daddy Jim roared at the man's wife, his face getting redder all the time. "Do you want to live with this man —this goat! That fornicates before the eyes of children?" Daddy Jim grabbed Crystal by the scruff of her shirt, dangling her in front of the woman. Crystal howled and Mom began to cry, reaching for her.

"Oh-h!" the woman cried, pulling at her husband. "Let's get out of here. Take me upstairs—"

"Hey," the man said. "Let's try to settle this without hurting the baby. Okay?"

"Don't . . . touch . . . her," Daddy Jim threatened. "Do you think my hands could damage her after what she's seen?"

"Jim, you're wrong!" Mom struggled to speak in a quieter voice. "So wrong. Please. Put her down. Don't hurt her."

Daddy Jim swung Crystal up higher, holding her flat against the wall. Her face was dark as a beet; drool spilled from her mouth as she wailed on. Daddy Jim didn't seem to notice.

"Jim, how can you do this to her," Mom screamed.

"Tell me, Nora!"

"No—o!" Mom screamed, rushing to grab Crystal. He lifted his free arm in a slow, almost casual backswing and knocked Mom to the floor.

"Mom." I heard my own voice as I ran to help her up, a voice that was strangely undisturbed. "Mom."

"Help me," she appealed to the neighbors, "my baby. Please!"

They didn't make a move.

"Jim," Mom pleaded, "you're frightening her. Look at your baby daughter's face—"

"Put that child down," a deep voice ordered.

Officer Aarons, the father of one of my new classmates, moved into the doorway, a stick like a short bat in his hand. Crystal's screams faded to hiccuping sobs as Daddy Jim slowly lowered her to the floor. "You'll have to come with us now," Officer Aarons said quietly.

"We're charging you with disturbing the peace on the part of your neighbor, Mrs. Kelly," another officer said from behind me, having come in the back. "And it appears that these people may want to sign a complaint as well."

But the upstairs neighbor shook his head. Officer Aarons didn't look too pleased at that.

"Does this mean . . . he'll go to jail?" Mom asked breathlessly.

"For the night, ma'am."

"This was a misunderstanding. Jim wouldn't hurt—" Mom broke off, tears choking her.

"Now, ma'am, this is just for the night," Officer Aarons said to soothe her. "Although it seems advisable that you sign a com——"

"Oh, I couldn't do that!"

"You're not to come there, Nora," Daddy Jim spoke up. "I won't have you embarrassed that way."

"Jim." Mom threw her arms around him and wept. Crystal stood between them, blubbering.

"Let's go." The other policeman stepped forward to take Daddy Jim by the elbow. Mom looked lost and unhappy.

"Da-a-ah," Crystal wailed, latching onto Daddy Jim's leg. The policeman tried to dislodge her as Daddy Jim dragged the leg she clung to. Her screams grew louder as she realized her small weight didn't stop his progress. Daddy Jim made no effort to remove her himself but stood at the top of the porch steps while the upstairs neighbor told his story to the policemen.

Mom stayed inside after seeing people bunched up in front of the house. She knew they would talk to the upstairs neighbors and soon someone would mention that my name is different than my mother's. People do seem to get a lot of pleasure out of talking about a divorced woman.

"Crystal." I knelt beside her on the front porch. "I bought cookies at the grocery store." She shook her head, setting her loose blond curls bobbing. She was firmly attached to Daddy Jim's leg and crying strongly, her mouth wide open, her face scrunched up with misery. She was crying tearlessly, the way babies so often do.

"I was thinking of having some cookies while I look at my doll collection," I said as if there was nothing special going on. Crystal stopped bawling but she didn't take her face out of position to start in again.

"Mom said I could look at them if I was careful to smooth out their dresses when I put them back. You could help with that." She gave out with another howl, looking mournfully up at Daddy Jim. She sure hates to look like she's giving in too easy.

"The cookies are chocolate. With white icing sandwiched in between."

Crystal sank to the porch floor with a moan, her fat little hands sliding down Daddy Jim's pants leg. "Mine Daddy," she whimpered. "Mine."

"We could even have a cookie right now."

Crystal's last howl was loud and long, so's not to leave the impression she'd forgotten her troubles. She let me gather her

4 5

up, a faintly smelly bundle that was soggy from head to toe, but she wouldn't help in any way, lying limp in my arms without holding on. Daddy Jim was still staring down at his feet. Seeing him like that made me feel sorry for him. He'd brought it all on himself, I guess, making accusations and starting arguments, but he looked like he was feeling pretty bad. I took Crystal inside, sliding her past Mom's eagerly waiting arms, and gave her the promised cookie. It wasn't until Mom ran crying into the bedroom that I believed Daddy Jim was going to jail.

Mom walked us into town and called Grandma Drew first thing the next morning. "It's Nora, Mavis. Yes, we're all fine. She'd like to come out a little early if that's all right with you." She rocked from foot to foot. "Today. Yes, today. Unless you can't make it." Mom chewed nervously on a fingernail. "Fine. She'll be ready."

Mom's mood hadn't improved any on the walk home, having carried Crystal most of the way. But I had to ask. "When will Daddy Jim be home, Mom?"

"Sometime today, I guess," she said. "I don't want you telling your grandma anything about this."

"Is he going to be mad?" I must have touched on the thing she was worried about, because she got angrier than my questioning usually made her.

"Allie, I don't want you to start in! You're going to your grandma. What goes on when you're not here is none of your concern, hear?"

I hate packing. It always has to be done when you're leaving someone to see someone else. Mom makes sure she tells me not to annoy people with my questions. Then she tells me what I'm not supposed to tell anybody. This time she had an especially long list. Between don't ask and don't tell I don't know why they bothered to teach me to talk. After packing is the waiting. Halfway here, halfway there and nothing to do in between; it's as if I've already left for wherever I'm going. I wandered into Mom's bedroom, climbing onto the bed to watch for Grandma.

She'd be driving Grandpa's new car, Mom said. She's the

4 6

only lady I know of who drives a car besides Mrs. Kelly, our neighbor. My mother says Mrs. Kelly needs to drive herself, Mr. Kelly being a salesman who travels during the week. My mother says Grandma Drew is gallivanting. Grandma Drew says God gave women the same hands and the same brains as men and likely as not, He expected women to use them.

I watched her come up the walk, shoulders back and head held high, as tall and squared off as Grandma Taylor is small and plump. She wore her hair brushed back from her sharp face, rolled tightly around the sides of her head. It was a matter of some pride to her that she always matched her popbeads to her dress. She carried a present for Crystal.

I got to the living room just as Mom opened the door. Grandma gave Mom one of her dry hugs as she said, "Sorry to hear about Darryl, Nora. Such a good boy, I know." Mom's smile tightened around the edges as she offered Grandma a place on the couch.

"Allie, are you going to give me a kiss?" Grandma asked as she settled her big pocketbook against her hip. Her eyes were soft behind her silver-rimmed glasses, but Grandma didn't make you feel like giving any more than she asked you for. I sort of think she liked it that way. So I gave her a peck on her floury cheek and stood back for her to look me over.

"Getting taller all the time, Allie. You're going to be a tall girl," she said with satisfaction. "Much taller than your momma." My eyes slid toward my mother, returning from the kitchen with iced tea flavored with the mint from her garden. "That's all right, Allie. Your momma would like for you to be tall. Isn't that right, Nora?"

"It's nice to be tall," Mom said, careful not to look at Grandma, "but I do like that she isn't going to be big boned."

I knew Grandma Drew felt some advantage in being taller and wider than anyone else in the family, including Grandpa. But now her eyes narrowed. She remained carefully polite as she accepted the iced tea.

"This one," Grandma patted Crystal's blond curls, not noticing or just plain ignoring the way Crystal's mouth began to pucker up. "Why, her hair will be as long as Allie's before she's six." Crystal was some put off by Grandma Drew's eyeglasses last summer, and she wasn't going to tolerate any overtures today.

"Yes," Mom agreed as she pulled Crystal into her lap.

"Allie," Grandma's manner had gone crisp, "if you're all packed?"

I didn't waste any time.

I knew my mother was worried about divorce. It was what she always worried about. It scared me too. Not what I knew of it: the talking about what the other had done and still did (Your father's plane is late. He'll be late to his own funeral just to have the satisfaction of knowing everyone's waiting on him), or the eyes and ears turned on me to see and strike out the moving shadow of the other parent (Use your napkin, Allie. . . . Then in an aggrieved voice, Your mother's brothers wiped their hands on their pants and your mother will raise you to do the same). I was frightened by what I didn't know, by what my mother asked herself with her face hidden behind her hands: Who will take care of us? How will we live?

The police had taken Daddy Jim away and all that was different to my eyes was the smoothness of his pillow in the morning. Mom told me he would be back, over and over, as if she thought I must be afraid that he was gone forever. As I look back on it now, I realize I believed the police put an end to the trouble. That was as shortsighted as my mother's idea that God would work a miracle.

3

Getting to Grandma Drew's is always the same. Aunt Bonnie clears a drawer for me to put my stuff in just like I live there all the time. I share the same room with her that she lived in with Aunt Charlotte since they were three and eleven. Aunt Bonnie is a latecomer, although Grandma Drew never calls her that. Grandma Drew says Aunt Bonnie is her Foster Daughter. She says Daddy went with her to the orphanage, choosing Aunt Bonnie himself for her blond hair and blue eyes. I don't know that Aunt Charlotte cares for this part of the story and not only because her hair is mouse brown.

Grandma also says she took Aunt Bonnie in because God called upon her to help him when His children were in need. Aunt Bonnie says Aunt Charlotte apparently never heard the call because she used to pinch Aunt Bonnie at night. When Daddy found out what Aunt Charlotte was doing, Aunt Bonnie's tears meant bruises for Aunt Charlotte. Things quieted down some then.

Once I'm unpacked I carry my empty suitcase up to the attic. I spend a lot of time there. Now and then I find something, like letters Daddy wrote to Grandma when he was away to the war. Or Aunt Charlotte's prom dress. Best are the old Sears catalogs, made up of the slickest, thinnest pages I ever saw. I can draw paper dolls and cut up the catalogs to make clothes for them. While I'm visiting, the attic takes to smelling of freshly sharpened pencils and minty white paste.

Grandma Drew lets me make my own lunch, peanut butter sandwiches, and she always has Coca-Cola, which I'm pretty fond of. So along about noon, when it's getting too hot to stay in the attic, I head for the porch swing with my lunch. Grandma Drew is usually there, stringing beans or crocheting little white doilies. She asks about school and about my friends. But never about Mom and Daddy Jim. There were plenty of things I could've said about moving and being the new kid in school but I thought it best not to.

Last summer I went from Brownies to Girl Scouts, which meant I could go to summer camp. It started out okay that first day. We stood in a circle, learning the names of the girls on each side of us and said our new pledge. We went for a nature walk, then settled ourselves under a tree to eat our lunches.

About halfway through, one of the girls found a tick stuck to her leg. The leader touched it with a burned match to make it fall off. Two more girls found ticks on themselves and while the leader was lighting matches, more girls found ticks. I looked too, and was grateful not to find any. But one thing I know is, ticks live in bushes and trees. Likely as not, we picked them up on the nature walk but it didn't make sense to sit under that tree any longer.

I got up and moved out into the sun. The leader said I should sit with them in the shade where I wouldn't get sunburned. I said no thank you, as politely as I could, but she got some annoyed. She wanted to know why I insisted on sitting in the sun. I said I wasn't insisting, and I told her what I knew about ticks. She went on lighting matches as she nattered on about obedience being important in the Girl Scouts. After a while some of the girls started in, so I took my lunch into the tent the leaders had set up. There wasn't much room, it being full of cartons of paper plates and marshmallows and stuff.

It wasn't long before another girl joined me in the tent.

"She's telling stories under there now. It was bad enough we had to eat there, but *stories?*" It didn't matter that this was one of the girls who'd been jeering at me.

The drone of storytelling went on, interrupted by the occasional screech. After a while there were four of us in the tent. We were just saying to each other that not one more girl would fit when the leader yanked open the tent flap.

"Come out of there, all of you!" Her face was dark red except right around her mouth, which was very white. "I want you three to know I'm very disappointed in you. Girl Scouts pride themselves in the good sense to know a bad influence when they see it and the strength of character to ignore it. Please, join the other girls at the lakeside." I turned like she'd included me, though I knew better. "Not you, Alexandra. I want to speak to you."

I watched with a sick feeling in my stomach while the others marched off with that look of the saved. It's a look made up of the relief you feel when something hasn't been as bad as you feared and of the warm feeling it gives you to be accepted back into the fold of the Righteous.

"Who was your Brownie leader?"

I didn't care for being spoken to like I was something that'd just crawled out from under a rock. I didn't answer right away. The leader reached out and pinched me, hard, on the soft part of my upper arm. "Mrs. Johnson."

"Mm." Her face pocked up like she was sucking on a lemon. "Mrs. Johnson is a good leader, but she devotes more time to the arts and crafts period than most. She may be neglecting to pass on the philosophy that turns Brownies into Girl Scout

51

material." I wanted to say that Mrs. Johnson had better sense than to make her girls sit under a tree with ticks dropping out of it.

"You would do well to keep quiet for the next few days." I looked up at her through my eyelashes as she went on. "Pay attention and do as you're told, Alexandra."

"Allie."

"I beg your—"

"My name is Allie."

"Alexandra suits me fine. Summer camp isn't a place that gives you license to behave like a hooligan instead of a young lady. Backtalk is the last thing. . . ." She went on for a while and, to tell you the truth, I just stopped listening. I didn't mean to, but that's what happened. I had plenty to think about.

I'd been looking forward to camp, and now it was beginning to be worse than school. No matter how hard I would try, and I would, there was no doubt in my mind that things weren't going to get any better. So this was it. My mother would see to it I was here every day right up to the time I was to visit Grandma Drew, because you don't Start Something and not finish it.

"Are you listening to me, Alexandra?"

I nodded.

"What are you going to say when the girls ask about this conversation?"

I stood there, fishing for an answer.

"You are to say you made a mistake. You are to say you're sorry to have—"

"I'm going to tell my mother," I blurted out.

Her mouth dropped open, then clamped shut again. She gave me a long cold stare. "What is your full name?"

"Alexandra Drew."

"Well, Alexandra, I'm going to speak to Mrs. Johnson about you. She's going to know how you've behaved here today, and —is your mother Nora Drew?" Her face took on a sly look I didn't like at all. Mean-teacher looks haven't scared me since fourth grade, but this was something different.

"Nora Benton."

"Well, that explains a great many things," she said, her sly look spreading into a nasty smile.

I wanted to say something back. Instead I started down to the lake where the other girls were waiting, keeping well ahead of the leader. To tell the truth, I was afraid I was going to cry. Just then, when I wanted to be that brat she so clearly thought I was, I was going to cry. It was downright discouraging.

She came by the house that evening. She stood out front with my mother for quite a while, but I couldn't hear what was being said. When Mom came in, she was a lot angrier than the Girl Scout leader had been that afternoon. "You aren't in the Girl Scouts anymore. Get ready for bed."

"It wasn't my fault. Won't you even—?"

"There's no call for a big girl like you to act like she was raised in a barn. No, Allie, don't say a word! One of that woman's complaints was your sassing mouth. I'm putting Crystal to bed, and you're going at the same time till you start behaving better."

She found a tick in my sock when she took my laundry. And in the morning there was one on my pillow. That's when she asked what we had done in the park the day before. She didn't say anything, but she didn't put me to bed early that night.

The thing is, I told Grandma some of it. Not about almost crying and not what the leader said about Mom, but the rest of it. Grandma said, "Some people will never admit they're wrong."

"Who? I mean, which one, the leader or Mom?"

Grandma chuckled. "Both of them, now that I think of it. But your mother found a way to put her mistake right."

We gave the swing a little push and let the talk die out. It's easy to sit out there till the afternoon begins to get that faded look. Then Grandma goes in to start dinner and I walk to town to walk back with Aunt Bonnie. This time, just as we were getting up from the swing, Uncle George drove in with Aunt Charlotte. "There's a movie tonight. Wanna come with us?"

"Grandma?"

"I don't see why not. Bonnie's going with Calvin. I'll be able to go to the Friday night meeting with Dad. Just see to it you leave the porch light on when you go." By now Uncle George had maneuvered his wide pear-shaped body out of the car and as so often happened, Aunt Charlotte was already on her way to someplace else. "We'll be by to pick you up a little before dark. Let's go, George."

The movie was shown in the grass lot between the post office and the luncheonette. Uncle George and Aunt Charlotte would watch from their car, one of several parked crosswise on Main Street.

"There's Regina Cochran," Aunt Charlotte told me as Uncle George opened up a paper bag full of snacks.

"She let her hair grow long."

"That's 'cause it's sexier," Aunt Charlotte confided.

"Is that what she said?"

"That's how she acts."

"It doesn't mean much. She's only older than me by a month."

"In some ways," Aunt Charlotte said quietly.

"It's starting," Uncle George said with a meaningful look as the cartoon popped on the screen. I took the hint and got out of the car. It still wasn't quite dark when I found a niche in the post office wall to throw down a scatter rug.

Regina took the spot next to me, registering some disappointment at finding me there. She made a big deal of unrolling her blanket and spreading it out, crawling around on her hands and knees with her rear end waggling around in the air.

"You're getting real pretty, Allie," she said as she arranged herself on the blanket with equal care. I didn't answer, not knowing quite what the reply to that was. She tossed her head, looking around like she was waiting for someone.

Along about the middle of the second cartoon, Aunt Bonnie arrived with Calvin, bringing me a bottle of orange-pineapple soda. It was the first I'd seen of Calvin, and I liked him immediately. A great bush of dark hair sprang from his head, reaching nearly to his broad shoulders, and his eyebrows all but met

54

over his nose. Goodness seemed to flow right out of him to wrap itself around Aunt Bonnie. What I noticed about him while I was getting used to the way he looked, was his voice. It was soft, not in a girlish way, but soft all the same.

They spread their blanket out in the middle of the lot along with a group that had been doing a lot of talking and laughing. Everyone quieted down as it got dark enough for the movie to begin. It was pretty boring, a lot of men trying to get a sword out of a stone, though I never did care enough to know why. After a while, one of the young men from Aunt Bonnie's group joined Regina on her blanket. They did some talking, too low for me to hear. He put an arm around her shoulder. It wasn't much, but it was better than the movie.

I shifted to see what else was going on in the lot. It was helpful that the place I'd chosen to sit put me in the shadow of the building. Aunt Bonnie leaned against Calvin's big chest, his arms crossed around her, his face half-buried in her hair. It made me feel good to see them like that, so close and comfortable. There were a few couples kissing openly in the middle of the lot. I knew what my mother would say to that, and I wondered they weren't worried about hearing it from theirs. My eyes worked their way back to Regina's blanket.

His arm still lay over her shoulders, his back hiding her from the eyes of people sitting nearby. Except mine. I could see his other hand as it wandered up her arm to play with the ringlets lying at her neck. When his hand moved downward again, it slipped inside her blouse. Regina swelled her chest out with a deep breath, smiling at the movie screen all the while. I looked around as one more bold hero set his hands upon the sword and realized no one else had witnessed this.

Regina's eyes closed, her face turned toward his as he gently kneaded her breast. He bent to kiss her cheek and then her lips, molasses slow. As he kissed her he bent his leg at the knee, making a place for her in the curve of his body. As the kiss ended, he raised his head and looked around. I sat so still I could hardly breathe, not knowing whether it would be worse to be caught watching or to go unnoticed.

Satisfied that no one was looking their way, he passed his hand over her clothes, coming to rest on her leg. He began to kiss her again, moving in that slow way that drew no one's attention but mine, and allowed his hand to stroke her thigh. I wondered if he had only this morning told someone next time will be *it* like Uncle Little Mike told Uncle Joe. The idea made me grin, but it didn't last long.

He slid his hand inside the leg of her shorts to rub between her legs. It was beginning to be uncomfortable to watch, but I couldn't take my eyes away. Regina seemed to be shaking just the littlest bit, and once I thought I heard a tiny sound from her. He whispered in her ear and she shook her head no. It's strange to say it here, but I could feel a warmth between my own legs, watching his hand rub her so. He kept up that rubbing and pretty soon he whispered again. This time she nodded.

He kissed her again, letting his open mouth trail over her face. His hand slowed down, then slipped out from beneath her shorts. He whispered and she reached up to button her blouse. Then he got up and left, moving like he'd got the urge for a soda and had to have it.

Regina watched the picture screen for a few seconds before she let her eyes slide over to me. I know she couldn't see me there in the shadows, not so clearly to tell if I was looking at her. But she knew. My cheeks burned with shame. I can't explain why I was somehow more guilty of something now that I realized she'd seen me peeping at them.

After a minute or two Regina made like she'd begun to wonder where he'd got to, and soon she followed him out. I sucked in a deep breath, turning back to the screen. It sure gave me something to think about, Regina being barely thirteen.

They didn't come back until the movie was over and people were rolling up their blankets. I found it hard to look in Regina's direction as she took her blanket, but I did notice that she was alone, the young man returning to sit near Calvin and Aunt Bonnie.

Uncle George noticed I was quieter than usual on the short

ride back to Grandma's. "I'm tired is all," I told him. "I'll be livelier tomorrow." Tomorrow would usually be the day to look up old Regina and some of her friends. Hi, Regina, want to play paper dolls?

Fat chance.

I laid next to Aunt Bonnie, enjoying the softness of the summer blanket as we whispered in the darkness. The june bugs bumped and buzzed around the light fixture and when one would escape, he'd zoom around the room until he'd knock himself out. I don't know when I fell asleep. I only know I was suddenly wide awake. The june bugs were quiet, an owl hooted long and low, and Aunt Bonnie was gone. The outhouse, I guessed, and I needed to go, too. I've always preferred to make these trips with some company. I've heard too many stories of meeting up with a skunk in the yard or a snake that found a way into the outhouse on a cold night.

Aunt Bonnie wasn't in the outhouse. A man laughed softly, and I heard Aunt Bonnie's voice. They were somewhere in the blueberry bushes, tall shadowy clumps that dotted the back-yard and thickened into a kind of orchard on one side. It didn't have to be that they were doing anything like Regina had been. But on the other hand it was something that teenagers found pretty interesting. There was no good reason for Aunt Bonnie to be any different. My feeling was, I could wait a while to be a teenager.

I woke up before Aunt Bonnie the next morning. This is silly, I know, but I looked to see if she looked any different. Her face was pretty in the usual ways, maybe a little rounder and cuter than most. But I think she seemed prettier because she liked most people, always looking happy to see them. She woke up, yawning and stretching, and when she saw I was sitting up she grinned. "An early bird." She didn't look any different to me except maybe sparklier. "You can come help me in the luncheonette today, how's that?"

"Maybe later. I have stuff to do this morning."

"Whenever you like. Oh! Look what time it is. I'll have to

hurry." She leaped up and pulled her grass-stained nightgown off over her head.

"You have a tick on your bottom," I said, staring at what looked like a heavy brown mole.

"Oh, no!" She twisted to see it in the mirror. "Ma? Is Dad home?" Aunt Bonnie called out as she pulled a fresh nightgown out of her drawer. "I need some privacy in the kitchen."

I followed her through the house and in the kitchen, she hiked up her nightgown again.

"Aunt Bonnie has a tick," I said in answer to Grandma's raised eyebrows.

Grandma reached for a match. "Land sakes, Bonnie, couldn't you feel it crawling on you to get up there?"

"No, ma'am. The movie was pretty exciting."

"Must've been," Grandma commented as she lit another match to dislodge the stubborn creature. Her face was taking on a doubtful expression.

"I had two ticks on me last summer, and I couldn't feel them, either."

"That's true," Grandma said, her brow smoothing over. "Did Allie tell you her tick story, Bonnie?"

"No, I don't think so," Bonnie looked over her shoulder as she let her nightgown fall. "You will, won't you, Allie? You can tell me over the chocolate milkshake I'm gonna make for you."

"Strawberry."

"Strawberry it is."

I'd enjoy that strawberry milkshake. But I had a feeling Aunt Bonnie had the best tick story.

It turned out I didn't feel too anxious to go down to the luncheonette. Every time I thought about Aunt Bonnie I saw her smoothly rounded bottom peeking out from under that nightgown. I wondered if she let Calvin slide his hairy hand under it to rub against her. I spent the day in the attic.

I thought about writing a letter to my father, something I can't do at home. Mom always reads everything I write down, in case I wrote something about her. Once I got hold of an envelope with my father's return address on it. I wrote him, mailing the letter in secret. By the time it reached Belgium, he'd moved on with the show. The post office sent it on to Germany but it missed him there too, and that's when it came back to me. I hadn't said anything about Mom or Daddy Jim except that they were fine, but it was some time before I was sitting comfortably.

I wandered around the attic, thinking about Aunt Bonnie. And Regina. I wrote a story about a girl working in a garden. A dark, handsome stranger comes along and offers to help her if she'll share her lunch with him. While they're eating, he tells her how pretty she is (she looks a lot like Aunt Bonnie), and she notices how handsome he is (he looks a lot like Calvin). He asks if he can kiss her. She says no (just like in *True Confessions*) but she doesn't mean it and lets him kiss her . . . but that's all.

To tell you the truth, I was getting into areas I didn't care to think about. *True Confessions* always skips over that part too, but I couldn't remember just how. I decided to go meet Aunt Bonnie so I could hang around the magazine rack. I skittered down the stairs and out to the kitchen, just in time to bump into Aunt Bonnie coming home from work.

"Hi, where's Ma?" she asked, setting down a brown paper bag.

"She's in her room. Making herself a new dress."

"Are you feeling okay? You look a little feverish."

"I stayed in the attic too long. It's hot up there."

Aunt Bonnie began to empty the bag onto the table. I reached for the bread and a package of hamburger rolls. "Leave me a roll," she told me. "And one for yourself if you're feeling hungry."

I shook my head. "I ate three peanut butter sandwiches today."

Aunt Bonnie's eyebrows lifted. "What else did you do today?"

"Thought about things."

"What sort of things?" she asked as she salted the big black frying pan. I opened the breadbox, breathing in its sweet, grainy smell before I put away the bread. "Allie? Do you want to talk to me?"

"Tell me about your day."

"My day." She shook her head. "My back hurts. My feet hurt. I had the same conversations I have every day, with the same people I always have them with." She used the pancake turner to flatten the hamburgers. "The funny thing is, I've been working for six years in that place and I finally have enough money to get myself a place in Des Moines. Then right on the Saturday I planned to quit, Calvin and a couple of his buddies came in for lunch. He didn't take his eyes off me, Allie," she said with a smile. "Even when his friends started to tease him."

"So he asked you out?"

"He was back on Monday for lunch. He had to drive so far, he could only take ten minutes to eat in order to get back to work on time. He did that every day until the next Saturday. He came in for breakfast and stayed all day, playing the jukebox and drinking Coca-Cola."

"Then he asked you out," I said.

"We hadn't been properly introduced," Aunt Bonnie said, grinning. "He followed me home, telling me everything he could think of about his folks and where he went to school and why he's here. When I thought to play hard to get some more" —and here she blushed a little—"he apologized for the use of my time. Humble as can be, he said he was sure he wouldn't be the last moonstruck man I'd be forced to turn away."

"What did you do?"

"I ran after him, of course! He was impossible to me, asking a lot of questions as if I was courting him now."

"Like what?"

"Like, was I of any use in the kitchen? After eating my cooking all week long! And did I have all my teeth?" Aunt Bonnie made an exasperated sound. "I finally had to ask him, was he going to take me out or wasn't he?"

"You did that?"

6 0

"Keep a secret?" Her whole face lit up in such a way I felt it warm my own heart.

"Sure."

"We're going to get married."

"Wow! Did you tell Grandma?"

"Ssh-h! No. I'm hoping she'll warm up to Calvin some."

"She doesn't care for him?"

"His folks are from the Ozarks. Ma thinks that makes him white trash."

"It's awful hard to change Grandma's mind."

"She'll see when he buys me a house."

"You asked him to?"

"No, Allie. He feels its the right way to do things. Buy a house, then announce our intentions. Then, he says, Ma can hold her head up whenever she tells someone I'm going to be married. He's real sweet, Allie, the way he thinks of things like that."

I nodded. He had Grandma's number.

"I could help him with the money I've saved, but he won't touch a penny of it," she went on, taking the hamburger bun out of the frying pan. "He says it'll be mine to rely on in case something should happen to him." She proceeded to stack onion and tomato on the hamburger before she closed it up with the bun. "One thing I know, he'll take care of me." She sat down gratefully, gathering the hamburger up to take the first bite. I swallowed hard. "You changed your mind."

"No."

"I can see it on your face, Allie."

"Never mind. I said no and you're too tired—"

"Not that tired," she said, sliding the plate over to me. "You start so it doesn't get cold. It'll only take a couple of minutes to do another."

"At least have a bite while the other one fries."

"Thanks." Aunt Bonnie is the only person I know who looks good with ketchup on her chin. "Oh, is that good."

"Aunt Bonnie, do you know Regina?"

"I know who she is."

6 1

"What do you think of her?"

"I don't know her very well. I get the impression she could use a friend."

"I think she has one," I said around another mouthful.

"What do you mean?"

So I told Aunt Bonnie about Regina, leaving out some of the juicier details. By that time, we'd finished the first hamburger, starting in on the second one.

"So what exactly is the question?" Aunt Bonnie asked.

I shrugged. I hardly knew where to begin.

"Do you think someone should tell her mama?"

"That would only get her in trouble." I chewed thoughtfully on my next bite. "Do you think people should be married to do what Regina's doing?"

"Is that what your mama told you?"

"No. I never asked her about it. But I get the feeling it's why people are sneaking around to do it."

"What people?" Aunt Bonnie asked, two telltale pink spots rising in her cheeks.

"Uncle Collin. Uncle Little Mike," I said, thinking further. "They're not doing the sneaking, though. They talk to each other about it. Girls don't talk about it, do they? I've listened and they don't."

"I guess it's what people expect. That girls wait till they're married. Boys don't have to."

"Is that what you think, too?"

"Allie, I don't know that I'm the one should be answering these questions."

"Mom won't answer them. Who else can I ask?"

"I don't know that your mama would agree with me."

"I'll keep that in mind."

"Okay." Aunt Bonnie got up to get a Coke for each of us. It was a thrilling moment. I was eating Aunt Bonnie's glorious hamburgers, drinking Coca-Cola, and someone was finally willing to answer my questions.

"I don't think it's the being married that matters," Aunt Bonnie said as she sat down again. "What matters is why two people are together." She took a bite and chewed. "In Regina's case, it's probably loneliness."

"She came back to get her blanket all by herself," I remembered.

Aunt Bonnie nodded sympathetically. "Maybe a nicer boy will take up with her."

"Not everybody is like Regina," I said, thinking of Uncle Collin and his wife. "Some get married."

"Mm-hmm. Most girls wait, you know, till they're married. They feel it's wrong not to. Others don't see the good in holding themselves back, teasing like, if they know a man loves them."

"And some do some stuff, but not everything."

Aunt Bonnie laughed. "Seems to me you've been listening to some advantage. That's what I meant by teasing. It's a poor way to get a man to the church."

"I guess that's so."

Aunt Bonnie frowned. "You have a little while to wait before you have that to worry about."

"I don't want her carrying those things into church this morning."

"She gets bored, Dad," Grandma told him patiently.

"She's old enough not to get bored. She can listen to the service like the rest of the congregation."

"She fidgets."

"I don't care. It's embarrassing to have my granddaughter sitting in plain view, reading"—he grabbed the stack of comics from my hands—"Donald Duck," he finished disgustedly.

Grandpa Drew didn't Put His Foot Down very often. So Grandma didn't say anything more while I took the comics back to the bedroom. To tell you the truth, this was terrible news. Sunday morning services would have been bad enough, but Grandma and Grandpa also attended Sunday evening services, Wednesday night prayer meeting and Friday night hymn meetings. And the occasional Saturday afternoon revival picnic. Don't let the word *picnic* fool you.

All this interest in prayer meetings could be something of a surprise if you were to meet Reverend Allen and see that he isn't much more than a teenager himself. But then Reverend Allen is full of surprises. His hair, both that on his head and that of the beard he's grown since his arrival here, is a yellow brown color, his eyes being yellow to match. He's tall and very thin, enough so that you might dare to turn and look at him on the street. His clothing seems to have been meant for someone both taller and wider than himself. When a strong breeze touches him, the pants ripple against his thin legs like a robe. It's my opinion that it's no coincidence that he's come to look a lot like the painting of Jesus that hangs on the wall of the church.

Reverend Allen likes to make an entrance. He lets everyone get inside and find a seat before he leaves the door, coming down the aisle like a slow parade. By the time he reaches the pulpit the whole place has a hushed-up waiting sound in it. He takes a long look around, checking to see if any one person is making that sound. When he's satisfied it's coming from so many people with their mouths shut, he lets out a sigh you can hear to the backmost pew. He starts off with the week's news, his voice strong and deep. In a place as small as Swan, everyone knows who got married or who died. But Reverend Allen seems to feel it's his place to do the telling. Then the kids are sent off to the Sunday school rooms. There's one for dotkins like Crystal, on up to kindergarten age; the other one is for kids up to eleven. They tell Bible stories like they're fairy tales and sing "Jesus Loves Me." There is absolutely no chance to read comic books.

Reverend Allen usually starts out slow and quiet, getting louder, then turns red in the face and gets louder still. This Sunday he was pretty low key. Several times toward the beginning of services he asked us to rise and sing, a sure sign he was having trouble getting started. It was during one of these times that I opened the hymnal for Grandma, neglecting to turn to the right page. Midway through the hymn I decided to join in on the singing and I looked down to see my mistake. Now what

I found amazing, my grandmother seemed to be reading the words right out of the hymnal. It occurred to me that I'd never seen her reading anything but the Bible, and as far as I knew, she did that only in church.

On the next one I made a point of turning to the wrong page. She didn't notice, but not for a lack of looking at the book. Reverend Allen had us sit down again, and I waited impatiently for the next hymn. When it came, I turned the hymnal upside down and held it out in front of us. Grandma began to sing, a confused expression on her face. She continued to sing uninterrupted, looking all over that page, sure there was something wrong with it but unable to say just what it might be. All of a sudden she realized what I'd done and reached out to turn the book around. Her face reddened, but she didn't miss a word of the hymn. That was when Reverend Allen asked us to be seated once more and began to preach in earnest. He intended to make up in devotion the time he'd lost to this morning's lack of purpose.

Things picked up along toward the end of the service. There were two boys from the reform school who'd asked to be baptized. Reverend Allen spoke to them from the pulpit, concerning forgiveness and following the Lord's path. When he finally asked them to step up beside him, I was pretty interested in having a look at them. These two boys not only got out of the reform school for the day, but they got someone else to get up on Sunday morning to drive them better than twenty miles, sit through Reverend Allen's sermon, and drive them back again. I can't even get out of the classroom to go to the restroom more than once in a day.

They turned out to be a little disappointing. One of them had a big grin on his face. I don't think he knew it was there, because it stayed when Reverend Allen was saying some pretty solemn stuff about how unfortunate they were to be led astray in their young lives. It was still there when he told them how their actions that day were their first steps toward God. The other one looked embarrassed, as if this had seemed like a good idea when his friend suggested it but not anymore.

6 5

Reverend Allen took them into the little room behind the pulpit, parting the curtains so we could see them from the waist up. There's a baptistery back there about the size of two bathtubs next to each other. They removed their shoes and Reverend Allen took them one at a time. The grinning one forgot to close his mouth or hold his breath or something. He like to drowned before Reverend Allen could get him on his feet again. He asked Brother Lester to come up and give him a hand with the next young man.

That one looked really upset by now, and you could see he regretted his decision. But Brother Lester's feet were wet and he was going to be satisfied he'd saved a soul that day. It went all right until they just about reached the point where that boy's head touched water. He must have been taken with a sudden change of mind. We heard a yelp, followed by the reverend's voice uttering a word rarely heard in a house of God and, for the second time that morning, an assortment of noises generally associated with drowning. There was a fair amount of splashing before they all rose, drenched and flushed with their exertions.

I can honestly say that the only happy face to return to the pulpit was Brother Lester's. The boys were still sniveling and coughing as they received their blessing and headed back to their seats. Both of them looked like they wouldn't be asking to leave reform school again too soon. Reverend Allen stood before us in his wet socks and bony knees and asked everyone to rise and sing.

Sunday afternoons are quiet, so I climbed to the attic to write a story. It was my intention to write about the baptism. I started the story over and over but it just wouldn't come. It turned out that I wrote about what happened during the movie. It sounds like Regina is telling the story, just the way *True Confessions* are written. Unlike those, nobody finds out, she doesn't get pregnant and she doesn't have to roll up her blanket alone after.

Aunt Bonnie didn't sneak out on Sunday night. I was so nervous thinking she might that I didn't sleep for hours, and then I woke up practically every time she turned over. By Monday night I was tired, and pretty sure that Aunt Bonnie would stay put. I was someplace between awake and asleep when she slid out of bed and out the door. I lay there in the dark, listening for Grandma's bedsprings, announcing her nightly trip. I'm grateful to say it didn't come that early. I pretended I was asleep when Aunt Bonnie slipped back in. Then we could both sleep.

Tuesday night was the same.

I could hardly stay awake through the Wednesday night prayer meeting, not that I was afraid to miss anything. But I was wide awake at midnight when the cuckoo clock went off. I heard the back screen creak some time after and I knew Aunt Bonnie was on her way in. I heard the shuffle of Grandma's bedroom slippers on the wood floor as she started down the hall. I sat bolt upright in the bed, imagining no end of awful possibilities.

"G'night, Bonnie."

"Goodnight, Ma," Aunt Bonnie whispered as she ducked into our room. I let out a shaky breath which I hoped would be taken for deep sleep.

"What are you doing up here so much of the time, child?"

"Nothing."

Grandma chuckled. "You've never been one to do nothing, Allie." She sat down in her old parlor chair, relegated to the attic when she got her new horsehair living room set. That was about the time I was born. "You're not doing anything you shouldn't be, are you?"

The decision was made very quickly. One thing about Grandma Drew could be counted on: if she didn't get an answer to a question, she'd be rooting around for it until your hair turned gray and fell out. "I'm writing stories."

"Stories!" She shifted around in her chair the way she must

have been shifting the idea around in her mind. "I guess that makes sense. Somebody who draws pictures would naturally want to tell stories."

"I don't write very good ones."

"Never you mind. You keep at it and soon you'll be writing fine stories. Practice makes perfect." Said right out like that, it sounded like a good idea. If I could manage to write a story every day. . . .

"I have a letter from your father. I thought you might like to read it." She held the letter out, but didn't let go of it until she'd given me a long look. "It would be nice if you'd read it out loud. I'd like to hear it again."

I read the whole letter very slowly, the way you eat something you don't want to get to the end of. Grandma seemed to feel the same way. Hearing that Daddy would arrive on Saturday made her as happy as if she'd never read it herself.

"We have a mountain of things to do by Saturday," Grandma told me. "Let's go get your Aunt Charlotte over here to help."

I heard Grandma give a screech and then I heard Aunt Bonnie, moaning and crying. I raced through the well-black darkness of the dining room toward the back porch. I pasted myself to the screen door in time to see Grandma rushing Aunt Bonnie up the path, yanking on a fistful of long blond hair. Calvin followed from some distance, running and hopping as he tried to pull his pants on.

Grandma pushed Aunt Bonnie through the door, grabbing me up as she went by. She slammed the heavy kitchen door behind her and flipped on the light. We blinked against the sudden brilliance, frozen for an instant. Grandma looked wild.

"Please, Ma, you don't—"

Grandma slapped Aunt Bonnie. I sprang for Grandma's arm as it swung back again. "Don't!" But she wasn't going to hit Aunt Bonnie again. Her face crumpled up like a piece of paper.

Calvin pounded on the back door.

Grandma opened it, snatching up her big black frying pan.

Calvin, shirtless and hair flying, turned tail and shot through the screen door to dive for cover as Grandma swung. "Git off this property!" Grandma screamed. "You came and got what you wanted, you Ozark thief, but you ain't gonna get no more. Get away!" Grandma's voice ended on a thin shriek.

"What in blazes is going on out here?" Grandpa was some sight in his blue-and-white-striped nightshirt, his clean white hair standing on shocked ends. He'd pulled his robe onto one arm, then left it to drag behind him.

"They were out there on the ground, Noah, rutting like two animals," Grandma told him hysterically. "I knew something like this would happen if you took up with the likes of him," she screamed at Aunt Bonnie. "Setting himself up in one of those old mining shacks like he was a man of property. Know nothing of him and nothing to know if we did," she sneered.

"Ma, that's not fair. Calvin's tried—"

"Tried to weasel his way into my good graces! Why couldn't you take up with one of the local boys? One who'd treat you decent and marry you?" Grandma wailed.

"He does, Ma," Aunt Bonnie sobbed. "He's good to me."

"A-ahh!" Grandma screamed, beyond even trying to make sense.

"Stop it, woman!" Grandpa didn't yell but we all heard him just fine. "We have troubles enough without you flying off the handle."

Grandma dropped heavily into a kitchen chair.

There was a knock on the door, a firm knock, determined. Grandma half raised herself as if to start in again, but Grandpa put up a hand. "Let's hear what he has to say for hisself."

Calvin stood on the back porch looking like no one could chase him off again. His shirt was on now, but he'd buttoned it all wrong. His feet were bare in his shoes. "I need to speak to you, sir. Will you ask me in?"

Grandpa stepped back, a dignified figure now in his neatly tied robe. That was as close to an invitation as Calvin would get. Aunt Bonnie started to cry. "Please, sir, don't hold this against Bonnie. We're in love. We want to be married."

"Have you made her pregnant?"

"No, sir, I don't believe so."

"Why haven't you spoken to me before?"

"I . . . I know you're some distrustful of me," Calvin said, having the good grace to blush. But he kept looking Grandpa straight in the eye. "So I thought to do something that would demonstrate my prospects. I'm buying us a house. I wanted it to be mine before I announced my intentions."

"Where would this house be?" Grandpa asked in a way that suggested he didn't know whether to believe Calvin or not.

"Over to the development where I'm working," Calvin said with some pride. "I'm assistant to the foreman now."

"How old are you, Calvin?"

"Twenty-four, sir."

Grandpa was quiet, the way he is when he's digesting things. He didn't take his eyes off Calvin.

"I'm a good worker, sir. Bonnie will always be taken care of."

"That's what you say now!" Grandma yelled, rising from her chair. "Anyone knows there's no need to buy the cow iffen you've already taken the milk."

Calvin looked shocked.

"How many of our town boys have you been bragging to? How long—"

"Now just a dang minute there! You may be Bonnie's mother, but you got no call to talk like that! I wouldn't spoil the name of the woman who'll be my wife, or that of her family!" Calvin seemed to be bristling with porcupine quills. "And I'll thank you not to refer to Bonnie as livestock."

"That's enough!" Grandpa's temper was beginning to show itself.

"No, sir, it isn't. I came to say something, and I'll say it now!" No one ever backtalks Grandpa. He was struck silent, taking it in. "I love Bonnie. I'd marry her tomorrow if I had a place to take her. It'll be three months till I can sign my name to paper and give her a home. I love her." His voice shook as he said, "I love her all the more for loving me back.

70

"If you'll allow it, we'll make our announcements and I'll visit her in your parlour till we can be wed. You have no need to fear she'll be sneaking out at night. You have my word."

Grandpa rocked back and forth on his heels a few times, ruminating, he calls it. Just about the time I thought I'd burst, he nodded. "Seven o'clock, Saturday evenings. And you take to eating lunch somewheres else."

"Yes, sir."

Things had settled down some by Saturday. Mostly because Grandma had too much to do to work herself up over Aunt Bonnie and Calvin more than once a day. Still, I had hopes that I'd be around to hear it if Grandma had anything further to say on the subject. I was in the attic when the conversation turned to me.

"She doesn't look good to me, Dad. She's spending too much time to herself, up there writing stories and making paper dolls."

"I don't think it serves any purpose to aggravate yourself." Grandpa's ideas about raising children began and ended with whether you had a rash.

"She's been through a terrible experience. It may have affected her in some way."

"I'm not denying that." A coat hanger scraped across the closet rod. "Has she said anything about it?"

"No."

"There you are. You can't help her by making her drag it all out again." I heard the soft flap of the polishing rag over his shoes. "She'll make her peace with it in time."

"I seem to remember Darryl being a favorite of hers," Grandma worried. "She mentioned him a time or two and you could just see—"

"People are thick as ants at a picnic in that house."

"Noah!"

"All I'm saying is, she'll find another favorite."

"I think she's deeper than that. Some people are. Look at Robert, f'r instance. He never got over what Nora did to him."

"He married again, didn't he?" Grandpa asked. "He musta got over most of it."

"That woman didn't want to have Robert's children."

"My impression was that she didn't want anyone's children after spending her own childhood sharing her mother's duties!" Grandpa was losing patience with this conversation.

"It didn't stop her having a child by Jim Benton!"

"They were eight years married when that child was born. We could hardly accuse Nora of being overeager."

"She resented caring for Allie!" Grandma went on. "She lets Crystal cling to her like a spider to a ceiling."

"Robert didn't marry her for children or for her ways with them. He married her for her beauty. He left her when that couldn't hold him anymore."

"I remember why Robert left her!" Grandma's voice had gone shrill.

"That's what this is about, isn't it? Be honest, woman."

"She was brass bold, moving that man into their house two days after Robert went off to war in Europe. Every tongue in three counties wagged. She couldn't even go into a grocery store that someone didn't point her out to somebody else."

"I remember it being our son's idea that she take in a boarder until he could start sending her money, her having to be home with the baby. I also remember he as much as said she could keep it up and save the money for when he came home," Grandpa said in a voice ripe with disgust. "He had nothing to say concerning who she should rent it to. So she let the room. She slept in the baby's room. We saw that ourself."

"We saw an empty cot," Grandma argued. "We don't know how long she slept in it before she moved back to share Robert's bed with her boarder."

"Her neighbors either never saw that empty cot or they made out they saw more."

"You sound like she was all but forced to take up with him!"

"She was a young woman foolish enough to rent out her bedroom to a young man, but she'd have to be hard pressed

7 2

to look to her boarder for comfort," Grandpa said. "I'm saying she was hard pressed by those tongues you spoke of."

"She went on seeing him after our son came back."

"Not for some time. It may be that Robert was no better at living with those wagging tongues than Nora."

"Are you suggesting no one should have told him?"

"I'm saying we have to shoulder the responsibility for the damage our words do."

"What do you mean?"

Grandpa didn't say anything out loud. He can say more than enough with a look.

"Better to speak up and be sorry than to hush and wish we had," Grandma told him.

"All of which comes to what? You got something on your mind."

"I'm thinking only of Allie." Grandma sounded like she felt herself on the losing end of this conversation.

"Get to the point."

"We ought to talk to Robert."

"You don't want to talk. You want to tattle."

"If you're referring to that piece in the newspaper"—I could hear the clink of toilet water bottles as Grandma put on her Finishing Touches as she spoke—"I think we have a duty to tell Robert that things are getting bad in that house again."

"Just what good do you think that will do?"

"He has a right to know his daughter is under the care of a man who gets drunk and gets himself arrested." Grandma finished the sentence as if it were a question.

"Jim Benton has been getting drunk for years. If Robert hasn't seen fit to take his daughter out of there in all that time, I don't believe he'll do any different this time."

"What are you saying?"

"Just that we're likely to cause an upset that no one will thank us for. When our son gets up to go, it will still be Jim Benton who's taking care of his daughter."

"Each thing you say is more cruel than what you said before it!"

7 3

"I know some things about fathering, woman! I fathered mine, I raised them and I expected my children would care for theirs. Speaking as a man who has raised another man's child, I'd feel damned unkindly toward her parent interfering with my family. For all of Jim Benton's mistakes, he's done what he could for Allie and his own child, too. His faults are more obvious than mine, but I'm not prepared to say they're worst!"

"Noah Drew, are you saying our son isn't a good father?"

"I haven't seen enough of him being a father to venture an opinion," Grandpa said, shutting the bedroom door firmly behind him.

When you listen in on what people have to say, you take a chance that you'll hear something you wish you hadn't. Myself, I think I'm losing my taste for it.

The trip back from the airport seemed twice as long as it took to get there in the first place. Probably because I shared the backseat with my father's wife, Lisa, and her hatboxes and Grandma. Daddy sat up front with Grandpa. It was eight o'-clock when we finally pulled into the driveway where Aunt Charlotte waited with Uncle George. Calvin stood beside Aunt Bonnie. Grandma, who'd forgotten all about Calvin, gave a startled gasp.

Daddy turned around to look her over. "You all right, Mom?"

"Just fine, son. A little stitch from so much settin.'" It didn't ease her stitch to find Calvin at her side to help her out of the car. Grandpa introduced him as Bonnie's intended as if Calvin had asked for Aunt Bonnie's hand in the usual manner.

Daddy and Lisa talked through most of dinner. I kept hoping Daddy'd find a few minutes just for me, for the two of us to sit on the porch swing in the dark and talk. Of course I know Grandma was hoping for the same thing and probably Aunt Charlotte and Aunt Bonnie as well. Since we were all together, there was clearly no reason for him to take each of us aside.

I noticed Grandma kept a close eye on Calvin. Though he only had eyes for Aunt Bonnie, he made no attempt to be familiar except to hold her chair when she sat down. He showed himself to be a quiet man with an eye to helpfulness in the kitchen. When Uncle George suggested that that might be because Aunt Bonnie was in the kitchen, Calvin cleared his name in a voice that soothed even Grandma's bristling sensitivities.

"My Daddy said he thought the reason so many women aged early and died tired deaths is because they're still on their feet doing women's work long after they've settled their men down with a pipe and the Bible. He was always one to help in the kitchen after dinner and put us kids to bed. Then he and Ma could set down together to share the evening. I don't see that it should be any different for Bonnie and me."

It was an answer that held some appeal for everyone except Uncle George. I saw the briefest smile touch Grandma's lips. Not that she was giving in just yet. But Calvin had definitely gotten a toehold.

We were just about through the ice cream before there was what you'd call a lull in the conversation. "It'll be nice to have you here for such a nice long visit, Lisa," Grandma said.

"Well, we'd better talk about that, Mom," Daddy said, laying down his spoon.

"You'll be here through the fair, won't you?" Grandma's voice held a trembly note.

"I will, yes. Lisa is going on out to see her folks in Los Angeles. She'll only be here a few days."

"Why, we've hardly seen anything of her ourselves!" Grandma said.

"I realize you haven't had much time to get to know Lisa, Ma, a week here or there and some years of not seeing us at all. But she hasn't seen her folks in three years, same as me. We have to meet the show in Arizona as soon as the fair is over, that being the end of our vacation time. It's hard enough to get when the show is getting ready to leave the country."

"Well," Grandma prepared to give in gracefully, but Daddy wasn't finished.

"We have some news, Ma, that will make you happy." Lisa's

cheeks took on a rosier color as Daddy put his hand over hers. "We're expecting a baby."

There were surprised faces all around the table, an instant when they hung there wondering what to say. Suddenly everyone was talking at once, congratulating them and asking when.

"Well, I guess you'll be looking to settle down," Uncle George bellowed. Everything went quiet again.

"We aren't quite sure how we'll work things out, George," Daddy answered. He looked over at me and with that same careful voice held brightly cheerful, he asked, "Aren't you excited to have a little brother or sister, Allie?"

My mind seemed to blink with surprise. "I already have one." Then, realizing that wasn't the kind of answer he'd been looking for, I added, "A brother would be nice." When Aunt Bonnie touched my shoulder and asked would I help her do the dessert dishes, I was happy to go.

Daddy and Lisa planned to spend the night with friends in Altoona. They would pick me up and take me back to Carlisle late on Sunday. In that way I would be close enough to Des Moines to be with Daddy every day.

Reverend Allen was feeling particularly vigorous this Sunday. His eyes burned with impatience as we filed past him to be seated. His mood wasn't lost on many, and there was an air of anticipation as the church filled. He strode to the pulpit and, skipping right over the news of deaths and babies, told us of an attack on a woman in Pleasantville. "He was after the money in her pocketbook and before he was through, he'd taken more than that!" I gathered he felt there was little sympathy being offered her due to the nature of her work. In fact, that was the subject of his sermon: Who Among Us Shall Judge?

The congregation was unusually quiet, listening to the recounting of the woman's sad experience. They coughed and shuffled their feet through the sermon, a sign of general unrest. It may have been that Reverend Allen felt that strongly about his subject. Or maybe he'd been charmed by the sound of his own voice. He looked over the unruffled faces that sat before him and reacted as if they'd thrown down a challenge. Turning his yellow eyes on Brother Lester, he allowed his voice to strike a reproachful note. "When Jesus fed bread and fish to the hungry, he did not ask their occupation."

Singled out in this way, and finding Reverend Allen's statement innocent of scandal, Brother Lester felt called upon to lend his support: "Amen, Brother Allen."

"Indeed, he did not ask them to believe!" he shouted, casting a critical eye over his flock. Reverend Allen came from behind the pulpit and singled out Mrs. MacInntyre, the postmistress, speaking to her in a conversational tone. "If called upon to feed the hungry, would you withhold your riches from those blemished with canker sores?" Mrs. MacInntyre, paling at the suggestion that she might face such infection, but anxious to earn Reverend Allen's approval, shook her head strenuously.

Continuing across the front row, the seating preferred by the especially devout, he looked into the face of the elderly Miss Harley. He asked, "Can you, madam, refuse this woman the milk of your kindness because she lacks your virtue?" Miss Harley quaked like an aspen sapling, her wan complexion darkening under the warmth of Reverend Allen's gaze.

"They came to believe," he cried out, "the miracles He laid at their feet! And the love He offered so freely."

"Bless the Lord," a woman's voice called out.

Encouraged, his voice roughened with unspent emotion, Reverend Allen moved on to Mr. Kravitt, the blacksmith. "Is there a man among us who has never known a lapse of good intention? Who has never entertained thoughts of a downfallen woman?"

Mr. Kravitt was stunned.

Reverend Allen considered himself unchallenged. He closed his eyes and begged for our understanding. "If we can forgive ourselves our masculine nature, can we not extend the hand of forgiveness to a woman who accepts us, knowing so fully as she does the nature of the beast?"

Behind me, a man called out, "Say yea unto the Lord."

Several more voices rose to accommodate Reverend Allen. He returned to the pulpit, confident that God's truth would ring out for all to hear. And yet, as I looked around, there were a few faces, stony and silent, that let you know they didn't agree with Reverend Allen's sentiments, but felt that the church wasn't a place to say so.

During a burst of amens and hallelujahs, Uncle George passed Grandpa the keys to his car, saying he and Aunt Charlotte were walking back to the house. Sandwiched between Grandma and Aunt Charlotte as I was, I could see that Grandma took this as something of an embarrassment. "You can't leave in the middle of his sermon!"

"I'm sure not gonna sit here and listen to this . . . this—"

"What will he think?"

"Tell him I was taken sick! Tell that son of yours to return your car or plan to drive you here next Sunday and sit through this hisself!" Uncle George, as good as his word, proceeded to march Aunt Charlotte down the center aisle. Grandma blanched, but turned a sweet smile in Reverend Allen's direction.

I had no reason to feel that this concerned me. I joined in on the singing of hymns with a fresh enthusiasm. I was none too far from enjoying my own long-awaited freedom.

Then things took a turn for the worse.

We'd sung our hearts out. Now came the time when Reverend Allen bowed his head in a fervent prayer for the week ahead, finishing with the wish that we'd all enjoy a fine dinner and a peaceful afternoon. That let everyone know two things: that we could stand and go, and that he expected to see us back there for the Sunday night meeting.

But when Reverend Allen bowed his head to pray, he stayed silent. Everyone waited, heads bowed, eyes closed, and probably most did what I did—opened one eye to see that Reverend Allen was still with us. What had been a silence became a chorus of shuffling feet and cleared throats. When Reverend

Allen's voice came, it was deeper than it had been and dark with shame.

"Lord, I've failed you this Sunday morning. I want to touch the hearts of these good people, to awaken them to the true meaning of your love. I cannot find the way—"

The good Mrs. Allen was so moved by the force of her husband's words that she began to rock back and forth in the front pew. As Reverend Allen warmed to a new theme I felt my own spirits begin to droop. I put my hands on the pew in front of me and leaned forward to rest my heavy head on my arms. It relieved the headache that had begun to threaten and eased the misery of my poor bottom.

"Don't fidget, Allie," Grandma whispered, her irritation over the early departure of Uncle George and Aunt Charlotte making her sharp tempered.

"Yes, ma'am." Now it occurred to me that Uncle George, in his conversation with Aunt Charlotte, would've made it perfectly clear what this morning's sermon was all about. I was sorry I hadn't made it my business to go with them, since I would shortly be on Grandma's wrong side anyway.

The reverend's voice had taken on a quality that made it seem to come from the bottom of a barrel, raising goosebumps on my arms. It was a sound that belonged to God himself. Beside me, Grandma squeezed her eyes shut and moaned, "Bless him oh bless him." Other voices called out encouragement and someone began to hum "Amazing Grace," to themselves at first, then louder, and they were joined by another, and it all became some kind of rhythm that moved through the body of worshipers, gathering them up and gaining strength as it moved on.

Grandma tapped me on the back.

I stifled a yawn as I sat up, bringing tears to my eyes that blurred the approving smile Grandma gave me and the swaying figures in the pews around me. I turned dutifully toward Reverend Allen, his face tormented as he offered a tense appeal. "It can only be my failure, friends, if I have not found the words to open your hearts." Mrs. Allen gave forth with a sound that fell somewhere between a groan and a sob. "The Lord loves you. Open your arms and let him in," Reverend Allen's voice rang out. "Come forward, brothers and sisters, and ask for his forgiveness."

There was a moment, only that, in which Reverend Allen saw there wasn't going to be a rush forward and he stepped quickly into the breach. "Come forward and be saved," he said, placing his hands around the flushed face of Mrs. Whiddon, a dedicated porch sitter known to trade orange popsicles for half an hour's conversation, a woman who was in no way prepared to withstand the full force of the Lord's attentions. She rose to a half-standing position, gabbling and crying over Reverend Allen's hands before she fell back into the pew.

My grandmother was breathing heavily now and rocking rapidly back and forth beside me as Reverend Allen came down the aisle. "Come forward and be saved," he urged. And his sheep flocked toward him, eager to receive his blessing. One after another they crowded to the end of the pews seeking Reverend Allen's hands, and he spoke quickly to each of them, "Blessed be ye who offers thy services to our Lord, in His name's sake, amen," as he passed us and worked his slow progress toward the back of the church.

A woman threw herself in Reverend Allen's path as he turned to make his way back and he knelt with her to pray. Which is not to say that it quieted down any. Reverend Allen prayed with a fire and a force that whipped the congregation into a pulsing mass that surged toward him. As he prayed, the sun moved across the sky to shine brilliantly through the windows of God's house, as it had last Sunday and would again next Sunday, but never before had it found Reverend Allen prostrate on the floor of the church, and as the sun set its golden light upon Reverend Allen's head, it struck the fevered congregation as a Christlike spectacle, expressed in a great sigh that seemed to come from the bowels of the church.

Reverend Allen, bathed in sweat and trembling, slowly stood and ran his sharp eyes over each row of pews. "What is

80

done here today is God's work," he whispered hoarsely. Adoring eyes followed him back up the aisle, yearning hands plucking at his sleeves and clinging to him as the frenzy to touch and be touched grew. Reverend Allen bore it all, bent almost double with the weight of their love, treading slowly, unceasingly toward the pulpit. When he reached it, climbing onto his small platform as if it were the highest mountain, he called out to the congregation, "Good ladies, raise your voices to the Lord. Come forward, ye believers and reaffirm your faith." His arms opened outward as the church was filled with the joyous voices of the pure in heart. Mrs. Lowell, a widow of two years, stumbled into the aisle and all but ran toward the pulpit, hampered only by her advanced years. Reverend Allen reached for her and lifted her onto the platform, his arms still lovingly wrapped about her as they went into the baptismal tank.

I allowed myself one long miserable groan. He was turning this into a revival meeting.

The parishioners began to trickle down the aisle a few at a time, and the ladies still sang on at Reverend Allen's urging. Mrs. Lowell returned to her seat, dripping enchantment. Grandma was pressed against me in her eagerness to reach the aisle, and I drew back into the pew to give her room to pass. "Brother Allen!" she cried out. "Help me, Brother Allen, to ask God's mercy." Pushing me into the aisle, she threw herself down on her knees. "Save her! My granddaughter has never been baptized."

I had only a moment to look at her, hardly believing my eyes and ears, before two huge hands gripped my shoulders. When I tried to back away, there was another hand at my back and one at my elbow and I was carried suspended toward the baptistery. It seems to me there were a lot of things I could have done; I could have screamed or kicked or something. But there were all kinds of things running through my mind. The little gold cross Grandma Taylor draped over Uncle Darryl's still hands, saying he'd brought it with him and she thought he might want it now. Brother Wayne leering at my mother as he clutched her elbow. Those two boys from the reform school, choking and sniveling, wanting so much to be a part of something they hardly understood. And around and around the edges of my mind, like a dog that runs around sheep, ran this idea that my grandmother had to make up for Aunt Charlotte and Uncle George leaving early.

A great bulging horror swelled in my chest as I was handed over to Reverend Allen, and it may be that I remember it wrong, but I don't think any of those hands let go of me but began to push me down into the water, and even though I tried to wriggle away I felt the cold creep up my legs and into my clothing. It's an odd thing how your mind has an idea about what to do, and your body starts to carry it out while your mind is still working on it, deciding that it would be better to do something else. I think that's what was happening to me, that there was some tiny part of me that knew they wouldn't drown me, that this would be over in a minute if I would just hold my breath. But what I did as the water flowed across my face, I reached up and grabbed a handful of Reverend Allen's cheek, beard and all, twisting so hard I felt it lift up off the bone. I hardly gave it a thought when he screeched and let go of me, just scrambled out of the baptistery and tore down the aisle. It was only later that I remembered how suddenly the singing stopped except for one quavery voice still holding a fading note as I ran out the door.

4

Aunt Bonnie brought Sunday dinner up to the attic for me. I stayed there most of the day; not so much because I was sulking like Grandma said to Grandpa as they sat down to eat, but because the mood downstairs was fidgety, real fidgety.

Aunt Charlotte made Uncle George back down enough to say that if he was to be driving them around during the time that Daddy needed their car, they could plan to be at the Methodist church on Sunday mornings.

Grandma defended Reverend Allen, and Grandpa said all that's done is God's will, that it's not for us to be critical of His works.

Aunt Bonnie answered that by saying she never thought

she'd see three grown men force a child's head under water in God's name.

Aunt Charlotte, anxious to get back into Grandma's good graces, said she'd always thought Nora planned to raise me as a heathen just to strike out at their family.

When I'd heard enough, I abandoned the attic for the space beneath the front porch. I stayed there when Daddy and Lisa drove up, thinking I'd hear what Grandma had to say to him. I'd had the better part of the afternoon to think things over and I'd discovered I was angry. But they used the back door, and I heard nothing but the tail end of a conversation between Daddy and Aunt Bonnie.

". . . what good it will do? It's over now."

"That woman got herself beat up nearly a week ago, Robert Drew. Look what fresh disaster Timothy Allen made of it today! There's no such thing as over."

"If I were to see to her upbringing from week to week, it would be one thing, Bonnie. It serves no purpose for me to come in here after a three-year absence, saying I don't like the way things are being done."

"You expectin' Nora to stand up to them on this? You left your child with her and now the outcome rests on her shoulders, is that it?"

"For God's sake, Bonnie, I didn't abandon her. I left her to be raised by her mother, which seemed the best thing to do at the time." Then he said, more firmly, "It was the best. What could I do about raising a two-year-old? I had to think of making a living."

"You could have come back here, that's what. Your mother and your sisters could have cared for Allie."

"That's enough. We started out talking about what pain Mom caused her and now you're saying, what? That Mom should have had Allie all along?"

"Allie's caught between now. That's why this happened."

"And if I'd stayed? I'd be a coal miner. Probably out of work, from what I've been hearing from Pop. Living in one of these little shingled houses up the road here. Allie would spend weekends with her mother or Nora would come out to visit for an afternoon." He made an impatient sound. "How's that for caught between?"

"She needs her father now," Aunt Bonnie pleaded.

"I'm doing what I can to make life better for her. She'll be able to go to college, she'll—"

"You have it all planned out for her."

"It's the best I can do in this situation, Bonnie."

"But you won't have her."

"It would have been unfair to saddle Lisa with a half-grown child. She was unprepared. And now—well. . . ."

"Robert Drew, you're not the man you were at fifteen." The swing creaked as Aunt Bonnie got up.

"Bonnie—" and the screen door slammed shut.

Daddy planned to take Lisa and me shopping on Monday; that is, he takes us, drops us off and goes about his business. But Lisa spent most of Monday morning in the bathroom. It was noon before they got to Grandma's to pick me up. Lisa didn't look like she was in any condition to shop. After the car started moving, she laid her head back on the seat. Daddy started to plan the rest of the week, planning being one of the things he does best. "Is there anything you'll be needing besides school clothes?" Daddy asked.

"Like what?"

"Oh, like art supplies," he said, smiling to let me know he had a surprise.

"You mean like colored pencils?"

"Is that all you're using?"

"I don't have any. I used them up coloring in the maps for geography."

Daddy looked a little taken aback. "I'm surprised to hear that. I'd expected you'd be using paints or pastels."

"Pastels?" I wondered aloud.

"Tell me, did you ever take any art lessons?"

"Not me."

"Did you ever want to?"

"I guess I'd like that fine. I don't know that I ever heard of it before." He looked pretty unhappy with my answer, and for a minute I thought I'd said something wrong.

"Your mother and I always planned that you should have the opportunity to learn things. Like dancing. Did you ever take dancing lessons?"

"They taught us to square dance in school," I said, thinking to go on to tell him how much I liked it.

"I meant something different. Ballet?"

I could see he didn't want to hear about square dancing. "I was in the Brownies," I offered.

"Well, good! You must be about ready for Girl Scouts."

Uh-oh. "Daddy Jim took me on his bicycle because we had to go into town, to the church."

"Bicycle?"

"I rode on the handlebars. Some of the others wanted to, but their fathers only had cars."

"What did you do in the winter? In the cold weather, I mean."

"We bundled up with scarves and gloves. It worked out except when the snow was too deep. Then we walked and Daddy Jim waited upstairs in the church to take me home."

"Were Brownies so important?"

"Not Brownies, exactly." I tried to explain. "We were sticking papier-mâché on cardboard that last year and painting on it. I did a vase of flowers that looked almost real. We made paper-mâché puppets the year before that. Daddy Jim knows I like that sort of thing."

"So those were art lessons."

"I never thought of it that way."

"You had to buy paints and things, I guess."

"No. Mrs. Johnson had everything."

Daddy didn't seem to be in a mood to talk after that, and I let him alone. It was pretty funny when you think of how full of questions he was at the beginning of the ride.

By the time we reached Des Moines, Lisa had begun to perk up. I was more than a little relieved because shopping is the thing we do best together. Lisa stops looking at me like a growth that appeared on her nose, and I stop worrying about whether I'll hiccup at the table or say something Inappropriate. Because I have a Chic Figure, which suits her fine when she starts buying dresses. Except for this year when practically everything is too long because Hemlines Are Going Up and even the S & L department store should reflect that fact. I was just happy that S & L was taking the blame.

Better than the dresses were the coats. One was a loosely flowing, teal blue corduroy artist's smock, Lisa said. It looked as wonderful as it sounded. The other was hooded, with a circular skirt. No buttons, it wrapped and tied. Both were unlike anything I'd had before. I refused to even think about what my mother would have to say about one person having two coats. We were finishing up when Lisa said, "Your mother can take those hems up, I suppose."

"I guess." I knew what my mother would have to say to that. It might be that the hemlines were shorter in New York, but it would take Carlisle, Iowa, some time to catch up. And Carlisle, Iowa, is good enough for me.

It turned out Daddy did have a surprise for me. A paper pad and colored pencils. He delivered me to the door with my packages, and I listened with less than the usual interest as he talked with my mother. And once I knew I'd be going to the fair the next day, I settled myself on the front step with the pencils.

I didn't notice I had company until the boy came right up to me. "Hi."

I frowned up at him and went back to my drawing. I'd seen him before, when I transferred to the school here. He was in one of the upper grades, always walking with a different girl, and for reasons that escaped me, he'd made a point of saying "Hi" to me for the few days before school let out. I never said anything to him.

When he didn't go away, I frowned harder, trying to impart the notion that I had no time for talk. He just stood there.

I looked up at him like he was in my light.

He didn't look discouraged in any way. In fact, he sat down beside me like he wanted to get a better look at my drawing, then took a long look at the tree. He had nice eyes. He was good looking enough to be the subject of girls who stand around in schoolyards discussing such things. His hair dipped low over his forehead, an effect achieved by careful combing and the liberal use of hair cream.

"So go ahead," he said.

It was no good. I couldn't concentrate.

"Your problem is, you're trying to draw more than you can see." I gave him a look from under my eyebrows. "This branch. You've drawn it all the way to the top of the tree. But look," he pointed to the actual branch, "it's covered by leaves so you can't see it from here on," he said, tracing a finger across the page.

"I can too."

"Nope. You see its shadow. Right? Behind the leaves."

"Yeah. I guess."

"Your line has to stop here, where the leaves cover it. When you color it in, you'll make a shadow. You using crayons?"

"Colored pencils."

"Whoa. Fancy stuff. Let's see."

I pulled them out of my bag and passed them to him.

He took a moment to admire the colors. Then he did what I would have done; he opened the case to smell them.

"Terrific. I used to love these. You used them in school, right?"

"For maps."

"Me, too. Can I have a piece of paper?"

"What for?"

"I'll show you how to shadow it in."

"I know how."

"Oh. Sorry." But he didn't look sorry. Just a little surprised. He passed the pencils back. "Okay. I'll watch."

I turned away, trying to pick up where I'd left off. I had to erase a couple of times. It's really annoying to have to erase. It leaves marks on the paper no matter how careful you are.

Also, your new lines come in too dark. I scribbled across the drawing. "You think you can just walk up to people sitting in their own yards and bother them?"

He didn't answer.

"Who are you anyway? You don't live on this road. You have no business telling me how to draw a tree or anything else." He stared dead at me. Then he stood up and walked away, shoulders slouched, thumbs hooked in his belt loops.

Typical.

It was Mom's laundry day, and I didn't care to be called on for help. I took Crystal way off to the back of the yard, right to the edge of the cornfield. That must sound sweet, me being old enough to be some help around the house. Well, I am. But that washing machine is more than I can bear.

It's some sight, the cord stretched straight out from this fat red and white machine, straining and slogging in place. Like a dog at the end of a short leash. You have to feed the wet clothes through these two rollers that squeeze them dry. In order to get the clothes to go in, you have to get your fingers close to the rollers. Sometimes they grab hold of you along with the clothes. Don't for a minute think you can just pull your hand back.

It's gone.

And your arm follows right behind it. This happened to my mother the first time she used it, the rollers finally popping open at her elbow. When it happened to me, it didn't pop open at all. When it got to my shoulder I just hung there, screaming, while that thing kept trying to suck me in. Mom tried to release the rollers, but they wouldn't let go until she hit the knob with a hammer. My arm wasn't broken, but it was better than a month before it plumped out to normal. You can understand why I'm none too anxious to help with the laundry.

"Allie!"

I got up and headed back toward the house, leaving Crystal to her play.

"That's the third time I called you, young lady." I opened

my mouth. "Don't you tell me you couldn't hear me. I liked to tore out a lung screaming for you."

"I'm here now."

"Don't you get smart," she warned, her head poked through the basement door like an angry groundhog. "Go around and see who's at the door."

I started for the back porch.

"Don't track through the house. Go around."

Daddy was already on his way to the backyard. We gave each other a businessy hug, quick and not too close. He was early by half the day, but he already acted like someone late getting somewhere.

"Hello, Nora."

Mom nodded. I could see she wasn't happy that he'd caught her in old clothes, wetted by the laundry, and her hair looking like she might not have combed it yet. She likes to put on a dress and act like she doesn't do housework any other way.

"I thought we might talk, Nora. Then I'd like to take Allie to the fairgrounds with me."

"I guess that would be all right." Mom had a different way with Daddy, more ladylike I guess you'd say. I was glad Daddy Jim wasn't home to see it. "You wait outside, Allie. Keep an eye on Crystal for me."

"Maybe it's best, Allie," Daddy said. He followed her in, remembering to wipe his feet.

Crystal still squatted over the hole she was digging in the soft soil of the flowerbed. I didn't think she'd miss me. The basement was cool and damp and, as I scooted through, darker and darker. I slowed to a crawl in Daddy Jim's workroom, being careful not to bang into anything that would make a noise. A little light filtered through the living room grate, making it easy to find. Standing there, I could hear everything they said.

As my eyes adjusted to the dim room, I made a discovery. There were pictures on the wall in front of me, pictures on a glossy paper like you find in magazines. Carefully, I felt for Daddy Jim's flashlight. Pictures of naked women turning bare bottoms to the camera or holding their heavy breasts up with spread hands. They'd been cut out very carefully, not just torn out, and taped up all around the room. It looked so . . . orderly, all the pages lined up. Every inch of the walls was covered. I know they were only pictures, but they gave me the creeps.

It sure gave me something to think about. But that was for later. Daddy had gotten to something interesting.

"I want to take her to Brazil."

"These trips you take her on . . ." Mom said unhappily.

"What about them?"

"It's just . . . well, she comes back so different."

"How do you mean?"

"She doesn't act the same way. She talks like she's Mrs. Astor, about what she's seen, what she's been doing."

"She's excited, Nora—"

"It's more . . . what she knows. She uses such words."

"About what? Are you suggesting—"

"It's just that most children her age haven't traveled around the way she has, not—"

"That's not true, Nora. There are children all over this country whose families take—"

"It's not the same, Robert, and you know it. We aren't talking about Disneyland. I put her on a plane for Paris—"

"She was alone only as far as New York!"

"The point is, I put her on the plane and you meet her when it lands. She's traveling alone."

"Ah!"

"It makes her act different, Robert. She gets to acting so important—"

"Independent."

"You can dress it up whatever way you like!"

"I have a lot of responsibilities when we're moving a show. It's better for her to come later—"

"She spends an hour or more in the Chicago airport every time she leaves here."

"She has supervision—"

"The stewardesses take her off the plane—"

9 1

"And take her to an office to wait," my father finished, drowning out my mother's last few words.

"You think she stays in there? She told me about it last time. They put her in an empty office and told her they'd be back for her in three hours. They leave and she leaves!"

"She has a watch."

"Robert! She has the run of the airport till she meets them back at that office."

"So what? She buys magazines, she gets something to eat—"

"And walks around with an old lady who lives in the airport, begging off people and sleeping in the bathroom! She showed Allie how to get people to give her money—Robert Drew, it's not funny! Allie earned thirty-two dollars that she gave to the—"

Daddy laughed out loud, drowning out my mother's next few words.

"—not the only one! Did she tell you about the old man who rode up and down elevators all day, hoping to find someone to talk to? Or the people who sit around hotel lobbies—"

"Maybe they're retired people, I don't know—"

"Allie should know better than to go off with strangers!"

"You can take that up with her as well as I can—"

"When she's with you, she doesn't think of what I have to say! Another thing. A child shouldn't have twenty-five dollars in her hand as spending money. We aren't the kind of people who—"

"Oh, come on! No one is spoiling her."

"Open her closet, if you don't think so. There's a silk dress hanging there."

"She was six!"

"What six-year-old did you ever know who had a silk dress? And the dolls. A new one every few months, the likes of which I've never seen. Real hair and some of those have silk dresses! They aren't even toys."

"They're for her to enjoy."

"They're for her to brag on!"

9 2

"Ah, Nora." I could imagine him rubbing a hand over his face the way Grandpa Drew did. "Look, let's not talk about dolls or clothes, okay?"

"Whatever you say."

"This trip to Brazil," he began.

"Is the same as dolls and fancy clothes."

"You know, Nora, there was a time when we both wanted her to have these things."

"It's different now."

"For us, Nora. It doesn't have to be different for her."

"It already *is* different for her. If she misbehaves in school, her teachers say she's wild, that it's the result of divorce. If she talks about what she's seen, people say she's bragging. No matter about families taking their kids places, those aren't the families who are raising the kids she knows!"

"Are you finished?"

"No. You may not have thought of it yet, Robert, but she'll be picking a husband from around here."

"She has years yet before we have to think about who she'll marry."

"We were married at sixteen—"

"Nora, there's no reason to feel she has to pick a farmer."

"Or a coal miner?"

"That's right!"

"That's exactly what I'm talking about. You're putting ideas into her head. How can she be happy here, being somebody's wife and taking care of kids, if you're going to fill her up on foreign countries and big department stores, silk dresses and show girls with diamonds!"

"Just a minute. . . ."

"I'm not saying anything against your wife. She seems nice enough."

"But she bleaches her hair."

"Yes, she does. And don't forget, I didn't bring that up."

"You don't have to."

"As long as we're on the subject, I don't like that she tried to bribe Allie into getting her hair cut on that last trip."

9 3

"What?"

"She promised Allie an armful of comic books if she'd get a haircut. That woman better not touch a hair on Allie's head."

"That was months ago."

"My memory's fine."

"Then can you remember what you did with the extra money I sent for art lessons?" There was a brief silence. "Or dancing lessons."

"I fed your daughter, Robert Drew," Mom said angrily, but I could tell she was crying. "And I fed mine."

"Okay, okay. I'm sorry I brought it up." Mom went on crying quietly. "I'll try to send you a little more each month. But let's get back to this other thing. They aren't show girls in the way that you think. They're hard working. There are worse people for Allie to get to know."

"They have boyfriends—" Mom said chokily.

"They aren't in one place long enough! Most have families back home to send money to. Or they're married to one of the techs that travel with the show. Like Lisa and me."

"They tell Allie things a child shouldn't know."

"Who? Who ever told Allie something you disapprove of?"

"That last one, when Allie met you in Detroit. She had a strange name." Mom sounded stronger, like the tears were almost gone.

"Gitty?"

"She told Allie about concentration camps."

"What's wrong with that? Allie will learn about them in school."

"Maybe. So let her hear it there. She doesn't need to sit in a fancy restaurant with a pretty lady talking about her parents and sister dying in one and showing Allie the numbers on her arm."

"That's enough! Gitty is a twenty-five-year-old woman who looks closer to forty when you see her close up. She has her own act and doesn't have to be backstage all day like the chorus line. She was fond of Allie, and she took her to lunch whenever Lisa and I had to be at rehearsals all day."

"Not that you mentioned anything about that when you wanted me to send her—"

"Let's stick to one grievance at a time. Gitty never told Allie enough to upset her. Allie liked her very much."

"Why wouldn't Allie like her? The woman fed her lobster and bought her presents, let her put on lipstick and false eyelashes."

"In the dressing room, Nora."

"On the stage."

"Right. You're right. Gitty let Allie assist her in the last few shows."

"Oh, I like hearing that!"

"She was not wearing false eyelashes, Nora!"

"She brought them home with her, Robert."

"Look, Nora, I can't talk about this anymore."

"There's nothing to talk about."

"Oh, yes there is. We will talk again, Nora—about Brazil."

"I won't let her go, Robert."

"I pay for her support, and I'll take her wherever I please."

"If that's the kind of—"

"I have to get to the fairgrounds. I'll get Allie."

I turned and ran back outside. Crystal was on the back steps. I sat down beside her just before the screen door opened.

"Allie? Come on; it's time to go." I looked back at Crystal as Daddy pulled me around the corner of the house. She looked like the last kitten in the box, the one no one ever takes.

The boy was back the next day, about the same time. I would never have seen him, but I was playing hide and seek with Crystal. We'd played until I was tired of it and I hid on the front steps. Crystal likes looking better than finding anyway.

He passed by once, then turned around to walk past again. He stopped a couple of houses down and waited. He could hang there for all I cared. Crystal came running around the corner of the house. "Find!"

"I'll race you to the back, Crystal. First one there gets two cookies. Get ready, set"—I crouched like I was in a real race; Crystal's eyes sparkled with excitement—*"go!"*

He was back the day after that. I waited out front to see. He carried something under his arm as he came up the street. Quicker than yesterday, purposeful, you might say. He came up the walk and sat down beside me, flipped open a notebook, a blank notebook, and started to draw.

Whenever I've seen a person draw, it was by starting a line in one place and ending it in another, catching the picture inside. This boy used lots of short, quick strokes, hardly letting his pencil touch the paper. Paper thicker than I'd ever seen. Creamy looking, like it would be a real treat to touch.

On its surface, a tree began to take shape. Not that you looked at it and said, oh, a drawing of a tree. As he looked from paper to tree, tree to paper, a pale gray tree began to grow. There were leaves, you could see them, or bits of them, one over the other. There was the bright space where the sunlight bleached them out. And there was the shadow of the branches behind them, like he'd said. The tree trunk was a solid weight that supported gnarled branches beneath the delicacy of the leaves, dancing in the summer breeze. He tore off the page and handed it to me, stood up and strode off the way he'd come.

I stayed on the porch a long time after he'd gone, letting Crystal take advantage of the opportunity to play on the front lawn. The paper was wonderful. I fingered it again, testing, unbelieving. It was more than a drawing. It was the tree. Only when I touched it could I be sure it was flat.

"What've you got there?" Daddy Jim asked, coming out onto the porch.

I held it out for him to see.

"You draw that?"

"Nope. Some boy."

He reached for the picture as he sat down. "A boy. You know him?"

"Not real well."

His eyes shifted restlessly over the paper, taking on a fevered look as he handed it back. "A friend, then."

"I guess so."

He took my hand in his, the way he did when I was little. "I wouldn't like to think you had yourself a boyfriend already."

"He's not a boyfriend."

"I still think of you as my little girlfriend, you know," he said, resting my hand on his knee and covering it with his again. "You don't come to me for those long talks like you used to."

"What talks are those?" Crystal had wandered back in our direction. She climbed up a couple of steps to sit near us.

"Oh, about dinosaurs or whatever else you were reading."

"I haven't been reading those lately."

"What are you reading?" He was rubbing my hand back and forth over his knee.

"Nothing. Nothing much, anyway."

"Maybe you're getting too old for that stuff," he suggested. His eyes burned with a kind of purpose.

"Maybe," I said, starting to pull my hand away.

"Don't be so quick, there," he said, tightening his hand over mine. "You'll have me wonderin' just what you are readin'."

"Nothing, like I said." I caught a whiff of liquor on his breath.

"Some girls your age, they start lookin' for stuff about what girls and boys do together."

He didn't say anything more, just kept rubbing my hand back and forth. It seemed to me, I was feeling nervous enough to have imagined it, it seemed our hands moved higher and higher on his thigh.

"I have to go in, now. Mom will need my help with dinner."

"Don't rush off. We can finish our little talk first."

"What is it you wanted to say?" His hand was definitely pulling mine down to the inside of his leg.

"Just that if you have questions that need answerin', you can come to me." His jeans felt damp with sweat and too warm where his legs had been together. "You don't have to be em-

barrassed with me like you might be with your real Daddy,"
he said in a breathy voice.

"I don't have any questions," I told him, trying to pull my
hand away without making him mad.

"You will," he said quietly, then pulled my hand over the
bulge in his pants with a sudden movement. I panicked and
tried to stand up. I couldn't. His elbow was caught inside mine
in a way that held me fast unless he made up his mind to let
go.

"Jim—" My mother stepped out on the porch as she spoke.
"Bring the girls in for dinner, won't you?"

Daddy Jim slid our hands along his leg like nothing was
going on. This will sound crazy, but I went along with him, as
if I hadn't noticed anything either. It was that or turn around
and say to my mother, "Daddy Jim made me touch him."

What could she do? I couldn't imagine what Daddy Jim
would have to say to my mother or what would happen
after he did. What kind of faces would we be wearing when
we said those things? The most terrifying question of all—
what would be in my mother's eyes when she looked at me
after that?

So I went in to dinner like it was any other evening, helping
Mom with the dishes afterward. She said I was looking nervous as a cat lately. That it would open his eyes if Daddy could
see the difference his visits made in me. For the first time I can
remember, I was grateful to be sent early to bed.

We drove Lisa to the airport the next morning. I was quiet
for most of the trip, thinking over what I'd tell Daddy. There
was no doubt in my mind that this was the sort of thing that
needed telling, no matter how angry it made Mom. Then it
occurred to me that my silence could be taken for rudeness.
After all, we were seeing Lisa off. I sat forward so I could see
into the front seat.

"Thanks for taking me shopping, Lisa. All the stuff is really
nice."

"You're welcome," she said in a tiny voice. She was draped

across the seat, her head cradled in the niche between the seat and the car door.

"You have morning sickness real bad, huh?" I sympathized. Lisa's eyelids fluttered. "Aunt Lily was sick right through. She says she always delivered her babies with a smile because she knew it was the end of feeling so bad."

"Allie." Daddy gave me one of his warning looks. "I don't think Lisa wants to talk about feeling sick."

"Okay." I thought things over. "Did you think of a name yet?"

"Not yet," Daddy answered.

"Just so you don't pick a name you find on every Tom, Dick or Harry. Like Tom, Dick or Harry," I finished with a grin.

Lisa made an offended noise.

"Lisa's father's name is Thomas. We're considering it," Daddy told me. He was beginning to look like he was sorry he'd brought me along.

"It was a joke," I said, returning to the corner of the backseat.

"Pull over," Lisa said.

"We're running late, Lisa."

"Robert!"

Lisa was barely out of the car before she was sick. Daddy drummed his fingers on the steering wheel.

"Aren't you going to get out?"

Daddy looked like he'd forgotten I was there. "Why would I get out?"

"Mom always holds my head when I'm sick."

"Grown-ups don't do that," Daddy said in a comfortable voice. Lisa reached in for her pocketbook and fumbled for a tissue.

"Some do," I muttered as Lisa climbed back in and with what seemed to be a tremendous effort, pulled the car door closed. I don't know whether Daddy didn't hear me or he simply ignored me.

I was as nice to Lisa as I could be, not because she was Daddy's wife but because she seemed to need it. She thought

I was just being polite and she was polite back. She gave Daddy and me the same dry little kiss before she boarded the plane without looking back.

"You're unusually quiet," Daddy said.

"She doesn't like me a whole lot, does she?"

"She does. She likes you." Daddy sounded not entirely convinced. "It's just that she doesn't know much about children. She doesn't know what to say to you. You know."

"I know a lot about children. I help take care of Crystal and I've helped my aunts with their babies. I change diapers and I know how to give a bottle because Aunt Jill was sick after her first and her milk dried up."

A small smile appeared on Daddy's face, not the kind I'd been hoping for. "So, you're ready to do some baby-sitting, is that it?"

"Sure."

"Well, we'll be back here next summer. You'll get your chance." We stopped at the newsstand, where Daddy bought a paper. "Want a magazine?"

I shook my head. "Lisa will need someone to help her after the baby's born."

"She'll come back to stay with her mother for a while. I can pick her up when the show gets back to the states."

"Them."

"What?"

"There will be two. To pick up, I mean."

"Yes." A frown made a slow crease in his forehead.

"Then what?" I pressed.

"Well, I. . . ."

"If I was with you, I could take care of the baby while you and Lisa were at rehearsals."

"Oh, we couldn't do that."

"Why not?"

"Well, Allie, you have to go to school. Besides, it's one thing to baby-sit for an hour or so, but a baby needs its mother." I could see he was thinking over what I'd said. He wasn't happy.

100

I could feel my chest tightening up and I tried to take a deep breath.

We didn't say much until we were back on the highway. "A lot of kids your age start to feel unhappy with their life," Daddy said. "They start to blame it on their parents, the school, even where they live. It's part of growing up."

"It isn't that." Daddy's face set in a grim expression. "It's Daddy Jim," I went on. "He's acting funny."

"How do you mean?"

"He's drinking," I began, working up to the thing that was so hard to say.

"I've heard about that. He has before."

"He's drinking more," I said, annoyed that he thought I was tattling on Daddy Jim.

"I trust your mother to handle it, Allie. She's lived with this a long time now." I opened my mouth to try again. "Now, don't argue with me, Allie."

I stared straight ahead. This was not a good time to cry.

"It must look pretty good, the way Lisa and I go out to dinner all the time when you're visiting or when we come here. There's a lot of shopping going on and a lot of exciting people to meet." I didn't answer. "You know, when you see those people every day, they aren't so exciting," he said, sighing deeply. "We're just hard-working people who have to be at rehearsal on time, have to find a place to stay where we can do a little cooking in the room so we can save some money and —well, we're just ordinary."

"The drinking isn't all," I said through my teeth.

"All right," he said unhappily. "Tell me."

I lost my nerve. "He isn't so nice to me sometimes." I hated the way that came out, like I was making something up and saying it quick. I saw the look on Daddy's face, and I knew he thought so.

"It's the liquor," he said reluctantly. I was sure he shared my feeling that we were talking about something that my mother would disapprove of. I wanted to drop the whole thing, but I couldn't.

"He treats Mom bad." My voice shook, not so much with the thought of Daddy Jim's poor treatment of my mother as the fact that I'd spoken of something I knew I shouldn't. My mother would never forgive me. I drew in a deep breath and said it. "He hits her. He does worse than that."

"Allie."

"It's just—I can't explain it very well."

He shook his head. "Your mother told me you have a tendency to exaggerate."

I was angry now. "My mother says I lie."

His eyebrows lifted. "Yes, Allie, that's what she says."

I wouldn't be topped. "I also listen in. Are you taking me to Brazil?"

"It will be up to your mother, Allie."

"Uh-huh." That was a far cry from what he'd said to her.

We didn't have much to say for the remainder of the ride, and we separated quickly at the fairgrounds. The day before the first day of the fair was said to be the hottest day of any August for the last forty-two years. Dust hung in the air as people pitched tents, rolled in hot dog wagons and carried in exhibits. I began to think about sitting in the shade of the front porch and fiddling with colored pencils. Daddy was surprised when I asked to go home. "Are you feeling okay?"

"I think the excitement's been too much for me."

"Really?"

"The heat hasn't helped much. It makes me sick to my stomach."

I could see he was trying to work out how to get me home. "Nauseated," he said.

"What?"

"The word is nauseated. Say that, instead of sick to your stomach. It sounds better."

"It doesn't feel better."

On the way home, I remembered something that happened when I was maybe four years old. It was just after Mom and

Daddy Jim were married, I guess, because I was visiting Daddy at a new house. I was playing in the front yard when I realized I had to use the bathroom. I needed to go right away. I ran to the door, but it was locked. I yelled and knocked and yelled again. No one answered. The trip around to the back door was a long one for my short legs, too long to make it in time.

I hated to wet myself, hated not being able to wait. Hated the door that hadn't been locked when Daddy closed it behind me. "Shit," I said out loud.

That's when the door opened.

"What did I hear you say?" Daddy looked so tall, frowning down at me with that half-smile playing around his lips.

"Nothing."

"It was a bad word, Allie."

Urine trickled warmly down my leg.

I wanted to cry. I wanted to ask why I hadn't heard his steps approach the door, why he didn't answer while I stood there banging, but only long moments after I'd stopped. I felt I'd been tested and had come up short of his expectations. And in some way, that's how this visit was working out.

Next day was opening day at the fair. It was no surprise that Daddy found time too pressing to get around to picking me up. I thought, once, of walking over to Mrs. Kelly's and asking if I might use her phone to call the fairgrounds. Then, when my father was called to the phone, I'd ask if he was so busy he'd forgotten to pick me up. I could just see his face. I only thought about it. The use of Mrs. Kelly's phone was not to be Taken Advantage Of. I didn't matter. I got plenty of satisfaction just thinking about it.

I settled myself on the front steps once more, with two reasons in mind. One, I could draw in peace. Two, I'd be able to see Daddy Jim coming home from wherever he'd spent the night. I could make it my business to be near Mom before he could come around to sit beside me again.

It went better. I'd been practicing that tree in my head, not the same thing as drawing, I know, but it does seem to work. It also gives my mind something to do when my hands don't have a piece of paper or a pencil. That was when I spotted the boy coming along the road.

This time he stopped at the sidewalk and waited, as if he thought I might throw rocks. We looked at each other for a while, sometimes looking around at other things. Like we just happened to be in the same place at the same time. After a while, he raised one hand and half-waved, half-looked like he was trying to find a place to rest it before he put it back in his pocket.

I waved back. It would be hard to say exactly when I got so jittery. He came up the walk, keeping his eyes on me the whole distance. I wanted to jump up and run.

"Hi. You're Allie."

I didn't say anything.

"I'm Nate." I just stared at him, keeping my face as flat as a stone. "I saw you around school just before it let out. I know your cousin Tucker and I remembered seeing you with him." He sat down next to me. "I wanted to meet you."

"Why?"

"Tucker told me you're an artist." The word sounded natural in his mouth. Like he said it often enough that no one laughed or told him he was getting too big for his britches.

"I kept your drawing."

"I've been working on trees for a while," he said. "Why don't you show me some of your drawings?"

"Sometime, maybe."

"Come on. I know you have good stuff."

"Yours is probably better."

"Some of it," he said in a matter-of-fact way. "But I'm not good with people or animals. Tucker says you are."

"I can't bring them out now," I lied. "I guess you wasted the trip."

"You're going to hold that tree against me, aren't you?" When I said nothing, he stood up and started down the walk, moving fast. Miserably, I watched him go. I saw something appealing in the way his thin shirt lay over narrow shoulders. Something he kept hidden when you looked him full in the

104

face. He stopped at the end of the walk. "Tucker asked me to tell you he'll be at the fair, starting tomorrow." He spun around on his heel and left without a backward glance.

Tucker was at the fair to show his pig. Triumphant was handfed and cared for by Tucker himself when its mother rejected it as too little to bother with. I found Tucker in one of the open-ended barns, where the animals were housed. We talked, teasing, poking fingers into old wounds. It was comfortable. We groomed Triumphant the whole time, and for once I hardly noticed the way she smelled. But I didn't plan to stay for the show.

"I told my Dad I'd be back at the grandstand by noon. I'll see you later."

"Come back if you want."

I decided to wander through the rest of the farm buildings. They were cooler than some places I could be. "Allie," Tucker hollered. I looked back as he hooked a thumb over his shoulder. Nate stood in the sunlight at the other end of the barn, slouched in that way that boys seem to think is attractive. The pose was somewhat marred by a bundle under one arm. I guess I could have ignored him and gone on my way. I guess that would have been playing hard to get. I wasn't in the mood.

"Hi," I said, staying in the shade of the barn.

"Want to go for a walk?" he asked, looking not so confident of a yes as he had on my front steps.

"Where to?"

He shrugged. "We'll know when we get there."

It was a roll of papers that he carried under his arm. As we walked, I realized some of it was that drawing paper he'd used when he drew the tree. I didn't dare ask about it.

"You're here with your dad, huh?"

"Tucker told you?"

"I heard you. I was sitting outside the barn next to Triumphant's stall."

"Why didn't you tell us you were there?"

"I wanted to listen to you. I mean, how you are with

1 0 5

Tucker." First he eavesdrops, then he tells it right out like he thinks it's okay. "I wanted to find out how I make you so mad. Or maybe figure out why you don't like me. I thought I could do something different."

"And what did you find out?"

"One thing only," he answered. "It isn't me at all. You just have a real prickly personality."

Opinionated, that's what he was.

"Now if I could draw people, I'd put you on paper right this minute. How can anyone frown and grin at the same time?" he asked.

"Some people bring that out in other people."

His laughter was a surprise, a quiet kind of laugh as he shook his head. That was when I began to take an interest in him. Not that I was giving in just yet.

We found three oak trees on a rise, standing close enough together to offer some shade. This spot would attract a lot of overheated fairgoers as the afternoon wore on. At this time of the morning, we were the only two people with no business to attend to.

"What are those rolled-up papers?"

"A peace offering," he answered.

"How's that?"

"These are my drawings. Some good, some not so good." He flattened them out on the ground between us. "I'll show you mine, then you can show me yours," he said with a grin.

I don't know what it was that affected me so. Maybe it was looking at someone else's work for the first time, efforts so similar to my own. And the proof of a reward for those efforts, as I went from drawing to drawing.

Maybe it was how hard it had to be to give his beginning work over to a stranger's criticism. He could have held it back, showing only the best, to leave the impression that he'd been perfect from the start. My hands were shaking when I passed them back to him.

"I knew they'd be good."

"Some of them," he said, tossing away the compliment.

"All of them," I insisted. "Then they get better." The relief was so sudden on his face I had to smile. I decided I liked him.

"I have to get to work," he said. "Will you be here tomorrow morning?"

I nodded.

"Meet me?"

We met beneath the oaks for the next few days. We spent hours scratching away at the paper, shoulder to shoulder. I liked the feel of his cotton shirt on my skin when our arms touched. I liked the way he covered my hand with his to guide my pencil when words weren't enough. Nate left for work about noon, catching a bus that dropped him off at Walgreen's drugstore where he worked behind the soda counter.

I met Daddy for lunch. That meant I waited around the electrician's office for about forty minutes, until he could leave. Then he'd hurry me to the nearest hot dog stand, check that I had money, and race back to work. It was odd how the afternoon dragged. I felt like I'd seen everything and done everything the fair had to offer. The truth was, it just didn't compare with the mornings.

One afternoon I ran into a girl from school, Priscilla Thornton. She's a thin, long-faced girl whose pink and swollen upper lip looked like it had been stung by a bee. Everyone called her Prissy.

"Allie, hi, how are you?" Prissy is originally from Mississippi. She has a slight southern drawl to her speech.

"Fine."

"Are you enjoying the fair?"

"Yes."

"Well, haven't you got more to say than that? Whatcha been doing with yourself?"

"Seeing the fair, Prissy."

"You wouldn't mind if we saw some of it together, would you? My older brother and his girlfriend brought me, and now they've gone off by themselves. I hate going places alone, don't you?" But Prissy was off and running, letting me know what

1 0 7

she'd seen and done at the fair and what she planned for today. I didn't get in a word for ten minutes, and when I did they weren't the words she wanted to hear.

"I get sick on the rides, Prissy."

"Oh," she said in a way that implied she'd just friendlied up with the wrong person altogether. "Even the ferris wheel?" Still, I was all she had. "Well, there's plenty of things to look at in the air-conditioned buildings, aren't there? There's my brother, up ahead."

She pointed out a young man with a shock of straight blond hair, mowed like grass. He held a girl against his hip as they watched a carny's sampling of the wonders to be found in his, only his, tent. As we strolled toward them, Prissy's brother let his hand drift around to squeeze the girl's bottom.

"Oh, my God," Prissy groaned. She pushed me across the path where we joined another stream of people headed in a different direction. "You have to ask yourself, if that's how they behave in public, what are they doing when they're alone? That's what you want to ask, isn't it?" I didn't bother to respond. If there was one thing I knew, it was that Prissy didn't necessarily expect an answer to her questions. "Actually, Allie, I know precisely how they act when they're alone. I've witnessed it," she stage-whispered over the jumble of voices around us.

"How's that?" I asked casually.

"I can't say it here, Allie."

It didn't take much encouragement from me to find the right sort of place: an open tent selling greasy fried-chicken dinners. We took our cardboard trays to a table far from any listening ears. "All I can tell you, Allie, is, it's even more incredible than you've heard."

I was properly awed.

"There was one night, about a month ago, that I got hungry real late. So I sneaked down to the kitchen, rummaging around for something to get me through the night. Just as I'm on my way back to bed, I see my brother's truck pulling into the drive with the lights off! While I'm standing there wondering what's

108

going on, he and his girlfriend get out and start across the lawn in the moonlight. Now this is a new one on me! Mommy and Daddy sound asleep in the back bedroom, and as far as my brother knows, I'm asleep too. It's hardly a time to bring a caller around, is it?" Prissy bit into the breast of chicken, chewing steadfastly as she talked.

"They cracked the screen door just enough to creep through, being ever so quiet. Well, I trotted back to the living room to ask what was up. What do I see through the window, but the two of them settling onto the davenport Mama only this summer put on her porch! Whatever they were up to, they seemed to have been at it for a while, the way they had everything worked out, wouldn't you say? It didn't seem to be something that would meet with my parents' approval, did it?

"I tiptoed closer to the window—it happens it sits right over the davenport. I could just about make them out. What I couldn't see, I could hear. The things boys say, Allie!"

"Like what?"

Prissy gave me a scandalized look. " 'Let me just look at them, huh?' And when she unbuttons her blouse, so slow like she's teasing him, he says, 'They're so beautiful, couldn't I just touch 'em?' She kept saying no and pushing his hand away, but finally she gave in and let him. It was pure revolting, Allie, to hear him moaning over her."

"Revolting," I agreed.

"Well, he didn't stop there. No boy does."

"No." It was like *True Confessions*.

"The thing that got to me, Allie, was the sounds they made."

I couldn't ask. But it must have shown on my face.

"I mean the sucking," Prissy hissed. "He went to sucking on her like a baby."

"Oh."

"Both of them moaning and trying to slurp each other to death."

"Revolting."

"That's not the worst." Prissy leaned across the table to whisper, "He put a hand under her skirt. She yelps like she's burned herself on the iron, but careful like, because she knew my folks was sleeping not that far away. 'Oh, please, let me see,' he says. 'Just a look.' Did you ever hear such a thing?"

"Never." It was all I could do not to choke on the chicken.

" 'No, you can't,' she says. 'You'll want to do it and we can't. Not till we're married.' So he says, 'I won't. I just want to see.' " Prissy *tsk-tsked* and started in on another piece of chicken.

"I had to sit down, Allie, it was that disturbing," she said as she chewed. "It just so happened that from the side chair I could see her white panties and the dark shape of his hand as he tried to slide up under the panties. 'Silk, like silk,' he keeps whispering. I could only think how like that he'd sounded at the dinner table that same night. 'Heaven, like Heaven,' he told Mommy when he wanted the extra bowl of rice pudding." She put down the bare chicken bone hard enough to make the last piece of chicken jump off the plate. "Of course he got it!"

"Got what?" I asked, dry-mouthed.

"The rice pudding, silly."

"Oh."

"But the worst, Allie. This is the worst. Are you sure you can take it?"

"I'm sure."

"She says, 'No looking, 'cause I'd have to take my panties off, and there'd be no stopping you. But I'll let you touch. Just one finger to touch,' she tells him, Allie. Ain't that brass?"

I nodded.

"He could make her 'feel good,' he says, 'would she like that?' 'No,' she cries, 'we can't do it.' She rose him a foot off the davenport, squealing like that. 'We won't do it, I promise,' he whispers. 'Will you let me make you feel good?' He coaxes and coaxes, all the time kissing her and moaning till she says okay. Do you know what he did, Allie? Can you guess?"

I shook my head.

"He went down on her," Prissy whispered loudly.

"He what?"

"Shocking, isn't it?"

110

I guess it must have been, but to tell you the truth, I didn't have the faintest idea what she was talking about.

"Right there in front of his own sister," she said in a voice that mixed righteous indignation and gleeful horror.

"My God," I said, praying for the appropriate thing to say to come to mind.

"I should say so," Prissy agreed.

I renewed the attack on my fried chicken. After a few minutes of concentrated chewing and swallowing, our eyes met over the lemonade. "Was that all?" I asked, digging for a clue.

"Ain't that enough?" Prissy's eyebrows arched like two stallions. "But if you mean, did she keep her virginity, such as it was, the answer's yes."

I nodded, trying not to look disappointed.

"She let him hump up against her until he 'felt good' too," Prissy added with a leer. "All the time he was doing it, he kept saying how much better it will feel when they're married." She wadded up her napkin and dropped her trash into the bin behind her. "Married. When one of his friends was dating this same girl last summer, my brother said she was built like a prize heifer." Prissy took it upon herself to dispose of my trash as well. "This year he's talking about marrying her. It makes you wonder, don't it?"

"What?"

"How it is that all these big boys are being tied up and dragged to the altar by the thread of a pair of cotton panties."

I looked at Prissy with a new respect.

Daddy must have done some thinking during the week, because he took me out to breakfast to talk things over. I have to admit, I was distracted by the fact that I'd be late to the fairground.

"You don't seem too disappointed about Brazil."

"I wasn't counting on it."

He nodded. I went back to staring out the window. "Have you thought about what you want to do after high school?"

"Do?"

1 1 1

"Be. A secretary or—anything?"

"No."

"Would you like to go to college?"

"I don't know."

"I can pay for it. If somebody tells you it costs too much or something, don't worry about that."

I waited.

"You don't have to be here all your life, you know. There are other things you can do besides get married. After school, I mean. Of course you'll want to get married. Someday. I guess," he finished like a lame dog taking a last step.

"What could I do?" I asked.

"What do you like to do?"

Taking a chance, I said, "Draw."

He nodded. "Good. That's good. What else? Something practical, I mean."

"Practical?"

"You could be a teacher. Are you good with numbers?"

"Not especially."

"Well, you could think about nursing."

I just lost interest in the conversation, if you want to know the truth. I hardly heard what he had to say as we drove back to the fairground. Nate was there beneath the oaks; he saw me first, waved and ran toward me.

"What happened to you?"

"I didn't know I'd be late today," I said, trying not to smile at how pleased he'd been to see me. "Aren't you going to miss your bus?"

"I got the day off. I can stay as late as you can." He gave me a close look, the kind he has when he's drawing. Except that this had more the feeling of a cat studying a fish dinner. "Do you know your face is very pink all of a sudden?"

"Must be too much sun." I didn't try to wipe the grin off my face. "Do you want to see the fair?"

"I want to see food! I've been sitting there all morning, afraid I'd miss you if I left for a few minutes." After we ate, we went through the house of mirrors, a favorite of mine, and the house

112

of horrors, a first for me and a favorite of Nate's. It wasn't especially horrible. It was a kind of obstacle course in the dark. We threw rings, shot at plastic ducks in a pond and rode the bump cars.

Nate was a sucker for every carny on the strip. We saw Siamese twins, joined at the head and the hip, men of about my father's age to judge by the poster hanging out front. Inside the tent there were dead babies floating around in a bottle, in fact joined by a piece of skin at the hip.

We saw the bearded lady, a woman with a full beard down to her waist on the poster. She was a huge woman who did in fact have a few straggly hairs on her cheeks. They'd have done better to allow her the use of a tweezer, billing her as the fat lady.

The three-armed man was, I suppose, very nearly what they claimed. The sign showed him to be a spidery creature in a shirt with three sleeves who, because of the third hand, could cut his food with a knife and fork while drinking water. He turned out to be a tired little man with two good arms and a third shrivelled limb that flopped over the waistband of his pants where his shirt had been cut away. Unlike the bearded lady, who'd been reading a book as we filed past, this man's eyes caught at other people's and held on.

When a farmer stopped to speak to him for a minute, his manner was of the most accommodating sort. He explained how this accident comes about and showed that it caused him no real inconvenience in moving around. They shook hands heartily as the farmer took his leave, causing the third arm to jiggle up and down. The two women in line in front of us broke into giggles, nudging each other and then giggling some more. The little man tried to stare them down, but that only made them laugh harder. Someone in line behind us snorted like they were about to give way.

Nate stopped in front of the man, who was looking smaller and more tired than a few minutes before. Then Nate gripped his hand firmly, much as if they were passing the time of day in front of the church, and we moved on.

"I'm sorry. I could see you didn't like that stuff, the little tent shows, I mean. Even before the last one."

"I'd seen some of them before," I said.

"You don't have to say that. I could see you didn't like them. And that last one was pretty raw. I'm really sorry."

"They're tricks. They tell you you're going to see something, and they show you something else. You can't argue it because it all has to do with how they . . . I don't know."

"That's it?"

All of a sudden I was angry, not at Nate, but it shot out at him because he was there. "Not all. There's some things people ought to be able to keep to themselves. Or, if they can't, they ought to be able to hold their heads up." I pulled it back in, keeping myself to myself as we walked along.

"What else?" When I shook my head he said, "You look like you have something more to say."

It burst out, not loud but fast, like I wanted to get it out before I'd hear it and change my mind. "Did you ever notice how you go along thinking that something is what it looks like? Then you find out there's something else, underneath maybe, but you can't tell anyone about it?"

"What kind of things are we talking about?"

"Things . . . you believe in. People. Anything! Did you ever have that?"

"You mean like the sideshows?"

"Maybe. Maybe they aren't all in tents."

Nate wanted me to tell him more. When I wouldn't, he didn't keep at me the way Tucker or Dolly would have. It was getting dark when Nate got his next fine idea. "Just one more thing we have to try, Allie."

"What's that?"

He finished his lemonade with a loud slurp. "The Mad Mouse."

"Oh, no."

"You won't get sick. It doesn't go in a circle."

"It's like a roller coaster," I cried.

"Tucker says you aren't afraid of anything."

"Tucker doesn't know half what he claims."

"You're gonna love it."

The Mad Mouse isn't a whole string of cars, but one little car that carries one or two people around the track. That means you're always in front. The wheels are set back on the car so that when you come to the end of a piece of track, you're hanging out in space for an instant before the "Mouse" makes a sharp turn to whirl off along the next strip of track.

I insisted on sitting behind Nate, a fact that disappointed him some. It even seemed to be important to the fellow who ran the ride. But Nate gave a shrug and climbed in to sit in front of me. I couldn't quite bring myself to hug up close to him so I laid my arms along the sides of the car to hold on. When the car started with a jolt, he grabbed my hands and wrapped my arms around his chest. Every time we came to one of those sharp corners we screamed together and I could feel Nate's heart beat faster. It wasn't so bad, probably because I couldn't see that we were on the verge of death, but I could hardly say I took to it.

"Wasn't that fabulous?" Nate cried as he climbed out of the car.

"Never again."

"I think you enjoyed it," he said as he threw an arm around my shoulders and hugged. When he didn't take his arm away, it occurred to me, and I liked the idea, that this was the kind of thing Uncle Little Mike would've thought up. "Admit it. It grabbed you, right down in the pit of your stomach, didn't it grab you?"

"The pit of my stomach has better things to do than crawl into my throat."

Nate thought I was trying to be funny. I let him think so. "Come on. It's time we started back toward the grandstand," Nate said, grinning.

Not that we didn't make a few stops along the way. We were halfway through the line for the House of Mirrors and eating cotton candy when I heard my father call my name. "I'd better go," I said.

1 1 5

"I'll come with you."

"No, I'd better do this myself." I started to make my way back through the line. "I never told him I was with a boy."

"Oh. Well, maybe he won't notice."

"Nate."

"He's already seen me, Allie. Hey," he said, grabbing my hand so I couldn't get too far ahead of him. "It'll be okay. You'll see. I'm real good with fathers."

I didn't exactly share his confidence.

"Allie! Where have you been?"

"I'm afraid that's my fault, sir. Allie told me she needed to check in with you," Nate lied, "but I made her put it off until —well, it just slipped our minds. I'm sorry."

"And who are you?" Daddy's voice was just barely polite in a way I hadn't heard before.

"I'm Nathan Drummond, sir."

"Drummond." His attitude changed ever so slightly. "I've heard of a lawyer named Drummond."

"He's my father."

"How is it you and Allie happen to be together?"

"We ran into each other a few mornings ago. We've been getting together to sketch." He offered his drawing pad to Daddy, who took it and riffled through the pages, quickly at first, then more slowly as he realized the drawings were good.

"You ran into each other. Does that mean you just met?" Daddy asked as he handed Nate the pad.

"Oh, no, sir. I've known Allie for a while. We go to school together."

"I see." He looked a little uncomfortable, as if he wasn't sure what to say to that. "I have to get back to work, Allie. You should have met me more than an hour ago."

"I understand, Mr. Drew. My father isn't going to be pleased that we weren't more thoughtful, either."

"This wasn't deliberate, then," Daddy said, like he thought he shouldn't give in too easily.

"We got caught up in the fair, sir. Allie didn't mean to worry you."

1 1 6

"All right," Daddy said. "So. Do you two want to watch the last half of the show?" Afterward, he offered to drive Nate home. Daddy asked one question after another. Did Nate have brothers and sisters, how old were his brothers, what colleges did his brothers go to, what did Nate plan to do? I can see where I got my questioning ways, all right. Nate didn't seem to mind the questions, and he gave answers that clearly pleased Daddy.

"Can Allie meet me at the fair tomorrow, Mr. Drew?"

"I suppose so. Why don't you join us for the show tomorrow night? Or will you be working?"

"No, sir. I'd like that very much." Nate pulled my drawings from the back of his pad, giving them to me. "See you tomorrow. Early?"

"Why haven't you mentioned this boy, Allie?" Daddy asked as we watched Nate walk to his door. He didn't sound mad.

"I don't know. I didn't think to, I guess. I saw other kids this week, but I didn't think to mention them."

"Who else did you see?"

"Oh, Tucker. Prissy. She's from school."

"Nathan seems like a nice boy."

"He draws real well. He's been helping me with trees and flowers."

"I see," Daddy said. "Let me have a look at your drawings." He turned on the map light. "These are quite good. He's helping you with faces, too, I see."

"No, that's what I'm helping him with. And animals. He's not very good with animals," I said, sorting through the pictures. "But both our animals look better when they're shaded in the way he does his trees. See the difference?"

"I had no idea you could do this."

I could tell he was impressed by the way he said it. "Daddy Jim taught me in the beginning," I said, trying to be as modest as Nate had been.

"He draws?"

"He's good. He showed me a lot of stuff, like how to mea-

1 1 7

sure where to put the eyes on a face. Or where the elbows bend is where the waist falls on a body. Things like that."

Daddy nodded, sighing heavily. "You know, you're a little young for a boyfriend."

I didn't say a word.

"It's nothing like that, is it?"

"I don't know anyone else who likes to draw."

"I want you to know I don't think you should be giving boys much thought for the time being." He looked at me like he thought I might have something to say. When I didn't, he went on. "You ought to be sixteen before you start dating. I know this may seem early to talk about that, but it will save us any misunderstandings later on."

I didn't say anything. I know he meant well, being my father and all, but I had several other more pressing problems he could address himself to, if he was so interested.

The night before he left, Daddy took us all out to dinner. With the exception of Calvin, this being Tuesday night. What hit me early on was how much Daddy wanted to show Grandma and Grandpa something he thought they'd missed. This restaurant had two tablecloths and a small lamp on each of the tables. They served shrimp cocktail and everyone made a fuss over home-baked breads brought to the table on a cutting board. Daddy ordered for everyone, making sure it didn't escape anyone's notice that he ordered the most expensive thing on the menu.

It seemed to me, and not for the first time, that Daddy acted like a little kid who'd gotten into trouble and had to find a way to get back into everyone's good graces. To tell you the truth, I thought he was trying too hard. Not that I mean to criticize. But I could see that he only managed to outdo what he'd done the time before. He would end up doing that much more to impress them the next time.

It worked.

Grandma sat beside him, teary-eyed, and Aunt Charlotte managed to get to the chair on his other side before Daddy could say who he'd planned to put there. So Aunt Bonnie and I sat on either side of Uncle George, who said nothing while he went through three loaves of bread on his own. Grandpa was quiet, with an air of letting the children play.

Everyone sang when my birthday cake was brought out from the kitchen. It was the oddest thing. Daddy's face was more expectant than mine as I unwrapped my gifts. There were six pads of thick creamy paper and two big boxes of a soft chalk called pastels. I strained to put the biggest possible smile on my face, the most overjoyed note in my thank you. It was an effort that crushed my own real pleasure in his gift, as I tried to match his giving with my gratitude. Daddy'd even found a way to outdo himself for me.

The evening ended before nine due to the fact that Daddy's plane was leaving so early the next morning. He was too tired for one of the private talks we usually have at the end of a visit. He slept on the davenport in the dining room just as he had through most of his childhood. Aunt Bonnie and I went to sleep listening to him snore.

The next morning's breakfast was a sentimental affair, being, Grandma said, so much like the mornings when she had her boy at home. "Only yesterday, seems like," Grandma said at least half a dozen times. Aunt Bonnie rolled her eyes heavenward more than once, but only when Grandma wasn't looking.

In the car, Daddy sat up front with Grandpa. I found I wasn't surprised he never thought to share the backseat with me, nor did I find myself disappointed. There was little enough conversation on the way to the airport owing, for my part, to the early hour and for Grandma's, to her tendency to dissolve into tears while she was talking. Daddy gave each if us little pieces of advice, Parting Thoughts, I've heard my mother call them.

"Mom, I'd sure like to see you give up canning this year."

"There's too much in the garden, Robert."

"Plant a smaller garden, Mom. You're going to wear yourself down to nothing." Grandma simpered and fussed, pleased that

Daddy saw her as a fragile soul, in danger of being worn away by hard labor.

"Allie, you work hard this year in school and get good grades." I nodded. "Keep in mind what we talked about. There's plenty of things you could do." I was glad I was sitting behind him so he couldn't see the look that slipped out from beneath my eyebrows.

"I'm glad I got to spend this time with you, Dad, because it'll be a while before I get back again." Grandpa made a little sound in his throat that could've been taken for agreement. Or, if you knew Grandpa better, you thought about a three-week stay that allowed for only a few short visits with Grandpa and Grandma, and it could've been taken for a comment.

It could be said it was the only comment Grandpa made. He was stone silent as he drove me home, ignoring Grandma's mournful sobbing in the seat beside him. He had little more to say when my mother came out to the car to take my things. "Looking well, Nora."

"Summer weather agrees with me." Mom had a crisped-up look, only slightly worn with the waiting. I'll never understand the reason people   arrive forty-five minutes before take-off, only to   that's half   hour late. But Mom understood less than that; I knew she'd been waiting from the time we'd been eating breakfast, anxious to show herself at her best.

Grandma and Grandpa Drew left quickly. I slumped down on the front steps, halfheartedly poking around in the bag that held my birthday present from Daddy. It had suddenly lost much of its appeal. That's when Nate came strolling up the road. Things were looking up.

We sat across from each other on the top step drawing cartoon pictures of each other, coloring them in quickly with pastels. We were passing them across the space between us when Daddy Jim came out. Nate looked up first and began to rise. "Hey—wait—help—"

Daddy Jim shoved him with both hands. Nate flew through the air to land on the sidewalk with a sickening smack.

1 2 0

"No, Daddy, don't," I cried, flinging myself in front of him. When he tried to push me away, I clung to his arm.

"Get away from here," Daddy Jim bellowed as Nate pushed himself up on an elbow, gasping for air. "I've seen you here before, sniffin' around like some stray dog."

"No. No, sir, I wouldn't." Nate got to his feet. "We like to draw pictures together. I wouldn't . . . what you think. She's a little girl. I know that."

"You're lyin'," Daddy Jim snarled as he moved down a step. "Get off me!" he yelled, throwing me to the floor of the porch. "She ain't comin' out to play with the likes of you. You stay away from here."

"Go!" I told him, half-whispering, half-crying. I sounded too pitiful to my own ears to say anything more.

Nate glanced at me, then back to Daddy Jim. When my mother stepped out onto the porch, he decided to go. That's what was on his face, not fear, but the decision that the best thing to do was go away. When he reached the road, Mom bent to help me up. "Jim, you've hurt Allie," she said softly. "Jim."

"She has to understand," Daddy Jim told her in a voice loud enough to carry out to Nate, "we ain't raisin' no whores." Mom sucked in her breath with a hiss, but she didn't try to argue. "Just take her inside. I don't want her sittin' on the front steps anymore."

It wasn't until later on that same day that I took notice that my mother didn't go out to stand beside her flowers in the evening; hadn't for some time, I realized. Considering Daddy Jim's concern that my mother had set herself to attract the neighbor's attention, I believed I knew why.

5

THE first day of school was full of unpleasant little discoveries. The other girls were wearing their skirts up to their knees, as if Lisa had been foretelling the future. I was uncomfortable so I rolled my waistband up a couple of times. That made me look a little lumpy around the waist and the skirt still wasn't quite short enough. But it didn't look as odd as it did being too long.

There was a boy new to the district, an obnoxious creature to whom I took an immediate dislike. He spent most of his time finding fault with people, announcing his discoveries to one and all with a loud whinny that was meant to be a snicker. I made up my mind to avoid his attentions, no matter what. The least promising thing I learned about seventh grade is that there is homework every day, usually for every class. Prissy's locker was right next to mine. It's a sad reflection that that was the high point of the day.

I couldn't face the school bus. If anything, it would be rowdier than when we'd been dropped off in the morning. And since I was almost the first on, I'd be almost the last off. Aside from that, I knew Nate didn't take a bus home. He'd told me he liked to hang out around the school for a while. I decided to pin up my braid and stroll past the side of the building where the bigger kids seemed to stay. I did plenty of strolling, but I didn't see him.

"All the way from school? That's got to be two miles," Daddy Jim said over dinner. "I don't know that you can do that once the snow comes."

"You had so many books to carry," Mom said as if it made her tired to think of it.

"The kids throw stuff around on the bus. There's a lot of noise."

"You'll still have to take care of your chores. I don't want to hear any excuses," Daddy Jim warned.

By the third day of school, I hadn't seen Nate, but I'd made two discoveries. Good ones. Mom didn't think twice about me sitting down to do homework and staying there all evening writing away. Just so long as there was an open book beside me. Now and then I'd turn a few pages like I was looking for an answer in it. Also, it occurred to me that I had the perfect place to keep my stories. My locker. I started home in a pretty good mood.

Nate was waiting for me at the edge of the school grounds. I'd spent a lot of time wondering how I'd act if he said hello. And how I'd live through it if he didn't. He didn't waste time on hello. "I've been watching for you over by the schoolbuses."

I looked straight at him, waiting for something grown-up sounding to come out of my mouth. Something Lisa would say.

"Didn't you know I'd be looking for you?"

"I thought you'd be over on the other side somewhere," I admitted.

He looked surprised, then pleased. "Here, I'll carry your books."

"You have your own."

"Allie," he complained, pulling at them.

"No! Someone might think we're—" I stopped, embarrassed.

"Oh." He looked taken aback. "Well. We sure wouldn't want to give anyone that impression," he said, starting to walk fast.

I stayed with him. "I didn't mean it the way it sounded."

"I know." He slowed down. "I do know. I'm still sore about the other day, I guess."

"I'm sorry."

"Is he always like that?"

I didn't know how to answer him.

"Never mind. I want to talk to you about something." He dragged a couple of my books off the top, adding them to his own. "Have you been paying any attention to the announcements for after school clubs?"

"Some. I don't plan to join any."

"Why not tell your folks that you're joining a couple of them? Then we can hang around together for a while on those days."

"Okay," I said, managing to sound casual.

"What with that and the walk home, we'll get to see quite a lot of each other." He made me feel like a rabbit skin pinned to the barn wall, looking at me the way he did.

I nodded, breathless.

"That's a real pretty dress you're wearing."

"You think so?" It slipped out before I could stop myself.

"Sure."

"I don't care much for it." That wasn't much better, but at least it didn't sound like I was lapping up every word. I said it with a businesslike look that was meant to let him know I wasn't open to flattery.

"It's the color, I guess. It's one that isn't too appealing at

1 2 5

first." He leaned forward to catch my eye. "That is, until you put a pretty little redheaded girl in it."

"You better stop calling me a little girl!"

"Whoa! I think you're right," he said, looking me over and, I think, noticing that I'd pinned up my braid. "You look to be at least thirteen years and one week."

"How did you know?"

"Tucker told me." He slid a flat, prettily wrapped package out from between his books. "I lost the bow. I've been carrying it around for three days."

I sat down on the slope of someone's lawn to open it.

"Drawing pencils. 4B," I read the gold print on the side of the dark green stems.

"You'll see how much smoother they slide across your paper than those number twos you've been using." He started right in to talk about drawing as if a week ago had never happened.

You could just love a friend like Nate.

Daddy Jim always claimed to be sickened by the smell of cigarettes. To hate the choked-up feeling it gave him to breathe the smoke when it drifted his way. Now he'd taken it up and not in the way of having an occasional cigarette. He smoked all the time. The smell of it filtered up from the basement, a sharp dirtyish odor that clung to furniture, to clothing and even to our hair.

He put a large glass ashtray on the little table by his chair in the living room. He'd sit there after dinner, one foot nervously tapping the floor, a vein ticking away in his forehead. It was hard not to get caught up in watching that vein. His hands weren't relaxed in the way I knew them, sure and steady whether they held a jigsaw or a pencil. They took on a taut look, tugging at his moustache and flattening it against his upper lip. He'd sit there through two, maybe three cigarettes. Then he'd make an impatient sound with his mouth and stalk to the basement door, throwing us an ugly look as he left.

*　　*　　*

"Allie, aren't you ever going to clean out that locker?" Prissy asked, poking her nose in as I reached for my coat.

"What makes you think it's messy?" After all, I carried all my books so it would look like I had a lot of homework. That left only my stories, a pile that had grown deeper in the three weeks since school began.

"Those papers. What are they anyway?"

"Some are . . . notes. They're in a neat stack, Prissy."

"A neat garbage can is still a garbage can," was Prissy's pronouncement.

"I'll remember you said that when you're looking to borrow them for a test," I said, slamming the door shut. "Prissy, could I try your lipstick?"

Nate was waiting just outside the school. I felt truly grown up as I went through the door. A girl who didn't wonder if a ninth grade girl who smiled at Nate today would be walking with him tomorrow.

"Fancy. Very fancy," he said admiringly.

"I've worn it before," I said testily.

"It looks very pretty on you."

"Just so you know this isn't something new."

"It never entered my mind," Nate protested. I saw a suspicious glimmer in his eye. I let it pass when he was quick to change the subject. "Let's walk for a while and find a sunny place to sit, away from the school, okay?"

The leaves had begun to turn just as school started, turning the world into a patchwork quilt of yellows, oranges and reds. I never knew there were so many words for colors. Oranges became peach and pumpkin, apricot and burnt orange. They were all right there in my box of pastels. The more we mixed the colors the more words we needed.

"Let me try drawing you, Allie."

"No, find something else."

"I need to practice heads. C'mon, Allie, you never let me," he wheedled as we settled ourselves to lean a little against each other with the pastels at our feet.

"But I can't draw then. I have to sit still."

"Please."

"All right," I sighed, scooting away to rest against another tree. I turned my face up to the sun. I never used to do that, but Nate told me he likes freckles.

"Take the rubber band out of your hair."

"No, I don't like to leave my hair to fly all over." I didn't want to say I can't get it back the same way without my mother's help.

"C'mon, Allie."

"No. The braid makes my hair crinkly. It sticks out."

"Al-lie," he crooned.

"I'm sitting still. Are you drawing?"

"Okay," he gave in with a loud sigh. "I'll just have to use my imagination." He glanced at me then at the empty sheet, starting to see the drawing in his head. "I saw Tucker over the weekend," Nate said when he was sketching in earnest.

"How's he doing?"

"Hates school. Otherwise fine."

"That's the second time since school started, isn't it?"

"Third. I didn't think to mention last weekend."

"What do you two get up to on these nighttime forays?"

Nate raised his eyebrows. "Why, we're no better than we should be."

"What's that mean?"

He shrugged. "More or less the same thing it meant when you went with him that night."

I kept my face as flat as I could, but I took note that Tucker had talked out of turn. "You ever see girls?" I asked casually.

He shook his head over some mistake, erasing it vigorously. He looked it over, deciding whether or not he was satisfied. "You mean, do we see particular girls?"

"Maybe just girls that aren't with anybody in particular?"

"You care if we did?" he asked, pretending he was all wrapped up in his drawing.

I didn't answer.

"Do you care?" he repeated, glancing up as he drew and not looking away.

I felt my face growing warm. "No. I just wondered."

"Liar."

It was quick. So quiet I wasn't sure I heard right. "What?"

"I see the way you look for me, coming out of that school building," he said with a grin.

I think my heart stopped beating with the shock.

"It's the same way I watch for you when I'm waiting out there. So I know you'd care," he said quickly, looking back at his drawing.

"Nate . . ."

"Sit still," he said, his voice still rough with embarrassment. I kept quiet, knowing my face had turned an ugly shade of beetwater pink. He held the pad out to me. "Finished."

He'd begun seriously enough. The eyes and nose were distinctly familiar, like glancing into the mirror. Then he'd turned it into a cartoon with braids sticking up in the air and big freckles on fat cheeks.

"Oh, very flattering," I said, tearing off the sheet and crumpling it.

"Don't ruin it," he cried, leaping to the rescue. "I wanted to put it on my wall."

"Too late." I shoved it between my back and the tree. He snatched it back, getting too close to me for a breathless instant. He flattened it out, trying to smooth away the wrinkles.

"I'll have to do another."

"Not one that makes me look like Alfred E. Neuman. And not today. I sat long enough."

He tossed the drawing away, leaning on one arm, his hand planted in the grass on the other side of my legs. He was close enough for me to be aware of the clean but rather scruffy scent my uncles brought into breakfast. I'd noticed it before, but now it was bothersome in a way I hadn't felt when we sat elbow to elbow, working with our pencils.

"I'm glad I came by your house that first day." Nate looked into my eyes as if he was trying to touch something.

"Why did you?"

"Oh-h, things Tucker told me."

1 2 9

"That I draw?"

"Mm-hmm. Other stuff, too."

"Like?"

"He says you're silly when you're drunk."

"I didn't get drunk."

"Hell, you didn't," he argued, half-laughing.

"Tucker has a big mouth," I said weakly.

"I wouldn't tell him anything I didn't want the whole world to know."

"I wasn't very drunk."

"No, it didn't sound like it," he whispered, leaning in closer.

We watch people's lips all the time, when they're shaping the words we listen to and when we want to read the meaning of a silence. But there are certain things that don't get noticed. Like how warm other people's lips are. Or how they can be alive and full of their own interests when they touch yours. Some things can't be learned from the puckered-up kinds of kisses kids get.

Daddy Jim found some work at the end of September. As the first week finished and he was expected back on the job the next, my mother breathed easier. It was during the second week that Uncle Ted and Aunt Linda chose to pay us a visit. They stopped me at the side of the road just as I was waving good-bye to Nate.

"See you found yourself a companion for the long walk home," Uncle Ted said, grinning, pleased with his little joke.

I didn't say anything. I was thinking that it had done us little good to separate so long before we reached my road; that we'd been stupid to walk along the highway in the first place.

"Your mother said she was expecting you home on the bus," Aunt Linda put in, her little bird's eyes bright with interest. Nate had disappeared into the woods, looking back over his shoulder.

I shifted my stare to her. "I can choose not to ride it," I said flatly.

But she'd already come to some conclusions. "She's awful

proud of the way you've taken an interest in some of them school clubs," she said. "They musta let you off early today, that you'd have time to walk home."

"Must've," was all I could manage.

Uncle Ted had the good grace to look sorry he'd put me on the spot. And downright embarrassed as she went on.

"Nice to see that stepdaddy of yours is working again. We were just saying"—she rapped Uncle Ted on the arm—"how your mother's not looking too good. It must've come as some relief to her that he found something."

I didn't offer up any comment.

"I think we'd best be on our way," Uncle Ted said as Aunt Linda drew breath on another thought. I didn't wait to hear it.

"Say hey to Tucker for me," I said and turned away from the car.

Uncle Ted didn't drive away right off. I began to think, go away, go away, go away, as I passed Mrs. Kelly's house. Afraid Aunt Linda would find some reason to come back to the house and tell my mother I'd walked home. 'Such a nice-looking boy, Nora,' she'd say, letting my mother know that not only had she caught me in a lie, but she knew plenty my mother didn't. My mother would have to nod and smile, caught in Aunt Linda's sly trap.

I knew my uncle watched me in the mirror, worrying over what Aunt Linda had said and whether I would repeat it to my mother. I could see her in the near distance, hurrying across the yard to take the clothes from the line, Crystal running along behind her. Finally I heard the engine rev and the spit of gravel beneath the wheels. When Uncle Ted had gone, and Aunt Linda with him, I wanted in the worst way to go along. I wanted to sit in my grandmother's kitchen with Tucker pulling on my braid and my uncles playing poker at the old card table. And I would, come Thanksgiving. It was that thought that gave me some comfort as I walked home.

Daddy Jim was home for dinner and stayed upstairs for the evening, reading from my mother's bookcase. I saw my mother's hopeful glances in his direction and I thought of the things she'd told Aunt Linda. In the same way I wasn't the after-school student she'd spoken of, I had a feeling Daddy Jim's mood wouldn't last.

Nate and I found a couple of different ways to go home. There was a long way that gave us two good places to sit and draw if we didn't stay too long. Once the school bus went by, we hardly ever saw a car. My favorite way was the shortest, cutting across town, then through a field and some backyards until I crossed the highway to go down my road. Nate could stay with me longer, leaving us plenty of time to draw or to play around.

"Allie," he called from somewhere to my left. I pressed myself up against the tree, hoping my brown dress would help to hide me. I heard the snap of a twig, held my breath.

"Gotcha!" He wrapped his arms around the tree and me as well. I let out a real shriek, and when I laughed, I could feel my heart beating like a rabbit's.

"Hey! I didn't really scare you, did I?" Nate was chuckling as he came around the tree. He hadn't let go of me.

"I forget sometimes, that it's a game," I said as an excited shiver ran through me.

"You're funny." He wrapped his arms around me and held me close, letting his chin rest on top of my head.

"That doesn't mean you think I'm childish, does it?"

"No." He bent his head to put little kisses on the edge of my ear and, pressing his advantage, said, "Want to let your hair out?"

"No." It was all I could do to stand there quietly. I like kissing but so often I wanted to tell Nate, "Wait, give me a minute. Let me be ready." I'm not quite used to kissing yet.

"How often do your rubber bands break?" he whispered as he pulled me down into the grass.

"Not often," I said breathlessly.

"They're about to become old and dried out, all of them, and they're going to break often." He moved quickly over my mouth as if he expected a protest. Our tongues touched, and finding it wasn't as wet or as sloppy as it sounded, touched again. Wanting to please him, I let mine trace the inside edge of his lower lip. Nate drew in a sudden breath, almost a groan, and opened his mouth wider over mine. He pressed his tongue deeply, thrillingly alongside mine as he slid one hand quickly up between my breasts to rest on my throat. My heart beat faster and faster, and I thought I might scream, and I knew Nate could feel it all beneath his fingers. "OhGodohAllie," he whispered urgently as he roughed up my face with kisses. I arched against the weight of his arm until I felt his chest against mine, warm and hard and good. It was even better when he pressed himself down over me in another kiss. All at once he jumped up, saying, "We'd better quit."

The first thing, I was relieved. Caught up in it like that, I hadn't realized how scared I was. Nate was scared too, or at least he looked it. I was embarrassed as I sat up, my body absolutely electric, and knowing that Nate knew it. I needed to act like what we were doing was as casual for me as it was for him. "We have to go?" I asked.

"Yes." The determination in his voice had nothing to do with the time. He knelt to pluck some dry leaves from my hair, his hands shaking and his eyes not quite meeting mine, before he pulled me to my feet. We walked quietly for a while, holding hands. Meaning that we weren't talking. I don't think either one of us felt quiet in any way. The feelings that were so delicious when you were kissing ended up being sort of nungry after you'd stopped.

"Listen, Allie," Nate burst out. "If I get pushy or anything, don't be afraid to tell me to cut it out."

"I wouldn't."

"I just don't want you to think I'd stop caring for you or anything, if you said no to something."

"Do you think I should have said no?" I was amazed; he sounded almost angry. "To our tongues, maybe?"

"No. But I keep thinking—never mind."

"Tell me."

"Never mind," he said in a "that's final" tone.

*   *   *

133

I could write every night, looking like I was doing my homework. I could write in study periods at school and stack the pages in my locker. I began to do more writing about people I knew, taking little bits of conversations I'd heard and turning them over until they became a story.

By the middle of October, I couldn't bring myself to look at homework in the evening. So I began to do the history for first period, spending the rest of the evening writing. In history the next morning, I did my math homework to turn in second period. And in math I did my English homework, and so on. It worked out well enough, and the stories began to pile up in the bottom of my locker.

Daddy Jim began to fight more frequently with my mother, usually about the man who lived upstairs. I took Crystal into bed and stayed in there myself. Daddy Jim sat in the kitchen late into the night.

One night in particular, Daddy Jim was sitting up. It wasn't so much the fact that he was sitting there that made me uncomfortable. It was the fidgety way he'd been tugging and twisting his moustache. The way his eyebrows lowered over his eyes as he watched me cross the kitchen on my way to the bathroom. I took care of my business and returned to the kitchen, intent on getting back to bed as quickly as possible.

"You're up mighty late." He leaned his chair into the space between the table and the woodstove, blocking my way.

"Just for a minute."

"You're awful anxious to get back to bed." His eyes had that fevered look, directed at me in a kind of challenge.

"I have school tomorrow."

"It wouldn't be," he said slowly, rocking on the back legs of the chair, "that you don't care to talk to me." He smelled strongly of liquor.

"I just want to go back to sleep."

" 'Cause I'd be awful unhappy to get the feelin' you didn't love me anymore."

"I love you." I wasn't so much feeling love as feeling that

I had to say it. I could never guess how he'd act when he'd been drinking.

"You don't show it," he said, reaching for the braid that fell over my shoulder.

"I want to go to sleep now," I said, trying to ignore the way his fingers climbed.

"What could you do to show it?" he said, as the side of his hand brushed against my breast. His arm hung heavily from my hair.

"Well?" he asked, letting his breath wash over me. I started to get panicky. "How will I know?"

I said the first thing that came to mind. "You smell funny."

His startled eyes flicked over me.

"What's that smell all over you?" I said, louder.

"Allie?" my mother called from her room. "Why aren't you back in bed?"

Daddy Jim let his chair drop forward.

I moved around him but he caught at the back of my pajama top, holding me at arm's length. I just stood there, not daring to look around. After a moment he let go, and I went back to bed. I wanted to close my door. The look in Daddy Jim's eyes made me think better of it.

Several things happened toward the end of October. The upstairs neighbors moved away, Daddy Jim silently bidding them good riddance. Although my mother could once more go out in the evening, her flowers were dying.

My father sent me another doll that, not unexpectedly, my mother put directly into my closet along with all the others. He also sent an odd vest. Odd in that it didn't close down the sides but the two fronts came over the shoulders and a string belt tied around the waist. It was turquoise with bright bits of red and other colors. It made my eyes dance to look at it. Mom forbade me to wear it, looking on it like something hand-me-downed three times and with holes in it. I hung it in my closet —on the door, so I could see it every time I opened the door.

I got home late one afternoon. I rushed up the road worrying about whether Daddy Jim would be angry, and as I got near the house I saw Daddy Jim's bike lying in the front yard.

But Daddy Jim never thought to say anything to me. He'd lost his job again.

He lay at my mother's feet as she sewed. He didn't leave her side when she got up to cook dinner, slouching against one wall and then another until they sat down to eat. When we returned to the living room, he told her, "I feel so alone sometimes, Nora. Like you and the kids don't need me anymore, don't love me." My mother shook her head, sympathetic tears dripping onto her sewing. I made myself look back to my textbook. It wasn't his words that pulled at me. It was his eyes.

"You're good to me, Nora, and I know it. I don't know how many women could be so strong as you, so good to me."

"Jim," she said in a strangled voice, "I'm not being good to you. I love you. We all love you. You must know that."

"It can't be easy sometimes. I'm a hard man."

"No, Jim." Her hair had grown longer since the summer months, and now she swept it away from her face, sniffling.

"I want you to be able to depend on me, Nora. Our whole lives can't be like this."

All I could see were his eyes, looking like all he wanted was for us to help him and everything would be all right.

"It will get better. Lots of men are out of work."

"I know. Oh, I know. But—"

"Don't say it, Jim. It doesn't matter. You made a mistake. You won't take a drink again."

"I won't. I promise, Nora. I know I can't."

"You won't do it again," she assured him.

"I won't ever do it again." He rolled onto his side, facing away from me. "You're so precious to me, Nora."

"I love you, Jim. I do." Her face twisted like those words caused her pain.

"You won't leave me."

"Never." She found a hanky in her apron pocket and blew her nose.

I understood that this was what my mother wanted to hear. Some part of me wanted to hear it, too. At the same time I wanted it, I couldn't forget the way his eyes could change.

I got to write a story, legally, you might say.

"Class, I want you to write a story. It can be on one of three subjects. One, A Halloween Story. Two, Winter on a Farm . . ."

Okay, so the subjects didn't exactly give me a rash. But it was a chance to write a legitimate story that a teacher would read and grade. I could find out if I was writing anything worthwhile, if you know what I mean.

Since that afternoon in the woods, Nate insisted we spend most of our time in the schoolyard. I went to our usual place and dropped to the ground, with a satisfying crackle of dead leaves. Their colors were bright but darker, the crisp edges burnt black by the cold night air. The trees that still had leaves clinging to them took the worst of the frost. Colors were deepened to coppers and golds, spidery patterns etched on their surfaces. I itched to get to the pastels, to rub the colors into the paper until they took on the glossy metallic look of the leaves.

"Let me draw you like that," Nate said as he came up to me.

"If you're quick. I can't work if I'm sitting for you."

"Quick, okay. But I'm going to make it a good one." He began to set himself up with his pad on his knees. I took the rubber band off the end of my braid. His eyebrows rose. "You're leaving your hair loose?"

"I decided it's better than letting you draw me with my ears sticking out," I said nastily. He laughed outright, leaning against the tree with an interested gleam in his eye. I reached to separate the braid where it started at the top of my head. Something about the way we were sitting there, I don't know what exactly, made me feel like I was undressing in front of him. I looked away quickly. But he must have caught the feeling because he suddenly made a big deal of looking for his comb.

"Here," he offered in an embarrassed way. "It's a little greasy from my haircream."

"Maybe it'll help my hair lie down." I knew I was blushing. I ended up hoping I'd least turned a reasonably attractive color. Nate started to draw, and that made us both feel easier.

I remembered I had some news. "I have to write a story for English."

"Is that what's got you all nervous and jerky?" he teased.

"It's enough," I answered defensively.

"Yeah. You told me something about that once. That you liked writing stories."

"I've been writing a lot of them since school started."

"Could I read one?"

"Maybe the one I do for homework."

"Not the others?"

"No."

He glanced at me with raised eyebrows, holding the look a moment longer as he drew.

"I'd just like you to read a good one, that's all."

"How'd you get started? I mean, how'd you figure out what to write?"

"By looking at other stories. Then I wrote one like it and compared them, see what I'd left out. Now I just go by what sounds right."

"What kind of stories did you start out with?" he asked as he searched the grass for his eraser. "About yourself?"

I shook my head.

"Hold still. So what kind?"

"Just stories."

"Allie! That's like saying 'just drawings.' " He found the eraser in his shirt pocket. "Why won't you tell me about them? Are they dirty?" he guessed, glancing up in mid stroke.

"No!"

"All right then. Sexy?"

"Not exactly. They're private, that's what."

"Ho-ho-o," he crowed with delight.

"Don't you start!"

"Not a word. This is not a joking matter," he assured me joyously.

"Hey!" Someone called to Nate as they crossed the field. "Big game coming up." A tall sandy-haired boy moved into my line of vision.

"Yep," Nate answered indifferently.

"See you out here most afternoons." He made it sound like a question.

"That so?"

"Her too," he added, taking a look at Nate's drawing. "Didn't know that I'd seen her around before."

"Are you looking for an introduction, Bear?"

"Me? No, I have a girlfriend," he answered uncomfortably. Then he got to the point. "One my own age."

"Things are going good for you, huh, Bear?"

"I'd say so."

Nate continued to draw. Bear gave me a couple of long looks before he realized he was being ignored. He shuffled around for another minute, then he stalked off.

"He's a jerk," Nate said quietly. "Don't pay any attention to him."

I shrugged.

"I think he has a soft spot for redheads myself." A big grin broke out over his face.

"Something about Bear?" I asked.

"Nah. He's forgotten." He chuckled and began to make some strong wavy lines down his drawing.

"Are you making me look funny again?"

"Oh, no!"

I was certain he was. "Are you about finished?"

"Soon."

"It isn't funny, you know." I was angry all of a sudden and it surprised both of us.

"What?"

"The stories I'm writing. It isn't funny."

"I didn't think so," he said, looking at me in a measuring way.

139

"You're laughing outright. You were laughing before Bear came over."

"Hold still," he ordered, giving me that careful look again. He was looking at my eyes. He always finishes eyes right at the end of his drawing. "I'm not laughing at you. It's just that Bear . . . and you're—girls, that is, are so . . . here, it's finished."

He'd drawn me the way he drew the tree. I was better on paper. "I'm not so pretty."

"Fishing for a compliment?" he teased.

"No. I'm just saying, I don't have flowers in my hair."

"You should have," he said quietly.

I didn't know what to say, so I looked back at the picture.

"Allie," he said as he moved closer. "I'm really glad . . . you let me . . ." He stumbled over the words, embarrassed. "I didn't know you'd look like this," he finished in a whisper.

To tell you the truth, I was terrified. The next thing I knew I was on my feet gathering up my books and Nate was rushing to keep up with me. I couldn't have said what I was running from.

I was halfway home before I could slow to a normal walk. Nate swung along beside me, keeping his mouth shut. He hadn't tried to take my hand when he caught up.

"What're you going to do with that drawing?" I asked, hoping to break the silence.

"Roll it up. Stick it in a drawer," he said matter-of-factly. "What kind of story are you going to write?"

"I don't know." I didn't either. Winter on a Farm. God.

"You'll think of something," he said, looking at me with an expression far too sympathetic for my tastes.

"I can do it," I said defensively.

"I said I thought so!"

"Okay."

"Will I get to read it?"

"I guess so. After it's graded. If it's a good grade."

He cleared his throat. "I just want to say one thing."

"What's that?"

"About what you're writing." He switched around to walk

140

backward so he could see my face, talking fast all the while. "Guys think about sex all the time. It isn't hard to figure out girls do, too. Or else they wouldn't do all that giggling and whisper behind their hands when a guy passes them in his gym shorts." He took a deep breath and went on, easier.

"I wasn't laughing at you, Allie. I like that you aren't the kind of girl who acts like she's too clean minded to know how babies get started. Okay?"

"Okay." That was all I could say.

"Okay," he repeated, grinning, and reached for my hand.

"What happened to your hair, Allie?" Mom asked, squinting at me as she stirred something in a pot. I hated that squinty-eyed look. She reminded me of a dog that expected to get whipped.

"The rubber band broke up on top. It got sort of lumped up so I combed it out. That's all."

"It looks real pretty," she said wistfully as she began to pull potatoes out of boiling water.

"Real pretty," Daddy Jim said from the basement door.

Mom jumped, dropping a potato on the floor. It broke and a couple of pieces hit Crystal as they flew. She screamed and began to cry. Mom brushed them away, rushing to put Crystal's arm under cold water. Crystal screamed all the louder.

I picked up the hot pieces of potato. I had to pass through the narrow space left between Mom and Crystal at the sink to throw them away. Daddy Jim chose that moment to leave the basement door. I saw there wasn't enough room and I pressed myself against the edge of the table to make way. He was in no hurry to pass by and as he did, he pressed himself up against me so that the front of his pants rubbed against my belly.

I didn't say anything, I didn't even look up at him. When he got past me I dropped the pieces of potato into the wastebasket. My hands were shaking. In fact, I was shaking all over.

I didn't look in Daddy Jim's direction all through dinner. Not even when he started in about my hair. "Seems to me you've been coming home with your hair loose pretty often."

"Only this once." It seemed to me he looked at me closely, my mouth in particular. Although Prissy's lipstick was a pale pink, I worried about whether he could tell I'd been using it.

"We've been using the same rubber bands ever since we stopped the newspaper," Mom said, sort of thinking out loud.

"What?" Daddy Jim bellowed suddenly.

Mom snapped up straight in her chair, her eyes squinched up.

"Are you saying things are so bad you don't have a rubber band for her hair?"

"Jim!" The corner of my mother's mouth twitched nervously.

"It only broke this once!" I said again.

"It's a terrible thing to say to a man out of work, Nora! Don't you think this is hard enough on me already?" Daddy Jim's voice shook with outrage. "It's no wonder she acts like she's too good to give me the time of day. She learns that from you, Nora, from the things you tell her!"

"Allie? She loves you—"

"You don't see! Look how she slants her eyes away like the sight of me—" He began to sob, great harsh rasping sobs that tore at my mother's heart. For my part, I was unimpressed.

"Oh, Jim." She reached to encircle him with her arms and he shoved her away, nearly knocking her off her feet. Mom nodded toward the bedroom and I got up, taking Crystal with me when I saw the sympathetic tears in her eyes. Crystal will cry along with anyone because it's one of the things she does best.

I don't know what I meant to write when I sat down. I do know I planned to do my history homework first, but I had such an itch to write I never did get to it. In fact, I wrote till I had to go to bed. And I wrote right through history and math. I don't know that what I wrote even fit under one of the subject headings. But when I turned in the story at the beginning of English class I thought I'd done a good job.

"Did you do all of this since last night, Allie?"

"Yes, ma'am."

"How many pages do you have here?"

"Eleven."

She smiled and nodded and went on. I watched to see what everyone else gave her. No one had written more than three pages. I began to wonder if she'd even bother to read mine.

The worst was, by the end of class, I could hardly remember what I'd written. By the end of the day I was sure it wasn't much of a story at all. Nate did little to change my mood.

"Why not, Allie?"

"It makes trouble, that's why."

"How much trouble?" he teased.

"I don't feel like drawing today," I said, getting up.

"You're going home?"

"I guess so." I kept my tone businesslike as I picked up my stuff, hoping he'd have another suggestion. "You're going home" didn't sound like he was planning to walk me.

"Because I want you to let out your hair?" he said, teasing giving way to ridicule. It struck me to the quick. I fought a rush of tears as I snatched up my sweater and turned away.

He caught up with me at the edge of the schoolyard. "Hey, what's the matter?"

I didn't answer.

"I don't like it when people up and decide not to talk to me. It's babyish."

"That's not a nice thing to say!"

"Maybe not."

"You told me to say no! You told me—" I couldn't repeat it. I was going to cry. I hated it.

"You're right."

I gave him a quick look out of the corner of my eyes. I didn't know that we weren't still fighting. "What's so important about my hair anyway?"

"I like it, that's all."

"Suppose I was to say no to something else you like?"

"Don't be mad, Allie."

"Are you mad?"

143

"Nope. I'm just going to hope you'll give up that braid altogether."

That did it.

"Allie! Why are you crying?"

He started to take my books, passing me his handkerchief and looking for a place to stop, all at once. Even as miserable as I felt, I thought he was funny. "Jeez! Why are you laughing? One minute you're all—" A wise look slid across his face and he calmed down all of a sudden.

"I'm all what?" I asked, hiccupping.

"Maybe it's none of my business," he said. "I tell you what. Let's go past that old gas station. We can sit on that wicker thing if it isn't too broken down, and I can tell you about Tucker's girl."

"Tucker's got a girl?"

Things got better from there. I don't know exactly how it happened that we had nothing to fight about. I had the impression that Nate set himself to baby me along. I decided I could use some of that.

Things were okay at home, quiet for once because Daddy Jim had found another job. But when I sat down to do my homework, I started to think about my story all over again. It gave me a headache. I mean it. In the same way that I could hardly think what I'd written, I could now remember everything, practically word for word. They were all the wrong words and too many of them. Pages and pages of what happened, but not written in a way to make it a story, not bringing out any one point that the reader could hang on to at the end. After all this time writing stories, to mess up the first chance I had to see if one of them was any good. The noise in my head was worse than listening to a fight had ever been. I decided to take a bath. Turn off the light and soak in a hot tub. That was it. Drown my troubles.

Crystal made several trips in to drop something into the water: rubber toys, her bottle, a small stuffed duck that Aunt Lilly'd made her from a piece of an old quilt. I put that out on the floor as soon as she went out again.

It was strange to lay there in the warm water, seeing nothing, feeling nothing, listening to Mom and Crystal moving around the house. Daddy Jim had gone downstairs after dinner. It felt like one of the other times, when he'd be late home from work. It was the same yet so far away. Maybe that's what it felt like, being in the basement so much of the time.

Whispers. It did sound like whispering, now that I thought about it. I closed my eyes, as if that would help me listen harder. What would make that sound? I sat up with a slosh of water; a couple of Crystal's toys thumped around in the bottom of the tub.

The whispering stopped.

After a few moments I slid back down beneath the water.

"Jim?" my mother called from the kitchen.

"Jim, do you need something?" she asked, closer now.

"I need to use the bathroom."

I sat up more quietly this time, huddling up to cover myself.

"Allie's in the bathtub—"

"She's been in there an hour already."

"She'll be out in a minute."

"I can't see as that matters," he said, the way he'd been saying it for a year now. "It ain't like I didn't change her diapers often enough."

"Jim—"

He switched on the light. "You don't mind a little company, do you?" he asked, standing over me. He unbuckled his belt and opened his jeans, all with the same sharp, angry movements. "Do you?"

I shook my head without ever taking my chin off my knees. I stared at the rubber plug at the other end of the tub.

"Jim," my mother pleaded.

"All right, all right."

He turned to stand over the toilet, but he looked over his shoulder at me. "Hey! You gonna sit in there all night?"

I didn't look up.

"Don't you answer your daddy?"

"I'll come out soon."

145

"You're getting goosebumps."

"It's okay." I hugged myself more tightly.

"C'mon. I'll get you a towel."

"Jim, I don't think—"

"I'll dry you off like I did when you were little."

"Jim!" my mother almost screamed.

"Don't get excited," he sneered as he turned and dropped the towel on the floor. "We're just having a little conversation." He left the bathroom, walking in that slow, smart-alecky way some boys have when the teacher makes them leave the room. He turned into the bedroom, slamming the door behind him.

I sprang out of the tub and grabbed the towel. My mother stepped in and pleated my nightgown in her hands, dropping it over my head before I was dry. Crystal was bawling, but Mom ignored her. She reached up to pull the hairpins that secured the braid on top of my head. I set my face to uninterested as the bathroom door was pushed gently aside. Mom handed me the hairpins with shaking hands. I took my time putting them in the cabinet while she hung the towel.

Daddy Jim blocked the door.

"Excuse me." I tried that briskly cheerful voice that Lisa used whenever we were doing personal stuff.

No good.

He would stand there until he could be sure we were scared; he'd stand there longer, looking mad, until we'd look scared and he could smile. I looked up, ready to give him the same brittle "excuse me."

It was like an electric shock, a jolt that went right to my toes. Daddy Jim's lips were stretched over his teeth in a grin, his moustache quivering with held-in merriment as he stepped back to let me pass. My head began to ache horribly.

In the living room I turned back, hearing Daddy Jim's voice oddly gentle, cajoling. His hand was on my mother's shoulder, and as I watched, she nodded unhappily. He pulled her closer and turned her into the bedroom. My head throbbed. I needed to lie down.

I quieted Crystal, taking her into my bed. She cuddled right up, singing "twinkle, twinkle," to herself as I shivered beneath the blanket. It was almost daybreak when Mom crept through the bedroom. "Allie, what are you doing awake at this hour?"

"I can't sleep."

She sighed and sat down on the edge of my bed. "You shouldn't pay any attention to the way your daddy's behaving now. He isn't himself lately."

"He means to scare us." I raised myself onto an elbow, sure of my mother's ear.

"Allie, it's hard on him to put down the drink. It makes him act in ways that aren't his own. He's afraid to make a wrong step. He's scared." She put a hand to my head the way she did when I was little. "It's not right you should hold this time against him."

I kept shut. I didn't trust myself not to cry. I didn't know why I wanted to.

Mrs. Green had nothing to say about the stories on Monday. Or the day after that. I knew it was a lot of stories to read, of course, but I didn't think it was very funny when she came to class on the third day wearing a sign that said, "No, Allie, I haven't read the stories yet.."

Everyone else did.

That afternoon Nate told me I'd been in one of my prickly moods, about as prickly as he'd ever seen me. I had a feeling he thought he was pretty funny, about as funny as Mrs. Green. I told him what I thought.

That night I took my bath along with Crystal. Mom went along with it much more easily than I'd expected, looking awfully tired as she swept her hair away from her face. Crystal was delighted to have a life-size bath toy, even though I took up half the space. I hoped it would work so well every night.

Mrs. Green looked especially pretty coming into class the next day. Excited. "Class, we have an interesting day ahead of us. I have your stories here," she said, pulling open a drawer. "They were all so good that I know you're waiting anxiously to see them. Five of you wrote such outstanding stories that you got an A.

"I'm hoping the enthusiasm you showed for this assignment will result in a new club, a writing workshop to be held after school one day each week. Anyone who's interested may take one of these workbooks off my desk as they leave at the end of class. Tuesday afternoon. . . ."

I hardly heard what she said as she began to pass the stories back through the rows. I wanted an A so badly my stomach hurt. Two stories were passed to me. They belonged to the two people who sat behind me. I passed them back.

". . . to read one of the stories aloud."

Everyone looked around to see who wasn't holding a story. Some stopped looking and started listening. I saw one girl in the next row look at Prissy and shrug. Prissy pointed at me. The girl looked at me, listened for a minute, then poked someone else, telling them it was my story. It made me nervous. I tried to listen, hoping I wouldn't be embarrassed to find the story wasn't very good after all.

It was different than when I'd written it. That felt good. Like pulling off damp, sweaty clothes and rubbing yourself with a rough towel. Now, as I listened, I heard the clack-clack-clack of the thresher blades, repeated through my story. I felt the sun beating down on the back of my neck as Grandpa's pickup truck jounced over the ruts of a dry dirt road. I could see the tears rolling down Uncle Harry's face and the lines in Grandpa's forehead. Uncle Darryl's hand covered mine.

Perspiration stood on my forehead. Never mind the words, I told myself, just so many words. Telling about something that left me rubbed raw in a hundred secret places. I was going to be sick. Prissy's ponytail was a blur as I got to my feet and headed for the door. Mrs. Green looked up from her reading. "Allie?"

"I need a pass."

I don't remember getting to the restroom. I only remember vomiting up the remains of my breakfast.

"Allie? Are you all right?" Prissy called.

I locked the cubicle.

"Mrs. Green sent me to check on you."

"I'm fine. Leave me be."

"That's what all those papers are in the bottom of your locker, aren't they? Stories."

"Prissy. Leave me alone."

"I'm going back then. I'm missing the end."

I heard the door swing shut behind her. I slid down the wall of the cubicle and sat there. I couldn't go back. When the bell rang for the next class, I sat on the toilet and waited for the three-minute bell. No one noticed me as they rushed in and out. I sat there the rest of the day.

"Allie." Mrs. Green looked surprised to see me. "Why didn't you pick up your books earlier?"

"I didn't have time. Between classes, I mean." I collected my things, my hands shaking, just wanting to get out of there. But Mrs. Green didn't seem to notice.

"I'm sorry that it upset you to have your story read aloud. It's a fine story, Allie."

"It's all right. I wanted an A."

"You deserved it. Your story was very well written."

"Thank you." I edged toward the door.

"Prissy says you have several others."

I couldn't tell her about them, but I couldn't be rude to a teacher, either.

"You'll join our club, won't you?"

"I don't know."

"I realize this story was special to you. But the others wouldn't upset you so much when they were read, would they?"

"I don't know."

"Please think about it."

"I will." I reached the door and slipped out.

Prissy was waiting for me. "I thought you were never coming out of that bathroom."

"Restroom, Prissy."

"Don't stick your nose up at me, Allie Drew. I liked your story. I can't say that for everybody I know."

"What are you talking about?"

"About some people who didn't think much of your story, that's all."

"Who?" It came to mind so suddenly: no one liked it.

"Never mind, Allie."

"Prissy!"

"Oh, all right. It was that awful Sickles boy. I didn't see an A on his paper, you can believe me. It's no mystery why he'd be interested in taking a shot at yours."

Things got better and better. I wondered how long I would bear the brunt of Eddie Sickles's attentions.

"Could I read one of the others?" Prissy asked.

"No."

"That's what you write them for, isn't it? Don't you want someone to read them?"

"I'm just learning, Prissy. Most aren't very good."

"Allie, let me read one. Just one. Please?"

I didn't say anything as I pulled on my coat. I can't say I wasn't tempted.

"I'll give you a lipstick if you'll let me."

"I can buy my own lipstick."

"Well, then, maybe you should." She flounced down the hall and out the door.

It must have been a day with a black cloud over it, the way everything kept going wrong. Some of it was my own fault. We were walking home when a question popped into my head and I let it fall out of my mouth.

"Have you ever been with a girl?"

"Allie!" Nate went dark red immediately.

"I'm not asking anything about it. Just if."

"Well. Sure. I'm nearly sixteen, you know," he grumbled.

"More than one girl?"

"Only one girl at a time," he answered solemnly.

"Nathan!"

"What does it matter?"

"It helps me know. . . ."

"Know what?"

I shrugged. "One girl, one time. Three girls, three times. Or maybe . . . one girl more than once."

"I'm not telling you anything. You're probably writing one of those stories." He crossed to the other side of the road.

"So?" I raised my voice so it carried across to him. "Don't you want to be helpful?"

"I want my privacy."

"What if I wanted to know . . . so I'd know? I could want to know even if I didn't write stories."

"You could want to know, but that doesn't mean I'd have to tell you."

I should have dropped it right there. "Well then. I won't tell you anything, either."

He hooted. "What would you have to tell? You're only thirteen," he said, coming back toward me.

"It so happens I had a very interesting twelfth summer," I said haughtily. "But you wouldn't want to know about that."

"You're making it up."

"Don't be so sure," I said with a little smile. I was rewarded by a small frown between his eyebrows.

"I can ask Tucker, you know."

"Tucker wasn't with me when I visited my grandparents in Swan." And I knew Tucker liked to tout me as a girl who would try anything once.

He reached up to smooth his hair, making sure it still rolled neatly to dip over his forehead. "So you think we could make an even trade, is that it? You have a story for every one of mine?"

"Maybe. Maybe not."

"Are you talking about one guy or what?"

"Are you talking about one girl or what?" I parroted.

He walked faster, not saying anything until, "I could tell you anything I wanted. You wouldn't know any different." He was getting mad, I saw, but it only struck me as funny.

"I could do the same," I tossed off. "It only takes a little experience to back up a whole lot of stories."

"So you're saying you didn't do anything much, just. . . ." He let the sentence hang, hoping I'd finish it.

"I didn't say what I did. I said you only have to do a little to know about more."

"So what are you saying you did?" he yelled with a wild look in his eyes.

"I'm saying nothing about what I did," I said with a sense of triumph. I practically skipped the next few steps.

"Girls can't hide it, you know," he said in an offhand way. "Nothing shows on a guy, but that isn't true for girls."

"What can't I hide?" I asked, caught off guard.

"Whether you did it. I could lay you out on the ground without your panties and tell you in a minute whether you still have your cherry."

"If I'd let you." I was stung. He'd never spoken to me like that before.

"Yeah, all right. But I'd know."

"Not everything, you wouldn't," I said angrily.

"Like what?"

"Like how many times. Or," I reached for something particularly shocking, "whether he went down on me."

Nate grabbed my arm and yanked me around to face him. He was white, dead white.

"I was kidding," I whispered.

"How would you even know about that, Allie? Let alone talk about it?"

"True Confessions." No good. I could see it in his eyes. *"Playboy,* then," I pleaded. "I read it somewhere." I knew he'd never believe Prissy knew enough to talk about it.

"It's all right, Allie," he said, letting go of my arm. "I thought you were making it up."

"Look, I didn't mean for us to get mad over this. I only—"

"Don't say it, Allie. I told you I liked that you weren't pretending anything." He wouldn't look at me. "I can't get mad when you tell the truth."

"Nate, you have to believe me."

"Stop it, Allie," he snapped. "Listen, I'm going to turn off here. I told my dad I'd be home early." He passed me my books. "I'll see you on Monday, same as always." He gave me a quick peck on the cheek and started to walk away.

"Nate." But he was running then. I let him go. He might get used to the idea that I was an experienced woman, but I had a feeling he wouldn't ever get over letting me see him cry.

I walked the rest of the way home so slowly it was past dark when I got there. "Sit down to your dinner, Allie," Mom scolded. "We all waited till it was cold, as it was."

I slid into my chair. Daddy Jim pointed to a bowl.

"You'd better take the bus on Monday," he said.

"I'll be quicker on Monday. I was tired, I guess," I said as I passed him the mashed potatoes.

"She's been working very hard, Jim."

"I know! I see what goes on around here."

"Of course, Jim. I'm only saying—"

"I don't need you to say nothin'. I have eyes," he said, setting the bowl down too hard. I gave him a quick look, realizing he was drunk. "I'm not down in that basement all the time, you know."

"I didn't say that—"

"You were thinkin' it. It's only a matter of time before you start sayin' what you're thinkin'. You're one big-mouth woman, you know that, Nora?"

Mom sat silent. It was terrible to see her accept the things he said. Worse to see her nod in the face of his anger, stretching out a rubber band smile to show she understood what he said to be true.

The whole weekend was awful. When Daddy Jim was upstairs, we hoped he'd go back to the basement. When he was downstairs we waited, knowing he would come back up eventually. Even Crystal was quiet, playing near Mom and singing her little song over and over. Out of sight, out of mind, that's what we were being.

As it turned out, Daddy Jim was upstairs hardly at all except mealtimes. He complained about Mom's cooking, all the while eating like it was Thanksgiving dinner. Nobody else ate much. He got annoyed with Crystal's babyish ways, so that Mom and I started to pick at her more than he did. Which is probably why Crystal got whiny shortly before Sunday night supper.

"Can't you keep her quiet?"

Mom had already taken Crystal into her lap where she'd begun playing with food, wiping mashed potatoes over Mom's clothing and her own. "I can put her to bed after supper. If I do it now, she'll just cry louder."

"You sayin' you got no control over your own children?"

"She's a baby, Jim. She doesn't see anything wrong with what she's doing."

"You have to make her see it! She's messin' everything up."

Crystal's chin crumpled, always a sign that a bigger storm was on the way. "You let these children run you ragged. It's no wonder you're tired when you crawl into bed at night!"

Crystal began to wail mournfully, letting her body go limp. Mom dragged her up to sit again. She stiffened and threw herself over Mom's arm; her hand sideswiped my glass of milk and turned it over.

"Would you just look at that!"

Mom had already run for the dishtowel. The milk seeped through the crack where the two leaves of the table joined. Crystal wailed wholeheartedly, caught under Mom's arm like a load of laundry.

"We can't even eat in peace," Daddy Jim yelled, banging his fist down on the table. "Every time I come upstairs I have to thread my way through an obstacle course of abandoned toys and smelly bottles dripping—" Daddy Jim's voice broke as if he were going to cry.

"Jim, they're your children, too! Please don't talk as if—" The towel couldn't soak up the milk as fast as Mom pushed it across the table, forcing the milk over the edge in a stream.

"Stop it!" Daddy Jim screamed as the puddle of milk drooled into his lap. Daddy Jim reached for Mom's thin arm and snapped it like a pencil. Mom gasped and let Crystal slide to the floor. Crystal's mouth clapped shut in surprise. For a few moments she forgot to cry. Mom's eyes grew larger, rounder, in the silence that stretched tight over the kitchen. Her face had lost its color, sweating like a piece of warm cheese. She stared at her arm and said plainly, "Ow."

"Ah-h-h!" My scream brought Mom's eyes around to look at me before they rolled back in her head. She dropped to the floor. "You've killed her! Ah-h-h!"

Daddy Jim swung around to slam me up against the wall. I didn't stop screaming. My head felt like it was swelling up with the noise. He slapped me again, knocking me to the floor. I crawled beneath the table as dishes and silverware crashed around me. I dragged Crystal, who cried and kicked, beneath the table. Mom's pottered bowl smashed against the wall, leaving globs of mashed potatoes to slide slowly toward the floor.

The back door slammed so hard I could feel it in my knees. Crystal's breath sucked into her chest, caught and stayed there. I heard Daddy Jim go down the back steps, but there were no sounds of him going into the basement.

"Mom." She didn't answer, but pushed herself up on one elbow. Seeing her, Crystal let go with another wail.

"Allie, I think my arm is broken." I crawled out from beneath the table, helpless to do more than hold the baby. "Take her in the other room and rock her, Allie. Just keep it up till she sleeps. I'm going to ask Mrs. Kelly to take me to the hospital."

"I don't want to stay here," I said, loudly enough to be heard over Crystal.

"Allie, you're too big a girl to act like this." Mom got shakily to her feet.

"What if he comes back?"

"I don't want to hear any more talk like that. He's your daddy," she said angrily, turning away.

"Mo-om!"

"Enough!" She left, looking small and straight, even as she favored her arm. I wouldn't have been ashamed to argue her into taking us along if I thought I could do it.

Crystal and I rocked and rocked, and for a long time I worried that Daddy Jim would come in, spoiling for trouble. Crystal settled down to grizzling and whimpering, half-asleep as long as the rocker kept moving. It seemed like we'd been there all night when I heard a car come down the road. Mom came in alone, one arm covered in white plaster. She looked like she could barely stand up, she was so exhausted.

"Is it almost sunup?" I asked.

"It seems like such a long night, I know," Mom sat down on the end of my bed, sighing. "But it's only ten-thirty." I don't think she meant to do anything but rest a moment. I rocked back and forth, not really thinking anything that I can remember. When I looked up, she was asleep.

Daddy Jim was home when Mom woke me up for school. She kept a watchful eye on the bedroom door, her face pinched and tired looking. Crystal's bottle was ready, kept warm in a pot of water so there'd be no reason for her to fuss when she woke up. Clearly, Daddy Jim wouldn't be going to work today. "Sit down in your Daddy's chair, Allie, and eat your breakfast."

I tried, but when she left the room, I bent to pick up silverware from the floor. Cleaning things up would take hours, and Mom would have to get some dishes from someplace. Nearly everything was broken. "Allie, I'll take care of that," she said, returning. "Come here and sit."

I put the pieces on the table, unable to bring myself to throw them away. I couldn't think how my mother, so tidy in her kitchen, could walk around the mess like she didn't see it. "What are we doing?"

"Cutting bangs. You have a bruise on your forehead. Bangs will cover it," she said matter-of-factly. Questions popped into my head one after another. Mom was in no mood to put up with them, and I wasn't sure the answers would make me feel

1 5 6

any better if I were to get them. So I kept my mouth shut. I didn't even say I didn't want bangs.

"You're not to talk about this at school," she said, carefully separating a fringe of hair that fell over my face.

"I wouldn't."

"Someone might see the bruise. Or ask about the bangs."

"Nobody will ask me," I told her as the scissors cut slowly across the fringe. Long thin strands dropped into my lap.

Mom's hands were damp when she brushed my new bangs into place over the bruise. I was on the way out when she stopped me and whispered, "You remember what I said?"

"Yes." There was no point in repeating no one would ask.

"Don't dawdle on the way home. Right after your club, you get home."

"Okay." She licked her fingers and flattened the bangs over the bruise once more.

Mrs. Green complimented me on the fresh set of bangs, although I felt she did so with a kind of frown in her eyes. It may have been that Mom's concern made me oversensitive. I found myself licking my own fingers to pat at the bangs throughout the day.

Nate waited for me, just as he'd promised. He walked much faster than usual, and he didn't offer to carry any of my books. What little he had to say was said with a kind of edge to it that made me reluctant to do much more than nod my head. But I couldn't live with that for long.

"You're mad at me, aren't you?"

"No."

"What then?"

He shrugged. We walked some distance before he decided to answer. "I'm feeling stupid, that's what. I thought you were a kid, I guess. Not a child or anything. But a kid." He shifted his books and managed to walk even faster. "That was okay with me. I can wait a little while. I mean—" He crossed to the other side of the narrow road and kept on walking as if we were still together. I could see his Adam's apple sliding up and down.

I decided it was best to let him settle down. I fell a little behind, hoping he'd feel my absence. When he reached the old gas station, he stepped up onto the porch and dropped into the broken wicker settee. I walked a bit faster. But when I sat at the other end, I wondered what I ever thought I could say to change things.

"So maybe you're not a kid," he went on. "All right, you're not a kid, at least in some ways. Maybe you're even—" he broke off with an exasperated sound. And finally, as if he were talking to himself, "Maybe you are." My insides were shaking so hard my sweater set trembled where it laid against me.

"You aren't crying, are you?" Nate slid closer to me, his voice as soft as the first time he'd kissed me. I shook my head, trying to keep from doing just that.

"I won't tell you it wasn't upsetting. I sort of had a picture of how—what I'm saying is, I'll get over it." Tears started down my cheeks. I brushed them away, and they were followed right away by more. "Hey," Nate whispered, "I didn't mean for you to cry."

"I don't want to." My throat was so tight my voice was as deep as Nate's.

"It's that bad?"

Things were that bad. Worse. If I started crying, I didn't know how I'd ever stop. I swallowed down hard.

Nate slipped his arms beneath the loose panels of my corduroy coat and pulled me into the space where his jacket gapped open. He kissed me. "Allie," he whispered, his mouth moving over mine in a way that made mine open. His tongue ran over my lower lip, then darted away. He did it again, circling my lips and lingering there, drawing a whimper out of me. His hand slipped to my breast.

"No." My reaction was immediate, but the shock of what he'd done remained after I'd pushed his hand away. His kisses grew more insistent, his tongue finding its way to mine. I didn't pull away, but it wasn't the same. We were fighting now, in a close-up silent way that scared me.

He put his hand there again. When I pushed it away, he

moved his hand over to my other breast, tightening his arm around me, pulling me hard up against him. "Nate," I tried to say, but his lips were crushed up against mine.

I bit him.

He yelled, jumping back. I grabbed my books and ran.

"Allie!"

I just ran. I could taste his blood in my mouth, like sucking on a copper penny. He caught up, running beside me.

"Allie. Will you stop and talk to me?"

"I know I shouldn't have, Allie.

"It's just, I thought . . . since you already—never mind," he said, his voice fading. He ran with me, trying to make it up.

"This is silly, Allie. At least talk to me.

"Look. I only want what every other guy wants. So I tried. So what?"

Even as he began to sound scared, I kept going.

"Allie. I didn't mean for this to happen. I didn't think you'd be so mad.

"Please, Allie. Stop and talk to me."

After a while he dropped back. When I made the turn for my house, he was walking some distance behind me. I slowed down to catch my breath. Nate had been so different. Or did he just think I was?

What if he didn't wait for me tomorrow?

Maybe I should go back now.

No. I'd end up crying again. I didn't want to sit there blubbering that I didn't do it. He'd never believe me. He'd just say he did.

I had to be able to tell him, see, here's what I said. And here's what you said, that made me say the next thing. And so on. If I was going to have to admit to being childish, at least I didn't have to be bawling like a big baby.

The living room looked so dark, coming in from the afternoon sunshine. Mom was sitting in Daddy Jim's chair, working by the light that filtered through the blinds. She looked so strange there, struggling to sew a snap on Crystal's nightgown with fingers that were hampered by the cast.

"Want me to turn on a light?"

"The electric bill is high enough already," she said bitterly. "Your teacher was here, Allie."

"Mrs. Green?"

"She came right after school let out. She says you been writing stories." Mom looked stricken. She held her injured arm to her like a wounded bird.

"I got an A," I said warily.

"You wrote about what happened to Darryl."

"Did you read the story, Mom? Did she show it to you?" I heard the tears in my voice, choked them down.

"How could you do that? Write down something so baldly personal for a stranger to read?" She threw the nightgown to the floor by her sewing basket.

Suddenly I was too tired to care that she knew. "Did you even look at it?"

"I saw some. It was too terrible to read through," she said with a shudder.

"It was terrible," I whispered.

"Allie Drew! I'm ashamed of you! You don't even have the good grace to be sorry for what you done."

"I got an A," I said helplessly.

"That's not all," she went on. "She's upset that you wouldn't join her club. But it's not that you're so busy with them other clubs, is it? She says you don't belong to any at all. What are you doing after school, Allie Drew?"

"Drawing."

"But you're not in any clubs." Her eyes narrowed as she took that in. "You're meeting that boy?" she asked as a horrified expression came over her face.

"I'm drawing, nothing more."

"You are! I just know it." She sank deeper into Daddy Jim's chair, slowly folding in on herself like a damp rag left beside the sink.

"Mom, don't act like that!" It was scarier than if she'd gotten angry enough to chase me around with her wooden spoon. "I haven't done anything wrong."

160

"Wrong! You never do think you're wrong, Allie. You have a lot of your father in you."

"Won't you listen?"

"No. I listened too often to your father and too often regretted it. Today I spent the better part of an hour listening to your teacher's ideas about upbringing. From some fancy school back east. What does she know about living here and raising—" Mom's face twisted around the words she held in and her voice had gone high when she said, "I'm not about to listen to you."

"What's wrong up here?" Daddy Jim had come upstairs so quietly we hadn't heard him.

Mom drew in a shaky breath.

"Don't look at me that way," he said, stepping into the room. "You look at me like you're lookin' at your daddy." I tried. My eyes went back to my mother's face. "It's like that, is it? The two of you talkin' privately."

"No, Jim." I heard Crystal waking up, calling to Mom from her crib. Mom didn't make a move to get her.

"Cat got your tongue?" he asked, giving me a hard look.

"I wrote a story for English," I told him. "The teacher stopped by to ask if I could be in her club."

"Stories, is it? You know how your Ma feels about you making things up."

"It isn't like that," I said desperately. "Mrs. Green asked us to write a story down. We had to or we'd get a zero. I didn't make it up."

"She wrote about what happened to Darryl," Mom said in a faint voice.

Daddy Jim paid no attention to that. "What did I hear about that boy?"

"Nothing, Jim. I was jumping to conclusions."

One thing I do know is that if you don't want to think of something, if you just want to put it out of your mind, it starts to sprout up everywhere like so many mushrooms after a rainy spell. That was how it was with the thought of Nate's hand on my breast. I didn't dare look into Daddy Jim's face then, knowing he'd see that thought, bright as chalk on a blackboard.

"Have you been seein' that boy, Allie?"

Crystal began to cry, a whiny crying that rose and fell like a police siren. It would go on till someone let her out of her crib.

"We've been drawing pictures," I answered as clearly as I was able.

"I threw that boy off this place. Wasn't that enough for you?" he said harshly.

"Jim—"

"Be quiet. She was told to stay away from the boy and first thing, she goes waggin' her ass back to him."

"I don't think it was like that—"

"How long?" he demanded. "Since you started with these 'clubs'?"

Crystal was screaming now.

"I'm not sure exactly," I hedged. "Maybe a few weeks." It wasn't that I meant to lie. I simply didn't have the strength to tell the truth.

"This is the middle—no, damn near the end of November. You seein' so much of that boy you lost track of time?" he asked, coming closer. My mother crouched forward in the chair like she had some kind of cramps.

"I don't see that it matters, a week or two difference." It was a mistake. I knew as soon as I heard myself say it.

"What do you mean by that?"

"Nothing."

"Don't say 'nothing' to me! What makes you think you can talk to me like that?" he shouted.

"Noth——I didn't—"

"Jim, please!"

"Is that how you talk to your rich, no-account daddy? Or maybe you think you're too big to be answerin' to me?" His face twisted with anger, the vein in his forehead throbbing dangerously. "Maybe you're expectin' your boyfriend to come in here to protect you?"

"No!"

He swung his arm back as if to hit me.

My mother was up and between us. "Try not to get upset, Jim. Lots of girls her age—"

"I know what girls her age do. I know what you all do."

"Jim—"

"We haven't done anything but draw pictures," I said stubbornly. Knowing the rest was between Nate and me, private, like Nate said.

"And lie," he said in a voice that seemed to snarl. "You lied to your mother and me about those clubs. I told you to stay away from that boy."

I remembered him telling me, the day he'd come to sit beside me on the porch, and what he'd done. I'd been so wrapped up in trying not to think hand on breast thoughts that it was a shock when it broke through, coming to me in a rush of anger.

"He's my friend," I yelled. "You never said I couldn't have a friend."

"Allie," Mom warned.

"I said you couldn't have a boyfriend!" Daddy Jim said.

"Yeah, I remember that now! You think I don't know why you told me that. You think I don't know—"

He slashed out at me with such speed that I didn't even know it was coming. I felt the blow and a rush of warmth across the lower part of my face. I heard the crack as my head hit the floor. Everything went black for an instant. Not long enough so that it could be said he'd knocked me out, just long enough to be the opposite of a flash of lightning.

In that instant he hit my mother. I opened my eyes to see her fly up against the wall, hang there another second before she slid down to crumple to the floor. He kicked her hard in the side. She flipped into the air like a soft rag doll and she didn't make a sound.

"Mom," I cried, "oh, Mom." She didn't move, and I couldn't take back what I'd said.

"She can't help you now," Daddy Jim told me in a sly way. "You have something you want to say?"

"No, I don't." I took a deep breath. "I didn't mean it."

1 6 3

"What've you and that boy been doin' together?"

"Drawing, like I said." My head had started to throb.

"Nothing more?"

"No."

Daddy Jim stared at me, turning things this way and that, looking for a way to trap me. "You been havin' trouble with your rubber bands lately? I see you wearin' your hair down more often."

"Only once."

"Maybe your boyfriend likes it that way."

"He's not my boyfriend. We draw—"

"Pictures, I know." He seemed to mull that over, growing calmer. I thought maybe, just maybe, he was finished being angry. I wanted to look at Mom, I wanted to see if she'd moved, but I didn't dare take my eyes off his face. "And he kisses you, I guess," he said gently.

"No." I saw something flicker deep in his eyes, and I knew he could hear the lie. "Not real kisses like boyfriends give. Just a little one now and then."

His lips stretched into a wide thin smile. "He's a big boy, old enough to be wantin' more."

"He's not like that." His voice was still quiet, but I could feel a stirring inside me, a kind of winding up for something.

"You're lettin' your hair down for him, I've seen it before," he said, glancing at Mom. "Your mother was the same," he said thoughtfully, as if he'd come to some new understanding. "She let her hair loose in the sunshine, knowing it picked up little gold lights. A man had to want to touch it . . . touch her. But one man," his voice shook with anger as he went on, "would never be enough. A woman likes to see if she can do that again. Tempt a man and take him for a fool while she tries her wiles on some other poor sot!"

"Stop it! Don't you talk about my mother!"

He stopped. Maybe it was a time when all that happened could have been changed. If I'd taken a deep breath and tried to forget the things that had happened. But instead I felt that wound-up thing snap free.

164

"You're the one! You're drinking again and you can't hold a job more than a few weeks at a time. You hurt my mother and you—"

"Shut up!" he shouted, reaching for me. I stepped back, keeping plenty of space between us.

"You should never have made me touch you. Your pictures of naked ladies taped up on the wall. You're the kind they write about in *True Confessions,* and even then, they don't write about anyone as bad as you!"

He made another grab for me. I jumped away, knocking over the floor lamp.

"I'm going to tell my grandmother and she'll tell my real daddy what's going on here. He'll come back and take me away, take us all away!" I kept moving, seeing the hatred that pulled his face into a mask.

He laughed. "You think he'll fly all the way back here for you? Why, he barely thinks of you when he's gone." He edged closer. "Oh, sure, he sees a doll in a store window and buys it. How many dolls are in that closet? Twenty? Thirty? How many times in a year does that mean he thinks of you? Twice? Three times?" He shook his head as if at my stupidity.

"And the letters," he stepped closer, trying to force me into the corner. "A few lines, always the same: 'How are you?' " he mimicked in a stilted voice, " 'How is school? Hope all is going well.' Then pages filled with the glittery places he's seeing, all the fancy people he's meeting."

I hadn't known about the letters.

"They're like his visits." His lip curled up in a lopsided smile. "Full of himself. Your mother burns them after she reads them."

"You're wrong," I said, feeling that wound-up thing shrivel away.

"He don't take an interest in what's going on here," he said, taking another step toward me. "I'm your Daddy, and it's my duty to keep you from becoming one of those women in the pictures you talk about."

Something passed between us, a kind of knowing what the

1 6 5

other had in mind. It was only a second, a stretched-out second when I was listening to the heavy sound of Daddy Jim's breathing, before he snatched out at me.

I slid along the wall and came out on the other side of an easy chair, running for the kitchen. He was right behind me, reaching for me with a stream of words: "My duty to teach you right from wrong . . ." He grabbed my braid, pulling me up short, then using it to drag me back into the living room. ". . . for your own good . . ." I clung to the doorjamb and then to the chair, screaming all the while, and when I couldn't hold on I sank to the floor. ". . . once and for all . . ." Daddy Jim dragged me across the room where he reached into my mother's sewing basket for the scissors. ". . . make you remember this day . . ." I swung a leg, aiming for the hand that held the scissors. He hardly seemed to notice, just kept coming after me with a face that was rigid with fury, following me around the room as I scrabbled this way and that, trying to get away. ". . . see you for what you really are . . ." He began to saw away at my braid. I dropped to the floor again and tried to crawl toward my mother.

"Mom!" I screamed, and I saw her arm move, heard the thick white cast scrape against the floor. "Mom!" I could feel Daddy Jim's breath on my neck as he bent over me, sawing and sawing and I thought, I must be bleeding. How could this be happening and I must be bleeding. ". . . leave a mark that . . ." I sprang into the air, my head ramming into Daddy Jim's chin.

"Ah-h!" His head snapped back and he let go of me, dropping the scissors. "Son of a bitch!"

I ran for the kitchen, but he sprang for me, falling forward and flattening me beneath him, landing so heavily that it knocked my breath loose, but I didn't stop trying to break free. Not that it was something I was thinking, *be brave, keep trying,* but I was filled with such fear that I kept moving even as I felt Daddy Jim crawling up to lie over me.

I tried to call out for Mom again, but my voice would only come out in a squeal, like a baby pig's. I hated the sound of

166

it and I hated that it made Daddy Jim laugh, but I couldn't stop it.

"Is this how you and your boyfriend lay together? Is it? Is it?" he kept at me, his body holding mine to the floor. "Does he put his hands on you? All over you?"

I cried in that squealing voice, unable to fight any longer.

"Jim!" My mother. I tried to call out, but I couldn't find enough breath, ended up making a gaspy hiccupping sound that hurt my throat. "Jim!" she shouted.

Daddy Jim raised himself, took hold of my shirt as if to haul me up off the floor. "Leave her go!" Mom screamed.

"You bitch!" he spat as he started to get up, pulling me with him.

I saw my mother standing as if the cast weighed her down on one side, swaying as she swung the floor lamp around. When Daddy Jim reached for her, she raised it as if to hit him, but he jumped back. "You'll pay for that," he yelled. "You'll be sorry for even thinking of—"

Mom swung the lamp and hit him full in the face. He screamed, but he never let go of me. "Allie, get away!" Mom cried.

"I can't," I answered, trying to yank free.

He turned on me with fresh fury and hit me in the face.

"Jim!" Mom swung the lamp again. I heard it connect with a solid thunk. Daddy Jim fell, letting go of me, and I fell too.

He gathered himself into a ball, half-crying, dragging himself up onto the easy chair. I watched in amazement, expecting him to raise his head and scream at us, to throw himself across the room to take the lamp from my mother.

But he didn't.

He continued to sob, his face buried in the crook of his arm, as Mom crept past him into the kitchen. "We have to run," I whispered frantically to my mother.

She shook her head tiredly. "It's done now. It's all over." She leaned against the table and looked around. "We have to see to the baby."

1 6 7

I heard Daddy Jim getting to his feet, the scrape of his shoe, the creak of the old armchair as he leaned his weight against it. My eyes kept darting back to the doorway, expecting him to come through it. He didn't. He was still crying.

Crystal's crib was empty. "Crissy," Mom called. No answer.

I opened the closet. Crystal's big blue eyes were full of tears, and she let out a wail when she saw Mom. She clung to a stiff china doll from Spain, her fingers twisted tightly into the silky red dress and real hair. A brightly painted comb lay on the floor at her feet. Mom took her hand and walked her to my bed.

We were all huddled together on the end of my bed when Daddy Jim came to the bedroom door. "Nora, I'm sorry. I don't know what got into me."

Mom didn't even turn to look at him.

"Nora. Can you forgive me?"

"I can't talk to you now, Jim. Leave us be."

"Please, Nora."

"No," Mom said in the same tone she used to turn me down on a second helping of milk and cookies.

Daddy Jim shuffled away from the door and headed for the basement, crying all the way.

Mom didn't look hurt by it the way she usually did. Just tired. "Allie. Stay here with Crystal."

"Where are you going?"

"I have to be sick."

But Mom didn't make it to the bathroom. She was sick in the kitchen sink, holding her side and moaning. I helped Crystal put the comb in the doll's hair, trying to keep her busy.

I'd been afraid to think about my own hair, but I felt it hanging off to one side and flopping against the wrong part of my back. I swallowed against tears. It was silly to cry over hair.

"Go get the scissors, Allie," Mom said, limping back into the bedroom.

"What for?"

She didn't answer.

I went for the scissors.

They were lying where they'd been dropped. I picked them

up and set the lamp back up. The shade was crushed, but I put it on as best I could. The room seemed empty after so much noise and fear. I held in a nervous shudder and went back into the bedroom.

"Sit here," Mom indicated a spot on the floor between her feet.

"What are you going to do?"

"There are only a few strands holding your braid, Allie. We have to cut it off the rest of the way." Mom looked so sad about it herself I didn't have the heart to make a fuss. I sat, she cut, just one quick snip, and it was gone. She handed it to me. "Put it in your bottom drawer."

It was strange to see it nestled there among the outgrown clothes and things Mom felt were too fancy for me to have. It wasn't fair. I reached up to feel my head. Hair hung below my ears on both sides, but it was short across the back of my neck.

"Allie," Mom said softly.

My voice shook as I asked, "What does it look like?"

"We'll take you to the beauty parlor to have it fixed up," Mom said. "They can give you a permanent wave," she said anxiously when she saw my tears, "and it'll be nice and curly."

"I don't know."

"It'll look so grown-up, Allie. You'll like it, you'll see." When I didn't look enthusiastic, she said, "We don't have much choice, Allie. We can't leave it like that."

"Can we get it fixed tomorrow?"

"I don't think so."

"Then when?"

"You'll stay at home till it's fixed up nice."

At least I wouldn't have to go to school this way. But there would be no trip to Grandma Taylor's for Thanksgiving either, not with me looking like this. Resignation settled heavily in my chest. I pushed the drawer shut.

Daddy Jim stayed in the basement all night as far as I know. Mom fed us soup, and we all went to bed straight after, leaving the bowls on the table. I couldn't go to sleep. After a while I crept through the house, wondering if my mother might still be awake. As I neared her door, I heard her crying. All I can say is that there are different kinds of tears, just like there are kinds of everything else. I thought I knew my mother's, sometimes hurt, sometimes angry, and if those had been the tears my mother shed that night, I could have gone to her. Found some strength in her. But the hopeless sounds she made, all but smothered by her pillow, made me turn back to my room.

I sat at my window and stared out into the darkness of the cornfield behind the house. When we moved here in the spring and then again when the corn was cut, I'd seen that someone lived at the other side of that field. Someone whose lights were on late into the night and then again before sunup. They made a changing pattern of warm gold squares that I watched with some curiosity. I thought, *One day I'll walk across that cornfield to say "hey."*

Now I imagined that those lights were my father's, and when that didn't seem to bring him within my reach, they became Nate's. That was more painful yet, bringing me dangerously close to tears like my mother's, and I searched for someone else. Grandma Taylor came to mind, and I seized on her with a needy vengeance. I saw myself, elbows on the table, as she rolled piecrusts for Thanksgiving dinner, pouring out my troubles. She shook her head sadly, smiling her sweet smile that meant everything would be all right. And I tried to see myself feeling better. But I didn't. The thing that Grandma Taylor couldn't see, because I couldn't tell her, was that it wasn't over. Daddy Jim was still working himself up to something.

I went back to my bed, finally too tired to sit at the window. I woke up several times during the night, sometimes crying, sometimes shivering with cold.

I didn't get a look at myself until the next morning. It was no mystery why my mother wanted to wait a few days to take me for a permanent wave. One eye was bruised and purpled. My face was swollen on one side. When I opened my mouth wide, which wasn't easy, I could see my own teeth marks on the inside of my cheek.

The first thing that came to mind was what Nate would

think when he saw me. Right after that I thought, *I'll never let him see me again.* Then came the tears. I brushed them away angrily. I hate to hear girls moaning about a blotch here or there and how they'll *never* be able to face the world or whatever looking like *that.* Then they fuss and primp and ask everyone, "Okay, how do I look *now?''* And sometimes they go through the whole routine again.

I've never been one to look for an excuse to stand in front of the mirror. When I look, I know exactly what I'm going to see. Me. I won't have changed from the last time I looked in. Primping isn't going to make a difference. Not that I'm ugly. It's just that my face isn't the kind that makes you want to pinch or pat or fluff anything.

Now all I could think about was that face in the mirror. And the way my hair hung in limp strings at each side of it. It was fascinating in a horrible way. I must've been there every ten minutes or so just staring. Each time I walked away from that mirror there seemed to be less of me to hold on to.

"Mom." She was feeding Crystal some tapioca pudding. "I want to talk to my daddy."

"You can't," she answered right back, as if she'd been expecting this. "He's already in Brazil."

"You must know where he is," I cried.

"Not till he sends a support check. Usually he's moved on by the time we get those." She looked like she thought that ought to close the subject.

"I need to talk to him. Maybe Grandma Drew knows where he is."

"That's enough, Allie," she said as she set Crystal on the floor. "I know things are bad here. It's bad for all of us." She dropped back into her chair, worn-out looking. "Your Daddy Jim will get better. Please, Allie, I know what he did was . . . he'll stop the drinking and. . . . It's not all his fault. A lot of men are out of work."

"I need to talk to Daddy."

"I can't have you talking to your daddy about this," she said, annoyed now. "You think I want his family to be able to say they saw it coming? Saying I can't make a life for myself with anyone?" she cried.

"I want to go live with him," I said in desperation. "I don't want to stay here."

"Don't you ever say anything like that to me again, Allie Drew!" There was an angry clatter of dishes in the sink as she soaped them. "You're liable to hear some things you'd rather not. Now you just get back to your bed and leave me be."

I used to have a dog, a terrier kind with stand-up hair and legs like sticks. He'd wander away in the afternoon when I went in for a nap, and sometimes he didn't come back until after supper. One evening he didn't come back at all. It seems to me it was three or four days before I found out what happened to him.

I was sitting on the edge of the tub, balanced there because my feet weren't quite reaching the floor. My mother was getting ready to go out, I remember because she was putting on powder and lipstick. I was just sitting there, watching her against the clean white tile walls, so bright in the light over the sink. All of a sudden I was missing my dog. I'd been missing him for a while, but it had just that minute become more urgent.

"Where's my dog?"

"Allie, I don't want to hear any more about that dog. He's gone, and I don't think he's coming back."

That answer made my stomach hurt. "I just want to know," I whined.

"Daddy Jim walked all over looking for him, and he's gone."

"He can't be gone. He'd get hungry."

"Stop it about that dog!" She shut her lipstick case with a click. "Oh," she swore under her breath as she pulled the case apart. She'd crushed the lipstick into the cap. "If you must know," she said angrily, "the dog is dead. He was laying in the road a little way from here. He was hit by a car."

I felt the tears starting behind my eyes.

"Don't you cry, Allie. You've been nagging me about that

dog till I'm near crazy. Now you know what happened, you leave me be!" She stalked out of the bathroom, saying, "It was only a dog!"

Funny thing is, I took her word for it. I didn't cry, and I don't remember thinking much about it anymore. That was how it worked out about talking to my father.

Daddy Jim sulked for the first few days. He tried to talk to me a few times, but I stared at the floor. If he didn't go away from me, my chest tightened up and I started to cry. I don't think I was afraid of him, not just that minute, but I was still so shaken from the haircut thing that at the sound of his voice or footstep I could feel my insides slide around.

I even cried at the dinner table. I wasn't noisy about it. I just couldn't stop it. Sometimes Crystal joined in. Mom looked nervously in Daddy Jim's direction, but she didn't dare say anything. After a few minutes, Daddy Jim would send me to my room.

On Thursday he was up early and shaving like he was going out to look for work. But when he showed up at the breakfast table, he was dressed for church and he ate with the same big appetite and hearty ways that my Daddy used for Sunday brunch. Mom peered at him in a nervous way as she served him second helpings.

"I'm going to see her teachers," he said finally. "She's missing a lot of school." He didn't look my way. He might have been talking about anyone.

"What will you tell them?" Mom asked.

He didn't hesitate. "She has a cold. A bad cold. Kids get them all the time." He took a huge bite out of his toast.

"She could do with something to keep her busy," Mom said, agreeing with some reluctance, "and she will have to make up the work."

"That's it, then. Is there any particular thing you need?" Daddy Jim asked as I slipped away from the table.

I knew the asking was a kind of playing at being nasty, a way of letting me know I wasn't as invisible as I was trying to

173

be. "I have all my books here," I answered carefully. "I only need the assignments."

I made it back to the safety of my room, my heart beating loudly in my ears, my underarms dripping. "That is some unforgiving child you've raised, Nora," Daddy Jim said in a conversational way.

Mom didn't say anything. After a moment he got up and left. He was gone all day, missing dinner. Mom went from wondering what happened to him, shuffling from window to window for a view of the road, to the certainty that he'd stopped somewhere to drink. She was angry then, but that quickly gave way to worrying whether he'd get drunk enough to talk about what he'd done. I hoped he would. I hoped it so hard I could almost believe it was already true. Then I remembered the squealing pig sounds I'd made, the way I'd scrabbled around the floor in fear, and in a sudden rush of the deepest embarrassment I'd ever felt, I shared my mother's fear that he would tell.

He made no attempt to speak to me when he brought home several sheets of notebook paper that had been folded and stuffed into his back pocket. He smelled of beer. Later, much later, I heard him arguing with Mom. I pulled the covers over my head, trying not to hear. I'd tried to make myself believe the whole thing was over. Yet every time I thought of it, I was right back there, my scalp pulled tight over my skull, screaming and fighting as Daddy Jim hacked away my hair. It had finally occurred to me that it might never be completely over. Even when my hair grew back it might be something that is remembered all the time whether you think of it or not. Like divorce. Or being ugly. That was scary.

I sucked in a deep breath, angry with myself for crying. Now my nose was stuffed and my head ached.

Tap.

I had almost been asleep. But it wasn't one of the house's usual night noises.

Tap. Tap.

I got out of bed, going to the window, not sure whether to be frightened or not. I saw Nate outside, long narrow legs and a heavy jacket blousing out around his waist, easily recognizable even in the dark. He reached out a tentative hand to tap again. I didn't even think about it; I opened the window. He grinned, something I could be sure of only because his teeth picked up the moonlight for a moment.

"Rapunzel, Rapunzel, let down your hair."

Stunned, I didn't answer.

"It's you, isn't it?"

"Yes," I whispered.

He let out a shaky breath like he'd been holding it a long time. "For a second there I wasn't sure which room was yours. I figured it wouldn't be the one with the light on."

"What are you doing here?"

"Visiting a sick friend. Are you feeling better?"

"How'd you know I was sick? Anyway, I thought we were ma——"

"Prissy told me," he said in an annoyed way. "She didn't like to leave me standing in the cold too many afternoons in a row."

I smiled in spite of everything. "You waited for me?" But he wouldn't want to admit to that again.

"Come closer to the screen," he whispered. "I can't see you."

I did, but cautiously. "Can you see me now?"

"Barely. You look like a ghost. You know, a pale circle floating in midair?"

I relaxed a little, knowing he couldn't see my hair. "I'm better."

"You sound like you have a cold."

"That's what it is."

"You'll catch pneumonia, sitting at that window," he said, putting a hand up to the screen.

I put my hand over his, pressing fingertip to fingertip.

"I miss you," he said quietly.

"Me, too. I mean, I miss you."

"I'm tired of acting like a jerk. I apologize. Things will be better when you come back. Promise."

"It's okay."

"No, it's not. It'll be different."

"Not too different."

Nate grinned again, a flash of white teeth. "It must be true."

"What?"

"That girls mature quicker than boys."

"Who said so?"

"The schoolbooks. You get that in eighth grade. And my mother says it about twice a week."

I rested my chin on my hands. It was unbearably romantic, a boy at my window in the middle of the night. That it was Nate made my heart ache, happiness mixed with the dread of facing him in the daylight. Maybe I should break it to him before he could see it.

"Allie, what are you doing at that window?" Daddy Jim asked from the bedroom door.

"Nothing," I answered as invisible fingers tightened over my throat. "I was too warm."

"You'll get sick, sitting there in the draft." He started toward me. I got up, and out of the corner of my eye I saw Nate flatten himself against the house.

Daddy Jim looked around before he shut the window, and I had reason once more to be thankful for the screen that barred a really good look along the side of the house.

"You get to bed. Don't get out again till your mother calls you to breakfast." He left without waiting to see me into bed. I heard him go through the living room and shut the bedroom door.

It was tempting to see Nate off. But I got into my bed with a great creaking of springs. I knew Daddy Jim was out there in the darkness of the living room or kitchen, waiting for me to make a mistake. I rolled over on my side.

This was the first recent encounter with Daddy Jim that hadn't left me in tears. I realized that as I became aware of a hard little knot, like a kernel of dry corn, deep in my chest. It was something like the knot you get from a nervous stomach in that it was definitely there, almost touchable. But it wasn't nervous at all.

6

"STOP running your feet through the leaves, Allie. You'll ruin your shoes."

That was okay with me. Anything, so long as I didn't have to feel like I was being seen by anyone passing us on the road. We made some picture. The day was nearly as warm as summer, a point made by the fact that Crystal, being pulled along in my old red wagon, was only wearing a little sweater. I'd insisted on wearing my heavy coat. Mom had decided on a scarf when the hood didn't cover me well enough. I might as well have had a hump on my back.

The beauty salon was in the front room of a house belonging to a lady whose manner reminded me of my mother. That was what struck me hard. How much she was like my mother had been, and immediately after, how different my mother had become. I'd never seen it so clearly before.

Mom held herself so tightly around the shoulders that she appeared to be cringing, even when you knew she was standing straight. Little lines had come at the corners of her eyes from the way she squinted. And when Daddy Jim was upstairs, she blinked all the time. I remember thinking once that she didn't really want to look at him. Now it occurred to me that she didn't want him to be able to look into her eyes. Maybe she was afraid he'd see something that hadn't been there before.

I took off my scarf.

"Good Heavens! What has this child done to herself?"

I looked from the beauty operator to my mom, who started to talk right away, not hurriedly, just not giving me a chance to say anything. "You know how kids are. She thought she'd like it short, and she didn't stop to think about the right way to go about it." My mother's voice, calm and strong in a way I'd forgotten it could be, faded into the background as I thought about what she'd told this woman. It made me go weak all over.

"Here, honey, sit down. You're looking a little sick," she said, yanking my coat off. "It's much too warm a day," she muttered as she hung it up with a look of distaste.

It didn't matter that I knew why Mom had done it. I simply felt she could have made up something that didn't make me look so stupid.

"My lands, you are a nervous and jerky one."

"What?"

"You're jumping all over the place. It's only a little water."

"What did you say? Nervous and . . . ?"

"Jerky?" She laughed out loud. "It's something one of my customers says now and then. It certainly does call up a picture, don't it?"

I nodded. It comforted me somehow, as if Nate had reached out to hold my hand. It got me through the bad part.

"What are you going to cut?"

178

"I have to do something with it, honey. It's long around here, and short as a boy's up top here, where you must've had your ponytail. It's a mess, that's all. I have to even it out."

I took a deep breath. "Okay."

I had no idea what I was getting into. She spent most of the morning wrapping tiny little scraps of hair in paper, to be rolled around plastic clips. I thought she'd never finish. She mixed up some awful-smelling stuff in a dish and squeezed it over my hair with a cotton ball. It got so I could hardly breathe. The only relief I did get came when she put me out on the back porch with a sandwich and a Coke until it was "done."

She and Mom talked in low voices about Children Today. I was so mad I wanted to cry. I couldn't get over it. How could she tell that woman I did this to myself? How could she sit in there embroidering on that story, while I was out here with this evil-smelling mess in my hair? I was in some mood by the time they took me back in. It wasn't improved as she started to unwrap my hair. "Why is it doing that? It looks like wire springs!"

"That's the permanent, Allie. Don't get excited. We aren't finished yet." That was no lie. She rinsed my hair and proceeded to pincurl it, taking almost as long as she had with the rollers. She started to prepare me for the worst.

"The curl will be a little tightish for the first few days, not like a wire spring, no, but tightish. It takes a little while to settle in, and then the curl relaxes and it looks just beautiful."

She stuck me under a big helmet of a hair dryer that burned the tops of my ears and bits of my scalp where the hair was parted. I couldn't hear anything they had to say, which was probably just as well. But I didn't miss the darting looks my mother kept giving me. I knew how hard this was for her. It was all on her face, in the way she kept that polite little smile carefully in place while they chatted, in the way she began to blink as the afternoon wore on, and the nervous way she kept picking Crystal up and putting her down again. But I was mad. I glared out from beneath the hair dryer and let her stew about whether I would expose Daddy Jim. There was a certain satis-

1 7 9

faction in that. It was forgotten as soon as I came out from under the hair dryer.

The curls popped back to lay flat against my head as the bobby pins were drawn out. "That's the way they're supposed to look now. Don't worry," she told me. "Nora, you're going to have to bring her back in a month or so as the hair on the crown begins to grow out. Then I can shorten the sides a bit so it's all even."

Mom nodded, blinking.

"Comb it out from the top, Allie, the way I'm doing, so the short parts will blend right into the longer part," she said in a tone that I recognized from Lisa's "I know about these things" speech. It didn't sit well with me.

My hair didn't sit well with me, either. It made me think of a hat, the kind that fits tight to the top of your head and has a fur ruff that goes all around your face and ears and neck. There were no curls. Just an all-over frizz that suggested I didn't have the good sense to keep my fingers out of the electric sockets. I burst into tears.

"Oh, now, honey! It ain't so bad. It looks like one of them big city hairdos, almost, and it'll look even better in a week or so." She'd have gone on that way for a while, but Mom put my coat in my lap and gathered up Crystal as if she were being chased.

Outside and down the walk, she had only one thing to say. "It was the best we could do, Allie."

"The best! You said my hair would look like yours! It doesn't. You never, ever came home looking like this."

"It'll look nicer all the time. It will loosen up in only a couple of days, you'll see."

I went on crying about how it looked, telling my mother it would make me a laughingstock, and though I knew that to be true, I was more concerned that Nate would no longer think me pretty. There was some satisfaction in seeing how affected my mother was by my tears. To tell you the truth, the more my mother looked unhappy, the more I cried. It made me feel better to be the one doing the hurting.

1 8 0

But after a while, Mom stopped worrying about my hair, and she started thinking about my behavior. Her face closed up over the wound she felt and her mouth grew tight around the edges. Still I went on, long past crying for how I felt but childishly crying to see the mark on my mother's face. By the time we got home, I'd ceased to think about the reason for my tears. In fact there were no tears during that last mile or so, just an insistent wailing that failed to a moaning as we approached the house.

"Stop that sniveling, Allie! You've embarrassed me all the way home with that foolishness, and I won't put up with any more of it." Mom slammed the backdoor shut.

It seemed to knock something loose inside me. "Don't you say that to me! You told that woman I did this to myself!"

"Shut your mouth! You hadn't ought to talk to me like that."

"I'm going to talk to my father! You can't stop me. I'll write him a letter or call him or whatever I want."

She started toward me, her hand upraised.

"You better not hit me! I'm going to tell my father. And before I tell him, I'm going to tell Grandma Drew. Wait till she hears how you burned my daddy's letters!"

My mother gasped and covered her mouth with her hands. Her eyes were wide and frightened over them. Somehow it didn't make me feel any better to see that I could scare her so much. Not that I was feeling sorry for what I said. It just made me feel uncomfortable.

I went into my room and sat on the end of the bed. About those letters. They were my letters. She had no right to decide if I should have them. That was decided when they were written to me. Now I was nearly grown up. Why couldn't I talk to my father? Or write him a letter. Why couldn't I talk to my grandmother when I chose?

If I wanted to see my grandmother, I could damn well walk there. How long could it take anyway? That hard kernel could be felt in my chest again. It felt bigger in a way, but not uncomfortable the way you might think. I liked the feel of it.

181

Stronger. That was how it made me feel.

At first I stayed off the main road, thinking the trick would be to avoid being seen. I loped along in the darkness, being grateful for the unseasonal warmth in the air. It seemed to me I was making pretty good time. Then it occurred to me that there was no way I could go far enough, fast enough, on foot. I would have to get on the highway, risk being seen by someone who knew me, in the hope of getting a ride. Otherwise they would find me in the morning, only a few miles from home.

So that's what I did. I was real nervous at first, half-jumping into the ditch every time a car passed me. Then I started putting my thumb up like I'd seen hitchers do. All the time I made up stories in my head for what the driver might ask, what I could answer.

A car passed going the other way, slowed, started to speed up, slowed again to a stop and started to back up. I started to run, my heart hammering in my chest. The car ran backwards, right along beside me. It was a convertible, its top down on this warm night. It pulled over and a girl got out, laughing.

"See? She is a girl. I told you," she called back to the car as she crossed the road.

"Hi, Regina."

"Huh?" She leaned forward to peer at me. "My God! Allie, is that you?"

"It's me."

"I hardly recognized you, girl, with that cute little haircut. When'd you do that to yourself?"

I shrugged helplessly. Regina was too drunk to care.

"Can we give you a ride?" a boy asked as he came up behind Regina. He was tall and fat, and although he sounded very polite, I suspected he'd been drinking as well. A car whizzed by us.

"Hey! How long am I supposed to sit here?" called a boy from the car.

"This here's Larry," Regina said, and he made a little bow, "and that's Richie. He's my new boyfriend."

"Are you going home, Regina?"

182

"We're on our way to a party over in Des Moines. That's where these boys live."

"A new bar opened up. They're having a beer night with a band for dancing," Larry added.

"That sounds good," I decided. Regina had to go home sometime, didn't she?

"You sit in back with Larry," Regina told me. "Isn't this nice? Now we're all paired up."

Richie had nothing to say except for the snapping of his gum. Larry gracefully accepted the burden of conversation, difficult not only because of the company he kept but because we had to shout to be heard over the windstream.

"Where were you headed when we picked you up?" he asked, turning to me when he ran out of things to say to Regina.

"Over to Swan, where my grandmother lives. She's sick, and I'm going to see if there's anything I can do to help."

"Oh. I see," he said seriously.

Richie snorted loudly from the front seat.

Larry ignored him and so did I.

"So what do you do? Ordinarily, I mean."

"Do?"

"Your job. What do you do?"

"Oh. Uh . . ."

"She waits on tables, same as me," Regina put in.

"You look so little to be doing that," Larry said in surprise. Then, realizing he'd been less than tactful, he went on. "But then you girls probably don't have to be able to lift bales of hay, do you?" he joked.

I looked to Regina for help.

"We're working girls," Regina said in what was meant to be a lilting, sophisticated manner.

It drew another snort from Richie. "You girls aren't jailbait, are you?" he asked suspiciously.

"We're eighteen, both of us," Regina insisted.

"I know it's dark 'n' all, but you both look awful young to me."

"That's very flattering," Regina giggled. "Wouldn't you say so, Allie? Allie?"

"Yeah. Flattering." I didn't care for the sound of this at all.

"I think we oughta take a closer look before we show up in a bar with 'em," he said to Larry.

"There's no call to be rude, Rich."

"I'm not being rude," he said, slowing to turn down a narrow dirt road. "I'm not planning to be rude at all."

No one had anything to say while he chose a place to pull over. We'd passed a few houses, but by the time he stopped, there were no lights to be seen in any direction. We were sitting on the edge of someone's farmland, marked by a narrow strip of woods on this side of the road. Richie slid across the seat and put an arm around Regina.

"Hey," she said, "what do you think I am? I'm expecting to be taken to a party."

"We'll get to the party," he told her. "But I want to know what to expect in the way of entertainment later on." Regina giggled and gave a little shriek, giggling some more.

Nothing he said sounded all that hilarious to me.

Larry and I sat through maybe two or three minutes of nuzzling and bickering from the front seat. Richie stopped and looked into the back as if to say, what were we waiting for? Larry shifted in my direction, and I turned to face him, ready to fight if he tried any of the stuff Richie was up to. "I know this is rather sudden," he said in a low voice, "but I feel we've gotten to know each other pretty well."

I stared at his dark silhouette. The fight went right out of me. All that was left was this terrible sadness. I can't explain it, but suddenly I was feeling sorry for him. For myself.

"Hey," Regina protested as Richie pressed her down into the seat. "I'm not gonna do anything here. Not with company and all."

"What're they supposed to do?" Richie asked with another snort. "Wait outside?"

"Don't get me wrong," she said in a wheedling tone. "I'd like to and all. But we need a little privacy."

184

"Yeah. Well, as long as we're working out something, I ain't the only one looking for relaxation."

"And I ain't the only game in town," Regina snapped.

"Hey, look, Richie. This isn't neces——"

"I'll tell you what's necessary, Larry boy. You paid the gas, you picked the party, you said hey, lookit the girlie and we picked this one up," he said, motioning toward Regina. "You two social butterflies found the cue ball here, and I'm damned if I know how old either one of 'em are!"

"Lookit, I——"

"Shut up! I'm willing to play, and I'm willing to pay if that's what rolls around, but I won't be doin' either one by myself. This is put-up-or-shut-up time, for everybody in the car. Or these two lovelies get out right here, and you and I go on our way. What's it gonna be?"

"You can't leave us out here," Regina whined. "Besides, I'm only asking for some privacy. The woods are fine even. Listen, you have to at least take us into town someplace. . . ."

"What'll it be, Larry boy?" Richie said as if he hadn't even heard Regina.

Larry heaved a deep sigh.

"C'mon, you two," Regina urged. "You'll be feelin' like you're old buddies by the time we get to the party. You don't want to miss a great party, do you?" Her voice had taken on a scared tone. "Larry, you don't want to leave us out here, do you?"

"No. Sure I don't. It's just——"

"Fair's fair," Richie said. "If we're going to the woods, you're going to the woods. Maybe later, at the party, we can take turns in the car." He was out the door and pulling the seat forward to reach for me.

I pulled back. "Regina's going with you."

"We'll get out this side," Larry said, putting an arm heavily over my shoulders. "Thanks anyway."

We walked into the woods a way, Richie and Regina several feet off on another path. "This looks like a good spot," Larry said. He'd found a grassy area around a fallen tree. He knelt

1 8 5

to brush it clean, then stood aside politely. I stared at the cleaned-up spot, mostly because I thought I might be expected to. There was little enough I could tell in the dark. I thought about running away, but there didn't seem to be much use in that.

"You want to take off your panties?"

He was too well-mannered to watch, and he fiddled with a candy wrapper. "I'm finished," I told him as I gave my skirt another quick brush to be sure it covered me.

He offered me a piece of candy. I didn't want any.

"Well, I guess we ought to lie down." When I didn't make a move, he said, "You first."

"God!" I heard Regina's voice carried through the night air as clearly as if she were standing next to me. I laid down quickly, holding my skirt tightly against my legs. The ground was wet, making me think of things that live there and come out at night. I swallowed against something in my throat.

He fumbled at his jeans for what seemed a long time, and then I heard the whispery sound of his zipper. I was holding my breath as he stretched out beside me, leaning on one elbow. "You ever done this before?"

"Yes." I don't know why I lied.

"You like it?"

"Sometimes."

He sighed deeply and moved over me. A sound gurgled up out of my throat, hardly anything to hear because I choked it back so hard and fast.

"It's okay," he said hurriedly, misunderstanding. "I won't be too heavy. It's okay."

I could feel his belt buckle on the inside of my leg, just above the knee, and his warm orange-flavored breath on my face as he settled himself on his elbows. He reached back to push his pants down some, scooching up over me so that my skirt rode up and left me nearly bare.

I squeezed my eyes shut and waited. His hand brushed over my face. I opened my eyes in surprise. It was strange that it seemed like he wasn't touching me at all. His hands might have been a doctor's, feeling for a heartbeat, for all the interest I had in what they were doing. I couldn't have said if they were rough or smooth, dry or sweaty. He kissed my cheek a couple of times, leading over to my mouth.

Richie laughed a little way off. It had a nasty sound. Larry must have thought so too, because he made a disgusted kind of sound, pressing his face against mine. Then he started kissing me again. His hand dropped lower to slip beneath my sweater. Only when his hand went under my skirt did I think about how unhappy I was to be here. He brought his hand back out and licked it a couple of times, then went back under my skirt. "You aren't too wet. Maybe you're a little nervous."

"Maybe."

His body touched up against me and his fingers were there, searching for the place. "Can you lift your knees?" I did. He pressed up against me, rubbing a little, as if coaxing it to go inside. Something was wrong. He made a couple of more tries before he collapsed on me, his face pressed into my shoulder. "I can't do this."

"It's okay," I told him, sensing his embarrassment.

"I . . . it must be the way—" His voice cracked as if he might be about to cry.

"I think it's kind of nice that you can't."

Hesitantly, he asked, "You won't say anything?"

"No."

Right then we heard Richie and Regina coming toward us. "Lay still," Larry whispered. "I'll keep you covered up."

"Hey, you done anything over here?"

"Get away, Richie. We aren't finished."

"Who you think you're kidding?"

"Not everybody just sticks it in and pulls it out."

Regina giggled, then shut up quick when Richie raised his arm like he'd hit her.

"Yeah, like you'd know," he said, his attention returning to us.

"We're going to ignore you, Richie. If you're any kind of man at all, you'll walk away and leave us to it." He lifted his body a little, pressing up against me. He did that again and moaned painfully.

"Let's go," Regina whined, pulling at Richie's sleeve. "We don't have to stand around watching."

Larry heaved again and I arched with him, throwing my arms around his neck. The next time I managed a shaky moan of my own. We eased back to the ground and Larry's mouth met mine in a grateful kiss.

"Whoa," Richie breathed aloud.

"Hsst! Let's get out of here." Regina started back through the woods on her own. Richie backed off slowly, and we went through our act once more.

Then Larry began to laugh, all in a whisper with his chest shaking and his face buried in my shoulder. I caught it then, a quivering, shaken-up feeling from deep in my stomach that erupted in a hiccup-whimper as tears rolled down the sides of my face and into my hair.

"You should hear them now," Richie's awed voice carried back to us, "they're crazy with it."

We hugged each other, trying to keep the laughter inside. When we had it under control, Larry whispered, "Don't laugh now, no matter what." Then he began to groan in short bursts that got longer, an imitation of the sounds we'd heard Richie making some minutes before.

"You know what's funny?" Larry whispered.

I shook my head.

"I could almost do it now. We're sort of friends."

We held hands on the way back to the car, partly because it looked good, partly to make the trip through the brush easier. Richie and Regina were thunderstruck, there's no other word for it. Larry reached over and squeezed my hand when we got into the backseat. It felt good.

Richie would have nothing to do with taking us to a party. Larry had to insist that Richie take us as far as the city limits. Richie kept saying he didn't feel he got his money's worth, and Larry shut him up finally by telling him, "You got as good as you gave."

188

They dropped us off at a gas station. Larry gave me his phone number on a piece of paper, a couple of dollars and a handful of dimes and nickels.

"Larry," I began, "this is really nice but—"

"I can't go home wondering how you'll eat or what will happen to you if you run into another—just take it."

The station owner eyed us through all of this as he started to close his place up. "Well, I guess it's you and me now," Regina said as Richie drove off. "Listen, before we hunt up a ride back, let's use the bathroom here."

"I don't think we ought to. That guy's been giving us funny looks."

"We know that look, don't we? Maybe he'll give us a ride."

The restroom was none too clean, and Regina was far too cheerful to bear. I decided to wait outside. That's where I was when the police car drove up.

There were a lot of questions before Regina and I were taken to the police station, and more questions when we got there. None of them could be answered to anyone's satisfaction. That was in part due to the fact that Regina stuck to her story about being a waitress. I said nothing at all. Finally Regina told the police her name and where she lived and because her mother had a phone, she was shortly on her way home. Her mother told them where I lived. It wasn't long before they realized they couldn't reach my mother by phone and they called Officer Aarons in Carlisle, no doubt raising him out of bed. I spent the rest of the night waiting up in a hard wooden chair, dreading what my mother would have to say.

It was past sunup when Daddy Jim came to collect me. Mrs. Kelly waited anxiously in the doorway while he talked with the police. I chewed my nails, wondering why my mother hadn't come, wondering what Daddy Jim had told Mrs. Kelly, wondering what was being said that I couldn't hear. The policeman who'd picked me up looked awfully mad. It never occurred to me to scream out what Daddy Jim had done.

The ride home was done without one word to pass anyone's lips. We got home at just about breakfast time and Mom put me to giving Crystal her cereal. Neither Mom nor Daddy Jim asked me why I ran off. They didn't seem particularly interested in how I got as far as Des Moines. They didn't say not to do it again. Although my mother's eyes were full of worry, she showed no anger at what I'd done. As the morning wore on, Daddy Jim took himself off to the basement, and I waited tiredly to hear her views on so great an offense. It was with some surprise that I realized she was only relieved to have me home. In the end, although I'd hardly say I was in a frame of mind to be grateful, that may have been the reason I didn't try again to tell anyone how things were.

I knew the first day would be hard.

I put aside the dress my mother chose for me. I looked for the apricot-and-gold plaid skirt that Lisa bought for me and found it hanging in the back of the closet. The fuzzy gold sweater that went with it was in my bottom drawer. My braid looked dead, like the century-old scalps that lay in the glass case of a museum in Des Moines. I tried not to look at it while I dug for the sweater.

One good thing. This skirt was almost as short as the ones the other girls wore. So was that royal blue jumper that I'd picked and the olive green dress I hadn't liked. Mom had put them all away, deciding they were too short. I looked in the closet and found them. Good again. I jumped when I heard my mother behind me.

"What are you doing with those things on, Allie?"

"I felt like wearing them."

"They aren't for you."

"They were bought for me."

"Don't you be smart with me. You know what I mean."

That hard kernel lodged itself in the center of my chest. I looked straight at Mom and said, "I'm wearing them to school."

"I'm going to talk to your daddy about you," she threatened.

"You do that," I said quietly and got my books from the chair.

190

"You haven't had any breakfast yet." She was looking sorry she'd said anything.

I didn't care. I walked out the door without another word to say. I had reason to be grateful for that fuzzy sweater because I never even thought of a jacket. The warm spell was breaking and although the sun was strong, there was a winter chill in the breeze when it came.

I sat right up front in the school bus, figuring it was better to have being seen be over with as quickly as possible. Each person who got on gave me a long look as they passed. One or two girls giggled once they were behind me.

Prissy was at her locker when I got to school. "My Lord, Allie, what have you done to yourself?" she asked loudly.

Several people turned to look our way.

It was an inspiration born of the knowledge that this terrible day had only begun and I had already had a gutful.

"I had the chicken pox," I said as loudly as I could manage. I don't think my voice carried as well as Prissy's, but it was good enough. "My head itched till I like to tore my hair out so my mother cut it off."

"Lord," she said again, less loudly now that the first shock had worn off. "I don't know that I've ever seen anything like it."

I had nothing to say to that and I began to open my locker.

"Uh . . . Allie, I have to tell you—"

The floor of my locker was bare.

"I think your stories are good, Allie," she said quickly.

I couldn't take my eyes off the bottom of my locker. It was a sensation much like looking at myself in the mirror had given me.

"A lot of kids think they're awful good."

"How'd you get them?"

"The lady in the office gave me your combination when she sent down for your books."

"Where are they?" My voice croaked out of me, leaving a pain in my throat after it passed through.

"Oh, here and there. I'll get them back quick. I'd've put them back by now, but I didn't know . . . I mean. . . ."

"Prissy." It took all of my strength not to leap on her and beat her to the floor. She must have seen it on my face.

"I'll get them all back, Allie, I promise." She turned and ran down the hall.

Eddie Sickles was in my first class. It took him a moment to recognize me, but he's one of those blessed with quick recovery. "Egad!"—he looked truly astonished—"if it isn't our little storyteller! And don't she look like someone who had a run-in with a thresher herself?"

I sat at my desk and looked at the board to copy homework, ignoring him for all I was worth. But he saw everything that happened in class as a golden opportunity. The teacher made a mistake at the board and reached for her eraser. "Use Allie's head, why don'cha? It's the soo-peer-ior eraser," he said like a radio announcer. Even the teacher looked like he wanted to laugh. One of the boys started to scratch his back, trying for a hard to reach place. "Just go rub up against Allie's hairdo, Ned, that'll take care of that itch."

I didn't cry. It was hard to bear, but it was only what I expected. In some way I can't explain, it made me feel right in what I'd done, running away. Every time someone opened their mouth to me, it was another finger pointed at my mother's part in this, even if I was the only person who could appreciate that fact. Each time angrier with her, I put my chin in the air and acted like I didn't care. Now and then I even believed I didn't.

But in the hallway, I watched for Nate. I had it all worked out in my mind, the way he'd stop and stare, shocked at what they'd done to me. He'd forget the thing he'd done and the way I'd treated him, feeling sorry for me the way he would. He'd pretend everything was just the same. So I crept along, checking the faces of the older kids that went past, holding myself ready to duck into a classroom or turn quickly before he would see me coming.

Mrs. Green looked once, then again, her glance cheerfully expecting to greet a new student. It was only as the look drew out that I saw something there that reached into me and

192

twisted. It was all I could do to get to my seat and concentrate on sitting there and looking like it didn't matter. I didn't look at Mrs. Green again.

It was only when I left her classroom that I felt safe to think again. And all I thought was, I could never bear to see that look in Nate's eyes.

By the end of the day the long looks had turned to pointing and whispered comments. Nervous giggles had become two girls leaning against each other, laughing helplessly. I was exhausted by the time I was standing in line to get on the bus. The only thing on my mind was to get home and go straight to bed. Maybe things would be better tomorrow. They'd have gotten it out of their systems.

That's when I looked up and saw Nate.

He was standing at the corner of the school building so he could see me whether I went out to the buses or out the door where we usually met.

He looked angry. There was something else, I don't know what. Not the look I'd dreaded. I turned away, looking back only once. He stood there until I got on the bus. When I got to a seat and looked out, he was gone.

So stupid. I'd spent the whole day imagining the worst. The worst. Only now did it occur to me that he might not have stood at the corner of that building to watch for me. That he'd seen me at all was an accident. I felt like I'd been hollowed out inside.

I didn't even cry. I was only dimly aware of the jeers as I got off the bus. At home, I got into bed and stayed there, skipping dinner and homework. My mother came in to stand over me every so often, her eyes full of wishing things were different. I paid her no attention. All day I'd thought of letting everything out in a good cry, but now that I could I was numb. Everything was worse even than I'd imagined.

It was very late when I needed to get up to pee. The thing that stopped me was the thought of finding Daddy Jim out there somewhere in the dark. Still, I couldn't wait until morning. I crept out of bed and sneaked into the kitchen for a jar which I brought back to my room. I peed in that and hid it under my bed. I crawled under the covers with a relieved sigh. Maybe I could go to sleep now.

Tap.

The muscles in my stomach wrenched into a knot.

Tap. Tap.

I wouldn't get up. That was all.

Tap.

If he'd had something to say, he could've said it that afternoon instead of staring at me like I'd turned into something slimy.

Tap. Tap. Tap. Tap.

If he stood there all night, he'd freeze.

Tap.

I turned over on my side. After a long time I slept.

He was waiting for me at the bus stop in the morning. Half an hour tapping at my window hadn't been enough for him. I put my chin in the air. In the end he'd see me and say whatever he wanted, if that's what he meant to do.

Nate didn't take his eyes off me as I walked up to him. He had that looking close, measuring eye at work. I wouldn't give him the satisfaction of looking away first. I brushed nervously at my skirt, thinking all at once of taking my panties off in the bushes and brushing that other skirt down. I pulled my coat closed.

"Are you okay?"

I didn't answer.

"Let's walk to school?" He looked okay to me. Not in any way like he'd made up his mind to take pity on me.

"We'll be late," I said finally.

"So we'll be late."

I thought about missing first period and Eddie Sickles. I nodded. I didn't refuse when Nate took my books, leaving me only my notebook to carry.

"I didn't know what to make of it when I heard you'd run off."

"You know about that?"

194

"Not till after you'd been picked up." We walked for a while and then he said, "I was mad about it, I guess. That's why I didn't come over to you yesterday. That, and I had some things to think over." He put a hand on my arm to stop me. "He did that to you, didn't he, Allie?"

My eyes filled with tears, two fat drops running down my cheeks before I could stop them. There weren't any more.

"I knew it had to be that. He cut your hair because you took the braid out for me. That's it, isn't it? He's crazy enough to do something like that!"

"Shut up!"

He stared at me in a shocked way. After a moment we both began to walk again. "I'm sorry," he said in a low voice. "I shouldn't have said that about him." His hand was warm and strong over mine and I refused to think about anything but that.

"I'm right. About the other?" When I didn't say anything, he said, "If you don't say no, I'm going to know I'm right."

I felt the tears starting to swim again. I looked away, but there was nothing I could see clearly. Nate squeezed my hand, making it okay to walk along without trying to talk. We'd almost reached the school when Nate pulled me over to sit on somebody's steps. "Can you walk with me after school?"

"I have to ride the bus."

"Will you meet me at lunchtime?"

"We aren't supposed to."

"Nobody will pay any attention. You'll just walk off like you have to go home for lunch, and we'll sit on my back steps."

"Your Mom—"

"Nobody's home at my house during the day. My Mom works."

I wasn't sure it was a good idea.

"Please, Allie. When else can we see each other?"

"We have to be careful to get to school on time," I decided. "Or else there'll be trouble."

"I agree. We always have to get to school on time."

"We'd better go."

"We'll wait until after lunch. We don't want to start off on the wrong foot our first day, do we?" he said with a glint in his eye.

"You mean play hooky all morning?"

"Only in the interest of being on time."

"Uh-huh." I felt a small trying-it-out smile work its way onto my face. I thought about getting into trouble, but only for a moment. We wrote excuses for each other to turn in after lunch. I can't say I really expected it to work, but I didn't allow myself to think about it. I wanted to be with Nate.

The morning stretched on and on without classes to mark the time. We kept moving in the cold, walking with the wind at our back. Talking about the things we'd been careful to avoid when we thought of ourselves as on the way to school.

"I only wanted to have something to say back," I explained.

"I would have known it if you'd picked almost anything else to say!"

"It had to be something you couldn't laugh off."

"I was crazy the whole weekend, seeing you in the backseat of somebody's car, raising your arms to let out your. . . ." I felt my face grow warm with the heat in his voice, but we were talking about something lost forever. The memory of that time in the autumn sun seemed to belong to someone else. My throat was tight, too tight to let easy words pass through.

Nate reached out to touch my hair. I watched his face for I don't know what, maybe for whatever he'd keep hidden if he thought it would hurt me. "It's like baby fuzz," he said with a smile. When it faded, there was something like pain on his face. "It'll grow."

"What?"

"It'll grow again. Your hair."

"Oh."

"It looks pretty this way, you know."

"You don't have to say that."

"I know that! I like it."

Just hearing him say it made my chest ache.

"I like the way it fluffs out all around your face, like angel hair. I like the way it curls around your ear." He ran a finger around my ear as he spoke. The wind suddenly changed direction, biting at our faces now, and I moved closer to Nate, hoping he'd think the wind caused the tears in my eyes. He put an arm around me, making a chuckly sound deep in his throat. "Your ears don't really stick out. I just draw them that way."

I swallowed noisily. "It got cold so fast," I said, trying to change the subject.

"We could go by my house to eat our lunch," Nate suggested. "We'll get warm."

But once there, I didn't want to go inside. Nate was clearly disappointed, but he made the best of it. "Not bad," he said, as we sat on the back steps. "We're in the sun and out of the wind."

"I think it's going to snow." My voice held a ridiculously grateful note and I didn't like it. Better he'd made some complaint. I wanted it to be we'd had a fight, and now it was over, and we were still standing nose to nose. But my hair had changed all that.

"Not yet."

There was nothing obnoxious in the way he said it, but I was smarting over the idea that he might be feeling sorry for me, that he would make allowances for me. That I would want him to. "What would you know about it?"

His eyebrows shot up in surprise. "I read the almanac."

"Which is good for what?" I sneered.

"The farmers go by it, Allie," he said in an easy voice. He wasn't going to be goaded into a fight. He wasn't going to let me get away with anything, either. "It said winter would be late in coming and hard to die."

I didn't say anything.

"Hard to die. I guess a farmer would think of winter that way."

He wanted total surrender. His and mine. I gave in with a sigh.

Nate put his arm around my shoulders and held me close, burying his face in my hair. "What made him think to do it?"

he asked after a time. "What made him think to do that?"

"My mother liked it," I said, realizing the truth only as I spoke. "She liked my long hair, and he wanted to do something that would hurt her. It was what you said, about letting my hair out for you and him not wanting me to have a boyfriend —" the word was out before I thought to catch it, a word that had never come up between us. "But that's all twisted with something that's going on with him and Mom," I finished quickly, pulling away.

"I like being your boyfriend." I could see that in his eyes. It wasn't a look that had anything to do with what boys and girls do together. I loved him for it. I pulled my knees up beneath my chin and crossed my arms over my legs, liking that he sat so close. The leather smell of his jacket filled my nostrils.

I pressed my face against my knees, trying to hide the tears. "Allie, don't cry." Nate wrapped his arms around me, legs and all.

"It was so awful."

He held me tighter. "Tell me."

"I can't." I couldn't stop the tears either. Nate didn't let go. After a time the pain in my chest faded, and the tears dried up.

"Don't do that again."

"Do what?"

"Run off. Don't do it again."

"I couldn't help it, Nate."

"You come to me. I'll hide you or something. We'll figure out what to do. Promise me."

"If I can come to you, I will. But I won't promise. I couldn't have come to you then. You don't know what—" what I looked like, I wanted to say, but that would never begin to make him understand the way I felt.

"He didn't—didn't do anything else?" His arms tightened around me.

"No," I mumbled, embarrassed. "That wasn't what I meant."

"I'm afraid for you, Allie. Anything else happens, you come to me."

198

"I'll try."

He shook his head. "It isn't good enough."

"I don't know what you want from me."

"Not from you. All the stupid stuff that goes through my head. Knight in shining armor stuff. Nothing that I could do. So I think, what could I do *really?* And I think, we could run off together. Maybe we wouldn't get caught. Then I think, we wouldn't have to run off if I got you pregnant. They'd make us get married." He made a disgusted sound. "Then I think, look what happened to you when we haven't done anything. How could getting you pregnant be the answer? So I think of going to my parents and saying, see what a terrible man this is, see what he's done to Allie—"

"Nate, you wouldn't."

"I won't. Not yet."

"You can't."

"It could've been worse, Allie. He could do worse than cut your hair," Nate said in a frightened way.

"No. Mom says he'll get better. He always does."

"Oh, God, Allie." He was nearly crushing me but when he let go of me, I felt lost. "We'd better start out. We don't want to be late for class," he said in not much more than a whisper.

We were late, but Mrs. Green pretended to take no notice of me or of the wave of snickers that followed me to my seat. She stopped me after class, and after a few awkward moments, said what she meant to say.

"Allie, I know you're having some difficulty with the other students. It's hard when these things happen but—"

"It'll pass," I said, feeling tears too close to the surface.

"Yes," she agreed, "it will. But, Allie. . . ."

"Ma'am?" I'd already turned to the door as if we'd finished our conversation.

"If you need to talk to someone," she said kindly, "I have some time after school. . . ."

"I have to be on the bus directly after school," I said.

*　　*　　*

I was called down to the office the next day, passing Nate on his way out as I went in.

"I'm sorry, Allie."

"What'd they say?"

"Nothing much. They just hand out a detention for this sort of thing." But I could see the worry on his face. "Maybe if you tell them you have to be home—"

"Nathan," Mrs. Reardon said as she came out of her office. "Don't you have someplace you're supposed to be?"

"I'll try," I whispered and slipped past him.

But Mrs. Reardon had plenty she wanted to say to me. "This is the second time I've been told you missed classes, Allie, although you were absent so long after the first time, I attributed it to illness. Now I see I was being too kind."

I sat at attention, hearing something more in her voice.

"Your grades haven't been very good since you moved here, Allie, and as I looked back over your records," she said, riffling through some papers on her desk, "I noticed you didn't do well the last year or so at your last school. Now, with this"—her mouth tightened as she lifted the note Nate had written for me—"well, this is a pattern we've seen before." She gave me a long look, one meant to measure the effect her words had on me. It may be that it would have been wise to show some shame at my misdoings, but Mrs. Reardon's manner made me want to stick my chin out. "A girl losing interest in school and taking up with boys," she said firmly, "results in that young girl leaving school before graduation." I felt my face grow hot. "If she's fortunate"—she raised an eyebrow—"one of the boys will marry her."

I sat silent, although Mrs. Reardon clearly meant this to be a time for me to speak up for myself. There was nothing that would've helped anyway. Mrs. Reardon's daughter, in the next grade up, was friendly with Prissy. I didn't imagine it would be long before Mrs. Reardon would know about my stories.

"It's one thing to discover a boy's interest in such things," she went on. "But when the girl involved is as young as you are, it seems wise to have a talk with her parents."

"You can't do that!"

Mrs. Reardon's face registered a certain approval over my alarm and I realized she'd meant to scare me. She was satisfied she'd done that. "I don't know how you girls get yourselves into these situations and never give a thought to what will happen."

I nodded.

"I want to see an immediate improvement in your grades. I don't care that you don't see any use in it, Allie; I'll take that improvement to be a sign that you're keeping yourself out of trouble. Maybe there will be no need for me to speak to your mother. Further, you'll serve detention for the morning. . . ."

I tried to think of some excuse I could offer, one that she wouldn't be tempted to check. I couldn't come up with anything. "I can't serve detention," I said desperately.

She didn't say anything, just sat there looking surprised.

"My daddy said I have to be home right after school. He gets mad if I'm late."

"I can understand his concern," she said in a tight voice. She looked at the records spread on her desk. "I see you have a neighbor's phone number down here. Do you have a phone now?"

I shook my head.

"Well, I'll assign you to detention for tomorrow. That will give you a chance to let your daddy know where you are."

I sat frozen, seeing the opportunity she offered, but wondering whether it would do me any good.

"I hope I'm going to feel my own efforts are well placed, Allie," she said in a way that suggested she thought it unlikely.

I was in no position to chance seeming rude but I couldn't bring myself to do so much as nod my head. She told me I could go.

Nate and I met outside at lunchtime as we had planned, but he insisted that we eat in school. "Just until we serve our detentions and they stop thinking about us."

I nodded, wondering if I was likely to escape Mrs. Reardon's notice. But I didn't speak to Nate about what she'd had to say.

That evening I told my mother I needed to stay after school.

"Allie, you aren't thinking to see that boy!"

"No! I promised I'd help hang stuff up in the classroom. Posters and things. Please let me."

"No."

"Mo-om!"

"I don't want to hear another thing about it," she said through clenched teeth. "I have enough without worrying what your daddy'd do if you were to come late home from school!"

I gave it up.

Prissy was able to give back most of my stories over the next few days. She'd kept most of them at home for herself, and it was only a matter of bringing them to school. As for the stories she'd given out, she'd been unable to find two.

"I'm sorry about this, Allie. I sure didn't mean to cause you any embarrassment. I wanted to read them, that's all."

"You didn't have to give them to anybody else."

"It wasn't like that," Prissy whined. "I was reading one on the bus and somebody said, 'What're all those papers?' so I said what they were and they said, 'Oh, I know her, lemme see one.' It was like someone asking for part of the Sunday papers. I never thought—"

I slammed my locker door. "I don't want to hear any more, Prissy."

"No one told you to write stories like that and leave them in your locker, Allie Drew."

I ignored her. All day I'd thought about just staying and getting detention over with, hoping it wouldn't come to Daddy Jim's notice. It wasn't an idea I took seriously. I had to get to the bus.

"Stories like that should be left at home," Prissy yelled after me.

Nate was standing at the bus, but there was no time for us to talk.

I didn't know what to expect when I got to school the next

day. I was too nervous during first period to know what was going on around me. Nate must have known how I'd feel, and he made it his business to find me in the hallway.

"I don't think you're going to be in any trouble."

There was something too sure in the way he said that. "Why?"

"I asked my dad to call."

I was too mortified to speak. I could only stand there, staring at him.

"I told him I had a friend who had some trouble and we cut school to talk about it." The bell rang. "See you later." And he ran down the hall.

I was in a kind of heat all morning, embarrassed that Nate's father would no doubt hear Mrs. Reardon's version of my absences. That led to wondering what Nate had told him to get him to act on my behalf. At lunch, I found a corner and sat down with a carton of milk and the sandwich I'd brought from home. In some way, I expected to be left alone there. Maybe I'd even forgotten about Nate, his part in my humiliation fading in the overall sense of catastrophe.

So it was a shock when he sat down across the table from me, smiling. "Hi."

I watched as he started to unwrap his lunch. He caught my eye and said, "Hey, you aren't still mad?"

It was the way he said it, half-teasing, half-sure I wouldn't stay mad at him, that pushed me over the edge. I wadded up my paper bag and threw it at him, hitting him square in the chest. Someone seated nearby laughed. Nate just stared at me, too surprised to speak. I picked up my sandwich and threw it, and the the open carton of milk followed right after.

"Hey!" he cried, standing up. I ran out of the lunchroom.

He caught up with me outside, maybe only because I'd stopped running. There was no place to go.

"Allie! What are you so mad about?" He stood there, milk splashed on his face and soaked into his shirt.

"How could you tell your father stuff about me?" I yelled, overcome by the feeling that it wasn't enough to say about

203

how I felt. And I was worried that it wasn't enough of a reason to have Nate standing there in that condition.

"I told him what we did, cutting school to talk over some trouble you've had," Nate said slowly. "I told him your dad isn't a man to listen to reason and that he wouldn't understand about detention."

"You didn't tell him"—my face went hot with embarrassment—"about my hair?"

"No!"

"He didn't think anything of your friend being a girl?"

That stopped him. I could see he'd been prepared for my questions to be like the first one, did you tell him this or that, after hearing it. Finally, he said, "He wanted to know if you were nice."

I didn't have anything to say to that.

"Of course, that was before I knew you throw things."

I didn't know whether to laugh or cry. "Mrs. Reardon is likely to tell him otherwise. You know what she thinks we were doing that morning?"

Nate pulled me up against the door and when I expected him to hug me, he took me by the arms and said, "When we go back inside, I'm going to go sit someplace else. Near the teacher who's on duty. This is all going to get back to the office, anyway. We might as well have some say in what they think is going on."

"And tomorrow?"

"I'll eat outside somewhere. Then in a couple of days they won't notice when you aren't in the lunchroom, either. If we stay on the other side of the building, they'll never see our comings and goings."

"How long?" We weren't walking home together, now we weren't eating lunch together. Things couldn't get much worse.

"You should be able to meet me on Monday. They'll have gone on to something else."

Right or wrong, that's what we did.

During the week, whispers followed me wherever I went.

2 0 4

Boys gave me knowing looks, then passed remarks to get a pat on the back from their buddies. Girls who never spoke to me before would say "Hi," then collapse into a fit of giggles as they walked on. The teachers' puzzled expressions had given way to embarrassed glances as they came to conclusions about the whispering. But no one questioned the idea that we were each going home for lunch.

On Friday, Nate and I were almost late getting back to school.

"Nick of time," Eddie Sickles warned.

I ignored him.

"Had a heavy date for lunch?"

One of the other boys heard him and snickered.

"I read a great story today," Eddie said, poking someone else. "You be int'rested in reading a really good story? For maybe twenty-five cents?"

That boy looked at Eddie like the snail he was, but he laughed anyway. His eyes traveled over me as he turned to face the front of the room. The teacher asked Eddie if he had anything interesting to tell the class.

Eddie didn't have anything to say.

I kept my eyes on my homework.

I'd known the whole mess with the stories wouldn't be forgotten right away. But I had no idea it would keep on getting worse. Twice during the next week, Eddie Sickles and some of his friends walked behind me on the way to class and called me a whore. Girls stopped talking to me, as if being seen with me would contaminate them.

Soon there was talk that I was pregnant.

It was too humiliating to tell Nate what was going on. I consoled myself with the thought that it was my imagination that the whole school was talking about me, or else Nate would know. The kids in my classes would get tired of this soon. They'd go on to something, or someone, else. That's what I was telling myself as I got into line for the bus on Friday afternoon.

I felt someone's breath on the back of my neck. "Got a date tonight, sweet stuff?"

2 0 5

It was one of the older boys who rode the bus.

"You know what I think that is on top of your head?" he went on. "Pussy hair. That's what it looks like—"

I decided to take the shortcut home. I'd be there in time to help with dinner. It had started to snow, a first snow of the season breath of snow, falling so slowly you had to keep watching to know it wasn't just hanging in the air. Something about it made me feel better. I was halfway home when I saw Nate. He was leaning against the tree we so often sat under. It was like something out of a story, I thought, finding him there.

He heard me coming, and seeing me, looked away very quickly.

I thought, *he's going to tell me he doesn't like me anymore.* "Nate?"

"I thought you had to ride the bus," he muttered, glancing at me from the corner of his eye.

"I missed it," I lied. His hair was a mess, like he'd run his hand through it over and over.

"I wish you'd picked a different day to miss it."

He turned his head so I saw the ugly raised cut over his eye and the swelling around his mouth. There was blood all over his shirt. I wanted to say something, touch him, help. But I thought of how much Tucker would hate that. "What did you do? Get into a fight?"

"Not only that," he said sheepishly. "I didn't win."

"Who?"

"Bear."

"Oh, Nate. He doesn't count. He's not human."

Nate laughed at that, and though I hadn't meant it to be funny, I was glad. But the laughter faded fast, and he began to look worried. "Are you going to be in trouble when you get home?"

"I don't know."

"Come on. If we walk fast, you might be able to say the bus was late."

"I don't think we can make it that fast."

"We can try."

"Why are you rushing me home?" I was all but running to keep up.

"Why?! Because I worry about you."

"That's nice."

"No, it's not. Especially on Friday night it's not." He dragged me along behind him. "It'll be Monday morning before I can stop worrying again."

"Oh, Nate."

"Don't you dare."

"What?" I had to run to keep up with Nate's long legs.

"Tell me that's such a nice thing to say."

I wouldn't have said it right out, but that's exactly what I'd been thinking. "Tell me about the fight?"

"I did."

"Tell me what it was about."

"You have enough."

"Was it about me?" That cramped-up feeling in my stomach was getting to be all too familiar. "It had to be about me or you'd say."

"Look," he said, stopping short. "Somebody's likely to say something to you anyway. You have to try not to be upset."

"All right." I sounded choked as I tried to catch my breath.

"Bear told me . . . exactly what he said was, 'Hear your girlfriend's pregnant.'" Nate made his voice slow and shuffly like Bear's.

"Oh."

"So I said, 'No, she's not.'" Nate's voice was firm, telling me he knew that was true.

"And he hit you?" I whispered.

"Then he said—this is where he got ugly—he said, 'I didn't say it's yours. I just said she's pregnant.'" Nate shrugged. "So I hit him."

"You hit him first?"

"I'm glad I did. 'Course, he about pounded me to death after. This cut"—he pointed to his eyebrow—"bled so much he took pity on me and stopped. He probably thought he was leaving me to die," he finished, trying to make a joke out of it.

2 0 7

"I'm sorry. It's my fault, Nate."

"How do you figure that?" He started walking again.

"I didn't tell you. I should've."

"Tell me what?" He stopped again. "I know you aren't pregnant, Allie. We had this conversation before, and I'm not going to make an ass out of myself again."

So I told him the whole miserable thing, about the stories and Prissy going into my locker and Eddie Sickles. All of it. But I told it with this big smile on my face because of what he'd said. He had faith in me. I just love Nate.

"I wish you'd told me right off, Allie." He slipped an arm around my shoulders so we could walk close together.

"I didn't know how bad it would get."

"The only thing to do is get those two stories back, even if the whole school's read them by now. They can't keep going around."

"How can I do that?"

"I can. I think I can."

"Don't get into any more fights," I pleaded.

"Tell me one thing. In these stories, is there anything about . . . ?" His arm tightened around my shoulders.

"What?"

"I mean, where did you hear about," he lowered his voice, "you know, going down. You know."

"From Prissy," I whispered loudly.

"Oh, no," he said aloud.

"I swear. She claims she saw her brother do it."

"Allie!" Nate looked a little sick at the idea.

"I'm not making it up!"

"Oh, God."

"Tell me one thing?" I asked, imitating his lowered voice.

"Yeah?"

"What does it mean?"

He looked at me straight on, then let a smile show. It was a rather crooked one because of the swelling. "You really don't know?"

"Don't get funny, Nate."

"I'm not telling you," he said, shaking his head.

"You thought I did it! Now you won't tell me what it is?"

"Nope." He gave me a teasing look. "I will tell you one thing."

"What's that?"

"It's delicious," he said, licking his lips like Sylvester looking at Tweety. He could only do one side. It looked like it hurt. And it wasn't particularly informative.

"Then you've done it?"

He laughed out loud.

"What's funny?" I knew I'd missed something, but I couldn't figure out what it was.

"Oh, no," was all he would say with this big grin, and he'd look at me and say, "oh, no," again.

"Nate! What is it?"

He wouldn't tell me. He kept chuckling over it, though, as he walked me home in the snow. I didn't mind. In a way, it was one of the best times we'd had so far. It made me think of staying overnight with my cousin Dolly and talking in the darkness, long after the grown-ups had gone to bed. It was like that. But better.

7

I DON'T think Crystal missed Christmas. You can't miss what you don't know you're supposed to have. It was Mom who felt the lack of a tree and presents, complaining that this Christmas Crystal was old enough to wait for Santa, to open her own presents, to. . . . On and on. She started in on that a week before Christmas, first with a comment to me, then bringing it up at dinner. Each evening, she had more to say than the night before. Daddy Jim's face went flat and quiet, but he didn't answer back. He'd been none too inclined to start trouble since he'd had to pick me up at the police station.

The good thing was, Nate got back one story, the one I'd written during the summer, about Regina. The bad thing was, vacation began. It would be next year before we'd see each other again. We stretched out the walk home as much as we dared, stopping often to open our coats and press our bodies together. We were more than halfway home when he caught me up against a tree for another kiss. When he let his hips slide against mine, I could feel how much he was holding back, how much he wanted more.

"Do you know," he whispered, "that we could do it like this, against a tree? You could wrap your legs around—I'm sorry." He buried his burning face in my hair. "I'm sorry. I don't know how that came out."

I was astonished. My curiosity was only whetted by the picture his words drew.

"Let me take you home before I get myself in big trouble," he said, stepping away.

I pulled him back. "Will you miss me?"

"Miss you?" His eyes grew wide. "Allie, don't play with me. Not now."

"I don't mean to. I just wonder—" I hesitated, "who you do that with."

He looked startled, then he grinned. The grin turned into a laugh as he sort of danced away, pleased as could be.

"Nate."

"Yeah?" When I didn't say anything else, he came back to put his arms around me. "There's no one right now."

"What are you grinning about?"

"What you said. It's nice to hear."

"What is?"

"That you . . ." He gave up and kissed me again.

The first day, my mood soared high whenever I remembered that last afternoon with Nate. And plunged satisfyingly into a heavyhearted gloom when I thought of the long days that stretched ahead of me. Then I began to realize that missing Nate wasn't the only problem I had. Christmas was coming. Bad enough we weren't sharing in it, but Mom kept harping on that fact, not just at dinner but every time Daddy Jim would show his face. It was the first time I'd had occasion to realize the fighting didn't stop when I was in school.

Mom kept at Daddy Jim unmercifully, finding and using the words she'd held in for so many months. By the end of the second day, she only had to open her mouth and the vein in his forehead would leap out, measuring the tread of his heartbeat as it began to race. My mouth went dry. My mother went on and on unheeding, her face working as she ran down his faults as a father and a man, her eyes screwed up against the blows her mouth invited.

The next day was no better.

Daddy Jim got up quietly, leaving his Christmas dinner half-eaten. He didn't come back that night. I didn't sleep much, thinking that Daddy Jim couldn't take much more, but to tell you the truth, I didn't know how things could be any worse than we'd already seen.

I slept late the next day, then stayed in bed long after I was awake. Daddy Jim came home late in the afternoon. He was drunk. Loudly, gleefully drunk. Carrying a bottle of something not half-finished. My mother must have heard him coming down the road, because she was in the kitchen before me. Her hair was wild, standing out at the back of her head as if something nested there. She wore an old nightgown, stained and gray. "Stay in bed," she hissed and pulled the bedroom door closed.

Crystal's chin crumpled immediately. I searched hurriedly for her bottle, hoping she hadn't finished it. She refused it, sitting down hard in her crib and letting out an uncertain cry. I dashed for the closet, snatching the box that held a prickly bear, dressed in green cloth pants and a leather vest, complete with a tiny pipe.

Crystal reached for it, paying no attention to Daddy Jim's singing or the accusations my mother hurled at him. I stood with my back against the door, hands shaking and sweating, knowing this was going to be bad. My mother's voice grew angrier and more daring as Daddy Jim told her he wasn't drunk, his voice at once cajoling and challenging.

Standing there, I could see this could be all there was, today, tomorrow, on and on. Daddy Jim wouldn't get better, no matter how much my mother wanted it. Each time was worse, no matter that I couldn't imagine it. This wasn't the stuff of stories, with endings that cautioned you against Going Too Far before marriage. Or warned you of God's final punishment should you stray too far afield. God hadn't laid any restraining hand on Daddy Jim.

Things had reached fever pitch in the kitchen, interrupted by a single squawk from my mother followed by a scuffling noise. I pulled the door back to peer through a hairline crack. Daddy Jim held my mother in a close embrace, her arm twisted behind her as he forced the neck of a bottle into her mouth. Liquid drooled down the side of her face as she fought against swallowing it, choking and crying together. I stayed there, somehow less horrified to watch than to listen to it through the door.

It went on and on, but that bottle never seemed to empty, even held straight up and down as it was. When I thought to look, there was almost none on the floor. Daddy Jim laughed, louder and more reckless than I'd ever heard it. I looked at him and his eyes bored into mine, freezing my hand to the doorknob.

He knew I was there and watching.

Like a child playing at something he shouldn't he laughed again. Like a child who fears no punishment, he set the bottle down on the table with a bang. He pressed his mouth over my mother's, moaning as he smeared the liquor over both their faces. Forcing her further and further back until I thought she'd break, he lifted eyes shining with delight in finding an audience as he put a hand to her breast and squeezed. She cried out, but he only laughed and crushed her breast until she screamed.

I shut the door, not caring that he heard, and ran to the other side of the room. I heard my own breathing, fast and catchy, like I'd been running a long time. I didn't like to hear it; I put my hands over my mouth and pressed, hoping to hold it in, and with it the scream that wanted to echo my mother's. I was shaking so hard my teeth clacked together. I don't know how long I stood there.

The fighting had moved into the living room, and for a time, seemed to be dying down.

Crystal had slipped into a fitful sleep, clutching the prickly bear so tightly that its fur was pressed into the soft skin of her cheek. It had grown dark outside, and I tucked Crystal's blanket around her.

Now my mother's voice had grown louder, raging at Daddy Jim in a way she'd never before dared. I went back to the door and opened it, wider this time because it didn't seem to matter, an opening that I stood back from. I could see clearly into the living room where my mother stood facing Daddy Jim. Listening, I wondered if she'd swallowed much of the nearly empty bottle that Daddy Jim now tipped up and poured into his own throat. She had never been so inflamed, so crazed, that she wasn't afraid of him. He offered it to her, laughing, and she threw out her cast-covered arm, knocking the bottle out of his hand. She took no notice, but continued her tirade until he threw her to the floor.

Terrified, but unable to do any different, I left the bedroom and ran to the woodstove. I grabbed my mother's big iron frying pan and pressed myself to the wall, my heart hammering in my chest. I was hidden where I stood. Before I went around that stove I had to be very certain I could raise that pan against Daddy Jim.

"Take it back," he said, not much louder than his speaking voice.

"You're less," my mother screamed back hoarsely. "You're nothing, nothing, nothing."

"Take it back," he roared, and I could feel it vibrate in my ears, all but drowning out the sudden squeal from my mother. I stepped haltingly away from the wall, starting to cry, seeing myself defeated before I'd begun.

"I'll show you, you bitch. You want a man, you'll get a man!" I heard his buckle clink and the crack of his belt as it snapped free. I gripped the pan tightly, so tightly I could feel it in my neck, but I couldn't make my feet move.

"Leave me alone," my mother yelled, fear finally edging into her voice.

"No, bitch, you asked for it, you're going to get it," his voice cracked with the strain on his throat. "Animal? I'll give you whatever you want!"

There was a struggle at the doorway, and Daddy Jim laughed nastily, calling out, "Here pussy pussy pussy, come on sweet little pussy." I pressed myself back into the corner as my mother scrambled into the kitchen on her hands and knees. Daddy Jim caught at her, laughing and calling, "Pussy, pussy?" laughing all the while but looking like he hated her. When she tried to pull away, crying and tearing at the floor, he dropped on top of her, pinning her to the floor with an arm across her shoulders.

"Pussywannit?" Daddy Jim's words ground through his teeth as he tugged at her nightgown. My hands were clamped tightly, helpless, sweating streams down the black handle of the frying pan as Daddy Jim crouched bare-legged over my mother, his shirt open and hanging free, his coarse voice muttering foul things until he finally succeeded in pushing her nightgown up past her waist.

"All right, bitch, here it comes," he yelled, dropping on her and pushing, grunting up against her, his face red and redder as he swore and called her names. "Don't fight me, bitch, you got it coming. It's a long time coming," he panted, and my mother reached out for the table leg, trying to pull herself away, maybe trying to pull it down on top of him.

"No, bitch," he snarled and snatched at her wrist, but my mother had her fingers locked around the leg so tightly that he had to tug and tug, and finally he dragged himself up over her and pulled her hand away, slowly, slowly, her fingernails so deeply embedded in the paint that they tore it away, leaving bare wood exposed. His breathing was harsh and mixed with bits of his voice as he twisted her arm over her back. My mother cried loudly, an angry, helpless sound that gasped for

2 1 6

breath as Daddy Jim raised himself and began to swear again, "Bitch bitch bitch." He tried to stop her writhing with pressure on her arm. When she continued to fight him, he set his knee into the back of hers, ripping a scream out of her. "Ha," he yelled, releasing her arm only to grab her around the hips, leaning over her to mutter into her ear as she sobbed, gasping.

But not before I saw.

In that instant that he straightened and his shirt fell back, I saw the angry red thing that hid as he bent to tell my mother what he was going to do. He laughed and reared back, baring it to me again, and with his fingers twisted in my mother's flesh, he stabbed it into her, ignoring her shriek of pain; he wrenched her body back and forth, stabbing into her again and again, his lips stretched back over his teeth, straining as he spat, "Animal bitch animals do it bitch like this bitch you want to talk bitch animals," a litany that ran beneath my mother's groaning cries, together with a high keening wail that I finally understood to belong to me, my own voice that caught sharply as he pushed her further away and it sprang out, an angry red glistening rod that he grabbed and forced into her, ramming into her harder and faster as he groaned loudly, his eyes rolling back into his head.

In that moment I understood Nate's fear. That could happen to me. My hands loosened around the handle of the frying pan, and it dropped to the floor. Daddy Jim's eyes snapped open and he stared at me, first in surprise, then slyly as his face twisted into an evil grin.

I ran.

I reached the door and fumbled with the knob, my hands were shaking so badly, and when I got it open at last, I ran without thinking across the frozen earth, aware of but ignoring the way the cold cut through my pajamas and the icy bite of the wind as I left the shelter of the house. The lights were on all over Mrs. Kelly's house, warm yellow beacons in the night, and I wondered as I ran toward it how it could look like a fortress, showing so welcoming a face to those coming out of the darkness. I ran, faster and faster, the cold burning in my lungs. I could see the Christmas tree through one window, blinking colored lights surprised to see me running with the howling of the wind. I could see Mrs. Kelly, sitting in a chair near the window, her head nodding as she spoke to someone, maybe Mr. Kelly, who was home for Christmas, and she tossed back her head and laughed. I saw but couldn't hear. I ran.

"Allie!"

He passed me and pulled up right in front of me. He was barefoot too, but he'd stopped to put on pants, his shirt still hanging open.

"Allie, I won't hurt you."

He sounded like the Daddy Jim of so many years ago, a voice that carried love and concern wrapped in words I wanted to hear. He shivered with cold.

"Allie. Come back now. You weren't meant to see. I'm sorry."

That voice brought fresh tears to my eyes, longing tears that wanted to believe him.

"I'm sorry. You don't know that, Allie, but it's true. I do a lot of things I'm sorry for."

But this was the Daddy Jim of now and I shouldn't be fooled.

"I won't hurt you," he whispered, his words barely reaching me like the hand he stretched out.

I shuddered suddenly, feeling the cold and the need to run.

"Don't, Little, don't," he said, pulling a sweet pet name out of memory.

He blocked my path. He'd caught up to me so easily, how could I outrun him now?

"I won't hurt you, Little. Look. I'll show you," he said, reaching out a slow hand to touch mine. I was tensed to bolt, but he didn't grab, didn't jump, and I shivered again violently.

"This is how we'll walk," he said gently, grasping my ring finger lightly between his thumb and forefinger.

I watched as he drew me closer slowly, and when I thought to run he stepped a long step back.

"See, I'm not even close to you."

Our arms were stretched out fully between us and we stood there, saying nothing. I looked at Mrs. Kelly as she shook her head, laughing again her merry laugh that never ceased to make me stop and listen, and then she rose from her chair, and all that could see me were the winking blinking colored lights, winking blinking ever less, calming as they saw how gently Daddy Jim held my finger as he turned me slowly back toward our house.

I wanted to scream.

"Easy, Allie."

All that came from my throat was a garbled sound and a sour taste.

"I won't hurt you, I promise."

When he stepped back, a small step, there was a slight tug on my finger.

I stepped forward, a small step.

"See? Not so bad," he said encouragingly.

He stepped back, inches.

I stepped forward, only inches.

"You remember, Little, how I used to hold your hand and walk you home when you got off the school bus that first year?"

I stared at him.

"I carried your finger paintings, your colored-in papers, your Kleenex roses."

He stepped back.

I stepped forward.

That was how we walked home. By inches, Daddy Jim leading me with words I didn't dare believe. Our hands linked by one thin finger, clearly visible in the pale moonlight. I couldn't take my eyes away. Only as we reached the back steps did the fear begin to rise again.

"Don't run, Allie. I won't hurt you. Aren't you cold?" He kept talking, a comfortingly worried note running through his voice. "We have to go inside so I can see to your mother." When I said nothing, he stepped up, coaxing me along. "I only hurt her with my knee, Allie. You know that."

My throat tightened painfully.

"The rest. It's only what men and women do together. You know that."

He tugged gently on my finger.

I stepped up.

"The fight. It was all because I was drinking. You know that."

When he pushed open the back door, I had to go in. I was shivering so badly Daddy Jim helped me through the door. My teeth chattered, rattling in my head until the pain stretched over my skull like a hair net. The kitchen was warm.

I went to stand by the woodstove, trying to soak in its heat. It was strange how much the same the room felt to me, as if it had been the scene of a bad dream, the kitchen itself in no way changed.

Except for the bare stripes in the paint of the table leg.

My mother came back into the kitchen, limping, dragging her rocking chair. "Get to bed," she snapped. "That's where I told you to stay."

I went, not knowing what else there was to do. I shivered beneath my blankets, my feet burning with the cold. When their voices started, low and coaxing from Daddy Jim, short and sharp from my mother, I pulled the pillow over my head so I wouldn't have to listen.

I don't know how many hours I lay there shivering. I just know it was an awful long time before I was warm. And then it didn't quite reach to my hands or feet. When I came out from under the pillow, it was quiet in the kitchen, but for the creak of the rocker on the floorboards. I got up to sit on my feet to warm them and tucked my fingers into my armpits. I was sitting like that when I heard it.

Tap.

Fear bolted through me like lightning.

Tap.

I sprang out of bed and opened the window, thinking only at the last instant to be quiet. "Go away!"

"Merry Christmas," he whispered, already working a tissue-wrapped cylinder through a hole in the screen.

I snatched it through. "Go away!"

"Allie? The lights are always on—"

"Don't come back," I whispered close to the screen. I shut the window as the bedroom door opened.

"Allie? What are you doing in here?"

"I needed some air," I answered, letting the gift hide in the fold of my pajama leg.

"Seems to me you've had enough air for one night," Mom said. "Get back to bed." She shut the door firmly. Then she opened it again. "Don't even think of leaving this house again. Don't you pick up a pen or paper," she said, her voice cracking on the last word. "What happened here is to stay here. Do you understand me?"

I nodded, breathless.

She shut the door again.

I stood in the darkness, breathing easier as I saw Nate leave the side of the window and walk quickly away. An explanation would have to wait.

Something rustled in the darkest corner of the room.

Terror held me rooted to the floor. But there was nothing there, I thought, no one could have come in without my knowing it. The sound came again, and I wanted to scream. I turned to face it only because I was too afraid of not knowing, too afraid of a hand reaching out unseen.

My heart lurched. Crystal stood there, a tiny frightened fairy figure who'd been hiding in the corner. "Beh," she said, showing it to me and snatching it quickly back behind her.

"You can keep it, Crystal," I whispered, tears starting in my eyes. "It's your bear, now." I took her into my bed, covering us both. "Santa came, Crystal," I said and handed her the tissue-wrapped gift. "Merry Christmas."

She accepted it, turning it over and over in her hands, not understanding. I reached out to tear a bit of the paper. She tried it, giggled, and tore it some more. They were candy sticks, and as Crystal and I lay there, sucking sweetly, I wished I could have gone with him. My throat hurt with the need to cry. Feeling sorry for myself. Missing him. Wanting something. Anything. Different.

Daddy Jim was on his best behavior the next morning, making breakfast and talking at Crystal and me like it was Saturday morning, all we had to do was spend our quarter, smile, everything would be okay. He was the only one who thought so.

Crystal picked over her cereal, sticking wet Cheerios all over her tray and finally spilling the milk. Mom, who'd spent the night in the rocker, watched the whole thing like it was some kind of picture show, never missing a beat as she rocked back and forth. After a glance at her, Daddy Jim mopped up the mess without a word, his moustache quivering with distaste.

Mom stayed in the rocker most of that day, keeping Crystal right next to her. If I went to the bathroom, she picked up the baby and found some reason to be there with me. When she took Crystal into the bedroom to change her diaper, she called me to come along. Saturday mornings were long gone, and by midafternoon Daddy Jim had gotten the point. He went down to the basement.

Mom had me heat some canned soup for lunch and she made panbread and bacon for dinner, falling back on the kind of quick cooking she used during tornado weather. She sometimes looked to be in a world of her own, but all it took to shatter it was a sound from the basement.

When Daddy Jim came upstairs, he was drinking. Mom stayed in the bedroom with Crystal and me, where we sat listening to the clink of bottle against glass. Daddy Jim muttered to himself, then called things in to us and getting no response, yelled at no one in particular about the bad treatment he got from his family. Mom slept with me that night, though I'd hardly claim either of us slept all that well.

She continued to keep us all together over the next few days. She hardly ever uttered a word. Although Daddy Jim made no move toward any one of us, he began to play with my mother, cat and mouse. He didn't come to the table at mealtimes, but called in to us from the living room, asking were we enjoying our dinner. Once he came into the kitchen while we sat frozen and took the panbread from the table, carrying it down to the basement. My mother said nothing, as if she hadn't noticed; just got up and made peanut butter sandwiches which she made us eat in bed.

In fact, Daddy Jim spent more time upstairs than he had for some weeks. He drank steadily and after a couple of days he gave up trying to talk to us, lowering his eyebrows and retreating into silence. The smoking seemed to ease off, but he didn't shave, and it's my guess he didn't wash either. It was like we all had a fever, miserable and lying abed, waiting for it to go away.

On New Year's Day I laid on my bed, trying to read a book I'd found in my closet. My mother had gone to the kitchen to make a bottle for Crystal, watered-down juice since the milk was gone. I heard the rumble of Daddy Jim's voice and the smash of glass in the sink. I jumped up.

"You have to get these children some food," my mother was screaming. "You can't make us go on this way!"

"You telling me something, woman?" Daddy Jim's voice was deep with a threat I could only guess at.

Mom was quiet immediately and when she spoke a moment later, it was with a meekness that caught me by surprise. "We need milk. There's no food in the house."

"Why's that?"

Mom stumbled over her words, then answered, "You haven't provided us with any."

"And why would that be?" he said, standing over her now. She cringed against the sink. "It wouldn't be that I'd be worried about being arrested, would it?"

My mother shook her head.

Daddy Jim smiled, a shockingly gentle smile. "I didn't really worry about that, Nora," he said, cupping one hand around her face. My heart ached to see that hand, so familiar and yet so often raised against her, now so sweet in its intention. My mother raised her face to his. "If you were to do that to me, Nora," he said in a voice too soft, "I'd never forgive you."

My mother's eyes widened, but she didn't make a sound.

"You know that, don't you, Nora?" His grip had tightened on my mother's face but she managed to nod her head. Daddy Jim smiled that gentle smile.

"I couldn't say a word against you, Jim," my mother said as he released her. "You don't have to try to scare me."

But my mother continued to sleep with me.

When the morning to go back to school finally arrived, Nate was waiting for me at the bus stop, knee deep in snow and with a new bright blue cap on his head.

"Okay, I can see it on your face," he said. "Just make all the jokes you're going to make and get it out of your system."

"Where'd you get it?"

"My mother gave it to me for Christmas. She knitted it, and I have to wear it."

"Then I better not say anything."

"What happened?" he asked as we started to walk to school, my hand and his deep in his pocket for warmth.

"Nothing."

"C'mon, Allie."

"My mom was in the kitchen. I was afraid she'd hear you."

"Don't come back? You expected her to be in the kitchen the whole vacation?" he said, exasperated. "I knew you were in trouble."

I slipped my hand into his. "Thanks."

"For what?" he said, giving in.

"Not coming back."

"Are you all right?"

"Yes."

"You don't want to talk about it."

"Not right now."

8

Iᴛ wasn't a good day. Easier than the ones that came before it maybe, but not good. The stories and the sniggering hadn't stopped. Two of my teachers let me know I wasn't doing passing work in their classes. When Nate met me at lunch, he said it didn't seem likely that he'd get the last story back. Whoever had it had as good as put it under their pillow.

Mom was in my room when I got home. She didn't look to have moved all day. Crystal lay exhausted in her crib, needing a dry diaper and seized every so often with a hic-cupy shudder, as if she'd been crying a good part of the afternoon. I took care of Crystal, and Mom roused herself to make some dinner.

Except for dinner, we were there all evening. I couldn't

write. I didn't feel like doing homework. I played with Crystal. Daddy Jim stayed in the kitchen.

By the middle of the week I was hurting. Boys and girls alike made wisecracks of one kind or another, not caring who heard. I became the subject of discussion for the teachers now that they knew of the talk among the students. They met each other in the hall between classes for a conversation that stopped when they noticed me.

The tension in Nate didn't fade, although he tried to hide it. It showed in the way he held onto me just that much longer after we kissed. And in the sidelong looks he gave me when he thought I didn't see. No one said anything about me, at least not out loud, when I was with him. He began to be late to his own classes in an effort to walk me to most of mine.

I'd stopped taking baths with Crystal when Daddy Jim took to spending his evenings in the kitchen. Now that school had started, Mom brought a pan of water into the bedroom and we washed one at a time, the other standing by the door. It was the only effort she made once I got home, leaving me to care for Crystal and make something for dinner.

Finally, I got home Thursday afternoon to find my mother crouched on my bed with tears running down her face. Daddy Jim wasn't at home that I could tell. "Mom, what is it?"

"I almost told her, Allie."

"Who?"

"Mary Kelly. She came here this afternoon, saying she hadn't seen a hair of us since she couldn't remember when." My mother trembled. "It was all I could do to find some pleasant thing to say."

Finding myself helpless to find something to say as well, I fell back on politeness. "Did you ask her in?"

My mother shook her head, not noticing anything odd in that question. "What would have happened to us, Allie, if I had spoken?"

"You look like you're being chased, Allie." Nate had been at me for several minutes now. "That's why everyone's giving you such a hard time. You're not fighting back."

I sighed tiredly, giving up on my lunch. I stuck it back in the bag.

"You have to ask somebody for help. Somebody who can make people listen."

"Nate—"

"Don't tell me you can't. You have to!"

"Let me get through today, okay? It's Friday."

"I would, Allie, if I thought Saturday would be better."

"Please."

"All right. But you have to talk to someone soon."

"Soon." That was a word I'd begun to use often, trying to avoid these talks. By the next week, Nate's "someone" had turned into someone more specific.

"You could talk to my dad. Or my mom, even, and she'll tell my dad what you can't."

"Stop it!"

"You can't handle this on your own."

I began to cry, knowing Nate would give in. For the moment. He wouldn't be put off much longer. So it was a relief of sorts when, a few days later, the principal and Mrs. Kelly came to take me out of class.

"You have to come home, Allie."

"What did he do to her?" I didn't really want to know. I asked only to have my worst fear confirmed.

"Crystal's fine," Mrs. Kelly said nervously. "Your momma's seeing the doctor."

"Will she be okay?"

"I can't rightly say, Allie. She's beat up pretty bad."

I cried. I'd like to say I didn't. But I stood in the hallway, clinging to Mrs. Kelly, and cried. The principal closed the classroom door right away, but I know everyone heard.

"I found Crystal in the road," Mrs. Kelly told me, crying along with me by then. "Wearing nothing more than a sweater and a diaper. She was just wandering along and calling out for I don't know who." The principal was moving us toward the stairs, making sympathetic noises that didn't ring true. "I thought to take her back to your momma and that's when I found her, lying in the snow in the strip of land between our houses. She must've been on her way to me."

My mother was one long bruise, so it was no surprise that Daddy Jim had been arrested once more. The doctor let her come home "against his better judgment," he said as he looked Crystal and me over for signs of a beating. And since she was already there, he took off Mom's cast, about a week overdue. Her arm was shrunken and scabby looking, the patches of flaking skin adding to her general appearance of mistreatment.

I knew my mother was humiliated. In a way I shared her feeling, but above all, I was glad someone had taken the situation in hand. So it was with certain misgivings that I nodded agreement when Mom told the doctor that Daddy Jim didn't mean to do these things, that he had only the best intentions toward his family. And it was with considerable relief that I saw that the doctor would not be swayed by my mother's pleadings.

Late in the evening a deputy came by, an Officer Sickles as it turned out, to say there were further charges being made against Daddy Jim. He'd hit a police officer. He would be held in Des Moines until his court date. What it meant, in the end, was that he wouldn't be coming home in a few days like my mother had expected. Officer Sickles had the same "bite you as soon as look at you" eyes that Eddie had, leading me to believe that the name was more than a coincidence. I wasn't unhappy to see him go. Mom took the news quietly enough while he was there, but when he left, she crumpled into a chair. "How bad will it be when he comes home?"

I had nothing to say to that. I wanted to go to bed. I slept soundly, and alone, for the first night in weeks.

In the morning, Nate knew Daddy Jim had been arrested. "How's your mom taking it?"

"I don't know. She cried at first. Now she's sitting around like she's waiting for a bus. I don't know that she'll think to feed Crystal today."

"It'll get better."

"I guess."

"Things will get better at school, too. You'll get your work done, your grades will improve, people will stop talking about you, about everything."

"They have something new, now."

"It won't last long."

"We'll see." That's what I said, knowing each day was longer than the one before it. But it was what I wanted to hear. It was what I wanted to believe. Still . . .

"Nate. How did you know?"

He looked at me quickly. "I didn't say a word to my dad, Allie, not since the detention. But he always hears when somebody gets arrested or—"

"Nate!"

"He was standing in the hallway talking to the doctor, Allie. He didn't know until then that it was your stepdaddy in question. And he didn't know I was anywhere around to listen."

"He knows now."

"He understands, Allie. Doesn't it help to know that?"

It didn't. But the talk didn't flow so freely in front of Nate again. Because it came as a surprise when, about a week later, Eddie Sickles came to school with something new to harp on. "Hear they're putting your daddy in the bughouse." I looked up, not so much because I'd understood what he said but because he had a particular tone of voice for talking to me.

"Look at this!" he hooted, pointing at me. "Are you in there? Yoo-hoo! I think she's visiting her daddy," Eddie went on, speaking to no one in particular. "He's in the looney bin, didja hear?"

That was when Mrs. Green told him to sit down and be quiet. I couldn't pay attention to anything she had to say after that. I had little interest and no energy for schoolwork lately, thinking only of the time I could spend with Nate. At home, taking care of Crystal, I waited for the occasional evening visit of one of my uncles or my grandparents, feeling slighted that I missed the more frequent daytime visits. I hadn't been able to improve my grades. The teachers had stopped talking to me

229

about it, stopped encouraging me to do better. Not that they were quite prepared to say I was stupid, the way most of my classmates seemed to think, but I was definitely being looked upon as a lost cause. So when Mrs. Green called on me and discovered I hadn't heard the question, she got angry enough to send me to the office.

I didn't go there. I walked home.

By then my mother's question had become, "What are we going to do, Allie? How will we live until he comes home?"

I'd given the matter some thought lately, and although it hurt me to think of leaving Nate, I said, "We could stay with Grandma Taylor. She said—"

"Allie! I'm a grown woman. I can't go live with my mother." She shook her head. "I could never go back to that."

"It wouldn't be like that! The little house is empty now."

"I don't want anyone saying they had to do for me because—" She began to cry. "I have to take care of us."

I wondered what more there was to suggest. I'd been pretty sure she'd be happy to be reminded of the little house. "Nate's mother works," I said finally.

"I have a baby to take care of, Allie. Just what do you think I'm going to do with her?"

One thing I know is this: when it's, first, useless to open your mouth and, second, likely to result in someone's taking offense at something you've said. Not a good combination if the someone is a grown-up. I decided to take a bath. A long, hot bath. I didn't know how long Daddy Jim would be gone, but I knew what use I intended to make of the time. When I went to bed, I felt better.

I woke from the dream fighting for breath. It was so clear, like something you see on a movie screen, the way I saw Mom and Crystal and me on the front porch, dressed up, family-portrait straight as we waved good-bye to Daddy Jim. He waved to us from a flat white truck, ambulance type, exactly the one I'd seen in a Daffy Duck cartoon, taking away a short, moustachioed character with big six-guns strapped around his chubby body. We didn't find it odd that the truck was a cartoon, or that Daddy Jim seemed happy to go, and we turned to go back into the house. Daddy Jim burst out of the front door, grinning a mad grin and brandishing a long knife. He stretched out his arm and cut my mother's throat. She fell without a sound, her throat slit like the bullpig that trampled one of Aunt Belle's children.

I served detention for leaving school early. That didn't bother me, but something else did. The teachers, the people in the office, all had a new attitude toward me. It made me think of the way the Girl Scout leader had said my mother's name. It seemed they thought our problems were over, now that Daddy Jim was gone, and in their opinion, we weren't showing ourselves capable of improving our circumstances. In the end, it didn't matter. They held me in particularly low regard.

Early in February I got home to find the house empty, a note from my mother on the table saying she'd gone with Mrs. Kelly. There was some relief on her face when she came home.

"We're all right for a while. We'll have money to eat, and we won't have to leave this house." She sank wearily onto the couch.

"Is Daddy Jim coming home?"

"He'll be well when he comes home, Allie," she said firmly.

"That place he's in—"

"He's wild when he's drinking. He won't get anything to drink there, and they'll see he's all right." She didn't seem so tired all of a sudden. "He'll stay until he doesn't hunger for it anymore. He won't be angry when he comes home, because he'll see how wrong he was," she said as she got up. "The doctor didn't say how long it would take—" She was moving around the kitchen with more energy than I'd seen in a long time. "Things will be like they always were. As soon as he gets better."

I nodded, knowing these were words she needed. They didn't make me feel any better.

"The doctor did say I couldn't visit for at least six weeks, so we know it'll be a long time. Three months maybe. Maybe more. What I was thinking, instead of— Well, I think I'll look for a job." She shifted some pots around noisily, waking Crystal, but she didn't seem to notice. "If I can find something in the evening, waitressing maybe, then you'll be here to see to the baby." She talked like that all evening, planning.

I went along with her, nodding and thinking about a long time without Daddy Jim. Maybe forever. I liked the sound of it.

It took another week, but Mom pulled herself together to go to work. She twisted her hair up in back the way Lisa sometimes wears hers. Dressed up, wearing my hooded coat instead of her old one, she looked entirely different than I had ever seen her. More than that, she was pretty again, a little tired or strained-looking, but pretty.

When she came home, she had a job as a cocktail waitress in a little place on the edge of Des Moines. She could ride back and forth with someone else who worked there. She dug up a black skirt and a white cotton blouse, hemming the skirt up till it was shorter than the ones she didn't like me to wear. I didn't say a word.

The first night, I played with Crystal long past her usual bedtime, putting off the moment when the house would be completely silent. It was no good. I couldn't sleep. Maybe it was the way that good dreams had of turning on me. Daddy Jim jumping out of corners to wield that knife, bad enough, but I never woke till my mother fell. Maybe it was just that Crystal and I were alone in the house. I went to bed at my usual time and lay awake till Mom got home. The next two nights, I got up after a while and wrote until it was almost time for her to come home. I got awfully sleepy in school.

Now it was Friday night, and I stayed up again. I was tired and almost falling asleep, right up until I turned the light off. Then I couldn't close my eyes.

Tap.

I sat up in bed.

Tap. Tap.

I crept over to the window, only half-believing.

Tap.

Nate leaned across the snow, piled high beneath my window, to knock, then straightened to wait on the icy path our feet had beaten into each fresh fall of snow. I opened the window, then pulled my pajamas up around my throat against the cold blast of air. "What are you doing out there?"

"Your mom's at work?"

"Yes."

"Can I come in?"

It took a moment to sink in. The decision was made when Nate let his teeth click together. I could feel a little smile twisting my mouth as I went to the kitchen and switched on the lamp. Nate might have made his teeth chatter on purpose, I knew. I didn't mind.

He brought the cold in with him. I pushed him toward the woodstove and then stood there, shivering in my pajamas. "This is great," he whispered, opening his jacket to let the heat in. His ears were red from the cold, and his hair, usually carefully combed to roll and dip low over his forehead, had blown messily off to one side. He ran his fingers through it and swept it back. "Maybe"—his eyes slid over me—"maybe you ought to put on a robe."

"I don't have one. I'll be warm in a minute." He nodded and took off his jacket. His eyes traveled over me again. "I'll get dressed," I whispered.

He shook his head. "Don't. It's nice. Sort of personal."

I was at a loss for anything to say. I just stood there looking back at him and stretching up on tiptoe.

"You have a checker game?"

I nodded. "I'll get it."

It was a good idea except that Nate won three games in a row. He sat cross-legged on the floor, grinning at me across the board. "I'll bring a Monopoly game tomorrow night," he said. "You got someplace to hide it?"

I eyed the board. He was going to beat me again. "I don't know how to play."

"You'll learn," he said in a firm voice.

233

"I'll find a place." I made a last-ditch effort to take one of his kings.

"Don't lean over like that, Allie. I can see right down the front of your pajamas."

We stared at each other, both of us with hot red faces. I didn't know how to act. I wasn't mad, exactly. Or embarrassed. "Why didn't you say something sooner?"

He shrugged.

"I'm tired of checkers," I said, clambering up onto the couch. He followed me, sitting at the other end.

"I couldn't see much."

"What does that mean?"

He slid across the couch. "Will you let me hold you?" We were both a little nervous. It was entirely different with me in pajamas. It took some getting used to. "I love you," Nate whispered.

"You never told me that before."

"Now seemed like a good time," he said with a laugh.

"I can see how you might think so."

But Nate's face had gone serious. "Tell me what happened, will you, Allie?"

But I didn't know what happened that day, and Nate asked what before that. I told him, which led to telling him what happened sometime earlier. Nate asked a couple of questions here and there, trying to place things that happened next to things we did together. It wasn't long before he knew everything. When I finished, he heaved a big sigh.

"Allie, I had no idea it was so bad."

"Me neither. Not till I said it all at once this way."

Nate was able to come over earlier Saturday night because his parents were visiting out of town. He did bring the Monopoly game, and we spread it out on the floor. I hardly heard a word about the rules, although he talked steadily. I'd been up too many nights waiting for Mom to come home, then getting up when Crystal cried in the morning. Mom had slept almost all of Saturday since I was home to watch Crystal. I spent the whole day thinking of being with Nate.

"Are you listening to me?" he asked, midway through his explanation.

"No."

Nate studied me for a while. I sat with my chin on my knees and stared back. "Pretty shirt," he said finally.

"Thanks. It was a birthday present."

"I'm going to miss the pajamas," he said with a grin.

I felt my cheeks go pink, but I didn't look away.

"We have to have something to do, Allie. If we sit around and neck, we're going to get ourselves into trouble."

I nodded. I agreed. Except at that moment in particular.

"What do you want to do?"

I smiled.

Nate groaned. And held out his arms. We moved up onto the sofa. Nate's kisses were what I'd waited all day for. But in fact I think we did more talking than kissing. "We have to take it easy," he whispered, "what with nobody knowing we're here alone."

"I know." I rolled onto my side so that my back rested against his chest.

"I don't want to grow you up too soon. My dad says—"

"Your dad!" My eyes sprang open.

"My mom and dad were sweethearts like us, from grade school even. Mom is four years younger than Dad, and he says it about drove him nuts, waiting for her to grow up."

"How old were they?"

"Mom was sixteen when they got married."

"Mine, too, the first time."

"Then she'd understand." I had my doubts about that, but before I had a chance to say so, he'd gotten up on an elbow and leaned over me. "I think—you won't tell anybody this, will you? Not Tucker or anybody?"

"No."

"My mom blushes so hard when Dad talks about waiting— I think they didn't. Couldn't."

"How long do you think they waited?" I asked, fitting myself snugly into the curve of his body.

235

"Mom and Dad?"

"Mm-hmm." I think I just wanted him to go on talking.

"She had to be fifteen, I guess. Maybe fourteen?" I smiled at the hopeful note in his voice.

"You won't get tired of waiting?" I wondered. "Or maybe you'll see somebody else when you're out with Tucker." My voice faded away. I was asking him to tell me something I didn't really want to hear.

"I guess it wouldn't hurt for one of us to know what they were doing."

"Nate!" I poked him with an elbow.

He kissed me roughly, tightening his arms around me. I had just about decided that was all the answer I was going to get when he spoke up again. "What I said to you that day, about being able to tell. It isn't exactly true."

"No?" All of a sudden I knew what he'd been telling me. "Are you saying you never—?"

"I'm not saying that," he said loudly. Then, in a lower voice, "It's just that I've never taken the time to look things over down there, and I don't know that I could be sure. Let's just leave it at that, okay?"

A grin started to crawl across my face. I tried to hold it in, I really did.

"Allie," he warned.

"I'm not saying a thing!"

"You'd hardly have to!"

"Why, then? Why'd you say you did it?"

He groaned. "I'm nearly sixteen, you know. Sixteen!" He looked at me expectantly.

I thought of Uncle Little Mike's hopeful "Next time will be *it.*" Uncle Little Mike was seventeen at the time. And Uncle Joe, sixteen, didn't even have a girl. For once, I kept my mouth shut. It was sort of nice to find that Nate wasn't so grown-up as I thought. It made it okay for me to be myself, just going along doing my best. More, I didn't have to worry that he was looking down on me from some higher place. He was stretching for it, same as me.

2 3 6

He leaned over and saw my smile. "You won't say anything to anybody, will you?"

"Don't be stupid." I cuddled up to him, happy with this new knowledge.

"Allie, wake up," Nate spoke into my ear, shaking me.

"What time is it?" I asked, waking up fast.

"Time for me to go home. You better get into your bed."

"Mom?"

"She should be here in another hour."

"Why didn't you wake me sooner? I slept all our time away."

He shrugged. "It was sort of nice." A smile slid over his face, but I don't think he knew it.

Nate wasn't in school on Monday. It was a long day, what with no one who'd talk to me and Eddie Sickles taking pot-shots at me in the hallway. I was tired enough to take the bus.

That was a big mistake.

Eddie Sickles got on the bus, riding home with a buddy. I was sitting up front so there was no way he could overlook me. It was probably because I was so tired that the sight of him brought tears to my eyes. I looked out the window to hide them as he came down the aisle.

"Hey, let's sit here."

"Nah, the best seats are in the back."

"Here," Eddie said, dropping heavily into the seat behind mine.

"Oh. Oh!" I knew Eddie was pointing me out. "Look, my friends all sit back there. You sure you wouldn't rather—"

"Siddown, will ya? You got a friend sitting here."

The other boy sat, sighing reluctantly.

Eddie was quiet till the bus started.

"Y'know what white trash is?"

"Huh? . . . No, I guess not."

"It's white niggers, if you know what I mean. Poor folk, living off other people's dollars—"

"Hey! Poor is what most people are."

"Yeah. That's so. But there's poor and there's poor. We ain't

2 3 7

talking God-fearing, hard-working poor. We're talking ain't worked last month, ain't looking to work next month poor. The state picks up the tab for 'em and they drink it down, letting their babies want for milk. Them babies grow up to do the same and bring more of the same into the world. White trash. Stupid and can't read, so they fall out of school and useless, so they can't get work, and drunk, so they beat up on their wife. . . ."

The hate poured out of Eddie's mouth, and the tears spilled down my face. I was mad at him, but I was furious with myself. Everyone was turning to listen to him as he got louder, and there was no way they wouldn't see the tears and think, *Yep, that's her, all right.*

"Look, Eddie, you don't know—"

"Sure, I do. My brother arrested her old man at least twice since we moved here. Always the same thing. He says it ain't bad enough her daddy's a drunk, but he's crazy besides—"

It was all one motion that I had nothing to do with, the books sliding off my notebook as I twisted around, the edge of the notebook catching him in the throat between his ear and his chin.

He hadn't seen it coming. Now he bent forward, coughing, choking, and his friend pounded him on the back, only at the last moment, putting his hand out to stop the notebook as it slammed down on the back of Eddie's head. Both boys yelled as it hit, then fell into the aisle along with me as the bus lurched to a stop.

"What's going on back here?" The bus driver dragged me up off the floor and pushed me back into my seat.

"She assaulted us," Eddie shouted.

"Find yourself a seat in the back, kid."

"Did you hear what—"

"Shut up!" the bus driver yelled. And then, in a more normal tone of voice, "You got a lot to learn, kid."

I didn't pick up my books; I couldn't stand the idea of bending over to pick them up with everyone watching and maybe Eddie finding something new to say. An older girl sitting across the aisle looked half-inclined to pick them up for me. I glared at her and she changed her mind. I got off at my stop, leaving them on the floor of the bus.

I walked to school the next morning, even though it meant I'd be late. Nate was waiting outside.

"Were you sick yesterday?" I asked.

"My mother thought I was coming down with something because I slept all day Sunday," he said, grinning. "She kept me home."

"I got in a fight."

"I thought you'd be on the bus this morning and—I heard. Your books are inside on the steps with mine."

"How'd you get them?"

"The bus driver was taking them into the office. I told him I'd give them to you."

So he'd heard it all from someone else again. I'd have liked, just once, for him not to have heard about me from someone else.

"You did the right thing, Allie."

"You think so."

"It was a little wild," he said with a grin. "They'll back off. After a while, someone will get the idea that they might have been wrong about you."

Later that week I was called down to the office. Mrs. Green said she thought I ought to take my books with me. I got there in time to see my mother going into Mrs. Reardon's office, hair neatly pulled back into a bun, shoulders rigid beneath her old coat, her rainboots slipping up and down on her ankles.

It gave me plenty to think about while I waited for them to speak to me. The school would have to write her a letter to let her know they wanted to see her. Had it come in the mail today? Or had she known yesterday and said nothing to me? Either way, it didn't look good.

There were plenty of things Mrs. Reardon might say to my mother. That I was doing poorly in school would be certain. That I wasn't where I should be to eat lunch was likely, that people were talking about me was possible. If Mrs. Reardon had heard about the fight, she'd be sure to bring that up.

I didn't know how my mother would take it. She'd always been quick to grab her wooden spoon and leave its mark on my behind, then no more said. This was a situation that required a certain formality, in that we had to walk all the way home before she could punish me.

They never did call me into the office. Just left me sitting outside to chew on my lip. Wondering how Eddie Sickles would turn this new development to his advantage. There are plenty of things to see when you have to wait in a place like that. For instance, the hands on a clock don't go around smoothly the way you'd imagine, but in little hops.

Mom's face was set, angry, as she came through the door. She didn't look back at Mrs. Reardon. She didn't look at me either, but walked quickly down the hallway. I caught up to her on the stairs. She gave me a look that was worse than if she'd reached out to slap me. I slowed a little, but she kept right on going, faster even, as if she wanted to put some distance between us.

That was how we walked home. Mom all but running away, me trailing behind, watching her get further and further ahead. At home she said she knew about the stories, that in fact the whole town knew about the stories; she was ashamed that I knew such filth and wrote it down. She told me they didn't want me back at school. Her manner, as she dressed for work, suggested she was none too happy to have me either and all that kept me was the lack of a place to send me. It definitely would've been better if we could've handled this with the wooden spoon.

I fell into bed right after I put Crystal down to sleep. There was little else to do unless I wrote a story. Somehow I didn't have a taste for that.

Tap.

I was up and at the window but Nate was already at the door, pulling off his boots and dropping them into the wood box. "What are you doing here?"

"I came to see you," he said, stripping off his jacket.

"It's a school night."

He shrugged. "How are you?"

"Okay, I guess." I felt awkward for some reason. If he'd said, "How about something hot to drink," we'd have been like that all night. If he'd said, "I still love you," I'd have had to say, "It's all right, I'm fine."

But what he said was, "Do you love me?" I started to cry and went right into his open arms. I cried for a long time, lying on the couch alongside Nate. When I was finished, he reached over to switch on the radio. We didn't say much, just stared at our bare feet propped up on the arm of the couch. "We could draw them," Nate said. "Family of feet."

I tried for a giggle, but it came out as a shudder.

We moved around, getting closer, and as we shifted, Nate's hand passed across my breast. He took it away, glancing at me, and then, I don't know exactly how it was decided, he put it back. It didn't seem like an outrageous thing for him to do. The radio played soft music. Nate's body was warm against mine and it was good. "You didn't do anything wrong, you have to know that. Those stories weren't nearly as racy as the ones in magazines and these same people go out and buy those. They just didn't know what to make of it, that a kid wrote them, that's all."

"They thought there were worse ones. They told Mom—"

"Did you say that was what other kids made up to talk about?"

"She wasn't listening."

"Maybe you ought to write her a story about it."

"Maybe I ought to stop writing stories."

"I don't think so. I like them."

"Good somebody does."

We shifted again, and Nate's hand moved to my shoulder. I couldn't see his face when he whispered, "Caught you in your pajamas again."

My mouth quirked up in a grin.

2 4 1

"You're beautiful," he said, moving again, his arms holding me in a way that made me feel like he was wrapping himself around me.

"You said you couldn't see much," I reminded him.

"I lied."

I laughed out loud, maybe because the answer was unexpected, maybe because I'd known all along and it hadn't been very important.

He ran his hand down my back and up again, moving his body down just enough for our mouths to meet. It wasn't frightening to feel his hand on my breast again, touching, gently kneading. His kiss made me dizzy, wanting something from me and taking it. This was different, the kind of kiss he'd held back for so long, waiting for me. I knew those things, but I couldn't really think about them. He pressed me back into the couch, moving over me so that our bodies touched everywhere.

"Nate," I whispered as he kissed my face.

"I love you," he whispered back and covered my mouth with his. His hands slipped over my arms and back and breasts. It was almost more than I could take; my skin sang, my breath came in whimpering gasps and I had no thought of stopping. Until I felt Nate press himself against me.

"Stop!" I scrambled out from under Nate. "Don't."

"Allie! Allie, it's all right," Nate said, holding me tightly. "We'll stop."

"I'm—it's too. . . ."

"Soon. I know," he said. "Let me hold you."

"You wanted to," I whispered.

"All the time," he told me. "I'll always stop when you say no."

"Always?"

"How about"—he hugged me tightly, then let go—"a game of checkers?"

"Nate."

"Yeah?"

I stared hard at the ceiling. "I want to see it."

"What?"

"You know."

"Allie?" He lifted himself up to rest on an elbow so he could look directly into my face. I refused to look away. "Are we talking about the same thing?"

"I need to," I whispered, angry that my voice nearly failed me.

He sat up. "Let me think about this, okay? Just let me think a minute." He stalked around the room, rubbing his arms. He stopped in front of me.

"This has to do with what they did—what happened—"

I nodded.

He put out his hands in a "wait" sign and went around the room a couple of more times before he said, "I don't know about this, Allie. It's a scary idea." I looked at him from under my eyebrows. "Just let me think some more, okay?"

I nodded.

"I'm going to think in the kitchen, okay?"

I nodded.

I could see him, sitting in Daddy Jim's chair, resting his head in his hands. He raised his eyebrows when he came to a decision; I had an idea his father did the same thing. "I—" He stopped short on the sentence the way he stopped in the middle of the living room. "I think I—" he tried and stopped again. "It looked bad, maybe worse than—is that it?" he asked in a rush, his face going pale.

I nodded, relieved.

He blew through his lips like someone standing in the cold, trying to warm their hands. He looked to be the thing he said so often, nervous and jerky. "Stand up, Allie." I did. He turned his back on me and lifted his arms. "Hold me. Like on the Mad Mouse." I slid my arms around him and he threaded my fingers through his, holding me against him. He relaxed after a few moments, but he didn't let go of me. He didn't do anything. After a while I could relax, too, leaning against him a little. "Stay there, okay, Allie? Don't let go of me."

"Okay." I was glad to be there, where I could hide my face

against his back when I heard him open his pants. He threaded his fingers through mine again and began to pull my right hand lower.

"Nate!"

"You can't be more nervous than I am, Allie," he pleaded. "You just can't. I think I'm going to faint."

I stopped fighting him. I felt the smooth cotton of his underwear as he slipped both our hands beneath it. He stopped, resting I guessed, from the way he drew in a trembly breath. It made me want to do the same. Hearing it, he said, "What does it feel like?"

"What?" I stiffened with shock.

"Easy. Just touch it," he urged, moving my fingers over it.

"Soft," I whispered in amazement.

"That all?"

"Like velvet," I said, exploring now without his help. "And hard, too."

"Oh, God," he said shakily, and I took my hand away. He grabbed it and pressed it back to his chest. "Not so scary now?"

"Nate?" I hesitated. "Is it red?"

"Red?" He turned suddenly in my arms, saying, "Cripes, Allie, it's like any other part—" He looked at me and seemed to understand. "Look then. It's no worse to look at than to touch," he said, nudging his jeans a little lower and pulling his underwear away from his body.

He just let me look. It wasn't scary. And it wasn't red.

"Blood fills up the veins. That makes it bigger, like now. But it's no longer than your hand," he said, reaching for me again. It was still the same velvety touch and, like Nate said, not so big after all. Alive, like kissing and—it spurted suddenly, spraying us both as Nate jumped back. "I'm sorry, Allie! I couldn't help it."

I looked on, astonished, as Nate covered it and pulled his pants closed even as it throbbed and spurted into his underwear. It was warm and sticky on my pajama top.

"Don't. I'll get tissue," he said, running into the bathroom and out again with the toilet paper trailing behind him. "It looks like milk when it dries. You'll have to tell your mother it's from Crystal's bottle." He dabbed frantically at my shirt, then his own.

"What will you tell your mother?" I wondered.

"I'll leave my shirt on, like I slept in it," he said, blushing darkly. "She won't ask."

"How do you know?"

"I have these dreams. All guys do. And in my sleep—I never thought I'd be telling you this," he said, too embarrassed to go on.

I slipped back into his arms.

"Anything else? You worried about anything else?" he said into my hair.

I shrugged.

"Haven't you ever heard girls talking about doing it?" he asked desperately.

"No."

He sighed. "So what aren't you worried about?"

"Does it hurt?"

"No. Well, maybe the first time, but—oh, God, Allie," he said in a thin voice, "this is very unusual."

I don't know what made me laugh so hard. The harried look on Nate's face gave way to a crooked grin, and soon he was laughing as hard as I was. We sank to the floor, roaring with laughter. Every time one of us would wind down, we'd see the other still rolling around, holding their aching sides, and it would start again, great shuddering sobs of laughter, wheezing laughter that squeezed out, sometimes without a sound, tearing at our insides, draining away that nervous feeling that had been building up around us. Finally Nate pulled me up on the couch, moving closer when we were breathing quietly.

"You won't be afraid, will you?" he whispered.

"No."

"It's a long time off but . . . I'll stop if it hurts, I promise." He shrugged. "It won't matter. Sometimes it takes a few tries."

"How do you know?" I teased.

"I do a lot of reading," he said with a grin.

*   *   *

My mother had more to say the next day. They'd told her I was often late to school or missed a morning entirely. I said I'd never been more than a few minutes late, and that only in the snow. It was out of the question to say I'd missed only one full morning and that Nate could say as much, being he walked me to school that day. It was no good saying I couldn't ride the bus.

"You can't ride the bus without getting into a fight, you mean."

"Only once!"

"My own daughter brawling in public with a boy! Like comes from like, that woman said to me." My mother's face reddened at the memory.

"He called me names," I said.

"She says you do things to attract the boys' attentions. That you distract them from their schoolwork."

"I don't care to attract that kind of attention!"

"Then you shouldn't have written those stories!"

There was more the day after that.

I didn't make an effort in my schoolwork, and I paid no attention when I was spoken to concerning it.

I'd taken to having my lunch off the school grounds, and it was Mrs. Reardon's opinion I used that time to keep company with boys.

Even more the day after that. And since it was Sunday and Nate would need his sleep for school, I couldn't ease the hours by thinking of the evening to come.

On Monday morning my mother went through it all again, not so angry this time but crying. No relief to come later in the day because she didn't have to go to work. I was my father's child more and more, the older I got, with little appreciation for the people who worked day to day to raise me. That likely as not I would grow up only to leave those who loved me behind, coming home only to measure the distance I'd put between us.

Mom gradually lost the inclination, or maybe the energy, to

246

natter at me. She slept the rest of the day and in the evening, she lay on the sofa to watch Crystal play while I made dinner. Which is not to say she was pleasant to me in any way. Her manner suggested there was plenty more she could tell me and would when she was feeling up to it. For my part, I was grateful for the silence.

I ended up going to bed early and trying to stay in bed late the next morning. She dragged me out, saying if I wasn't to go to school, I'd have to make myself useful around the house, no point in lying in bed all day. If I had time to become a public embarrassment, she'd see I had things to do with my time. She set me to cleaning the refrigerator, a project that kept me busy for the better part of the day and convenient to hear whatever she had to say about my shortcomings, although it did seem to me she had less to say. But by late afternoon I was not only tired, but tired of listening.

I sat down with a book and pretended to read. I'd been through my mother's bookcase and I knew it held little of interest. But until she went to work, I couldn't put pen to paper.

I fell asleep over the book. I fell asleep peeling the potatoes for dinner and again as soon as she left for work, never bothering to put on pajamas. I woke up fast, already sitting up, chilled but damp, as if I'd been perspiring only a short time before. It was the dream.

Tap.

Nate. I ran for the back door. "Come in quick. It's cold."

He grabbed a log from the woodbox and stuck it in the stove before he stripped off his jacket. "Fell asleep, huh? Waiting for me is old hat already."

"I was tired," I said, grinning. I ran my fingers through my hair self-consciously. "And I didn't know if you were coming, being it's a school night."

"Rumpled becomes you," he pulled me up close, making pointless any attempts at neatening myself up. His kisses were eager, and it took me some moments to notice the hand that crept beneath the tail of my shirt to settle on my back, skin to skin. I leaned back in his arms.

"What's in the bag?" I asked. He'd brought it in with him and dropped it at the side of the stove.

"A reward for one game of Monopoly," he said, letting me go look inside.

"Books!"

"Something to help you pass the time. There's all kinds of stuff there, but I can find you something else—"

"These are fine," I said as I shuffled through them. I eased myself onto the floor as I found one to look at.

"Monopoly first." I gave him a complaining look. "I know a short version," he said, giving in a little.

Nate stayed later than he should have that night, saying it was easier to do with no sleep than just a little. We sat at each end of the couch, our legs tangled in the middle as we read, petting each other with our bare feet. We slow danced around the living room, listening to an all-night radio station coming out of Chicago.

He left only minutes before my mother got home, planning to take a path through the backyards until he saw her ride turn down our road. I lay in the darkness listening to the occasional barking dog, knowing it marked his progress. I fell asleep as my mother came in the back door.

I kept the house as neat as my mother liked it to be, and I made sure Crystal always looked clean and pretty. Crystal loved it when I talked to her, smiling as if she understood everything and putting words together to hold up her end of the conversation. My mother didn't worry so much, now that she was working and bringing home money. Our lives took on a kind of order once more. And although I don't think she'd forgotten my transgressions, she didn't bring them up too often.

I did learn to play Monopoly, but Nate always won anyway. "It's a good thing I lose gracefully."

"Allie! You aren't going to get mad again, are you?"

"You brought this game because you beat me at checkers. Well, you always beat me at this game, too."

"I try not to."

"What does that mean?"

"It means I try to let you win," Nate said, smirking.

"Nathan Drummond! I'm not going to play with you anymore."

He slid the board aside and leaned in closer. "I guess we'll have to find something new."

"Don't press your luck," I muttered.

"Allie! You've really only played three times. How can you expect to win?"

"I don't even like this game."

After a moment he said, "I liked the look of those muffins your mother left on the table."

"I made those," I told him, still in the mood to grumble.

"Then I have to have one." He got to his feet, pulling me up with him. I had one and Nate had the rest, melting cheese over them that we carved off a big wedge my mother had brought home from work. That meant making more corn muffins because there was no way I could claim to have eaten seven on my own. We discovered we liked fiddling around in the kitchen, maybe as much as drawing together.

And as Nate pointed out, it allowed for plenty of kissing and rubbing up against each other without the hazards of lying together on the couch. "Nate," I said, grinning, "you mean all that bumping into me wasn't accidental?" I put the plate of corn muffins on the table.

"Some, maybe," he said as he put the other five muffins into a bag to take home. "Let's go discuss it on the couch. I have to leave in ten minutes."

"You took up all our time with that stupid game," I argued, letting him coax me into the living room.

As February passed, Mom took more of an interest in managing the house, even doing the shopping on her way to work and bringing a big bag of groceries home with her. She began to think of spring and with it, flowers. As I spread wood ash on the fresh fall of snow, my imagination wouldn't stretch to spring. But in fact that looked to be the last snow of winter, and it melted back to expose large patches of frozen earth over the next two weeks.

She also began to talk about school, and whether I might be allowed to go again next fall. Nate had begun to talk about that, too, saying my mother could insist that they let me back in, and sooner than next year. I was unwilling to talk to my mother about it, because I knew she saw it as something that would happen when Daddy Jim came home. I didn't want to think about that.

One Friday evening I couldn't wait for Mom to leave for work. When she did, I couldn't wait for it to be late enough for Nate to show up. Crystal must have caught my mood because I had a hard time getting her to sleep. She was up again in a couple of hours.

I was carrying her around on my hip when Nate tapped at the window. Crystal heard it. She heard him on the porch, too. She pointed, thinking I didn't know. I gave in, shrugging to myself. It was too cold for him to wait outside.

"Hey, look who's up!" Nate greeted her. Crystal gave him her widest tiny toothed grin. "I've never seen her up close, Allie. She's beautiful!"

"She's awake."

"Will she say anything?" he asked as he stood in front of the stove.

"I don't know."

Crystal stayed up for hours, bringing her toys to show Nate. When we played Monopoly, she moved the cards around the board to feel like she was playing. When we gave that up, she was there to put little fingers into the batter and, half an hour later, sample the freshly baked popovers. Nate sat back to draw, and Crystal fell asleep at the other end of the couch, draped over the prickly bear. He took her to bed and tucked her in, bending over her crib to put a kiss on her cheek.

"I'm glad she was up."

"Why's that?"

"I'm not sure we're—well, doing so good with all this time to ourselves. I thought we'd take a lot longer to get to the kind of kissing and touching we're doing."

"And?"

"All I'm saying is, it would be easier if we had all these hours together but not so many chances to—"

"It's all right. I know what you mean."

He looked down at Crystal again. "I wish I knew what to tell you to say."

"Mom won't know what she means."

"If Crystal talks about a boy, She's going to have questions."

I shrugged.

"I'll think of something," he said.

9

CRYSTAL let me sleep late the next morning. Mom was up before us, making breakfast. "Here, Allie, I'll feed her. It's kind of nice that she slept in," Mom said, tucking Crystal under her bathrobe as she stood at the stove, stirring hot cereal.

"You could've slept longer," I said, putting Crystal's bottle in a pot of water.

"It started to snow when we were on our way home. Everything looked so fresh, I couldn't wait to see it." All through breakfast, she chattered to Crystal about flowers that come up through the snow.

We'd finished the dishes when we realized we'd been hearing a snow shovel on the front walk. It was working its way around the house. "It's that boy, Allie," Mom said from the bedroom.

"Nate?"

"Get dressed. He'll be at the door before long."

He straightened and saw me looking out. He waved a mittened hand and went on shoveling.

"What'll we do?" I asked, thinking out loud.

"Give him a cup of hot cocoa!" Mom answered as if the question had been meant for her. "Hurry up and get dressed."

Crystal pointed at Nate as he came in the back door, and curled her hand in a "come here" gesture. "What a flirt you're going to be," Mom said as she scooted back into the kitchen and freed Crystal from the high chair. She'd pinned up her hair and put on a pretty housedress that I hadn't seen in a while. "I appreciate you coming by to help out like this."

"No trouble," Nate said. "I was out anyway and I saw you hadn't gotten swept out yet, is all." He'd parted his hair on one side and combed it back, taking on the look of a freshly scrubbed little boy going to Sunday school. In some way I can't explain, he'd never stood out so clearly as a man. "It's not a heavy snow. It won't stay long."

"What were you doing out here on a day like this?" Mom asked with a little smile.

"Drawing. In fact, I left my paper on your front porch. Maybe I ought to go around to get—"

"Oh, you don't have to go out again. Allie, reach out the front door and get it, won't you?"

I was dazed. Not even the cold air cleared my head, and I knew Nate saw it when I handed him the pad. There was a funny little glint in his eye when he passed it right over to my mother. It wasn't long before I understood.

Tucked into the middle of the pad was a sketch he'd done in the fall, placed so that anyone paging through would have to see it. My mother didn't notice that it was the only loose sheet or the thumbtack marks in the corners. She only saw my long hair, freed from a braid and wearing the flowers of Nate's imagination.

Tears sprang to her eyes.

"I've been meaning to give you that drawing, Allie," Nate

254

said as he lifted the cup of cocoa to his lips. "I forgot it was in there." So it was that his eyes were closed to the hot steam rising as my mother swiped at her eyes and put a look of polite interest on her face.

"You do draw so nicely. I don't think I realized it from what Allie said."

"You wouldn't mind that we got together some afternoons, then," Nate asked her. "I don't know anyone else who even takes an interest."

"I . . . suppose that would be all right."

Nate wasn't one to press his luck. He didn't stay any longer than it took to finish his cocoa and make a quick sketch of Crystal. Mom went off to pin the drawings to the wall in her bedroom, and I waited at the open door while he pulled on his boots. "What's with your hair?" I asked him.

"Like it?"

"I think so."

"You only think so?"

"You look older."

He laughed to himself. "The other—I thought it looked more grown up. Just lately, I'm feeling grown up. It didn't seem to fit me anymore." He shook his head and stepped up close to me. "Funny, huh?"

I didn't say anything. Something of my feelings must have been on my face.

"I'm not feeling too grown up for you."

I'd like to have denied that I'd even given that a thought. But the tears in my eyes gave me away.

"I'll be back tomorrow, Allie, and I'll stay longer."

"You aren't coming tonight?"

"I'd like to. And I'm not saying we won't do it again. Probably next week," he added with a chuckle. "But as long as she'll let us see each other, well, maybe we ought to. . . ."

"You think we ought to be good," I said helpfully.

He grinned. "I don't think I'll feel like I have to be so good if I'm not sneaking into your house at night."

"Is that a warning?"

"Absolutely." He leaned in to kiss me good-bye, lingering over my mouth until we heard my mother coming back. "I appreciate the hot cocoa, Mrs. Benton," he called and started off.

The afternoon passed quietly. So many times, Mom stood at a window, looking out at the snow, the hint of a smile playing at her lips. She did the dinner meal before she went off to work, saying she felt more like eating than she had in a while.

I was enjoying myself. No school meant plenty of time to draw and in the evenings, to write. Time to play with Crystal, making toys out of tin cans and milk cartons and stuffed socks. Time to wait for Nate, who stretched the afternoon visits into full days, being at the back door long before Mom got out of bed and leaving only a bit before she got ready for work.

He turned up one Wednesday afternoon toward the end of March, as I came in from the woodpile. I felt funny, caught in a sweatshirt way too large for me and pants with knees dirtied by the wood ash. He was staring openly at my hair, usually hanging in loose ringlets all around my face. I knew it would be standing up all over the rest of my head, the curls tightened up in the moist air. "You look cute," he said, grinning.

"What are those?" I asked, making something out of dropping the wood next to the stove.

"Your books. And your missed assignments. If you turn those in, you can go back to school next week."

I know what I said about being home—and I remembered how difficult school had been in those last days—but it did sound good. That was nothing to the excitement it created in my mother. "How do you know that?" she asked, still standing in the doorway between the living room and the kitchen.

"My father says I spend more time here than I do at home," he said with a grin that went some way to ease the lines that deepened around her eyes so quickly. "He wanted to know a little bit more about Allie, so I told him about her problem at school," Nate said. "He had a little talk with someone on the school board and "—with a shrug—"next thing I know, I'm given your books and asked to bring them to you."

"Your father must've been a little unhappy if he knows the kind of story Mrs. Reardon showed me," Mom said carefully. I could see she was asking what Nate's father thought of me now. And whether he wanted Nate to associate himself with me. In the end, she was asking what people were saying about her. She was none too sure she wanted to hear the answers.

Nate took care of all of them with a carefully offhand answer. "He didn't appear to be."

Mom made him a cup of hot cocoa to warm him and declared one end of the kitchen table my homework area, putting my books and things there to be worked on every day. Crystal clung to Nate's leg, ending by sitting in his lap until he had to leave. It seemed we couldn't keep our eyes off each other. Before he left, he said, "Maybe you'd like to go out for a walk the next time I come over, Allie."

We both looked to my mother for her answer. "I suppose that would be all right," she said with a little smile.

He grabbed a quick kiss by the door, whispering, "I don't know that I can wait till Saturday to see you." He let his fingers slide along my collarbone where the sweatshirt hung lower. My heart beat faster. Then he shook his head. "But don't look for me."

That night I couldn't sleep. I'd turn off the light, lay down and stare into the darkness. I'd wonder if Nate was feeling the same way. Knowing he did. Then I'd get up, search through the books beneath my bed and find something good to read for two chapters or so. Back to bed. No good.

I finally moved the kitchen lamp into my room and turned it on, dropping a towel over the shade. Enough light to read by but not enough to wake Crystal. My eyes ran over each page, seeing the words but not understanding. It was like my blood was excited. Worked up the way I was, sleep was out of the question.

Tap.

The barest flick of a finger to let me know he'd come. I leapt out of bed and closed the door quietly behind me, so we wouldn't wake Crystal. We'd pull out the Monopoly board. We wouldn't play. We'd listen to music. Nate would hold me in a slow dance around the living room. It was all running through my mind in a blur of anticipation as I swung the door wide.

Daddy Jim stood there.

I can't say I screamed. It was more of a drawn out "Ha."

He stepped inside, looking around the room, and I saw that in some way I couldn't quite place, his face had changed. There was the fresh pink scar on his upper lip, as if something had pinched out a piece of flesh and I wondered that I could see it, his upper lip being a new sight in itself, and then of course, I knew.

They'd shaved off his moustache.

I knew it could never happen that he would shave it off. Not the way he brushed it so carefully, spending as much time on it as on his whole head of hair. He'd never have shaved it off. My hand went to the back of my own neck.

"Where's your mother?"

"She's not here." There was a sudden spark in those eyes as they snapped back to me. "She's at work," I added.

He didn't say anything but headed for the bedroom. Maybe he thought I was lying, I don't know. I backed toward my room, letting him pass.

It took me a moment to make the decision, a moment wasted, but that was all. I went for Crystal, quickly wrapping her blanket around her as I lifted her from her crib. Mrs. Kelly would have to call Mom—

"Where do you think you're going?"

My spine stiffened. Caught, I was caught. How had he come back so fast except to catch me? "Putting Crystal in my bed," I said, turning. Hoping the huff-puff of my voice could be taken for exertion. "She likes to wake up there in the morning." Thinking that when my chance came again I'd be able to move faster, just grab Crystal and run.

"Make me some coffee," he said, pulling a pack of cigarettes from his shirt pocket and lighting up. "Anything to eat around here?"

"There's chicken in the refrigerator."

"What kind of answer is that?"

"Just what you asked—"

"Get me something to eat. You think I came all this way to be treated like a common tramp?"

Better not to answer. I found cold chicken and cornbread, put it on the table with a knife and butter. He went for it like he hadn't eaten for days, but it didn't stop him from picking at me. "Don't you have anything to say to your daddy?"

"I have to get back to bed." Then, on inspiration, "Tomorrow's a school day." I wanted to avoid looking at his face, put off by the lack of a moustache. But the very strangeness of it drew my eyes back.

"You'll stay home," he said, buttering the cornbread. "Anyway, didn't your mother write that you'd been thrown out of school?"

Write? She'd been writing him? I went numb all over.

"Don't you know enough to answer your daddy?"

"I'm just real tired."

He made a humphing sound in his throat, his eyes brushing over me in a tired way. "Where's your mother workin'?"

"She's waiting tables," I said, hoping to avoid telling him it was mainly a bar.

"She home soon?"

"Soon."

"You know where I been?" he asked suddenly. "You know where she put me?"

"Mom? Not Mom. The court—"

"She stood up in that court and said I wasn't fit to live with. She said I drank and beat her." He put out his cigarette, stabbing it into his plate.

"Maybe she had to say that." Desperation made my voice shrill.

"Nobody has to say anything they don't want to," he yelled. I thought I smelled beer on his breath.

2 5 9

"She didn't mean to hurt you."

"You know what they do to you in those places, state hospitals? Asylums?" he asked, rising from his chair. "They stick a piece of rubber between your teeth and knock the hell outa you. They hook you up to the electric current and run it through your body, knocking the hell outa you, so's you wake up not even knowing your own name! Treatments, they call it." He leaned over me; the vein in his forehead stood out like a great blue worm moving beneath his skin.

"You know how many days it takes to come back to yourself after one of their treatments?" I backed up, but he stayed right with me.

"Days, layin' in a fog, not knowin' who you are or how you got there."

I heard my own voice, raised in panic, telling him I hadn't done it, I wouldn't do it, I was sorry, didn't he see?

"You know how many times they did that to me?" he went on, his sweating face twisted into a mask of midnight horrors.

I don't think either of our voices stopped, although it seemed to me neither of us knew what we said, certainly I didn't, just saying whatever fell out of my mouth. I'd trapped myself in the narrow space between the table and the sink, backing toward the door, and he was still coming at me. I didn't think about what to do but grabbed a cup and threw it at him, a halfhearted throw that couldn't possibly have hurt him. It caught him by surprise. Amazingly, he stopped yelling, stopped in his tracks, staring at me for a minute before he turned around to sit down again.

I don't know how long I stood there, my heart whamming in my chest, hardly believing I'd done such a thing. Hardly believing that this was all that would come of it.

He didn't look at me again, didn't pick up any food or drink his coffee, just sat in his chair, staring at the stove. It wasn't that he was ignoring me. I don't think he knew I was there after a while, he was so deep inside himself. When he began to cry, a whispery sobbing that he seemed to want to keep to himself, I went back to my room.

2 6 0

The light still burned beneath the towel. Crystal slept in my bed, not her trusting outstretched arms sleep, but in a curled up, hiding-in-here stupor that didn't change as I crawled in beside her.

I felt for the sweet thump of her little baby heart, trying to draw courage from it. Could we get out of here, get to Mrs. Kelly's phone? Or would Daddy Jim, and this now seemed likelier, sit out there until Mom came home. What would happen then?

And this is the part that is so strange.

I fell asleep.

Curled around Crystal and trying to think of what to do about Daddy Jim, I fell asleep. I slept right through until morning, late morning to judge from the sunlight in the room. Crystal was awake and playing quietly beside me. The bedroom door was closed. The silence outside that door was unbearable. I found my mother in the kitchen, slumped in a chair, her hair hanging limply to cover her face. She looked up slowly, almost painfully. "Allie? Don't you have to go to school?"

My mouth went dry. "Not till next week," I said, my voice caught in my throat. "I have to get all the work done first."

She nodded, her attention wandering to the window.

"Where is he?" I asked in a low voice.

"Sleeping."

"What happened?"

"Happened. Nothing happened," she answered, staring outside with eyes too bright.

"How come he's here?" I asked impatiently.

Her face drew in, twisted with an eerie soundless weeping.

"Don't do that!" I cried. "He doesn't have to stay."

Her head bent low, and she began to make a mewling sound that became long weak sobs, torn from her against her will. The sight of her, broken and breaking apart, made me shake like the victim of a long fever as I lay back down on my bed.

I read a story once about someone who fell down a well. They struggled for hours, climbing out stone by stone, bleeding fingers slipping as they clung to the wall, only to fall back

261

as daylight touched their face. That's what was happening to my mother. To me. Back at the bottom of the well after a long hard climb. I didn't see why it had to be that way.

When Daddy Jim got up, I decided to make it my business to be in the kitchen. Crystal crawled off the bed to follow me. I stayed over by the sink, making peanut butter and jellies for Crystal and myself. Mom spoke quietly to Daddy Jim, in a manner that suggested he'd only been gone the weekend. Telling him that Crystal had a cold, that the damper often stuck in the stovepipe. Telling him these things with a hopeful note hidden in the words like a question she didn't dare ask any other way.

Daddy Jim ate the bread and eggs and coffee Mom put in front of him without comment. He took no notice of us, hardly seemed aware of his food, chewing steadily and without a change in the muscular spasms of his jaw whether he bit into the heavy crust of bread or the softness of the egg. Crystal lounged against his thigh, poking her finger into her sandwich to fish out the jelly.

"How is it that I didn't know you were coming home?" Mom asked as he pushed his plate away.

"You expect me to know the answer to that?"

"I just wondered that no one told me." Her voice wavered uncertainly.

"You expected some kind of warning?" Crystal moved away from him, going to cling to my mother's skirt the way she used to do. "You don't want me here? Is that what you're telling me, Nora?"

"No, Jim. You know I didn't mean that—"

"Why don't you just keep shut, Nora, and let a man enjoy his home? You think where I been they show you any comforts? You think the last two months have been easy for me, Nora?" he yelled, getting up from his chair so fast it fell backward.

"Jim!"

"It ain't right, the way you're treatin' me, Nora," he told her in a tortured voice. His face worked with all the things he

262

wanted to scream out. But he turned and stomped down the basement stairs.

I hoped Mom would say, "Quick, run to Mrs. Kelly." She looked shaky as her eyes met mine, but she swept her hair back and tried to secure it with a pin. I saw she was just glad it wasn't worse, that he'd said what he had to say and left her alone. I grabbed Crystal and washed her hands at the sink, trying not to be too rough. If I'd stood there with my mother any longer, I'd've said something mean. I needed to. But I didn't want to see her cry like that again.

He came back upstairs with a bottle, his breath already heavy with liquor. I thought I saw something like regret flash across my mother's face. Then it was gone, her features set for no nonsense as she told me, "Put Crystal down for her nap." We both knew Crystal didn't take a nap anymore, but it didn't matter. I stayed in the bedroom with her, knowing that was my mother's intention and having no desire to be in the kitchen, anyway. But I kept an ear cocked to the conversation.

"Jim, you know that only causes trouble," Mom said gently.

"It's not the trouble, Nora!" And then, quietly. "It's what I need to forget the trouble."

"You promised you'd stop."

"You promised you loved me, that you'd always love me."

"And I do."

"You didn't say that in front of the judge," he shouted. "You're trying to get shed of me, Nora!"

"That's not true."

"You turned away from me in bed, you—"

"Jim!" she hissed. "Don't talk so Allie can hear."

An uneasy silence fell over the kitchen as Daddy Jim continued to drink. We'd come back to the waiting. Cruel in that it didn't seep in slowly as it did before, but came suddenly, dreadfully, a waiting for something to happen that tightened like a band over my chest.

"You remember how you used to love me, Nora?" he asked, as the drink began to soften him.

"I haven't stopped."

I moved to a spot near the door now, giving no thought to whether it was right or wrong, just needing to know.

"Please, Nora, don't you remember how it was?" he asked fearfully. He plucked at his barren upper lip with trembling fingers.

"It was a long time ago," she said, like the words were attached to a string he was pulling.

"What made you change so quickly, Nora?" He raised watery eyes to plead with her. "A year, two, we had together that were so good."

"Stop," my mother cried in a tearful voice. "Stop this!"

"You're still beautiful, Nora," he said, each word slipping into the next as he reached for her. "I want you to love me the way you did when—"

"You don't know love when you're drinking that stuff," Mom said angrily, and the bottle crashed to the floor.

"Don't try to blame it on drink, Nora! The drink didn't come first!"

"You drank before I married you. You drank before I met you!" I could hardly breathe. She didn't understand. She didn't know how angry he was, down beneath the drink.

"I stopped!" he shouted, his voice cracking. "I'd stopped before I came to your house."

"I never caused you to take a drink! I loved you."

"Not in the way you loved him."

"I left him!"

"Because he knew! How long would you have let me live that way, meeting you in the afternoon when any other man would be working? Standing in dark corners to watch the windows, lit here, then there, watching till the lights went out. I went back to drinking in those months, Nora," he accused, "standing in the cold after the lights went out, wondering if you'd ever leave him."

"I can't talk to you," she sounded tired of the subject. "Anyway, I have to get ready to go to work."

"I'm home now," he said in an oddly frightened way. "You can stay here."

"Jim, we don't have any money if I don't work. Until you get a job—"

"I will! You know I always get work."

"Until you do, then—"

"Don't start in on me, Nora! Always trying to drag me down, that's—"

"No! I'm saying we need the money I'm bringing in till you can find work!"

"Shut up! I don't want to hear any more of your naggin'."

"Listen to me, Jim—" But he ran heavily across the kitchen, and the basement door slammed shut. With a tired sigh, Mom brought out the wedge of cheddar and, with a long knife, cut slices to make grilled sandwiches.

We'd nearly finished eating when I heard the car draw up out front, the horn beeping twice as usual. Mom jumped up, saying, "I'll just wave them on." I followed her to the door, suddenly too nervous to sit still. The horn sounded again as she stuck her head out and waved. There was one short beep like a question mark; the car didn't move on. Mom waved again, frantically. In a moment, I saw why. A man had gotten out of the car, and he'd started up the walk. "I'm not coming in tonight," she called out to him.

"You sure you can't?" he called back. "Millie's not coming in either."

"One of my kids got sick," Mom said as he reached the steps.

"You're not looking so good yourself."

Mom's eyes flicked back toward the kitchen where Daddy Jim stood now.

"Just tired," Mom said quickly. "I have to get back inside."

"Yeah, well, make sure you got plenty of wood near the door. It's getting colder." She closed the door, clipping his last word short.

"So that's him."

"Listen to me, Ji——"

He struck out at her, smacking her in the face with the back of his hand. "I don't have to listen to you! I can see!"

265

"Jim, don't!" she screamed. "Oh, don't, please don't," she whimpered. "That's why they took you away," she cried, her voice rising as he lifted his arm to hit her again.

He stopped.

"He drives me and another woman to work, no more," she said, letting her body sag against the door.

"So where's she at?"

"You heard him say Millie's not going in. Maybe she's sick. I don't know."

"You expect me to believe that?"

Mom's shoulders began to shake then, her strength giving out. Daddy Jim stood there watching her cry a long time, then he began to search his pockets. His lips were too dry to hold the cigarette at first. Then his hands shook so badly he couldn't keep the match at the end of the cigarette. He gave it up, throwing the cigarette and matches to the floor.

"Jim," my mother said, moving toward him. "You have to stop drinking so we can talk this thing over."

"No, I don't," he said, going into the kitchen.

"Jim, please!"

He grabbed his coat and left, slamming the back door hard enough to crack the window glass.

We had a hard time settling down that night. I had no thought of catching up on my schoolwork. Mom made no effort to clean up the kitchen. She waved me away when I thought to do it. Crystal dragged her toys into the other rooms, too restless to play with them in any other way. When we finally went to bed, Mom kept walking through the house, checking Crystal, then rocking a while, then getting up to walk again. I dozed now and then, waking up suddenly, listening.

I had the impression I'd slept more deeply, longer this last time, before I knew Daddy Jim was in the house. I got out of bed and went into the kitchen, squinting against the lamplight. He was in the middle of the living room, weaving slightly even though he stood with feet apart.

"You can't come in here with that bottle."

"What're you sayin'?" Daddy Jim's words slurred together.

2 6 6

"I'm saying I won't have you drinking and scaring our children and making our lives a misery any longer." Mom didn't yell, just sat calmly in her rocker as she told him.

"You can't keep me out," he told her, swaggering over to the couch and spreading himself across it.

Mom ignored that. "You ran away from that place, didn't you, Jim? That's why you didn't show yourself at the door. That's why you didn't want me to go to work. It was only the drink you wanted that drove you out tonight, wasn't it?"

"Shut up, Nora."

"I can have you put away again, and this ti—" Daddy Jim's foot shot out and connected with the arm of Mom's rocker, nearly knocking it over sideways. "You can beat me again, Jim, but only once."

Daddy Jim kicked the chair again but with less force. "Don't you talk that way to me."

"I'll leave you if you put a hand on me."

"You don't mean that."

"I mean it."

"I live here." Daddy Jim got to his feet. "I'll drink if I want to, and I'll slap you down if you nag me."

"I've said what I'll do." My mother's voice rose anxiously as he moved to stand in front of her.

"Tell me again."

"I'll leave you," she said, her voice faltering.

He slapped her. Hard.

"I'll have you put away," she yelled, sobbing.

He slapped her again.

I slipped back into the darkness of the bedroom to lean against the wall, my whole body shaking, tears running down my face. It was starting. I heard myself whimpering, crying, knowing my mother couldn't keep inviting this and knowing, too, that she had taken all that she could. Like a cornered animal, she would fight back. It would be as bad as the last time.

Their voices were raised in the living room, my mother threatening, Daddy Jim meeting each threat with more abuse.

In my chest that knot of defiance could be felt again. I let it grow. It had a strength of sorts.

I couldn't just lay there in my bed, listening to the yelling. I couldn't sit and do nothing while he beat up my mother again. I felt around in the dark for my corduroy pants, pulling them on right over my pajama bottoms. Crystal stood up in her crib, the better to keep an eye on my activities. In a spirit of, I don't know—rebellion, maybe—I wrapped that Brazilian poncho around her, tying it over the bulge of her diaper. She seemed cheered by that, reaching for the prickly bear and offering it to me for a kiss. I gave it a loud smack and pulled a big turtle-y sweater over my head before I gave her a kiss, too.

I felt better as I slipped my bare feet into my old tennis shoes. It might not make any difference that I was dressed to run to Mrs. Kelly, but it felt good. Like the summer I was seven or eight, when we had tornadoes every few days. After a couple of weeks I carried lots of food and toys down to the basement of the apartment house to put in front of the shelter. The threat of tornadoes hung over us all summer, but I was less afraid. I was prepared.

"Jim, give those back," my mother shrieked.

"You're bringin' your daughter up to use your wiles, Nora. It ain't right." Daddy Jim sounded strong as he came into the kitchen. Less at the mercy of the liquor, and confident he'd found a weapon to use against my mother. I went to stand behind the door.

"They're only pictures," she cried hoarsely.

"You brought that boy into this house after I said he wasn't to come around. You're teachin' her she don't have to listen to what I say."

"You're drunk, Jim." Mom tried to sound sure of herself, sure that he would do as she told him. "Give me those."

"Sure, I'm drunk." He laughed at her, easily holding the drawings out of her reach. "But that don't stop me from knowin' what you're up to." He swung the stove door open. "I'm gonna put a stop to this—"

"I'll never forgive you," she said through her teeth as she snatched at the paper, succeeding only in tearing off a large piece.

"—once and for all." He threw them in.

My mother's lips drew back over her teeth, and with a cry from the back of her throat she fought to retrieve the pieces. When Daddy Jim grabbed her wrists, she clawed at his face. He pushed her aside, but she scrabbled back to the stove and reached in, pulling out a burning piece of paper that she tried to save, smothering the fire with her hands.

"Mom!"

My shout went unheard. Mom kept making these sharp angry cries that never quite became sobs as Daddy Jim shouted, "They're gone. You can't save them stupid woman they're gone," all in one long breath that left his face red. It was over for him then, ended with his triumph and the evidence of my mother's defeat. Suddenly she grabbed a burning stick from the stove. Daddy Jim didn't see it coming, going through the doorway. She caught him on the side of the head and neck, a solid blow, and the smell of singed hair filled the room.

He howled in pain and a red welt had raised on his neck, even as my mother pulled the stick back. Daddy Jim was rocked, whether from the blow or the shock that Mom would hit him like that, I don't know. He put a slow moving hand up to his head, as if he had to touch it to believe what had happened. "Ah-h!" he cried, snatching his hand away. Daddy Jim's mouth quivered, looking for one moment like he might laugh, then like he might cry. I thought it was over, that he was going to weep and ask my mother to forgive him.

Until the muscles in his face began to work, cords standing out on his neck as he screamed.

Mom swung again, hitting him under the chin. He did fall back a step, screaming, but when she swung a third time, Daddy Jim raised his arm to fend off the blow and the stick fell from her hands. It lay on the kitchen floor, still burning as she threw herself upon him, kicking and screeching and hitting. They used no words to fight with each other, just the sounds that came from their throats as they struggled. Daddy Jim seemed unable to push her away, letting one arm hang at his side. The skin on his neck had begun to puff up like a blister and when she raked her fingers over it he screamed horribly and tried to beat her off. Mom had the fingers of one hand twisted into his hair so that even when he hit her and she should have fallen, she hung on and reached to scratch out his eyes with the other hand. Blood ran down his neck.

It was time to run to Mrs. Kelly. I knew I could go unnoticed, but the piece of wood was burning into the floor. I stamped the fire out. The stick was hot, so hot that I had to drop it. I didn't know how my mother held it. I got a towel to wrap the end and threw the whole thing into the stove. I started for the back door.

In the living room Mom and Daddy Jim grappled, teeth bared, wild animal snarlings all the voice they remembered, and in that instant that I meant to run, Daddy Jim's arm raised into the air and I saw Mom's long kitchen knife clutched in his hand. Every muscle in my body stood ready to run, still geared to make the dark run to a telephone while my mind let go of that idea, just let it go, knowing this to be the natural outcome, the one it had prepared to face with all those weeks of dreaming, and waited unsurprised, just simply watched. Daddy Jim plunged the knife into my mother's throat. Blood spurted up as from a fountain, spraying into the air to splatter over Daddy Jim.

I let those charged-up arms and legs take over, and it seemed to me that even as I saw my mother's face shift from rage to stunned surprise, I was snatching Crystal from her crib, complete with the blanket she held in an attempt to wrap the prickly bear, even as the strength ebbed from my mother's body and she slipped from Daddy Jim's hands, collapsing like a rubber toy with a hole in it, I was running from the bedroom, and as Daddy Jim sank to his knees before my mother's limp body, I was racing through the night, my mind remarking calmly on the events of the evening, after all, it was no surprise, isn't that what anyone might have known would happen, hadn't my mother said so herself on hearing of someone else's doing, maybe more than once, and I ran along the path to Mrs. Kelly's house, Crystal caught in my arms like sun-warmed sheets off the line, a loud hoarse sound reaching my ears unrecognized, until I slowed to find the steps in the dark-ness, and I knew it was my own ragged sobbing that chased me to Mrs. Kelly's door.

I was screaming, pounding on Mrs. Kelly's door with a fist, keeping Crystal tightly clutched under my other arm. The noise was terrible. I had to stop that screaming. It scared Crystal. It would tell him right where we were. I stopped pounding for a minute and touched my mouth.

Open, it was open, but the screaming had stopped. A light went on in an upstairs window. I raised my fist to beat at the door, *please, Mrs. Kelly, let us in.* That's when I heard him. He must have slipped, because what I heard first was the whump of a fall, then he swore.

Close, he was too close.

I ran to the end of the porch and squeezed behind a wicker settee. Crystal was rigid in my arms. I saw her frightened eyes as I pulled her up on my lap, raking her knees across the wooden slats of the porch railings. She didn't complain.

Daddy Jim ran up the porch steps just as Mrs. Kelly opened her door. She screamed and tried to slam the door shut on him, but he got in. I heard him running through the house as I left my hiding place. I saw Mrs. Kelly picking herself up off the floor. Daddy Jim was banging around somewhere inside. Our eyes met as I stepped off her porch. I think she knew what had happened when she saw me there, and I hoped it would be warning enough that she shouldn't stand in his way.

But I didn't stop. For one fleeting moment I was sorry I'd come to her, sorry I'd brought this trouble to her. But it wasn't something I could dwell on. I was running.

The first thing I thought to do was to head for the road, just like the first thing I thought of was to go to Mrs. Kelly. Even if I reached the highway, it would likely be a while before a car would come along. My only choice was to cross the cornfield that lay behind our houses, hoping to gain time while Daddy Jim searched for us on the road.

The way I'm saying I did this, then I did that and then I did something else, it seems like I was planning out each step. It sounds a little cold, even to me, that I could keep moving, making decisions, however little thought I was conscious of giving them—and think only of keeping us out of Daddy Jim's hands. There isn't much here about sadness. It seems a little odd that there wasn't more of it. Maybe it was deep inside me somewhere, but when I started out across that field I didn't feel anything, not even the cold.

I had my eyes wide open, thinking about the far-off lights I saw from my bedroom window on winter nights. I couldn't see them now. I wondered how far to the left or right the farm might be from where I was. It finally occurred to me that I could keep myself on a straight path by looking back at the lights that now burned not only in our kitchen, but in Mrs. Kelly's. I took a moment to get my bearings, gratefully sucking cold air deep into my chest. It felt like I'd forgotten to breathe for a while.

A light snow began to fall. I couldn't really see it—just felt it melting on my face. I stuck one foot in front of the other, walking blind not only because of the darkness, but because I carried Crystal against me. I felt for flat ground, letting my feet find their way over the plowed-under rubble of corn stalks. It wasn't easy—many were broken and sticking out at different angles, tangled places to catch my feet. It was a little farther along, with the corn stubble poking into the bottoms of my feet, sharp even through the soles of my shoes, that I first noticed the cold eating into my skin. I thought about Crystal. Her little teeth were chattering, and she shivered all the time. I remembered someone telling me that shivering is good, and that's how a dog keeps warm. I wondered how long it would work for Crystal. That's when I began to get mad.

Really mad.

At my mother.

How could she have let things get so bad? Not that I didn't

know her reasons. But there was something wrong with Daddy Jim. Too wrong to talk about him getting better, about things being the same someday. Her reasons weren't good enough, certainly didn't seem to mean anything while I trudged through a cornfield in the middle of the night. There were cold angry tears on my face.

I didn't want to be thirteen, carrying a baby to safety. I wanted to be thirteen with Nate coming to visit on a Saturday afternoon, taking me to a movie in a grass lot. Kissing me good night in some corner of the yard where the porchlight didn't reach.

I wanted it and I saw no good reason why I shouldn't have it.

I wanted to be thirteen with a friend and parties to go to and what will I be when I grow up. I could be something different than those who came before me. Not more. Different. In that I could put on paper something that I knew. When I died, I would have left something more than one of my children carrying the other across a cornfield, sick with fear that if she failed there would be nothing at all to show for her mother's life.

Why hadn't my mother ever thought of that? Why hadn't she seen us as something she'd leave behind her, a marker far more meaningful than the flat stone in the ground that showed where Uncle Darryl lay? A wave of despair rose in me and I let it out in a couple of loud sobs, trying to force them out really, so that they had a phony sound to my ears. They didn't encourage me to repeat them. I shifted Crystal to lay against my shoulder. She'd begun to weigh heavily on my arms. The feeling in my chest had grown stronger when I was angry, making me feel stronger, and I intended to turn my thoughts back to that anger.

I looked back across the field again, to see the lights burning in the houses behind me. There were lights on all over Mrs. Kelly's house now, and it seemed to me they were as far away as the light's I'd seen across the field and now ran toward. I wondered at the meaning of the lights in the upstairs windows.

Did it mean Mrs. Kelly was okay? Did it mean she had been able to call for help?

That's when I heard his voice, raised to call out to me, raised to scream out his intentions. I could hear the far-off noise of his feet on the frozen corn stubble. He'd probably found me in the same way. Then I saw the thin white sheet of snow that covered the ground, and I knew I was leaving footprints. A clear trail for him to follow.

It had a numbing effect, the realization that there were only the three of us in this field, and unless I got to the other side of it first, we might was well be the only three people in the world. There'd be no fairy-tale rescuers for Crystal and me.

He screamed again, a cry of rage as he made his way across the field toward us. I ran, but the running wasn't much faster than the walking for fear of falling. One of the things Crystal and I had going for us was her silence. I didn't care to change that.

Once I'd thought of it, it began to worry me. Crystal lay so still on my shoulder, not even shivering anymore. My arms ached, my back was tired, my feet were so sore I might have been walking on rocks, but I'd forgotten the cold. I stopped, although I was nervous about doing it, to make sure her blanket was still wrapped around her. Her breath came in shallow little puffs from her open mouth. She seemed unaware of the carrying, or of the cold. I put her against my other shoulder and hurried on.

In a funny way, it helped that I was frightened by Daddy Jim being so close behind us. Each time my feet slowed, each time my resolve weakened, I had only to think of him: longer, stronger legs and unhampered by Crystal's weight.

I thought of the red light of the radio tower that I used to point out to Daddy Jim when we'd lived in Des Moines. He'd always say, that's miles away, Allie. More miles than you are years old. What if that farmhouse was like that light? What if it was more than one cornfield away? What if I came to a fence, how would I ever climb that fence, and on the other side was another cornfield just like this one?

274

It was in one of these low moments that I felt the corn stubble give way to a few feet of flat earth. I walked right into the barbed-wire fencing. I felt it pull at my sweater, but I don't think it hurt Crystal. I looked along the fencing, dark against the snow, alerting me to the fact that the night was no longer thick or black.

I looked over my shoulder, suddenly afraid that Daddy Jim could see us, could know exactly where we stood and head straight for us.

It was cold. Standing still for a moment, I could feel it. The snow fell all around me with a soft ticking sound.

I couldn't even hear him. It was like he was hiding. He was hiding and any moment, he would reach out to grab me.

I looked along the fencing again. No gate that I could see.

I knelt on the ground and lay Crystal there, taking the opportunity to wrap her blanket around her more tightly. I was shivering now, as I pushed her under, reaching through the fence to pull her through without rolling her over. She didn't move an arm or seem to waken at all. For one terrifying moment I saw no breath fogging the air. I reached through the fence, scratching my face on the barbed wire as I felt for her heartbeat, my own breath coming in fast whimpering gasps until I found it.

Then I flattened myself on the ground to slither under, catching my sweater on the twisted wire. Laying there with my face against the frozen ground, I heard Daddy Jim coming. We were the only sounds in the world, he and I, and I heard him coming closer, his steps slower and heavier than mine. I pulled free, snatching Crystal up again, and began to run.

Grass beneath my feet. Flat earth and frozen grass that crunched beneath the light coating of snow. Ahead, I could see the dark shape of the barn and beyond that, less clearly, the house. I ran. Halfway across, I plunged something more than ankle deep into a stream, crusted over with ice and hidden under the snow. My ankle turned as my foot slid across the wet stones. I went down in a skid across those same stones, tearing open my pants at the knee. Water swirled icily around

275

my bare ankle and slithered into my shoe. Crystal didn't stir.

I stayed like that, half-kneeling in the stream until I could trust myself not to cry, hearing an odd whimpering sound that came with each straining breath, feeling my insides begin to shake with the cold that I had been able to ignore until now. My ankle wouldn't bear the weight I had to put on it to stand, and in the end I had to sit down in the stream, letting the icy black water soak my pants and creep upward. The end of Crystal's blanket dragged through the water, sucking it in as fast as my clothing, but I couldn't be bothered. Crystal didn't feel the cold.

I could see the house now, part of it anyway, at the other side of the barn, dark against a sky growing pale. I pushed myself up, sobbing with the effort, knowing it was light enough for us to be seen, knowing I was losing time.

My ankle throbbed with each step. I couldn't run. The cold burned my feet, and as I stumbled along, the snow stuck to my wet shoes so that in only a few minutes I had heavy clumps clinging to each foot. The water-soaked corduroy had begun to freeze, scraping loudly with each step and rubbing against the inside of my legs like sandpaper. I gave in to the crying because it was stealing my strength to hold it in. I cried, allowing that I was cold and tired and hurting. Allowing that I was scared for Crystal, for the way she lay on my shoulder, pale and silent.

But I was being chased across that field. I'd carried Crystal all the way only to have it turn into something like running to Mrs. Kelly's if I didn't get to those people in time to tell them. In time for them to call the sheriff. Time to know that trouble was coming right behind me. It was getting lighter all the time, and now my dark pants could be seen moving against the snow if Daddy Jim was looking.

That's what was driving me on when I passed the opening in the side of the barn. A low, narrow cutout like the one Uncle Zeke cut for his lady goats to let themselves out into the pasture in the morning. This one had a board set up against it, maybe to keep in the heat. I felt the warmth in the air as I

passed and looking, saw that the board was set to one side.
It was warm inside, dusky sweet smell of animals, making me want to lie down to do my crying. I tripped over something on the floor. When I put out a hand to catch myself, I felt something deeply furred and moving. Woolly. Sheep. They were all around me in the darkness as I felt my way toward the other side of the stall. My feet were so bad I could hardly feel the ground beneath them, but the pain didn't ease up, each step making me grind my teeth. I fell again, this time against a broken bale of hay, staying where I'd fallen. I gave in and cried, clutching Crystal to me. It didn't help. Feeling around in the darkness, I found a nuzzling response from one of the furry bodies. Sheep. Yes. Working with my one free hand, I hollowed out a little nest in the hay for Crystal. She'd be safe here. Warm. I covered her with the blanket and some of the hay. Each thing I did to hide her, to leave her, made me more afraid that I was doing the wrong thing, then made me move faster to be finished. I could bring help faster than I could carry her to it, once I was freed of her weight.

I stumbled back to the hole, moving through the slow stirrings of the animals I'd wakened, taking a look around before I crawled out. The snow was falling faster, making it hard to pick out a dark form against a dark cornfield.

The snow was deeper. Slippery because of the ice crusted on the bottom of my shoes. The rickety gate was held closed by a loop of frozen rope, and as I reached for it, a light went on in the house. It held me there, seen in the space between the gate and the post it was tied to for only a second or two, precious seconds that I was afraid to waste, but it took me that long to tear my eyes away from the warmth of that yellow light.

That was when I saw him.

He was coming up on the house from the other side. Somehow he'd veered way off to the side in his trek across the cornfield. That was why I hadn't seen him before. Now that I thought of it, it meant he hadn't been following the tracks I left in the snow. But it was nearing sunrise now, and he could see me if I stepped away from the gate. He was closer to the house than I was. A light sprang on in another room, making his head jerk up. He stood for a moment, arms out from the sides of his body, like a gunfighter ready to draw. He was an eerie figure in the falling snow, black on one side, lit by a dull yellow light on the other. He hadn't realized he was so close to the house, I thought; he wasn't even particularly watchful. When he moved again, in a stiff shambling way, I wondered if he was hurt.

He went to the door, going directly in; what's the use of locking the door out in the middle of nowhere, Grandpa always says, and there was a moment when all was quiet. Then the voices started. Outraged, angry. After the woman's scream, fearful. Another scream.

I was running.

Each slipping sliding step sent a dull pain through my leg, but there was no way I could stop.

It was worse than Mrs. Kelly's, worse and beyond that, my one chance at help was gone. Because I didn't believe they would overpower Daddy Jim now. To beat him, you had to know he was coming; you had to know what he could do. When he was finished, he would be looking for us again. He'd go straight for the barn. I slid back through the hole and covered it up behind me. I sat just inside, rocking back and forth holding my ankle, gulping long whooping breaths that sounded like I'd been running a long time. I couldn't do much more running, I knew, even if I didn't have Crystal to carry. But there was no question of leaving her behind now.

I began to crawl toward the front of the stall. It was like a game, hide and seek, and Tucker always found me. Now I was hiding for real. I had to know this place by the time Daddy Jim came looking for me. The best way was to keep moving. First one hiding place, then another. It would be easy in the dark.

One of the sheep let herself out of the stall alongside me and although I tried, there was nothing I could do about it. I closed the gate, not wanting the rest to follow. They were Crystal's hiding place, and I needed them there.

There was another stall closer to the front of the barn, smaller, empty, and I guessed it might be used for animals delivering babies. A pitchfork stood against its gate and although my spirits rose at finding something so clearly a weapon, I didn't allow myself to entertain any thoughts of what it would mean to use it. I took it with me, leaning on it like a crutch as I continued my exploration.

Most of the floor space was used to store hay, which likely as not meant there was no loft. The bales were stacked like uneven stairsteps toward the ceiling. One side much steeper than the other, hardly offering footholds where I felt around the bottom. The highest point would be at the back corner of the barn. My eyes had adjusted to the darkness, but I couldn't see clearly enough to know how high or how deep that meant, knowing only that it seemed mountainous.

The trick to winning, I thought, falling into words that made it a game, would be to move across it as much as possible, rather than up and into the corner. I was measuring it out when I thought I heard a door slam. I dropped the pitchfork and ran to the front of the barn, thinking I'd have time to look outside.

But I could hear him coming.

Moaning like an animal being rubbed raw by a piece of leather, swearing, calling out once as he neared the barn. I dove for the empty stall and pulled it shut as I dropped into the shadows.

He entered as quietly as he was able, using slow cautious movements to open the barn door, but for all his care, I could hear the quick heavy breathing that told me he was tired, maybe hurt like I'd thought earlier.

I waited for my chance.

He stood there in the darkness, listening, I guessed, listening for the slip of a child growing impatient with this game of hiding. The sheep trotted out of the darkness toward the open barn door. Daddy Jim jumped like it had frightened him, something running at him instead of away. Then he began to look for me. One foot dragged behind him. It meant he would be slowed, and that was good. I listened a little longer, trying to judge how badly he might be hurt. Hoping his injuries were worse than mine, and in that way I almost missed my chance.

I saw the movement of his darker form against the darkness. I was waiting too long. I pushed off on my good ankle and ran forward, leaning into the gate even as he began to turn around, gaining speed as it swung outward.

It caught him in the side and knocked him over.

My heart was racing, and panicked by my own daring, I ran straight out from the gate, never thinking to back away and make a wide circle around him. I ran straight past Daddy Jim. He reached out and snatched at my ankle with a grip so fierce that I fell face down on the floor of the barn. There was a red flash of pain and the scrape of the rough wooden floor against my cheek.

I heard his laughter, a hoarse, breathy kind of laughter.

He didn't let go.

His fingers pinched into the thin frozen skin of my ankle as he dragged himself up to his knees. When I couldn't pull away, I pushed myself up to sit, and when he leaned over me, I raked my fingers down his face. One finger caught at an eye, sliding under the lower lid. He shrieked when I dug my fingers in. It was a bad moment, that instant of wanting to pull my hand away, saying I was sorry; seeing myself as the attacker. In that moment of clawing fingers and his scream, he let go of me and I was able to roll to one side.

He made a grab for me but I pulled away, feeling his fingers slip from my wet shoe. I ran to get the pitchfork, and as shaken as I was, I was feeling pretty sure of myself, reckless even. It must sound like a strange thing to say, but I think it had to do with being caught for a moment and escaping him.

So when I turned back to face him, it didn't matter that he was already up and coming for me. I was ready.

He must be crazy, I thought, when I knew he could see that fork pointed straight at him and he just kept coming.

I backed up a couple of steps, then stopped myself. If I kept that up, let him back me any farther, I'd be cornered.

I started across the barn, trying to find my way in the darkness but moving as fast as I could. When I felt a bale behind my leg, I stepped up.

Daddy Jim chose that moment to make a run at me.

I swung the pitchfork, making him draw back even as he reached for it. He nearly caught it, would have if he'd been only a little faster, a little less afraid for his eyes.

I was lucky that time, I thought as I climbed higher.

If I was going to take little swipes at him, he was going to take that pitchfork away from me. If I let my nerve give way, if I messed up, even once, I didn't get any more tries.

"Get back," I screamed.

He put a foot on the next bale. When I didn't make a move, he stepped up.

His foot was still midstep when I stabbed at him with the pitchfork. He was fast, amazingly fast as he grabbed for it, caught it and sidestepped, nearly falling backward before he found a place for his feet.

I let go of the fork as soon as I felt myself being pulled toward him. I scrabbled backward as far as I could and began to climb again. He was following me with better speed than I'd expected from him, and although I moved sideways as much as I could, now it was necessary to climb higher in order to work my way across again.

"Thought you could run away, didn't you?" he said, panting harshly. "Thought you had me beat."

I stepped into a hole between two bales, sinking to the middle of my thigh with no place to stop my foot. The corduroy had bunched up around my knee, and I found as I tried to pull away that I had to stand up to free myself.

Daddy Jim was coming for me.

Gathering the other leg beneath me, I threw myself up to the next bale and rolled to face him, twisting my leg in the hole. Daddy Jim saw his chance but he was too far away to grab for me. He still had his hand around the handle, right above the fork. He struck at me, burying the end of the handle in the soft part of my stomach.

I heard my own voice crying out and with it I heard the air in my lungs escape, but I didn't stop moving.

I clawed my way up the side of two bales stacked one on the other to make a higher step. My breath began to return in long sobs.

He turned the pitchfork around so that when he went for me again I saw the glint of metal teeth bite into the bale.

I scrambled away, facing him all the while, and forced myself to climb again when I felt a bale behind me.

Daddy Jim didn't slow. He continued to plunge the fork into the hay, driving it closer to me each time, then used it to lever himself up before he pulled it free.

He flung himself forward again. This time the pitchfork came down over my leg like a snare, puncturing the fabric and biting into the skin of my leg.

I screamed.

Tried to wrench free.

Screamed again. Knowing once and for all, that he meant for me to die.

He put his hand high on my leg, putting his weight on it to pull himself up, panting with the effort.

I felt a shudder run through my body.

I twisted from side to side, arms outstretched, fingers frantically grasping for a crevice between the bales, for anything I could use to pull myself free. Maybe it was my imagination but it seemed that I did manage to gain a few inches.

He was snarling like an animal as he crawled up to lie across me. I screamed with the wild fear that he would tear out my throat with his teeth.

My arms were the only part of me that weren't pinned down. They scrabbled wildly across the rough surface of the bales; one hand caught at the wrist on something sticking out of the hay and still screaming senselessly in fear, I tried to pull that hand free while I used the other one to go for Daddy Jim's eyes again. He swore between clenched teeth, ending with a desperate gasp for air as he reared back.

Some small, still thinking part of my mind realized that my

hand wouldn't be trapped if I would close it, that it was caught in an angle by its own outstretched fingers.

He grabbed my free arm above the elbow and pressed it into the hay, breathing hoarsely against my cheek, his weight holding my struggling body beneath his.

I let the fingers of my other hand close around a wooden handle and pull. It didn't come loose right away, but shifted so that I knew it was caught in some way, then all at once it let go, weighty in my hand but small enough so that I could lift it and swing it up and over to hit Daddy Jim, feeling something give, not under my hand exactly but under the thing I held in my hand.

He stiffened and screamed, rolling away.

I was fighting back. Even thinking that that's what my mother did and knowing what happened to her, I wouldn't have changed anything right then, even if I could.

I swung it and hit him again, seeing the silver curve of the baling hook as it carved through the air and snagged in his shoulder.

He screamed again and fell back.

I scrambled across the hay, realizing that it was growing lighter outside, seeping through the roof of the barn. I kept my eyes on him as he abandoned the pitchfork and crawled toward me. I looked for a way down the steep side as he dragged himself up on his feet, muttering between clenched teeth and staggering toward me like a wound-up toy, breathing hard and swearing with each step.

I panicked and pushed away too fast, slipping past the next two or three bales until I caught myself with the baling hook.

Daddy Jim was right above me, climbing over the edge. I clambered up onto the jutting edge of a bale, clinging there on hands and knees while I tore the hook loose. He lost his footing and came slithering down, screaming and flailing his arms, knocking me to the floor with him.

I hit hard, wrong, landing on my shoulder first, bringing a sudden splintering pain that I couldn't fight. I lay face down, gasping, sobbing, consciousness flashing in and out behind my eyelids. I was terrified that he was standing over me, about to grab me again.

But he was hurt too.

After a time, my eyes focused and I could see him, lying face up, his breath coming fast, making his belly quickly rise and fall. His eyes were open, and as I watched he began to hitch himself up on his elbows, his face twisted with pain.

I tried to pull back to widen the space between us, but all that moved was one arm, and when it moved I heard the baling hook scrape over the rough wooden floor. I didn't know whether I still had the strength to use it, but it felt good to know I still had it in my hands.

"Allie?"

He sounded so normal. So—"Is anybody home?"

I had to get up.

It was terrible. Grinding pain as the broken ends of bones rubbed together. A wave of nausea washed over me. I swayed dizzily, using the baling hook to steady myself as I stood. My arm was heavy, so heavy. I wanted to cradle it in my other arm, but I needed it to wield the baling hook.

Daddy Jim was standing, too.

He didn't look to be in much better shape. It may be that he stood there, waiting, to see how much strength I had left before he began to come after me. I slid my feet backward a few inches at a time, feeling my way toward the door as I struggled to carry the sickening weight of my shoulder. Even breathing hurt.

I was afraid of falling.

Of not being able to get up again.

He began to come after me, stumbling, having trouble standing straight and then staggering in my direction.

"Allie!"

If it had been louder, I could say he screamed at me. As it was, I knew only from the tone that it was meant to be a scream. It was so pitiful it brought tears to my eyes.

"Stay back!" I shouted, raising the baling hook.

He didn't stop moving. He laughed. A ragged sound that made my skin creep. "You're like her. You know that?"

I backed away, each sliding step sending fresh pain through my shoulder.

Too slow.

I couldn't do any better.

"You're trying to get to that house, is that it? You think someone will be there to help you."

"Shut up!" I felt tears run down my face.

He made a sound like crumpling old paper in your hands, as he staggered toward me, a kind of laugh. "They're dead. Don't you . . . think they'd be out . . . here . . . if they weren't?"

"Stop it!"

"Just old folks . . . all they were."

"Mrs. Kelly—"

He just laughed.

I came up against the barn door. Not hard enough to move it, but enough to all but knock me to the floor. Pain shimmered in front of my eyes like a heat wave.

"Thinking . . . things over?" Daddy Jim said in a way that made me think he might be smiling.

I put my hip against the door and backed out.

Daddy Jim kept coming and as he left the darkness of the barn, I felt the shock crawl over my skin in tiny beads of perspiration. Running across the cornfield, it was the old face that hung in my memory. I'd forgotten this new naked face with its pink wedge of a scar. His eyes were swollen nearly shut and his dirty wet hair swung over his face as he lurched toward me, dragging his leg at each step. I was looking at a stranger.

There were blackened patches where my mother had hit him and in their centers, shiny wounds, oozing blood that he'd smeared across his face. Behind him the cornfield stretched out to meet the thin red line of the horizon. "You can't get away from me, Allie."

I felt my own face folding up, getting ready to cry.

285

He rushed for me, moving faster than I thought he could.

I turned and ran, or did what passed for running, as he loped behind me, breathing heavily. Gaining.

I tried to scream. Not enough left.

The ground swayed beneath my feet.

His ragged breath was in my ears.

Along with a desperate whining sound that was my own voice.

He reached out for me, a dark movement I saw from the corner of my eye.

I shunted to the side, but his fingers brushed roughly over my hurt shoulder and I wanted to stop him, wanted to end the vicious burning pain that shot through me as I turned and swung at him, hearing the whistle of the baling hook as it cut through the air and a wet punching sound as it connected, the sound of my mother's long knife chunking watermelon.

Daddy Jim grunted and came to a rigid stop as blood splashed over my hand, surged up around the steel stem of the baling hook I'd plunged into the hollow between his neck and shoulder, soaked into his flannel shirt, a bright spreading stain that grew as we stood there, closely joined by the weapon I still grasped so tightly. Daddy Jim was wide-eyed, breathing harshly, liquidly, his body held board stiff until he dropped suddenly to his knees.

The movement jerked the baling hook out of my hand, and I gasped at the ripple of pain that lapped at my shoulder.

His head lolled back to show me puffed eyelids and thin white slits of eyeball gleaming beneath them before he dropped back, collapsing against the snow, his chest rising and falling with a breathy whistle.

"Daddy . . . Jim," I whispered. I half-expected him to leap up and grab me; fear washed coldly over the back of my neck and over my shoulders. Even so, I stepped closer.

I wasn't aware of listening to the breathing, his and mine, until his stopped.

Just stopped.

In that moment of cold air and clear eyesight I saw everything the way it was. His head thrown back, chest arched away from the blood-stained snow, arms flung out, one above his head, one crooked at his side and the legs bent back at the knee. A pose so often glimpsed in the leaping figures of children.

But he was perfectly still.

He looked younger somehow. Maybe it was the bare upper lip, maybe the way his hair fell boyishly over his forehead and the surprised oval of his open mouth. The rosy color of his skin warmed by the fiery red light that rose high on the horizon. Marred by the blood that had spattered across his cheek.

I stood there until I could see the blood red edge of the sun. The sheep had begun to trail out into the pasture. Then I trudged slowly back to the barn, slow steps taken in the rhythm of my throbbing shoulder.

Crystal lay snugly in the hollowed-out bale, and although I knew her sleep was unnatural, I thought it was enough to know that she was breathing. I sat beside her. It wasn't even that my shoulder pained me so badly, though it made an impression on me. I was simply too weary to get up again.

That was where Officer Aarons found us.

10

For all the things that are different, and despite my mother and Daddy Jim being gone, it's amazing to look around me to see just how much the same everything is.

Grandpa still settles himself under his one oak tree on summer evenings. He looks out over his cornfields with some satisfaction, smiling and waving off the boys as they head out for an evening.

Aunt Florrie just got married and moved into the little house. They've been there less than a month, but we're raising a house for them because Uncle Little Mike plans to marry very shortly.

Daddy couldn't make it home for the fair, what with taking time off to come back in March. And the fact that the new baby

289

doesn't take to travel. He has two children to spread his attentions over now, and it no doubt means we'll each see him half as often. Although I'm sure Grandma Drew was some disappointed, she's been awfully busy this summer. This week she's setting up the nursery for the baby Aunt Bonnie and Uncle Calvin expect in the fall. It may be as Uncle George said, that she sees the wisdom of a bird in the hand.

It seems odd that it was only last summer that I stood in front of the mirror in Aunt Bonnie's room, looking for signs of the teenager I expected to turn into. One of the truest things Aunt Bonnie told me was, all of the growing changes that meant much could be seen in only one place. Calvin's eyes. I'll be fourteen tomorrow. Nate claims the very idea makes him drool. I just smile and tell him that it probably means that, like Crystal, he's getting a new tooth. He tries to look wounded, but I'm happy to see he isn't much put off.

It's due to Mr. Drummond's efforts that Crystal and I live with Grandma and Grandpa Taylor now, sleeping in the second bedroom. Crystal talks now and laughs a lot. She hardly ever cries. I didn't finish seventh grade last year, finding it hard to leave Grandpa's farm. But when Nate bought an old jalopy with the money he'd saved up, he wouldn't hear of doing anything with a Sunday afternoon but to drive all around, letting everyone see how good he looked at the wheel. Or at least that's why he claimed we were doing it. It seemed to me we always ran into someone we knew, but Nate never let go of my hand. It got easier. Soon I'll go to the school my mother went to, something that appeals to my sense of rightness. And while I won't get to enjoy Nate's company at the end of the day, the bus ride will likely prove uneventful.

Mr. Drummond says all that I wrote helped him decide what to say to the judge. If that's true, then it's good that I told him as much as I did, without stopping to worry about how he'd take it. It's awfully nice that he's never said one word to Nate about anything that's in it. Nate says it's nice that his father doesn't chain him to his bed at night.

Grandma says it'll get better, and I suppose she knows what

she's talking about. But I'm none too fond of that gray light that steals over the earth just before dawn. Or the way the air slithers along your skin as the first colors spread across the horizon. It may be what Tucker says, that I'll be someone who lays abed till the sun is up, waking to a world of bright sunshine and birds singing. That will help. Only yesterday, Dolly confided in me that she sometimes sits by herself and wonders, if she were to disappear right that minute, what would be different? I could see her discomfort as she spoke but I don't know that I was able to set her mind at ease. I've learned that the important questions don't come with easy answers. Maybe you can't even expect to answer them soon enough to do you any good. In that way I can understand that Grandpa Taylor listens to anything anybody has to say.

The one thing I'd been prepared for, from the moment I struck out across that cornfield right through to the time of this writing, was the sense of absence. I knew the pain of the sudden gripping remembrance of a loss as I moved through commonplace moments. I knew how to deal with the realization of what that loss meant to me, and the finality, the can't-ever-go-backness that would wash over me. Maybe that was enough to have learned when Uncle Darryl died.

Still, I don't know how it was that I missed the aloneness, the deep-in-your-bones alone that is all you're paying attention to, no matter that someone is talking to you. Their voices filter through, and you turn to look into the eyes of the speaker, maybe someone you know, and you give them the answer they're looking for. But in the eyes of those you love and need, there is that same aloneness and although you hold them and breathe in their sweet cinnamon scent, there's something in each of you that the other cannot touch and soothe.

I think Mr. Drummond knew that. Certainly he understood my silence when he came to the hospital, knew that I thought of him only as Nate's father and saw the way I plucked at the edges of the stiff hospital sheets, saw it long after I'd managed to still my fingers. He was still coming after everyone else's questions had been answered, or at least, had ceased to be repeated. He sat with me beside Grandma Taylor's woodstove, Crystal playing at our feet. When it was warm enough to move our chairs onto Grandpa's screened-in porch, he sat with me there, finally bringing me pen and paper. I wrote all the time, finding it rid me of the pictures that woke me in the night, and each time Mr. Drummond came, I could give him some of it to carry away.

I've had plenty of time to draw this summer, for the first time finding there's something to be said for a flower. My drawings don't capture the fragile beauty that Nate finds there. He says my flowers gathered strength to burst all at once from the earth, and they look to be going to last a long time. Grandma Taylor's practically papered her kitchen in my flowers. For all of that, I'm looking forward to the chance to draw some of them when their colors fade and the leaves lay close to earth. It may be that I have a better understanding of just how it is that dying is part of living.